December is here and it's time to celebrate the holidays with a romantic collection of contemporary stories from three of Arabesque's most cherished authors. Each of these talented authors will introduce us to a special couple who have discovered the holiday magic of true love blended with undeniable desire. Savor Shirley Hailstock's tale of Christmas's glad tidings, delight in the fruits of Kwanzaa with Rochelle Alers, and rejoice in Angela Benson's New Year's Eve story. These three unforgettable novellas will touch your soul and are bound to warm your heart during the chilly winter season.

Holiday Cheer

Rochelle Alers
Angela Benson
Shirley Hailstock

PINNACLE BOOKS
KENSINGTON PUBLISHING CORP.

PINNACLE BOOKS are published by

Kensington Publishing Corp.
850 Third Avenue
New York, NY 10022

First Printing: December, 1995

Printed in the United States of America

Contents

Invitation to Love

by
Shirley Hailstock

To Kim Lewis,
whose loyalty and support are as precious as gold,
frankincense, and myrrh

One

Elizabeth Gregory had vowed never to see James Hill again. Yet tonight, twelve days before Christmas, when her emotions were as raw as the wind whipping at her skirt, she found herself standing on his porch. Tiny white lights outlined the entire structure and she could see the tree, its lights blinking, through the huge picture window. The scene couldn't have been better set up if Hallmark had photographed it for one of their Christmas cards. "How could I have been so stupid?" Of all the addresses to mix up. How could she have pulled out *his* instead of the one behind it? Why hadn't she thrown it out three years ago, when she'd walked out of his life?

Elizabeth's finger punched the doorbell as if she wanted to push the Georgian colonial over with it. Inside she heard the musical notes of St. Michael's permeate the chilling air. He hadn't changed that, either, she thought. How often had she listened to that sound with a wide smile on her face? She shuddered, pulling her red velvet cape closer, knowing the coldness gripping her had more to do with anticipation than temperature.

"He's not here," she muttered, pushing the bell a second time. She should be relieved that he wasn't home, but she had to get that package back and deliver it to the right address. "Come on, James," she ordered. "You've got to be here."

It *was* the Christmas season. The sudden memory of a previous Christmas burst in her brain. They'd been curled up in front of the fire at his cabin in the Blue Ridge Mountains, just the two of them and a fake fur rug. Snow was piled up to the windows outside, yet neither of them noticed or cared. Elizabeth shook herself. She forced the image of their naked bodies out of her mind. The firelight was too hypnotizing for her not to remember James highlighted against the red-gold glow of leaping flames.

In three years she expected her anger would have cooled, but she found the prospect of facing him frightening. Pressing her fingers against her temples, she closed her eyes and forced herself to relax. She didn't need a headache tonight.

Ringing the bell a third time, she knew her luck had run out. James wasn't home. Even Mrs. Andrews, his part-time housekeeper, would be with her own family by now. She looked around the porch for the package. It wasn't there. Maybe the delivery hadn't been made. Silently she prayed for a tiny bit of luck. If James hadn't been home, the box could have been returned to the shop. Silently she prayed for the alternative to be true. It was worth a try.

Elizabeth turned to leave. She could phone Joanne, her temporary assistant, from her car. Mary, her usual assistant, had wanted two weeks off at Christmas. Elizabeth thought she could handle the load while Mary took the much deserved time. Everything had gone well until today, when she had pulled James Hill's address from the Rolodex instead of Jason Hillery's. The young college coed, away from home for the first time, was distressed over the mixup but didn't know the city well enough to find James's house. Admittedly, few people could negotiate Rock Creek Park during daylight hours. After dark, the poor girl would never have found the house nestled among giant rhododendrons on Redwood Terrace. And the very important delivery would have no chance of reaching the correct address in time. Chantel Hartman-Lawrence had been adamant about it arriving on time. Elizabeth had assured her that Invitation to Love had built a reputation on correct and prompt delivery. Now she was going to have to eat those words.

"Elizabeth!"

James Hill. His voice took her breath away. Elizabeth closed her eyes again as she gathered strength. Squaring her shoulders, she turned to face her former fiancé. He hadn't changed much, from what she could see of him silhouetted against the light of the doorway. At thirty-seven, his hair had not a hint of gray. His face was strong, his skin tight across his features. He had a square jaw that gave him a ruthless look, until he smiled; then any hint of severity disappeared. He was smiling now. Elizabeth's heart pounded in her ears. She stifled the urge to press her hands against her head. Her breath, congealing in the crisp December air, looked like a jerky staccato. She hoped James didn't notice it. He filled the doorway, dressed in tennis shoes and a sweatsuit. Even the bagginess of the outfit couldn't hide his powerful physique. She knew he exercised regularly. It appeared that even tonight, while most people were still frantically shopping, he'd gone to the gym. James had always been calm and exacting. He'd probably finished his shopping, wrapped everything, and stored it all under the tree.

"I wasn't expecting you," he said, raising an eyebrow. "I just got in."

"It's nice to see you, too," she said, her sarcasm undisguised as she swept past him without an invitation. The house looked the same. A roaring fire in the huge fireplace that dominated the high-ceilinged room made it warm and comfortable. Pine boughs scented the air. Entwined with the same white lights that decorated the outside, they arched from the mantel and the doorways and up the imposing stairwell, whose newel post was as large around as her waist. "Silent Night" played softly from the sound system in the back room. The house was beautiful, the kind Elizabeth often saw displayed in the holiday issue of *Architectural Digest.* The tree, its lights flashing in the window, was perfect, so much so that it brought tears to her eyes. Quickly she blinked them away. She loved this old house. It had been built before the turn of the century, and she'd imagined herself living here after she and James were married. They hadn't made it.

"Come in." He closed the door with a mock bow. Taking several steps into the room, he faced her.

Elizabeth turned to speak. James's nearness stopped her. She found her mouth too dry to utter a sound. In the brightness of the room, his tree-bark-brown skin radiated health. He crossed his arms, distributing his weight evenly on his legs. The action drew Elizabeth's attention to his broad shoulders and strong biceps hidden under the gray sweatshirt with a faded insignia of the Howard University athletic department. She could almost feel herself wrapped in his embrace. He stood three inches over six feet, and she had to tilt her head back to see his eyes. His strong, square jaw could be harsh and demanding, or tender and loving. The man exuded sex appeal. She nearly swayed toward him.

"Where is it?" Elizabeth asked, drawing on an inner strength she didn't recognize. She wanted to be out of here as soon as she could manage it. All he had to do was give her back the package and she'd be on her way.

"Where is what, sweetheart?"

"James, I don't have time to play games. It's Christmastime. I'm late for a party. Please give me the package and let me go. And don't call me sweetheart."

"My, you've changed, Elizabeth." She noticed him look her over. She fought the urge to gather the cape closer around her. It would show her fear, and she didn't want James to know how weak he made her just by being in her presence.

"You've cut your hair. It was longer when we—parted."

Elizabeth's head was splitting. Her attempts to ward off the pounding pain had failed. The day had been a disaster, and she still had to attend the Herefords' party.

"I don't want to talk about my hair." It had been long enough to touch her shoulders. Now she wore it cut above her ears, with wispy curls covering the top of her crown. "I want the box that was delivered here earlier tonight. It's been sent to the wrong address."

"I like it," James said, ignoring her demand. "It emphasizes your eyes."

He was making fun of her.

"I always said your eyes were your best feature."

He'd said lots of things, and gullible Elizabeth had believed every one of them. But not tonight. Ignoring him, she searched the room. The familiar white box with her logo on the side was nowhere to be seen. Leaving James, she went toward the library. Pushing the sliding mahogany doors open, she went into the dark room. The electric switch on the wall threw the room into brightness. Elizabeth blinked and immediately shaded her eyes until they became used to the light. The room was paneled with a rich brown wood. She could smell the lemon wax. Heavy, tufted leather sofas and floor-to-ceiling bookcases gave it a feeling of old money. James's antique desk dominated the room. In daylight Elizabeth expected the room would be dark, but the custom-made windows captured light and spread it around the room from all angles.

"Don't you want to take your coat off?" James followed her. He lifted the cape from her shoulders. Elizabeth swung around, backing away from him. His fingers, through the thick piled fabric, had touched her as surely as if she'd been naked.

"I see your fashion hasn't changed." He made a wide circle around her. Elizabeth forced herself to stand still. "You're still the best-dressed woman on Capitol Hill." Elizabeth held her breath. The fur-trimmed cape had been warm against the outside. Under it she wore a strapless gown with white fur adorning the straight-line bodice and circular hem of her Christmas-red gown. Under James's gaze, Elizabeth's lungs didn't work. The air was stifling. He was tall and lithe, a predator if ever she'd seen one. The urge to run was so strong she had to dig her heels into the Aubusson carpet. "Of course, the ruby necklace would go with that dress much better than that gold chain."

Elizabeth stopped her hand from going to her neck. James had given her a ruby necklace as an engagement present. She had dutifully returned it after they'd broken up.

"James—"

"What's it been, Elizabeth—three, four years?" he interrupted. "Can't we even have a drink before you rush out into the night?" James dropped her cape on the sofa and moved around her.

She moved away from the heat of him. "I don't want a drink; I'm driving." Did he really not know how long it had been? Why did that make her heart sink? How often did she think of him? When they'd parted, she'd thrown herself into Invitation to Love, using her business as a substitute for a broken relationship. Yet tonight, on some subliminal level, she'd pulled out his address and given it to Joanne. Did it have anything to do with Christmas? It had been another Christmas when she'd stormed out the door she'd swept through tonight.

Then she spied the current copy of *Black Enterprise* on the coffee table separating the two leather sofas sitting before the imposing fireplace. A smile stole across her mouth.

"You've been gone a while, right?" she led him.

"Until recently, my work meant I traveled a lot. Usually I spend Christmas in New York."

"You work there, too?" Elizabeth knew the answers to all these questions.

"Not anymore. I've been back in D.C. for several months."

She would have been disconcerted except that James's brother, Mark, made it a point to drop by at least once a month and give her regular updates. She supposed Mark did the same for James.

With deliberate slowness, Elizabeth crossed to the table. She bent forward, lifting the magazine with her face on the cover. The slick surface flapped up and down as Elizabeth walked to where James stood. She held the book toward him. As he reached for it, she let it go. It dropped at his feet.

They both looked down. The magazine lay open to a photo of her in the Oval Office. Next to her stood the President of the United States, a package of personalized invitations in his hand. They both smiled at the camera.

Her stare was level as he raised his eyes. She wanted to laugh at the small victory but decided against it.

James bent down and picked up the magazine. He stared at the photograph for a long time before closing the booklet and returning it to the table. "It says you bargained with the President to allow a wedding and reception to take place in the Red Room. In exchange, you got the White House business. In the world of small business, you pulled off the coup of the century. Do you know how many people wish they were in your shoes?"

Elizabeth did know. In reality, her negotiations had been with the White House advisers. It was happenstance that had the President within earshot of her request. She hadn't needed the article in *Black Enterprise* to bring in business. Twenty-four hours after the contract with the White House was signed, she had more business from the Washington elite than she and Mary could handle. But she loved it. After the initial overwhelming deluge, she'd taught Mary some of her calligraphy techniques. Her assistant seemed to excel in Spencerian penmanship. Together they were a team, and Mary's Christmas present this year would be a full partnership in Invitation to Love.

"James, I can't stay here talking to you all night. I need to get that package to the right address and then go to Charles and Lidia's. Please give it to me." She dropped her head. The pounding was getting worse, and soon she'd need to sit down. She didn't want to sit here. She wanted to be in her car, speeding away from Rock Creek Park.

"You're going to a party alone?" James's voice snapped her attention. "I thought you never went anywhere without an escort."

"Please, James." She held up her hands. "Let's not argue after so many years. Your address got mixed up with someone else's and a package was sent here. It really must get to the right man before eight o'clock."

"The right man?" His eyebrows rose. He approached her, watching her take a step back. Lifting her hand, he checked her ring finger. "Is he *your* right man?"

Elizabeth snatched her hand away. "You have no right to ask that question."

"I'm the man with the package you want. That gives me a lot of rights." James walked to the bar in the corner and set two crystal goblets on the leather surface. He reached under the counter where Elizabeth knew there was a small refrigerator and came up with two chilled bottles of Perrier. Pouring them into the globes, he walked back to her. Elizabeth accepted one.

Taking a sip, she hoped the cold water would help to cool her. "James, why don't you give me the package and I'll be out of your life?"

"You're assuming I want you out of my life. We were friends—once." He hesitated a moment. "Maybe I'd like to hear about you, what you've been doing in the past few years. Things that aren't covered in *Black Enterprise.*" He gestured toward the coffee table.

Elizabeth felt she was being manipulated. "You know damn well how business is. As for my personal life, it's none of your concern. Now, give me the box and let me go." She turned the glass up and drained it, then went to the bar and slammed the delicate crystal onto the leather top.

James lounged against the back of the tufted leather sofa, apparently in no hurry to give her what she wanted. "Why are you doing this? Do I have to search for the box?"

"You could start in our bedroom," he grinned.

Elizabeth stopped short of gasping. "*We* don't have a bedroom." The implication that they never would rang clear in the air between them. She wouldn't go to his bedroom. In fact, she wouldn't go another step. Chantel Hartman-Lawrence could have been a valuable contact for her business, but Invitation to Love had survived other mishaps. She'd simply go to the address and explain to Mr. Hillery. She knew she'd have to confront Ms. Hartman-Lawrence, but Elizabeth would rather fight her than James.

"It's that way." He pointed to the door behind her.

Elizabeth stared at him for a long moment. Then she grabbed her cape, swung it over her shoulder, and headed for the door.

"Elizabeth!" He vaulted over the sofa and reached the door in front of her. "Don't leave in anger. You left that way the last time. We were friends."

"That was a long time ago, James."

"Don't you think we could be friends again?"

"No, I don't. Please move. I'm late."

His shoulders dropped. Elizabeth's defenses told her to relax, but she held them tight. This could be another of his games.

James sighed. "Wait here. I'll get the package."

He disappeared into the back of the house. She knew there was a great-room there with enough windows to let the sun warm it on cold, wintry days. It, too, had a fireplace, as did all the rooms. Three Christmases ago, the two of them had drunk a toast to a room full of friends on their impending marriage. Elizabeth didn't know what made her move, but she walked to the arched entrance. In the dark the glass walls vaulted to the sky. Another lighted Christmas tree had been set up here. It was in the same space it had occupied when she'd stood before it, James at her side, a smile on her face.

"Do you know where you're standing?" James whispered. He moved in front of her. She hadn't seen him. She'd been lost in the past. Looking up, Elizabeth saw the ball of mistletoe hanging over her head. Moving her gaze back to James, she froze at the desire she saw in his eyes. She went to step back, but his arm encircled her waist and pulled her against him. "Merry Christmas," he murmured, then lightly touched his lips to hers. Elizabeth felt a tremor run through her. James lifted his head enough to look into her eyes. Then his mouth came down on hers in a ravishing kiss.

Three years of misery and frustration melted away as James's arms slipped inside the cape and it pooled to the floor in a heap of red velvet and fur. Elizabeth's arms connected around his neck as desire swept through her. It felt good to be held, to press herself against him, to feel his arms, the hard length of him, and know he was solidly there, not the elusive substance of her dreams. She leaned into the kiss, her mouth open as James devoured the inner contours. Elizabeth didn't know how long they stood there, just that she didn't want the moment to end. James slid his mouth from hers.

"Are you the woman at the door?" he whispered, his voice thick with emotion.

Confused and disoriented, Elizabeth frowned a moment. Then she realized the package had contained an acrylic rose with a man's wedding band hooked onto one of the leaves. A hand-engraved note inscribed with the message *Marry the woman at the door* was included. She pushed herself away from him.

"No!" she nearly shouted.

He held the rectangle of snow-white paper in his hand. Elizabeth knew her handwriting without looking at it.

"You opened it." Snatching the note and the box, Elizabeth rushed from the room, through the front door, and into her car. Her cape lay on the floor at James's feet. She refused to go back for it. She never planned to enter that house again—or to see him. In less than half an hour she'd found herself back in his arms, as soft and pliable as candlewax.

The chilling air made her shudder. She jumped into the car, throwing the hated parcel on the seat and gunning the motor in her effort to put distance between herself and James Hill.

Just as she came out of the park, Elizabeth passed the stone slab bathed in white light. "Welcome to Washington" had been carved deeply on one side of the marble square, while "Welcome to Maryland" adorned the other side. Cars skittered around the circle, their drivers unaware of the turmoil taking place inside the white Corvette that turned toward downtown Washington. Elizabeth pulled the car to the soft shoulder and cut the engine. She slumped over the steering wheel and cursed herself.

How had she let that happen? How could she let James revive feelings she'd fought to bury these last three years? She pounded the steering wheel, trying to keep the sensations he'd stirred from raging out of control.

* * *

James had no breath left after Elizabeth's hasty retreat. She was the last person he expected to find on his doorstep, wrapped like a present in a velvet coat trimmed in white fur. He remembered her with shoulder-length hair, eyes bright and dancing, a ready smile always present. Even in anger, her dark-champagne-colored skin glowed with health. Only her eyes betrayed her. He'd told her her eyes were her best feature. They were also her most revealing. Sometimes they were dark and mysterious, while at other times they were open and full of hurt. He hated to think he'd been responsible for putting the hurt there.

Their names had been linked since childhood. He'd been in love with her since the fifth grade, and three years ago he'd thought he'd be married to her, but then Claire had come and everything between them had changed. Tonight, when the package had arrived, he'd been too afraid to think, too afraid to do more than let it sit on the counter. Then she was the woman standing at the door; he thought the world had tilted in his favor; but she was only there to retrieve it and deliver it to its rightful owner.

He picked up the velvet cape. The white fur was soft and feathery, the way her hair had felt when he'd dug his fingers into it. He liked the way she looked now and the way her body knew the familiar contours of his.

Looking at the coat in his arms, he remembered another white fur and him wrapping her securely in it. Her brown eyes were huge and warm then, not like the cold ones that had looked at him tonight, but she still had the fire. The kiss had told him that. Her fire burned for him just as much as his burned for her.

"Damn!" he cursed. "Why did Claire have to pick that day to drop her bomb?"

Two

James guided the Lexus into the flow of traffic on 16th Street and headed downtown. His intention after the gym tonight had been to shower and turn in early. It had been a grueling week. Most industries, except retail sales, slowed down at this time of the year, but not the stock market. At the eleventh hour everyone panicked, buying and selling, pushing income into the new year or quickly investing in high-risk stocks.

He'd been tired both physically and mentally, but after Elizabeth's unexpected appearance, the thought of being alone between the cool sheets of the Lincoln-sized bed was unappealing. And as usual, thoughts of her forced all other women from his mind. Pulling out his tuxedo, he changed his mind about attending Charles and Lidia Hereford's annual Christmas dance. He'd refused their invitations for the past three years, yet an hour ago Charles Hereford had heartily laughed into the phone when James had asked if it was too late to accept.

Caught by the light at Military Road, he listened to the engine hum, then turned right, heading toward Wisconsin Avenue and his parents' house. The license tag reading MHH-MD on the Mercedes parked in the driveway told him his brother, Dr. Mark Howard Hill, was here. With three additional parking places available at the Cathedral Avenue address, James blocked him in, a grin spreading across his face. Leaving the car, he paused to study the red brick house next door—Elizabeth's house. The "For Sale" sign stood askew on the front lawn. No matter who bought it or how many families lived there, he'd always think of it as Elizabeth's house.

Pulling himself out of the past, he rang the doorbell of the house in which he'd grown up.

"James!" The look of surprise on Winton Hill's face quickly turned to joy as he faced his second son. "What are you doing here? I thought you were too tired for anything except an early night."

"I changed my mind," James said, following his father past the soft, muted shades of the gray and mauve living room to the one beyond. They entered the family room and library, where he'd practically grown up. As a family, this was the room they had lived in. It was where he'd told his parents he and Elizabeth were getting married. Where Mark announced he'd been accepted into Meharry Medical College, and where his mother, Opal, had told them she'd been diagnosed with breast cancer. It was also the room in which he'd notified them of his impending arrest. Happiness and crisis surrounded the book-lined room. James supposed it was why he'd come to his parents' house.

"James, I'm glad you're coming with us." Opal Hill walked into the room. Her gown was a glittering green. She lifted her cheek for his kiss. She rarely asked her sons for explanations. James's parents had instilled the values of right and wrong in their two sons. She accepted whatever they did as the right course of action for the time. Going to her husband, she reached up to fix his tie. Winton Hill lifted his chin and his wife tied a perfect bow. "You know, Elizabeth is going to be there," she said, glancing over her shoulder.

"I saw her tonight."

Opal's hands stilled. Slowly she turned to face him, the room completely silent. Three pairs of eyes bore into him.

"Where?" Mark was the first to speak.

"She came by the house."

Opal took a step toward him. He could see a mother's concern in her eyes. At thirty-seven he knew he'd always be her little boy and she'd always try to prevent anyone from hurting him. He went to her, putting his arm around her shoulders and looking down at her. "I'm fine," he said by way of explanation. "It was merely a case of misdirected mail, or I should say, a misdirected package. Invitation to Love sent a package to me by mistake. She came to get it, that's all."

It sounded simple, even to his ears. As if the earth-shattering kiss they shared hadn't occurred. As if her presence hadn't changed his conviction to forget her. Three years, and he hadn't found another woman to take her place. Three years, and all he ever did was remember Elizabeth, reliving the nightmare that had begun with Claire.

"How did she look?" Mark asked.

"I saw her a couple of weeks ago," his father said, relieving James of the need to tell them she looked better than cotton candy. He knew Mark saw Elizabeth regularly. "I bumped into her as I was leaving my office." Winton Hill was an economic adviser for the State Department. "We had lunch. She told me about her company. I'm proud of that young lady. She's really come a long way. It's too bad about that sister of hers. I'm amazed that two people growing up in the same house can be so different."

His mother concurred as James and Mark exchanged knowing glances. "I'm sorry things didn't work out between you two." She looked at James. "I'd have liked having her as a daughter-in-law."

"You know they call her 'the impossible lady' on the Hill," James's father told them.

"They discuss Elizabeth on the Hill?"

"You know Washington gossip, James. And anyone who's set up a parachute drop over the restricted airspace of the White House, arranged a wedding reception in the Capitol Rotunda, erected a waterfall at Carter Barron, and convinced the Buffalo Film Committee to allow a first-time director to use the Wilcox Mansion will be discussed on the Hill. And then there's—"

"Enough." James put his hands up.

"We'd better be going," James's mother said. His father lifted her coat and helped her into it. Minutes later James's father drove through the streets of the Washington. Wisconsin Avenue passed by in a blur. James's thoughts were on Elizabeth. He knew her accomplishments without his father itemizing them and without Mark's reports. Impossible missions were her trademark. He'd had an impossible task of his own—he'd tried to forget her. It was like forgetting he had a right hand . . . or a heart. Elizabeth made other people's dreams come true. She had dreams, too. James could only hope hers weren't impossible and he could convince her to try and make them come true.

The red and white gown brushed against Elizabeth's legs as she swirled to the music. The pounding in her head hadn't eased since she'd left James's house, although she had taken two Advil in the cold confines of her car. Kyle Gardner pulled her back into his arms, swirling her around as if she were a marionette. She'd been here an hour. One more and she could leave. Smiling at her partner, she followed his steps, but she felt no joy at the music. She had enjoyed dancing before Claire had died. Now Christmas brought only painful memories. Yet she went through the motions of buying and wrapping gifts, attending parties and smiling bravely.

She and Claire had had the best Christmases. They'd lost their parents when Elizabeth was only thirteen; Claire, barely over legal age, had supported her and made sure they always had food and clothes, a small apartment, and money to send her to college. Claire had taken care of her and made sure her Christmases were happy and that she always had at least one present. She could almost hear Claire telling her that somehow they would find the money.

Then things had changed, all because of—

"James! James Hill!"

Elizabeth lost her balance at the excited call of his name. Stepping on Kyle's foot, she looked toward the entrance. Lidia Hereford had just reached the three steps that separated the sunken ballroom from the entranceway. James's entire family stood in the archway. Lidia threw her arms around James's neck. Elizabeth stopped dancing and stared at the group near the door. Winton Hill at fifty-seven had only a few gray hairs. He stood an inch shorter than James's six foot three inches. Elizabeth had no doubt what James would look like when he was his father's age. Opal, James's mother, a petite woman with a wide smile that twinkled in her dark eyes, smiled at her hostess. In her green sequined gown, she looked more like a mature fashion model than a physics professor, yet she commanded several classes a day in the Death Valley building at Howard University. Elizabeth had liked her since she'd tasted her sugar cookies the first Christmas her family had moved to the house on Cathedral Avenue. And Mark, despite his antics and constant reports on James, she liked him. A happy guy building a reputation as a remarkable surgeon, Mark could charm his patients into getting well. They were a perfect family portrait framed by their love, which seemed to protect them. Even Elizabeth could see it from her vantage point. A stone ached in her heart for her own lost family.

"Elizabeth?" Kyle tried to recapture her hand and resume the assault he passed off as dancing.

Elizabeth pushed him away. "Excuse me, Kyle." She offered no further explanation, just turned and searched for an escape route.

"What is he doing here?" Elizabeth fumed as she slipped into a darkened room. The tiny men inside her head with sledgehammers stepped up the pace. She sat down, holding her head. She wasn't going to make it another hour. She needed to find Charles and Lidia and make her excuses now. Waiting in the darkness, she hoped the pain would ease a bit. Minutes later, she rose. By this time, James and his family should no longer be standing by the door. She could get out without them seeing her, she hoped.

Opening the door to return to the ballroom, Elizabeth blinked at the light. She'd find Charles and Lidia and use her headache as an excuse to leave early. Shading her eyes, she walked into a solid mass. Instinctively, her hands came out to support herself.

Grabbing hold of the arms that reached out for her, she looked up and into James's dark brown eyes.

"There you are, Elizabeth. I've been looking for you." He spoke as if they were the best of friends and had only been apart for a short time. "Dance with me."

Elizabeth wasn't given time to refuse. James took her hand and started for the crowded dance floor. He threaded through the crowd until he reached the center, then turned her into his arms. She wondered what he was up to. Before the dance ended, she knew they would be the talk of the town, but his arms around her felt good. For a moment her headache eased. She held herself stiffly, knowing if she relaxed she'd melt into him. She wanted to melt, wanted to let him support her without conviction.

Her eyes closed a moment. James ran his hand up her back. She felt his fingers on her skin and warmth spread through her.

"Relax," he whispered in her ear. "It's a crowded floor and it's only a dance."

Elizabeth couldn't fight the pain anymore. She relaxed just to give her head comfort. James's arms crisscrossed her back and he held her close until the last chords of Phyllis Hyman's "Somewhere in My Lifetime" ended. Even then Elizabeth didn't move. James leaned back and looked at her contorted face.

"Dancing with me couldn't be that bad."

She tilted her head back. Pain shot up her crown. She opened her mouth to say something, but nothing came out. A moment later she whispered, "Migraine."

"Come on," he said. "We're getting out of here."

Elizabeth didn't remember saying goodnight or seeing any stares follow them as they left the ballroom. The cold stabbed her bare shoulders as James wrapped her in the rough wool of his overcoat and took her out into the December weather.

"Where are your keys?" he asked.

"My purse," Elizabeth answered, clutching the small bag in her hands.

James pried it away, found the keys, and opened the door. He pushed her into the passenger seat. Elizabeth recognized her car.

As they drove along, it took a few minutes for the heat to reach her. Even then, Elizabeth kept her eyes closed to the flash of oncoming headlights and passing street lamps.

"How long have you been having migraine headaches?" he asked. His voice was disembodied and distant.

"I don't know," she murmured, her head pounding too much for her to try to think coherently. "Since . . . Claire . . ." she trailed off.

"Do you have any medicine?"

"I took it," she said, her head lolling back and forth. "After I left you."

James reached across, placing the back of his hand on her forehead. "Just relax," he told her. "Sleep."

The gentle rolling of the car over smooth road lulled her. After a while, the light and darkness stopped mixing and only blessed darkness remained. The road became smoother and shifting. James cradled her against his shoulder and she fell asleep.

Elizabeth opened her eyes to bright sunlight. Disoriented, she sat up in bed. A thick white satin comforter fell away from her like a cascading waterfall. She had on a pink nightgown, her own nightgown. She hadn't worn it in years, and this wasn't her bedroom. "Oh, my God!" she said aloud. She was in the guest room, James's guest room. Memory came back. She remembered the party, leaving with James, and the blinding headache. It was gone now. Sleep usually took them away. Why hadn't James taken her home? Why did he bring her here? She looked at the gown again. Had he kept it all these years, expecting her to return?

Surveying the room, done in shades of green and white, she found her dress and cape lying over a brass butler at the foot of the bed, the cape she'd left the previous night after her hasty exit. She paused, unsure what to do next. She had to get out of there. She didn't want to see James, be near him, have anything to do with him. Just as she stuck her foot from beneath the coverlet, the door opened. She pulled her foot back, instinctively raising the comforter to her chin.

"Good, you're awake." James's greeting sounded as if they were old friends who'd said goodnight only hours ago. He held a tray. Setting it across her lap, Elizabeth pushed her way up in the bed. She felt trapped. Her escape route had been blocked. Why did she sleep so long? Why hadn't she awakened, dressed, and left?

"What do you want, James?" Elizabeth didn't beat around the bush. James cocked his head to one side as if contemplating an answer. She realized the open implication of her question but refused to drop her gaze. "It's not like you to put up this show of masked enthusiasm unless you want something."

"I want you to eat your breakfast." He reached for the silver coffeepot and poured coffee into one of the two bone china cups.

"Did you cook this?" Elizabeth looked at the perfectly fried eggs, crisp bacon, and buttered toast. A single red rose in a crystal bud vase stood next to the linen napkin.

"Mrs. Andrews is in the kitchen," he smiled.

"Was she here last night?" Elizabeth dropped her head to glance at the nightgown. She wanted to know if he'd taken off her dress and put her in this nightgown.

"No," James said, all playfulness gone from his voice. "It's not the first time I've dressed or undressed you." He raised an eyebrow. "I must say, undressing you is more fun." He smiled that devastating smile that had first attracted her to him.

Elizabeth lifted her fork, covering her twitching lips. She liked the housekeeper and loved her cooking.

"Aren't you going to eat?"

"I had breakfast an hour ago." James pulled the Queen Anne chair from the antique desk and straddled it, careful of the delicate cup in his large hand. His casual jeans and white ski sweater didn't seem out of place across the centuries-old chair. "I'm willing to share yours." He reached for a slice of bacon. Elizabeth's fingers instinctively tapped his hand. They'd often done that in the past. The gesture wasn't thought out or conscious, it was just there, and both of them knew it. She then picked up the bacon and offered it to him. He took it, lifting it to his mouth.

Elizabeth couldn't help her gaze, drawn to his lips. They moved sensually as he chewed. She remembered them being on hers, the way they moved with such intimacy. Swallowing hard, she dismissed the image.

Elizabeth poured a cup of coffee, added cream and sugar, and drank, using the action to shadow the confusion she felt over her thoughts.

James stared at her. He still loved her. After three years, Elizabeth was the only woman he wanted in his life. She looked beautiful in the large bed. He had imagined her in *his* bed. It was where he'd wanted to put her last night, not in this guest room. This morning would have been quite different if she'd awakened to find herself wrapped in his arms.

She finished her breakfast and a second cup of the Irish Cream coffee Mrs. Andrews brewed each time she came. James took the tray and set it on the desk. Coming back, he sat on the satin cover next to her. Elizabeth quickly moved away from him. James noticed but said nothing.

"You asked what I wanted?" he began.

Elizabeth's gaze was level. The question was in her eyes, but she said nothing.

"There are eleven days left before Christmas. On Christmas Eve, I'm throwing a party. I want you to come."

"That's what this is about? You want me to come to a party?"

"It's more than that. I want you to come and *enjoy* yourself. Enjoy Christmas."

Elizabeth dropped her head. The riot of black curls were slightly straighter after she'd slept on them, but they still made him want to slip his fingers in them.

"I know what it's been like for the past three years." He paused. "I know you go through the motions as the holidays approach, smile in all the right places, attend all the right affairs, but you're having a miserable time."

James had always been able to read her. She thought she had hidden her real feelings under the act of enjoying herself. She wanted to deny his words but knew he could see through her lies, too.

"In less than two weeks, you expect me to enjoy the season again?"

James noted she didn't deny his statement. "I hope so."

"Are you suggesting therapy?"

James stared at the window. "In a manner of speaking."

"Therapy takes years. What could eleven days accomplish, even if I agreed?"

"It could change your entire life." He held his breath, knowing how much he was counting on changing her life.

"Why should this matter to you?" she asked.

"It matters," he said quietly. "I never wanted to hurt you, Elizabeth. And I don't want to be responsible for you disliking this time of year or only remembering the accident and Claire's death whenever Christmas approaches."

"I see," she said. "This therapy is really for you? You feel guilty and you're transferring it to me?"

His gaze went back to her. He hadn't thought of it like that, but in a way, it was true. If he'd left Claire alone that night, she might still be alive. And he'd be in jail.

"I'm not transferring it to you, Elizabeth, but we're both involved in this and it's only fair that we try to work it out."

"Exactly what are you suggesting?"

James looked directly at her. "In the next eleven days, I want the two of us to do some Christmas things. Remember the holidays we had before Claire died. Let those be the ones that carry us from season to season."

Elizabeth threw the cover aside, preparing to get out of bed. "No," she said.

James quickly put his hands on either side of her, trapping her in the satin folds. She looked back at him. She was close enough to kiss, close enough for him to smell her unique scent, feel her warmth. His mind was suddenly filled with memories of her. He wanted to touch her, pull her into his arms, and take her pain away, but if he acted, it would shatter any influence he had over getting her to agree to his plan.

Slowly he moved his hands and sat back on the bed. "Is this how you want to live the rest of your life, pretending you're happy and suffering through migraine headaches?"

Elizabeth turned completely away from him. Her shoulders slumped. James wanted to comfort her, but he did nothing. He hardly breathed.

"What did you have in mind?"

Three

The Stanford Arms Apartments sat on Connecticut Avenue, within striking distance of the Washington Hilton Hotel, where Ronald Reagan was shot during his presidency. Elizabeth occupied the corner apartment on the top floor of the pre-World War II building. The sand-colored brick structure looked stately and elegant in a neighborhood of stately and elegant apartment buildings. For all its old-world charm, Elizabeth's apartment had modern overstuffed sofas and carved cherrywood tables. Her kitchen was state of the art. The windows let in light and air and gave the place a feeling of openness. Living here was a far cry from the tiny two rooms she and Claire had occupied after their parents had died, leaving them debt-ridden and mortgaged. The bookcases were filled with books on handwriting, drawing, stenciling, and calligraphy. One of the extra bedrooms had an easel she often used to dabble in painting. Yet not a single Christmas decoration could be found in the two-bedroom suite.

At the offices of Invitation to Love, Elizabeth had a fully decorated tree, complete with wrapped boxes and mistletoe hanging from the ceiling. Here, she only had the memory of Claire and the agony of knowing that James had been part of her death. Here, she could let her pain be seen without the prying eyes of Washington.

Elizabeth lounged on the sofa, wearing black stretch pants and a green beaded sweater that fell a couple of inches above her knees. Near her feet lay an open book she hadn't been able to read. Though she stared through the windows, her mind was eight miles away, in a house nestled among the trees of Rock Creek Park. She'd agreed to James's plan before leaving this morning. He thought she was doing it to change her life and her view of the holiday season. How wrong he was. She was doing it to make his life miserable.

Three years ago he'd escaped. He'd gone to New York and stayed there, away from the memories, the streets, and people who looked at her with pity in their eyes. Even Theresa, Claire's best friend, had left for London. She'd felt alone and wretched, wishing she could somehow make it all different. It seemed ironic that she should spend her life making other people's dreams come true. Maybe she was trying all the time to forget she had dreams of her own that would never come true—either that, or hide from her own heartache.

Elizabeth jumped suddenly as the doorbell rang. Her foot kicked the book to the floor. Why was she so uptight? Getting up, she padded barefoot to the door. James's distorted features stared at her through the peephole. Elizabeth took a calming breath and pulled the door open.

"Hi." He smiled as he brushed by her. Behind him he dragged a huge pine tree. The apartment doorman followed him, loaded down with bags and boxes.

"Merry Christmas, Miss Gregory," he said under his strain. "Where do you want these?"

Flustered, Elizabeth said, "Anywhere."

"I'll take them." James grabbed a few of the bags and dropped them on the floor. He took the boxes and made a pile on the end of the sofa. Then he tipped the doorman, and they were suddenly alone.

"What is all this?" Elizabeth asked, turning around amid the chaos.

"We've only got eleven days." He pulled off his sheepskin jacket, throwing it casually aside. Standing in front of her, he said, "We're going to decorate your tree. I'd hoped you hadn't gotten one yet."

He meant he *knew* she hadn't gotten one yet. Elizabeth didn't have a tree and didn't want one.

"While we arrange bulbs and tinsel, I'm going to tell you all about the tradition," James ran on, as Elizabeth stood, unsure of what to say and do. "Where do you want it?"

"James, I don't want a tree. I spend so little time here." She paused. "There's one at the office, and—"

"You don't live at the office. Here, this looks like a good spot." He stood in front of the large picture window that faced the Capitol and downtown Washington.

"It blocks the view," she said weakly. Elizabeth loved that view. It was why she'd agreed to the exorbitant rent several years ago when she'd first seen it.

James leaned the tree against the wall and came toward her. Involuntarily she stepped back. He stopped. "You want this to work, don't you?" His eyes were serious, probing into hers as if he could look into her soul. "Don't you believe in Christmas anymore?"

Elizabeth nodded, not trusting her dry throat to speak. His approach told her he was going to touch her. Aching need revved inside her. She knew if she felt his touch she'd lose all reason.

"Then let's try to have some fun with it. It's what Christmas is all about," James said.

He reached up and his finger tapped the dangling earring on her left ear. Sensation ran through Elizabeth. The brush of the gold against her skin was as warm as James's fingers. Her hand came up and stopped the movement.

"I'll try," she agreed.

"Good. Now, where do you want the tree?"

Elizabeth told him to stand it in front of the window. While he positioned it for her approval, she watched him. She was still holding her ear. He'd always like to dangle the earrings she wore. There were times when she'd wait for him and he'd come up behind her and touch the earring or kiss her ear. Heat would warm her ear and spread through her body, just as it was doing now.

James pulled a tree stand from one of the boxes. Bending down, he quickly assembled it, humming "O Tannenbaum" while he worked.

"Why don't you put on some Christmas music?" James glanced over his shoulder.

"I don't have any."

He stopped and stood up. Elizabeth wished she were wearing shoes. She felt small next to his big frame. Stepping back, she tripped on the book and nearly lost her balance. She bent down, picked up the romance novel, and dropped it on the sofa.

"What happened to them?" James asked.

"I never . . . unpacked them . . . when I moved here."

"Why are you lying?" James accused. "You lived here before Claire died."

"All right, I packed them after she died. I didn't want to be reminded of Christmas. I hate it! I hate it!"

She turned away, her arms crossed in front of her in an effort to prevent herself from shaking. She stood there for several moments. Finally, her breathing returned to normal. Taking a deep breath, she turned back. James had not moved.

"Elizabeth, I'm sorry Claire's dead," he said softly. "I'm sorry I had any part in her death. I wish to God she'd never come into . . ." He stopped, leaving the thought incomplete. "In the past three years, Elizabeth, we've both been plagued by bad memories at Christmas. I want this year to be different."

Elizabeth suddenly felt guilty. Her goal had been to make him feel bad, yet she was the one who felt small, as if her actions were childish and petty.

Elizabeth tried to smile, but failed.

James stepped forward with a grin. "Smile," he said, then took her waist. "You'd better smile," he warned. Seconds later, his fingers squeezed inward, tickling her. "Come on," he urged.

Clamping her teeth together, Elizabeth tried to hold it in. She couldn't stop herself. Finally, the floodgates opened and she burst into uncontrollable laughter.

"Sto—opp," she cried, as she grabbed his hands and bent her

knees, slipping to the floor. James followed her, laughing with her.

He stopped tickling her, but she continued laughing. Only when she had no more breath left could she get control over her near-hysteria.

"Feel better?"

She nodded, wiping her eyes with the tips of her fingers.

He pulled her up, immediately releasing contact. From one of the bags on the floor he pulled a CD and offered it to her. "Put this on."

Elizabeth took the cellophane-wrapped package and went to the rack system in the corner. The disc contained a medley of Motown artists and a variety of Christmas songs. Gladys Knight's soulful rendition of "O Holy Night" filled the air.

"What's in the other bags?" she asked, returning to the center of the room.

"Open them," James told her absently. He'd finished the assembly of the stand and stood the tree in it. The room smelled pleasantly of pine.

Elizabeth loved surprises. As a child, the feeling of finding presents under the tree on Christmas morning always gave her a rush. She found tinsel, tree lights, colored bulbs, and garlands. Soon her living room was draped in colorful disarray.

When James was ready for the lights, Elizabeth found herself passing them back and forth as they draped the tree.

"I thought you were going to tell me all about Martin Luther and the tradition of decorating trees."

"Aha," he said, as if he were verbally flexing his muscles. "Many people attribute the tradition to Martin Luther. But long before the birth of Christ, people brought evergreens into their homes and decorated them. They held winter festivals and celebrated the winter solstice."

"Winter festivals?" Elizabeth glanced up from the box she'd opened. "Today we call them parties." She smiled at him, her first spontaneous action since he'd arrived. James smiled back as he stopped hanging glass icicles on the tree for an unguarded moment. Elizabeth turned back to the box and unwrapped several Victorian bulbs and placed them on the tree.

James returned to his story. "The festivals were thanks for a bountiful harvest and prayer that the next season would be plentiful. When Christianity became accepted, many people retained their winter rites, gradually changing them to honor Christ."

As James continued telling her about the tradition of Christmas trees, Elizabeth was mesmerized by the sound of his voice. A deep bass if he sang, the sound seemed to originate low in his body and flow forward. She had forgotten how much she loved hearing him talk. Opening another box of decorations, they filled the open spaces with bulbs, icicles, and Hallmark figures. When they got to the garland, the tree looked good enough for the cover of *House Beautiful* and James had reached the part of his story where the tradition came to the United States.

"The Hessians, German soldiers hired by the British to fight in the American Revolution, decorated trees during the holiday season and it caught on with the settlers."

"James," Elizabeth interrupted his story. "I know this part. I also know that President Franklin Pierce put up the first Christmas tree in the White House, that Calvin Coolidge lit the first outdoor tree, and that Eisenhower established the pageant of peace they hold on the Mall behind the White House."

"Good," James said. "That's the end of my story." He picked up the final unopened box. "How about putting the last decoration on?"

Elizabeth stared at the box. She knew it held an angel. They always topped the tree with an angel. "That was Claire's job. She always said the angel had been sent by our parents to watch over us."

"I'm sure she'd want you to do it."

Elizabeth lifted the lid. She gasped when she saw the delicate black doll, dressed in a white gown as sheer as gossamer. The box dropped to Elizabeth's feet as she lifted the angel, holding it as carefully as she would fine glass. Feathered wings extended from her back, arching up like summer clouds. Black eyes looked deep into Elizabeth's.

James touched the treetop ornament, his hand brushing Elizabeth's. "Put it on," he whispered.

"I can't reach it," she said, her head slowly rising to look at him.

"I'll help you."

Before she could stop him, James had lifted her from the carpeted floor and hoisted her to his shoulder. Vertigo claimed her momentarily. The floor looked miles away.

"Put me down!" She grabbed his shoulder, nearly dropping the doll.

"In a minute. Put the angel on the tree."

James stepped forward, his arms holding her firmly. Elizabeth reached for the top branch, unsure of her position. She felt as if she were going to fall. Quickly she stuck the angel on the extended branch.

"Put me down," she said, when she'd secured the ornament.

James's hands slid up her torso to grasp her arms. He slid her down his body. Elizabeth pointed her toes as if she were a ballet dancer and he was practicing a lift. Heat scorched her bottom as it rolled over James's chest. Elizabeth bit her bottom lip. Her heart hammered in her chest. Her brain told her to get to the floor fast, yet another part of her body savored the hard strength of him, remembered the hours of lovemaking, his arms wrapped around her, filling her with warmth and security.

Elizabeth mentally shook herself, trying to get control of her rampaging emotions. An eon passed before her toes felt the thick carpet pile. James turned her in his arms. She faced him, her voice caught below the lump in her throat.

"What do we do next?" he asked.

Four

Mrs. Andrews would have his head if she could see what he'd done to her kitchen. Bags of sugar lay strewn on the counter and an open one had spilled onto the floor. There were enough grains under his feet for him to perform a soft-shoe routine. The flour sack flopped over the moment he opened it, clouding the room and settling a powdery dust over everything. Chocolate sprinkles and rainbow toppers waited with red and green sugar crystals, bowls, spoons, a sifter, and half the spices from the supermarket shelf. James's previous excursions through the kitchen were to get to the barbecue pit in the backyard or to raid the refrigerator for fried chicken and cold milk in the middle of the night. He couldn't imagine baking Christmas cookies here. And why cookies?

When he'd asked Elizabeth what they should do next, baking had been the last thing on his mind. From the look in her eyes, it wasn't her first thought, either. Yet he *had* given her the option of picking the next Christmas tradition they should share. He couldn't back out of it now, even if he did hate cookies. He wondered if she remembered that and had chosen this as a punishment. He knew she'd agreed to his plan so she could turn the tables on him. Was this her way of doing it? It wasn't going to work; he loved her too much. Being in her company, even if she tried things he hated, was better than spending his days and nights without her.

His mother had made sugar cookies and they seemed to act like a homing device for Elizabeth whenever the oven was lit.

Tonight he'd spend the evening with cookie dough on his hands, letting Elizabeth instruct him on what to do with the sprinkles or any of the other items she'd had him buy. She'd given him a list of the things they'd need, and he'd come back from the grocery store with six bags of ingredients. He hoped he had enough.

Glancing at the clock, he knew Elizabeth would be here any moment. She'd always been prompt. He'd better at least get the sugar off the floor and get the counter back to a presentable state.

The doorbell pealed before he'd finished. Hastily he dumped the grains into the trash. Then he dropped the dustpan and broom into the closet and started for the door. At the archway where he'd kissed her, he stopped. His heart was beating wildly. Taking a deep breath, he waited a moment. He'd been nervous ever since hearing her voice on the other end of the phone this afternoon, when she'd itemized the things they'd need. After that, there was no way he could concentrate on futures, the Dow Jones Index, or whether NASDAQ was up or down. His thoughts were on his beautiful brown baby.

The bell rang again, startling him from his reverie.

"Hi," she said with a smile.

It was the old smile, the one that did strange things to his heart. James could do no more than grin. The wind was blowing hard. Elizabeth was wrapped in a fur coat and hat. Only her face showed, framed by the dark fur. Her eyes were dancing and her mouth was red and kissable. It was all he could do not to pull her into his arms and indulge in the urge at the forefront of his mind. He stood back and let her in. Helping her with the heavy coat, he stood close enough to smell the sensuous scent that was hers alone. His body grew warm, a prelude to the familiar reaction he had whenever he thought of her. With her so close, he'd have to be careful. Turning away, he took extra time hanging the coat in the closet.

"Did you get everything?" she asked.

"I found everything on the list."

"Good," she said. "Shall we begin?"

James took her arm as she turned toward the archway. Her eyes weren't just dancing, they were brilliant, as if she had a secret and was dying to tell it. "Can't we have a drink first?"

"Of course."

Her smile was so radiant, James couldn't help but be suspicious. She'd been reluctant to decorate the tree, but now she seemed to have done a complete reversal. Something was not as it seemed.

He went into the great-room, Elizabeth following him. At the bar, he watched her as he poured glasses of white wine. She pulled off the fur hat and used her fingers to pick the short curls. The act was so simple, yet fire alarms were going off inside James. He had to convince her how much he loved her, how much she loved him. He couldn't tell her everything she thought he'd done in the past had been Claire's doing. He wanted her to trust him enough to know he'd never have done anything to hurt her. Last night, decorating the tree, he felt he'd broken a little of the ice she had around her heart. Tonight he was going to have to turn the tables and let her know he knew where her ploy was leading.

Elizabeth dropped down on the padded bar stool and took the glass James offered.

"You're especially happy tonight," he said. "Something happen?"

Elizabeth took a sip. She was bubbling over with happiness. Something wonderful must have happened to her.

"I got a release today." She paused.

James waited. "A release from what?" he asked, after a long moment. He knew it had to be something spectacular. She had a client list that read like a Who's Who of Washington society, but Elizabeth was proud when she did something for people who had little power behind them.

"Not from what. *For* what." She grinned and took another sip. "The Department of the Interior gave permission today for the air show I've been planning."

James came around the bar. "Tell me about it."

"Three hundred hot-air balloonists are going to fly children over the Mall area on the Fourth of July. They'll take off and tour the monuments and Rock Creek Park, then land in RFK Stadium. The children will love it."

Elizabeth sat forward on the stool. Her body was poised with an excitement he hadn't seen in years. She glowed with the happiness reserved for children on Christmas morning.

"The balloonists are donating their time to help the Children's Fund." She stood up, leaving her glass on the bar. "You'll love it, James. It's going to be a perfect day for a child."

James recognized Elizabeth's favorite charity. He also heard the excitement in her voice include *him* in her future plans. He wondered if she knew she'd done it, if it was an unconscious slip of the tongue, or if she really wanted him in her life. He certainly hoped the latter was true. "What about the airport?"

"No planes in or out for three hours."

"Not even Air Force One?"

She grinned coming toward him. "Not Air Force One, not the military, not United Airlines, not anybody."

"How long have you been working on this?"

"Months," she said, her eyes rolling toward the ceiling. "But it's been worth it. I hadn't expected to hear anything until well into the new year. Then today I get a call saying everything's been approved." She looked at him, her face glowing. "I can't tell you how good I feel." Elizabeth wrapped her arms around herself and spun like a top. "Tomorrow night I get to announce it at the Fund's Christmas party."

"Congratulations," James said. Elizabeth's excitement reached him. He went to her and took her in his arms. He kissed her left ear where her earring dangled. Sensation flashed through him at the emotions that flared within him. "I'm almost afraid to ask how you did all this."

Elizabeth leaned back. "I don't know how I did it." Her arms reached around his neck and she pressed herself against him. "And I don't care. It's done, and I'm ecstatic."

James couldn't stop his arms from holding her close. He buried his face in her neck as she hugged him, smelling her scent and kissing her soft brown skin.

Elizabeth suddenly changed in his arms. Her body grew still and stiff as wood. He knew she remembered where she was. The excitement of telling him about the children was gone. She was aware of him, the changes in his body, and the heat gathering around them. He didn't move, didn't breathe. He knew he had to let whatever happened between them be her decision. He knew what his would be, but Elizabeth couldn't be rushed or pushed into a relationship. He didn't even know if she was still in love with him. He only knew when he'd kissed her, she'd reacted.

Slowly she leaned back. James didn't prevent her from moving out of his arms, if that was what she wanted. He hoped it wasn't. She stopped. He could feel her breath on his cheek. If he turned his head, his lips would brush hers. The urge to move was stronger than he was. Leaning back, he moved his head. Their breath mingled. His fingers reached into her soft hair. She angled her head toward him. "Thanks for sharing your news with me," he whispered. His lips took hers.

He wanted to take it slow, unhurried, tender, but his mouth touched hers and three years of hunger poured through him. His tongue found the sweet nectar of her mouth. Something inside Elizabeth snapped, too. She melted in his arms and together they battled for primal supremacy. His hands caressed her, finding familiar places, hearing familiar sounds. Elizabeth was thinner than he remembered, but she was just as hot and just as intoxicating. She tortured him with her mouth, her touch, the way she felt in his arms, the way her legs brushed against his. He needed to stop this torture or soon he'd lift her and carry her to the room he thought they'd share three years ago. Yet his mouth continued to find and battle with hers.

Finally, Elizabeth slid her mouth from his. *I love you, Elizabeth.* The words reverberated so loudly in his head he was sure he'd spoken them. How had he lived these past three years without her? If he couldn't make her fall in love with him before the party, how was he going to live the rest of his life? He'd grasped at the idea of trying to change her outlook on Christmas, but he really wanted her back in his life.

James's arms tightened around her. She didn't try to pull away. Her breath came in short gasps. James held her, trying to control his own raging emotions. Elizabeth's shoulders shook. At first he thought she was having as much trouble gaining control as he was. Then he realized she was crying.

Elizabeth had thought she could do this. She'd thought she could make James miserable. She knew better now. Her heart wasn't in it. Today, when clearance had come for the balloon show, she couldn't wait to tell him. He'd been the first person she'd thought of, not Mrs. McCaffrey, who ran the Children's Fund, or even Mary, with whom she shared practically everything. She hadn't even thought of the children who'd be thrilled when they found out. Her only thoughts had been of James Hill. But how could they have been? How could she still want to run to him, after what he'd done to Claire?

Nine more days. How was she going to survive them? Nine days in James's company, trying to remember how he'd lied about Claire, driven her until she'd fled from him and lost her life in an accident he'd walked away from. She knew what her brain told her, but her heart ruled when James walked in the door. Her heart remembered the love, not the pain. Tonight, they should be making cookies, a project she'd chosen because she knew he'd never eat them. James loved chocolate cake with chocolate icing, and even though his mother made the best cookies Elizabeth had ever tasted, James was the only family member who didn't eat them. Elizabeth didn't want to make the cookies now. It was petty. James had come to her with a tree and all the trimmings. His purpose had been to help her, while hers was to make him feel bad. She couldn't do it. She had to go.

"James," she said, pulling herself out of his arms. "I don't feel much like baking cookies now. Do you mind if we do it another night?"

"Why don't we just talk for a while?"

Elizabeth hesitated as if she were making a decision. Finally she nodded and James led her to a sofa. At first it was awkward. Neither of them knew what to say.

"I—I want to apologize," Elizabeth began.

"For what?"

"For the reason I agreed to your plan." She glanced at him, wondering what he was thinking. "I know you want to help me to deal with Claire's death. It was at Christmas, and I seem to relive it every year." James waited. He didn't say a thing, and Elizabeth found it difficult to read his thoughts.

"You wanted to make me pay for the way you felt, make me feel as sad as you do."

"You knew!" She stared at him, her eyes wide with surprise.

"I knew," he nodded. "If you hadn't tried to make any contact with me in the past three years, what else could be the reason for you suddenly agreeing to my company?"

"I know you didn't really have anything to do with Claire's death. At the time, I was so—"

"Why don't we try to forget it and begin again?"

Elizabeth smiled. She felt as if a weight had been lifted from her. "I'd like that," she said.

Elizabeth unconsciously lifted the receiver and spoke into it. "Invitation to Love. May I help you?" For the week before Christmas, she was unusually busy. Washington society, where the pace ran nonstop twenty-four hours a day, where emergency crises cropped up at least once a week, planned their parties well in advance, and neither world crisis nor war seemed to interfere. Elizabeth had just finished the three-hundredth calligraphic invitation for Mrs. Joy Carson's annual Valentine's Day ball.

"Well, Little Lizzie, how have you been?"

Only one person in the world called her that. "Theresa!" Elizabeth yelled into the phone. "Where are you—London? Or have you come home for the holidays?"

"I'm right here in the capital city."

"Are you going to be here long? Will we get a chance to have lunch or dinner and talk over old times?"

Elizabeth hadn't seen Theresa since Claire died. She and her sister has been the closest of friends. Although Claire knew many people, she had few friends, but she and Theresa had been inseparable. Claire's death had hit Theresa hard, and Elizabeth was sure it was part of the reason she'd accepted the position in England.

"I'll be here through the new year, but I'm afraid between family and previous invitations, I don't have a free moment to myself. I will be at James's party, so I'll see you there."

"I'll look forward to it."

Elizabeth replaced the receiver. She was smiling. A few days ago a call from Theresa would have brought the bad memories back to her, but today they didn't. Was this James's doing? Could his plan really work? She had enjoyed decorating the tree and spending the evening with him. The fire glowed against his skin with memories of their Christmas in the mountains. Happy thoughts of snowball fights and icicles hanging from the roof filled her mind, not the gruesome details of a policeman, Officer Robinson (she still remembered his name), coming to tell her Claire and James had been in an accident and Claire was dead. Not even noticing Claire's files when she'd pulled out her own stored Christmas decorations had put a damper on her night with James.

She looked forward to seeing Theresa and talking to her, even about Claire.

The small bell over the door rang, and Elizabeth got up. The day was nearly over, and Joanne had gone an hour ago. Elizabeth had to handle everything until she closed.

"Delivery," the uniformed Federal Express agent said. He handed Elizabeth a clipboard and showed her where to sign.

Elizabeth scribbled her name on the electronic pad and the agent slipped five large boxes from his hand truck.

"One more trip," he said. He left, returning moments later with another load of identical boxes.

"Thank you," Elizabeth said, her mind wondering about the delivery. She wasn't expecting anything, but at this time of year, she often received gifts from vendors, some of them elaborate and useless.

With a nod and a "Merry Christmas," the Federal Express agent left. Elizabeth pulled the tape away from the first box and opened the lid. The unmistakable smell of sugar filled the air. Dropping the lid to the floor, she opened the first tin inside. She found sugar cookies, gingerbread cookies, cookies shaped like bells, decorated Christmas trees, all sorts and varieties of Christmas cookies. They were perfect. James couldn't have done this, she thought, biting into a sugar cookie. After she'd left him, he couldn't have spent the night making these. She was sure in his world of buying and selling stocks and bonds, learning to bake wasn't at the top of his priority list. She took another bite. It was delicious.

Laughter bubbled up in her at the picture forming in her mind of James covered in white flour, rolling out cookie dough and cutting Christmas shapes. The laughter went on until her eyes were smarting and she thought her sides would split.

"I'm glad you're getting such a kick out of this, especially since you didn't help at all."

James stood in the doorway. He closed the door and came into the room.

Elizabeth took a cookie and went toward him with it. She raised it to his mouth. He brushed her hand aside and caught her around the waist. "I'd much prefer you to cookies," he said, before dropping his mouth to hers in a soul-spinning kiss. "I suppose it was worth a lost night's sleep for the reward I get."

"Did you do this all by yourself?" Elizabeth pushed herself out of his arms and went back to the boxes.

"I tried. Do you know how many cookies you can make from a five-pound bag of flour?"

Elizabeth looked up. "Dozens," she said.

"Twelve dozen," he told her.

Elizabeth stared at the cache on her floor. "How many cookies are in here?"

"At last count, that would have been about four o'clock this morning, there were twelve dozen of seven varieties, with more in the oven and even more to go in."

Elizabeth laughed.

"This is not a laughing matter, woman," he said with mock annoyance. "I intend to see that you eat each and every crumb before the next sun rises in the sky."

Elizabeth tried to stop, but each time the picture of James stacking dozens of cookies into tins and boxes came into her mind, mirth overcame her. "If I'd known you'd be so good at cookies, I'd have suggested English pudding cake, complete with charms." Elizabeth replaced the cover of a cookie tin and turned back to James.

"Somehow, I don't think I'd like the suggestion you're making."

"You like tradition. You'd loved it."

"Would I?" He raised an eyebrow.

Elizabeth had been waiting for him. It was time for her to close. Locking the front door, she walked about the shop, turning off lights and preparing to leave. "There are several charms, a wishbone, a horseshoe, a thimble, a coin, and a bell, each with a special meaning."

"The horseshoe and the wishbone could mean good luck and the coin good fortune. What do the others mean?"

"The horseshoe means good luck, the wishbone grants a wish, the coin does mean good fortune, the thimble blesses the owner, and the bell signifies an upcoming wedding."

Elizabeth turned off the lights that illuminated the window displays. Only one light remained, burning at the back of the counter.

"What do you do with these charms?"

"You bake them inside small cakes." She snapped off a counter light.

"I hope you tell people they're in there."

"Oh, you do." She smiled.

"I guess we'll leave that tradition for next year," James said. The anticipation of a continued relationship after this season ended was not lost on Elizabeth. He was a silhouette in the darkened room. She couldn't see his features and hoped he could not see hers. Elizabeth pulled her coat from the closet. James came to her and helped her into it. She felt his hands on her shoulders a moment longer than was necessary. Then he tapped her earring. Heat spiraled inside her and she wanted to step back into his embrace.

"What are you going to do with all these? You can't leave them here."

"I have the perfect place for them," Elizabeth said. Taking a tin from the box, she set it on the counter, then closed the crate. "Grab a box. We're going to load them in the van."

James did as she instructed and followed her to the back door. They quickly filled the space with the seven cases of cookies and climbed inside.

"Where are we going?" James asked, when Elizabeth pulled onto P Street and headed east toward Dupont Circle.

"To visit the one person I know who can get rid of eighty-four dozen cookies in less than an hour."

"Mark," he said.

"Mark," she confirmed.

Elizabeth smiled at her reflection. Green sequins twinkled as she moved and a row of them tingled her knees as she walked. Around her neck was a single gold chain, a cluster of diamonds at the end of it forming a present. The crossed ribbons were outlined in emeralds. Elizabeth remembered buying it the first year Invitation to Love had made money. It had been impetuous and impractical, but she loved it.

In the past, she'd have dreaded dressing to go to yet another Christmas party. Tonight she glowed as brightly as the first

Christmas star. James was picking her up in a few minutes and her thoughts had run to him since she'd made the mistake of selecting his card from her Rolodex. It felt like ages ago. Yet it had been only five days. Five wonderful, smiling, happy, lovely days.

Again she looked at the woman in the mirror. She couldn't help smiling. The doorbell rang. Elizabeth had given instructions at the desk for James to come right up. Opening the door, a rush of emotion washed over her. James stood there, looking better than any man had a right to. He stepped in the foyer and quickly kissed her cheek, a habit he'd taken to doing whenever he saw her. She had to admit she loved it, just as she loved all the things they did together.

"You look gorgeous," he said, coming into the room. "I can see I'm going to have trouble getting a dance with you tonight."

"I'll make sure to add your name to my dance card at least once," she promised.

The tree they'd decorated blinked at intervals, giving the room a festive look. The CD he'd left behind played in the background and a fire burned in the fireplace. Elizabeth had a sudden wish to stay home tonight, to ask James to forgo the party and spend the evening with them wrapped in each other's arms as they'd done countless times in the past.

She knew she couldn't. Tonight was her party for the Children's Fund. A few congressmen, hoping for reelection, would be there, along with the entire staff of the Fund. She was one of their champion fundraisers, and with the news she had to deliver tonight, delaying her appearance would be criminal.

"You look so good, I wish we could just stay here." James voiced her thoughts.

"I have to be there," she told him, glad he couldn't see the heat that poured into her face at his comment. "I have good news to tell them."

"I know. It's just that I'm jealous. I don't want to share you with anyone.

Elizabeth swallowed hard. Her eyes locked with his and they

stared at each other, sharing a moment only lovers could understand.

"Where's your coat?" James took the embarrassment out of the moment. He helped her into the fur coat and turned her to face him, his hands on her arms. He didn't say anything, just stared at her with the strangest look in his eyes. She felt something change between them but didn't know what it was or if it was good or bad.

"Is something wrong?" she asked.

He was quiet for a long moment, then he shook his head. "Nothing."

They left then. Elizabeth sat in the warm luxury of the Lexus. James was silent. He'd been in a different mood when he'd come to the apartment, but in the space of a few minutes something had changed between them and she didn't know what.

She didn't get to find out at the party. From the moment they arrived at the Daughters of the American Revolution hall, Elizabeth was pulled from one person to another. She grabbed James's hand and stayed near him, introducing him to people who pumped his hand and immediately tried to find out his position on fundraising.

After the dinner speeches began, Elizabeth made her announcement. When she left the podium, she was mobbed as if she were a rock star. James was pushed to the wall, where he watched and waited. Elizabeth kept track of him as she talked to everyone. James hadn't been in the best mood when they'd arrived. He was probably bored and needed to get out of there. Elizabeth finally got out of the crowd. She grabbed two glasses of champagne and came up behind him.

"Excuse me," she said. "You look a little lost. Can I help?" She smiled, hoping he wasn't angry, and offered him a glass.

"Do I know you?" he asked, continuing her joke. "Or are you trying to pick me up?"

She cocked her head to the side. "I haven't picked anyone up in years, but you look like a reputable character. Are you going my way?"

"I'd love to go with you, but you see, I didn't come here alone."

"And your mother taught you to always see the girl to her door?"

His eyebrows rose in mock surprise. "Do you know my mother?"

Elizabeth laughed. She hoped his mood was changing, that the man who'd entered her apartment tonight was coming back—not the one who'd left.

"Would you like to dance?"

"I'd love to dance," she said.

In the main salon, James turned her into his arms, and Elizabeth melted. She barely heard the sound of the band or the lounge singer. A music all her own played in her head. It felt good, being in James's arms again. She felt as if her life had been suspended since he'd left three years ago and she'd buried herself in her work. Tonight, work wasn't so important. Nothing was as important as the way she felt . . . the way James made her feel.

For hours they danced, talked, smiled at other people, and wondered if anyone was as happy as the two of them. Finally, it was time to leave. Elizabeth walked on air, humming softly to herself as they slipped into the elevator and ascended to the top floor of the Stanford Arms Apartments. James had his arm around her waist, and she'd never been happier.

"I had a *wonderful* time," she said at her door. She inserted the key and pushed inward. James followed her inside. She dropped the keys on the foyer table with her purse.

He grabbed her arms as she started to walk further into the apartment. "I think I'd better say goodnight."

Elizabeth frowned. She didn't want him to leave. "Don't you want a drink—some coffee or something?"

He stared at her. Elizabeth recognized the mood he'd had earlier, before they'd left. "Yes, Elizabeth," he said. "I would like something . . . If I stay . . ." he left the phrase hanging. "Goodnight, sweetheart. I'll see you tomorrow."

He kissed her on the mouth, a kiss so tender Elizabeth thought she'd float away. Then he left her. The door clicked as he closed it. She stood there stunned, staring at the closed portal, wondering why he'd left her alone. How had she gotten to this point? They'd shared only five days together, and not five whole days, just parts of them. Yet she'd changed. She'd hated James for years; in five days, he'd changed her into a woman who wanted him desperately—and when he could have had her, he left.

Why?

Five

James turned over for the hundredth time. The clock on the night table read three o'clock. Why couldn't he sleep? Wasn't everything going as he'd planned? Elizabeth was falling in love with him. He could have stayed tonight, made love to her. God knew he wanted to. Why didn't he? And why did he feel like such a heel? He'd done nothing wrong. She was the woman he loved, the one he wanted to spend his life with, the one he needed to complete himself.

"Claire," he breathed, with all the malice he could muster. Even from the grave she was between them. She'd always be between them, unless he could get Elizabeth to understand what Claire had been trying to do; how she'd manipulated people to get what she wanted; how she'd used everyone—himself, even Elizabeth, her loving sister. If it hadn't been for Theresa telling him Claire's plan, Elizabeth wouldn't even have had Invitation to Love. Claire would have seen to that.

Punching his pillow and flopping over on his stomach, James tried for a comfortable position and the inevitable coming of sleep, but both eluded him. Then he thought of Elizabeth. She had changed some in the last three years. Her appearance was markedly different, mostly due to the short haircut. She was thinner, and a sadness seemed to hang over her. She smiled in all the right places and appeared at the right events, but behind her eyes, there was reserved sadness. In the last few days, he'd seen some of it disappear. God, he hoped he was responsible for taking it away. He wanted it all gone, not a trace of it left. He wanted

Elizabeth happy. After spending her life trailing Claire from one tenement to another, she deserved a better life. Damn, she was there again—Claire, between them.

He turned back over, his arm across his forehead as if he could ward off the memories. What was Elizabeth doing now? he wondered. Was she awake, thinking of him? His body hardened at the thought. Now he wished he'd taken her up on her invitation to stay the night. She hardly knew she'd issued it, but it had been clear to him.

Listening to the quiet, he willed his body to calm down. In the distance, he heard a dog barking, the wind pushing at the windows, and the faint hum of a car engine. Kicking the covers aside, he turned on the lamp and got out of bed. Pushing his arms into the maroon velour robe, he belted it. He found his slippers and headed for the kitchen.

Hot milk might help, but he hated it. He was after cold milk and cold chicken.

At the bottom of the steps, something caught his eye. Sticking out of the mail slot was a white envelope. It hadn't been there when he'd come in. Mail was never delivered through the slot. He had a box at the edge of the property. The slot was merely for decoration. The door hadn't been part of the original purchase. When he'd bought the house, a year before Elizabeth had agreed to marry him, the entry door had been the only thing he hadn't liked. During a business trip to Charleston he'd found an old building being demolished. He'd bought the Corinthian-columned door and had it installed.

Grabbing the envelope, he recognized Elizabeth's precise handwriting. With all the styles of lettering she'd mastered, her own writing was almost straight up and down, with no slant and an economy of flamboyance. When had she delivered this? He'd left her at her apartment just after midnight. Suddenly, he remembered the engine hum. Yanking the door open, he scanned the area. She was there, near the curb.

"Elizabeth!"

She was almost in her car, but his shout drew her attention.

James dropped the envelope and ran. She wasn't in the driveway but had walked up from the street, some fifty yards away. Getting to her was the most important thing he'd ever done. She stood still, watching. He wasn't sure what had brought her here. He only knew he wasn't going to let her leave.

James's breath congealed in the cold air; his heart burst in his chest. He didn't ask why she'd come here. He didn't ask why she hadn't rung the bell. He took her in his arms and kissed her. The blowing wind, swirls of snow that threatened to turn into the capital's first snowfall, didn't touch him. He had Elizabeth; nothing else mattered. She shuddered against him. His lips grazed hers. He held the back of her head and ground his mouth into hers.

Elizabeth's arms went around his waist. She shifted, wedging herself against him. James's body tightened. Passion flared between them. His tongue swept into her mouth. He crushed her against him, knowing his strength could break her bones, yet feeling the weakness she caused in him. His hands moved over her, from her shoulder blades to her hips. James couldn't believe she was here, in his arms, returning his kiss. He was losing control. Her mouth was a seductive narcotic under his. He wanted her now!

Elizabeth returned his embrace with equal force and fervor. Moving her away from the car, he slammed the door and led her toward the open doorway.

"What are you doing here?" he asked between kisses, when they were inside and he held her against the closed door. He didn't give her time to answer. He took her mouth again, trading one hungry kiss for another. His hands wanted to explore every part of her body, but her coat inhibited him. Stepping back, he found the fasteners and released them, running his hands inside the fur and pulling her slender frame into contact with his.

Elizabeth's passion-filled eyes stared at him in the half-light. Her mouth was swollen from his kisses. Between them hung the oldest unspoken language in human history. Desire had gnawed at him for days. He couldn't resist it any longer. She was here—real, warm, soft, and filling his arms.

"Elizabeth," he groaned. "I'm so glad you came."

"I couldn't sleep," she told him, her body pressing into his.

He reached down, slipping his arm under her knees and lifting her from the floor. With her head resting against his shoulder, he mounted the wide staircase and entered the master suite.

Elizabeth hadn't been in this room in three years, yet she knew every inch of it. Maroon and green paisley drapes hung at the windows, perfectly matching the rumpled comforter on the king-sized bed. James held her close. She listened to his heart pounding strongly under her ear. He lowered her feet to the carpeted floor, keeping her close. She didn't move away from him. Her arms slid down his chest and she trembled at the sensation flowing through her body. She could feel the need pooling between her legs. Elizabeth told herself she had come to leave the letter; that it was a prank and James would get a good laugh out of it in the morning. She knew it was a lie. She wanted to find him. She wanted him to come to the door and see her. And she wanted to be here now. This is where she'd wanted to be for three years.

James's reentry into her life had shown her how much she'd missed him, enjoyed his smile, his playfulness. She wanted to forget the past and think only of the moment.

Her fingers inched to the opening of his robe. Fire burned her as she skimmed his chest, but she kept going. Holding her breath, Elizabeth leaned forward and placed her open mouth in the V of his robe. She felt a tremor shake him. Strong hands grasped her arms. Smoothing her fingertips over his hot skin, she undid the knot. With one fingernail she outlined his male breasts, then flattened her fingers and rubbed them across his nipples. Small nubs hardened under her caress. James's hands tightened around her arms.

"Elizabeth." His voice, thick with emotion, shook.

He brushed through her hair, angling her head upward. His eyes, dark and smoldering, looked almost painful with need.

"Are you sure?" he asked.

Elizabeth nodded.

Slowly his features blurred as he captured her mouth again. This time the kiss was slow, tender, passionate, the way their first kiss had been. Her arms circled his neck, her body melting into him.

James had never wanted a woman as much as he now wanted Elizabeth. He told himself there was too much between them that needed to be cleared up before they could go on with their lives. He told himself clearing the air was the honorable thing to do, stepping back and allowing his brain to lead him. But at that moment Elizabeth rubbed herself against him. Rapturous spasms coursed through him and all thought left him except the one that said this was the only woman in the world for him.

Bending down, he kissed her ear where the earring brushed her skin. Soft, delicious sound, like a purr, came from her throat. He liked hearing her moans and hoped they would continue. His hands brushed up and down her back, cupping her round hips and pulling her closer to his own hard body. She gasped at the action. A smile touched his lips at the rapture he saw on her face. Then he kissed her lips, unable to resist. Pushing her coat off her shoulders, he let it slide to the floor. Her sequined gown had been exchanged for a gray knit dress that hugged her curves. Finding the zipper at the back, he lowered it with restrained patience. Then he peeled the dress away, revealing skin as smooth and clear as wine.

When the dress joined her coat on the floor, Elizabeth stood in only a black teddy and stockings. Electricity suddenly snapped in the air, an obvious reaction to the furnace burning in his gut. His body, already erect and ready, was stabbed with a wave of desire so strong he was sure his control would erupt. Pushing her down, he sat her on the side of the bed. Kneeling before her, he unhooked her stockings, kissing the skin where the delicate nylon ended. Elizabeth's hands gently massaged his back. He felt his muscles contract at her touch. Intense emotions swept through him.

She closed her eyes and tried to breathe. Her skin was on fire.

Wherever James touched her she thought she'd incinerate, evaporating into a steaming gas. The torture he put her through was more than she could handle. Biting her lower lip, she tried desperately not to scream, but she could hear the moan coming from her throat. He removed her stockings with a slowness that knotted her stomach. Then, unable to continue at an unhurried pace, he made quick work of the teddy. The light behind him bathed his skin in a healthy glow of burnished brown. His robe joined forces with her discarded clothes at the foot of the bed.

James joined her, pushing her back and uncoiling his body down the length of hers. She splayed her hands over his broad shoulders, feeling his muscles contract and relax under her palms. Quickly she raked her nails down his back. He arched against her. She reveled in the feel of his naked skin next to hers, hot, like scented oil.

He kissed her shoulder, his hands running over her length in slow motion. Elizabeth caught her breath, burying her face in his skin. His hands worked erotically over her, pausing to sample spots he seemed to like. When the pads of his thumbs grazed her breasts, she called his name. His mouth replaced the exquisite torture of his hands, suckling the wine-colored strawberries as if it had been made for this task alone. Lingeringly, he went on, tasting her body in every detail. Elizabeth sank her fingers into his shoulders. Her mouth opened without sound as she struggled to control the screams threatening to break forth.

"God," she prayed. "I don't think I can wait any longer."

With lightning speed, James opened the bedside table and grabbed a foil pouch. Heat enveloped them as James leveled himself over her. Kneeing her legs apart, he entered her easily. Elizabeth let out a long breath filled with three years of yearning. Emotion welled up inside her strong enough to burst through her chest. His gentle movement took her by surprise as the intensity of feeling flooded her senses and threatened to overload.

"James," she moaned. "I've missed you."

"I've missed you too, honey."

She didn't know how much he'd missed her, how many nights

he'd dreamed of having her here in this room, in his bed, making love to her until she screamed. He wanted her to scream, wanted her to call out his name in hungry desire. He wanted to possess her and be possessed by her. He kissed her again, grasping her supple buttocks and lifting her onto him. Her legs anchored behind him, giving him room. He sank deeper and deeper into her folds with each powerful stroke. His control had long since gone. Elizabeth did that to him like no other woman ever had or ever could. With her, he couldn't hold anything back. He gave and took as she did. Together they created the perfect match, a union that had no beginning and no end. With her he made love.

James didn't remember how good she could feel. He touched her everywhere, cradling, crushing, kissing, massaging, until a great tide gripped him. His rhythm increased, intensified, as he cried her name over and over. He never thought he'd have this feeling again. Then it happened. Great bursts of electrified air imploded, carrying them into the mushroom cloud of magnificent pleasure.

She took his weight as the last aftershock ran through James and he collapsed onto her. They were both wet with perspiration and love. The room smelled sweet with the aftermath of their lovemaking. Elizabeth wrapped her arms around him. A smile curved her mouth as she closed her eyes, aware of every throbbing inch of his frame as it covered her, chest to chest, thigh to thigh. His heart pounded against hers.

After a time, James slid over to her. He gathered her close, kissed her eyes, her cheeks and her mouth as tenderly as if he were saying goodnight. Then, silently, they slept.

Dear James,

Your visit sparked good memories of Christmases past. It sent me to the storage room. While rummaging through old boxes of decorations, I found a card you sent to me several years ago. The cover had a reproduction of the scraggly handwriting of eight-year-old Virginia O'Han-

lon's letter to the editor of The New York Sun. *Inside was printed the famous editorial run by the paper on September 21, 1897.*

You asked me if I believed in Christmas, and like Virginia's question, I'd like to answer it.

Yes, James, I believe there is a Christmas. Last night a group of children came carolling in front of the shop. Their tiny faces were stung by the cold, their eyes were wide with innocence and wonder. My heart grew so large I thought I would cry. When they left, I walked through Georgetown looking in the store windows. The streets were crowded with shoppers. I watched them picking out gifts for loved ones, deciding whether something was right for Uncle Jim or Aunt Agnes. It was easy to pick out the faces of lovers, holding hands and walking through the cobblestone streets as they made and shared Christmas memories.

In every direction I looked, the windows were decorated with green and red for the holidays. In a small store close to M Street I found a black Santa mounted on his sleigh with eight reindeer and a sack full of presents. I bought it. It's the first decoration I've bought in three years. The purchase made me smile, and a warmth filled my insides. Nothing has done that in a long time.

At home, I dragged the Christmas decorations out of storage and into the living room, where I went through them all. Christmas is a time of sharing, of remembering old friends, and making new ones. Rereading the cards and carefully unpacking the bulbs we'd stored showed me how much I missed the merrymaking Christmas brings. The years I've spent without a Christmas seem empty compared to the ones where family and friends shared the joy.

Happy Holidays,
Elizabeth

James read the letter twice. In the wake of Elizabeth's unexpected arrival, he'd forgotten about it. It lay on the floor by the door, where he'd dropped it last night when he'd sprinted across the lawn. Taking it to the kitchen, he read it a third time as coffee filled the pot and the aroma permeated the crisp air. He remembered last night. Elizabeth had filled his arms and his world. He liked thinking of her sleeping upstairs—sharing his bed and his life. He wanted to come to her each evening, tell her his problems and share his happy moments. Had last night been the beginning of that?

"Good morning." Elizabeth's voice was husky.

James turned to find her leaning against the door. Her short curls were sleep-mussed and her eyes were only half open. The combination was so sexy his body hardened in response. She wore his green robe, its long sleeves and bulk dwarfing her.

"The coffee smells good."

He looked at the letter, then slowly brought his gaze back to her. She said nothing but levered herself away from the doorjamb and stood up straight. He went to her, folding her in his arms and kissing her ear. It was enough for the moment. He wanted, needed, to be close to her. She'd been in the shower. He could smell the soap on her clean skin, skin his mouth found soft as morning dew. "Sleep well?" he asked.

She nodded, snuggling against him. James slipped his fingers into her short curls and angled her head upward. He brushed her lips with his.

"I got your letter," he said, his body growing harder against her.

Elizabeth leaned back, smiling.

"Did you mean it?" he asked.

"You'll have to wait till Christmas and see if Santa leaves anything for you. Of course, you know he only leaves presents for *good* little boys." Sticking her finger in her mouth, she asked in a child's voice, "Have you been a good little boy?"

"I certainly hope so."

Six

The blue background of the computer screen didn't hold James's attention. For two days he'd thought of nothing but Elizabeth and their night of lovemaking. After she'd appeared in the doorway of the kitchen, and after they made breakfast, they made love again. For a second time they duplicated the fire that burned within them and refused to be extinguished after three years of separation. They were both late getting to the office that morning. Since then, he had done very little work. It was good the market was slow the last day or two, or he'd have had to fire himself.

With his jacket discarded and his sleeves already rolled up, he gave his full attention back to the screen. The price of Bristol-Myers Squibb stock had gone up while he'd been daydreaming. He had several clients who would find that favorable if it held through the end of the year.

"Hey?"

James looked up. Theresa Simmons stood in the doorway. Her coat, as yellow as a summer sun, was splashed with arcs of bright red and purple. Theresa hadn't changed. Only she could use color as a statement. Fortunately, for her, it worked.

"It's after five o'clock, the market's closed, but I knew I'd find you here." Her smile was as bright as her wardrobe. "When are you gonna get a life?"

"Theresa!" he called, getting up and rushing over to hug the six-foot-tall woman. "I didn't think I'd see you before the party."

"I should be at Blackie's," she told him, checking her watch.

"I'm meeting Janis and Harry for dinner, and then we're going to Ford's."

She mentioned her sister and brother-in-law as if they could wait. Theresa was forty-two, and Janis was her personal Cupid. Without Theresa saying so, James knew there would be a surprise guest at dinner to round out the couples.

"When I saw the light," Theresa went on, "I stopped so I could tell you to close up shop and go home."

James laughed. "I'll be leaving soon, and I *do* have a life." He thought of Elizabeth waiting for him. "Sit down a minute."

Theresa lowered herself into one of the leather-tufted chairs that stood before James's massive desk. James took a seat behind it.

"Anybody I know?"

He nodded, but offered nothing else. He tried to keep the smile off his face, but each time he thought of the dark-skinned woman, he couldn't help it.

"Is it Elizabeth?"

He nodded again.

"Well, why didn't you say so?" Her eyes were as large as gold coins. "It's about time. I thought after Claire's accident you two were doomed."

"Don't jump to conclusions," James cautioned. "I've only been back here a short time. After the funeral and the trade commission investigation—" He stopped, not wanting to think about the accusations made against him.

"We effectively covered that up," Theresa prompted, her voice softer and lower.

That they had, James thought, trying to keep the frown off his face. They'd reversed everything Claire had done and erased any record of it. They'd destroyed the forged power-of-attorney copy, giving Claire the right to act as agent for Invitation to Love. James shivered at what she could have done with that and how Elizabeth would have been devastated to find her beloved sister had ruined her business.

"You went to London and I went to New York," he finished. "I came back a few months ago."

"And Elizabeth?"

"I've only seen her five or six times."

"Well, what's wrong with you, man? I've never seen a woman as in love as Elizabeth was with you."

James's mind flew to Elizabeth. He almost felt her naked body curled against his. Quickly he glanced at the small clock on the desk. In an hour, he'd pick her up. They were going Christmas shopping tonight.

"She's different, Theresa. She took Claire's death hard and she still hasn't recovered. She puts up a strong front, and anyone who doesn't really know her can't tell how miserable she is underneath."

"So you're taking it slow?" Her expressive eyebrows rose.

"I'm trying," he told her. "Actually, I feel partly responsible."

"How? It was an accident. You didn't drive your car into Claire's on purpose."

"I don't feel responsible for the accident, but for abandoning Elizabeth."

Theresa set her rather large purse on the floor and leaned forward in the chair. "Talk to me," she said.

James appreciated the way her agile mind could read more in conversation than the words expressed. He knew she was trustworthy. Never had she broken a confidence, and if it hadn't been for her quick thinking, he might well be in jail this very minute.

"Why did you accept that job in London?" he asked, abruptly changing the subject. "It wasn't just the career move or being able to visit a foreign country. You had a perfectly good job here." He waved his arms about the room. Theresa had been the best broker he'd ever had. She had a knack for the market, could anticipate its changes with unerring accuracy. "Your salary was well above the norm. You had a score of friends and relatives and you lived comfortably." He stopped with a smile. "Despite Janis's tactics."

"I wanted to escape," Theresa said. "Claire was my best

friend. I knew her better than anyone, except maybe Elizabeth. brought her here and convinced you to give her a job and she betrayed us both. I thought leaving the city would help the wounds heal faster."

"So did I," James agreed. "I went to New York to manage the office there. The pace of this city is fast; New York runs on tomorrow's schedule. I thought I could lose myself, forget the police interrogations and defending myself before the Securities and Exchange Commission." He paused. "We found an avenue for our pain and grief. Elizabeth remained here, alone. She had no other family and no one to call on, only the memories of her sister and her parents, all of whom had died. Even her friends and her former fiancé had gone away."

"It doesn't matter that she lashed vile accusations at you. Said you were responsible for Claire's death and that she hoped you'd rot in jail."

"Claire had just died, leaving Elizabeth believing the lies she'd told her. Elizabeth's loyalties were divided. Her words were angry. I thought she'd get over them."

"And she hasn't," Theresa finished for him. "No wonder she's still mourning Claire."

"She's not exactly mourning. We have Mark to thank for that. He went to see her constantly. He'd drop by her shop to make sure everything was all right. He'd always mention her in his letters and phone calls to me. Finally, he called to say he couldn't go through another holiday seeing her acting instead of enjoying."

"So you came back?" Her voice held no censure, no incredulity, not even wonder. It held understanding. James was glad Theresa had returned. He needed her as much as he needed Elizabeth.

For a long moment they were both silent. James thought of the girl he'd met the day she and Claire had moved next door to them. Everybody walked around her, carrying boxes and lamps, books and furniture. She looked lost and alone then, too. James found out they'd told her she was too small to help. She sat in a lawn chair, her legs crossed Indian-style, a bowl of ice cream in her lap. He sat down and talked to her. After a few moments she smiled and offered him her bowl. The ice cream had melted to a warm paste. He ate it anyway. He was sure that was the moment when he'd fallen in love with her. James wondered what Theresa was thinking. Glancing at the clock again, he saw it was nearly time for him to go, and Theresa was going to have to skip dinner or be late for the curtain at Ford's.

"I talked to her on the phone a couple of days ago," Theresa mentioned. "She sounded fine."

"She is fine," he told her. "She just needs some time."

"She's had time, James," Theresa said dryly. "What she needs is love."

James watched his friend scrutinize him. He didn't attempt to hide his feelings.

"You're in love with her." It was a statement.

He nodded.

Invitation to Love was on 30th Street in Georgetown between N and O Streets. Several blocks away the tourist traffic moved as a human sea that waved toward the Wisconsin Avenue thoroughfare as if it was a welcoming shore. Parking was nonexistent as it was all over the District of Columbia. Fortunately, Elizabeth had secured the lot next to her shop, where four cars could park at the same time. Getting in and out of the small spaces required the kind of maneuvering that Washington drivers had come to know and understand. Behind the main shop were two additional spaces. Elizabeth's white corvette, gleaming under the halogen security lights, occupied one of them. James pulled his car into the other one.

The building that housed Invitation to Love had once been a residence. Elizabeth had kept the basic outside structure, not wanting to destroy the neighborhood design of stately row houses by adding display windows. From the front, the only designation of business was a prominent sign in the small yard etched in gold letters. Inside, the building had been kept mostly intact. A wall here and there had been removed or built to accommodate the need for workspace. When she'd begun the handwritten invitation business, she'd had to live upstairs. Now she used the space for storage.

Climbing out of the Lexus, James took the four steps to the back door two at a time. Opening the screen, he knocked lightly. Moments later Elizabeth pulled the lace curtain aside and smiled when she saw him. *Now, that's what I came through this hot, dusty summer day to hear.* A line from *The Long Hot Summer* ran through his head. It wasn't a hot summer day, but a blustery, wintry, cold one, and he hadn't heard anything, but had seen her smile and nearly dissolved.

"I brought you something," James said, when she opened the door. He passed through it, holding the paper bag up for her view.

"What is it?"

Elizabeth locked the door and pulled the bolt into place. She followed him back to her office, which was crowded with paper samples, cases of pen tips, boxes of greeting cards, and flowers. The smell of pine boughs permeated the air. James noticed the artificial tree sitting on her desk. The fireplace was lit and mistletoe had been hung over the door. He didn't comment. Elizabeth grabbed his arm. "What's in the bag?" she asked.

James caught her around the waist and pulled her against him. He kissed her quickly on the mouth. "Something you can't resist."

He let her take it from him when she reached for it. She tore it open and grabbed the contents.

"Ice cream?" she questioned.

"It's butter pecan," he said, as if that was an answer.

"Moving-in day." The memory hit her like a thunderbolt. "You remember."

"I'll never forget."

"Do you want to eat it now?"

"We haven't had dinner, and this'll certainly ruin your appetite."

He imitated her mother. Elizabeth remembered her mother telling her that whenever she found butter pecan ice cream in the grocery bag. Since they had often been in each other's houses, she knew James had heard her mother say that a hundred times.

"If I suggested we wait until after the mall, would you agree?" she asked, in her best parent's voice.

"No." He smiled.

"Then you get some bowls while I put on my jeans." She headed toward the door leading to the stairs. She'd hung an extra change of clothes there this morning.

"I'd much rather help you."

Elizabeth paused in the doorway. She turned back to James. "That might not be a bad idea, but then we'd have to eat ice cream paste." Her smile was sly. She turned again.

"We've done it before," he called after her.

James pressed the accelerator as the car shot pass the legal speed limit on its way to Tyson's Corner Mall. Elizabeth sat in the warm interior, smiling to herself. She wondered why he'd thought of the ice cream. They had shared it many times as children. When she was five, and still believed in Santa Claus, James had dressed in a red suit with white fur and surprised her. They'd eaten the bowl of warm ice cream she'd insisted on putting out for Santa instead of the traditional cookies and milk. Elizabeth laughed out loud.

"What's funny?" James asked, in the dark light of the car.

"I was remembering," she told him.

"Good memories, I hope."

"It had to do with a ten-year-old boy who had no whiskers at all, but he dressed up in a red suit to please a little girl who believed in the wonders of Christmas."

James's stomach knotted. He remembered doing that. In fact, after the Gregorys had moved next door to his parents, in one way or another, their families had always spent Christmas together. He had spent Christmases with Elizabeth. If he sifted through his memories, he could uncover all kinds of pleasant times they had spent together, including the winter in the Blue Ridge Mountains. They'd gone there on a whim, a quick ski trip a couple of days before the holiday. Then the snows had come, stranding them. Christmas had dawned as the embers in the fire had died and he and Elizabeth had found their own method of spontaneous combustion.

Hitting the brake, James swung the car onto the shoulder and threw the gearshift into park. Snapping the seatbelts that anchored them to the bucket seats, he hauled Elizabeth over the center console and into his arms. His mouth found hers and seared it with an electrifying kiss. What had made her remember that? He'd nearly forgotten about that Christmas. Elizabeth's arms tightened around his neck as passion flared between them. The interior of the car felt like a blast furnace. Yet his mouth devoured hers with a need so compelling he thought he'd die without her.

Breathing rapidly, he slid his mouth aside and kept her close to him. She smelled like a sweet flower. James tried to gather her closer, despite the barrier between them. What was he going to do when Christmas ended? Suppose Elizabeth decided she didn't want to see him after the holidays were over? She'd only made the deal with him for eleven days. On the twelfth day she'd have no reason to continue seeing him. Her memories would be in place. Her smile would be genuine. And Claire would still be dead. To Elizabeth, he would still be responsible. He couldn't change that fact.

"James." Elizabeth called him out of his reverie. "We can't stay here on the highway." Then she turned her mouth back to his and all was lost. James brushed her smooth skin, cradling her to him. He kissed her as if this was the last time they'd ever be together, sliding his tongue into her open mouth and drinking abundantly from the well. He held her reverently, giving and taking, communicating with his senses, trying to let Elizabeth know she was the only person in the world for him. He wasn't aware of how long they stayed together in the confines of the small space, just that he enjoyed holding her.

Tyson Corner's only distinction was that it was a sprawling developmental community created out of the wilderness of northern Virginia about thirty miles outside the nation's capital. It also contained one of the largest malls in the eastern United States. The parking lot that ringed the two-story facility had appeared adequate when the mall had opened twenty years ago. Then the Christmas shoppers had descended and finding an open space was like waiting for someone to die to get an apartment in New York.

James traveled up and down the rows of late-model cars, searching, following people who appeared to be leaving the crowded chaos of three shopping days before Christmas.

"There's somebody leaving." Elizabeth pointed to a car. James turned in time to see the exhaust fly from the tailpipe of a silver-gray Toyota. Snapping his blinker and hitting the brake in one fluid movement, he waited for the driver to vacate the space. Then he backed in and got out into the cold air. Each store appeared to outdecorate the next in the number of Christmas items on the outside of the mall. The total picture turned the buildings into a green-and-red light show.

James slipped his arm around Elizabeth's waist and they walked toward the entrance.

"Where should we go first?" Elizabeth asked, as they edged through the throngs of people inside.

"Who's at the top of your list?"

"No one," she said. "I'm done."

"Done?" James stopped walking and turned around to face her.

"Mary is the only person I need to shop for. I ordered gifts for my clients." She smiled, but James saw that it didn't reach her eyes. "Who's on the top of *your* list?"

He hesitated before deciding to let the remark go. "My mother and Mark," he said. "Let's find something for Mark first."

They proceeded through the crowds, slipping into and out of

men's stores. Elizabeth lifted and replaced ties, shirts, pajamas, books, gold chains, and bracelets. She appeared to get into the spirit, talking about the kind of person Mark was and what he was more apt to like and use. James was sure she put this kind of thought into her clients' needs; that was why she was as successful as she was. Finally, they decided on a caricature of a doctor with a huge needle in his hand and a frightened patient in the bed. Elizabeth borrowed a felt-tipped pen from the cashier, drew a name tag on the doctor's pocket, and printed Mark's name there. James selected an art deco frame of black and white and they agreed to pick it up before leaving.

The rest of his list was settled in the same manner, with Elizabeth going into the attributes of the person before deciding on the perfect gift. The only remaining name was his mother's. He and Elizabeth had traversed the mall twice without finding anything for her.

"When did the tradition of giving Christmas presents arise?" she asked, as they were jostled about.

"Why would I know that?" he asked. They had made their way to the center of the four-winged building. A display of Santa in a sleigh with his eight reindeer on a bed of white cotton snow had been set up in the center. The line of children was miraculously absent. It might be due to the late hour.

"Each time we do anything you tell me the history behind it. So far, I've learned that winter festivals were designed to entice a fertile spring and developed into a celebration of the birth of Christ; that Christmas trees were brought to the United States by Hessian soldiers keeping their winter traditions; that families hung mistletoe and kissed each other under it on Christmas morning; and that greeting cards were a way of saying hello to friends you hadn't seen in the past year. I thought gift-giving was next."

"I don't know the history behind gift-giving."

"Good," she smiled, taking his arm in intimate-lover fashion. "Something I can tell you. It started with the three kings—Balthasar, Melchior, and Gaspar, who came from Arabia, Persia, and India. They traveled over the desert to present gold, frankincense, and myrrh to the Christ child. After that, people made gifts and presented them to their family and friends at Christmastime. It wasn't until the Industrial Revolution that handmade gifts gave way to factory-produced goods."

They stopped, dodging a mother with a stroller. The child slept at an oddly bored angle. Overstuffed bags hung from the twin handles. Every other available space held packages and bags. The woman pushed it hard, like a manual lawn mower on an uphill plane. James pulled Elizabeth close and they walked on. "Even if they aren't handmade, a lot of thought goes into getting the right gift for the right person," Elizabeth continued.

James looked around. Even the harried expressions on some of the faces were tempered by a mask of goodwill.

"That's the part that makes the shopping fun." Elizabeth's light voice reached him.

James hoped she was having fun, that their trip was enjoyable and she wasn't thinking of being alone with no family at this time of year. She'd only had to shop for one present. He hoped she included his family as hers, since the spirit of Christmas was in the giving. Tonight he could see it. Elizabeth sparkled when she was caught in the spirit.

As they walked, Elizabeth suddenly stopped in front of a jewelry store. "Your mother," she said. "She'd love that."

In the window was a gold spider pin. The body was a huge diamond.

"A spider!" James frowned.

"Not that." She pointed to a statue in the corner. "That." It was of a jazz singer from the twenties. She wore a slick dress of blue that adhered to the curves of her body. Her ceramic skin was a creamed-coffee color. Her head was thrown back and her tight waves and curls cascaded to her shoulders. The details were soft, not harsh or straight, as with other statues he'd seen; this one spoke to him as he knew it would speak to his mother. James felt she'd just finished a song. The statue was wonderful. His mother would love it. Again Elizabeth had shown her ability to find exactly the right gift.

Elizabeth studied James as he talked to the clerk, a tall, thin woman of about fifty with soft blond hair and beautiful hands which set off the rings she wore. While James paid for the statue, which the clerk called "Blues Singer," Elizabeth browsed, looking into the glass cases. Rows of watches, birthstone rings, and gold chains glittered under the display lights. Crystal bowls and clocks set in a glass case shone brightly against one wall. She stopped now and then to take a closer look, then went on. Something caught her eye and she gasped.

The case held wedding bands and engagement rings. The ring she looked at had a set of geometric circles, seemingly designed by a drunk artist. The three levels were similar but unique in design and without end. They were crusted with small baguette-cut diamonds. The crowning stone must have been at least six carats, she thought. It stood like a statue on a pedestal of gold. Around it the circles were steps leading to an altar. It took her breath away.

"It is beautiful." The clerk who'd been helping James spoke to her. Elizabeth's absorption had been so complete she hadn't realized James's transaction had been finished and he was standing behind her. Suddenly she felt embarrassed, caught doing something she shouldn't do. She muttered something to the clerk and turned to him.

"Ready?" she asked.

He nodded and they left. On the way out, Elizabeth couldn't help glancing back at the display case. She couldn't see the ring, but its beauty was embedded in her brain.

Seven

The small bell over the door tinkled. The day had been slow and she'd been daydreaming about James. He filled her thoughts all the time these days. She came out of her reverie. Her body froze when she saw the man looking around the small shop. He wasn't wearing a uniform, but with or without it, Elizabeth recognized him. Officer Edward Robinson had been the policeman who'd come to tell her James was in the hospital and Claire was dead. He was probably a detective by now, she thought. He was dressed in a jacket with the familiar Indian insignia of the Washington Redskins football team. In his hand he held a baseball cap with the word "Jordan" written on it.

She stood up straight, forcing a blank expression to her face. "Good morning," she said. "Is there anything I can help you with?"

He looked her directly in the face, but she saw no sign of recognition. "My wife sent me here." He paused. "We decided to have a little New Year's Eve party, and she wanted a special invitation." He looked a little embarrassed. "She said the President comes here."

Elizabeth heard that a lot from people who'd never been to the shop before. "He doesn't come here."

"But he *does* get his invitations from you?" he probed.

"Some of them," she hedged. Often she got FBI agents in here trying to quietly investigate her. He didn't look like one of them.

He smiled as if he'd just made the arrest of the century. "Of course, we can't pay what he does, but we'd like them to be special."

"Is this your first party?" she asked, already knowing the answer. Newlyweds always wanted to have a party, and they never planned it far enough in advance. It wasn't a problem for her. Usually they didn't want more than thirty invitations and the lettering they chose was simple, but even if she had to create a crest for each invitation the order could be completed in a couple of hours.

"We were married last June, and Margaret—that's my wife—thought it would be fun to have some friends in to celebrate. We'll need about forty invitations."

Elizabeth began her standard speech, pulling out catalogs of samples and inviting him to browse through them until he found something he liked. He took about five minutes to decide. As she wrote the order, she noticed him studying her. He picked up one of her cards which sat on the counter and glanced from the scripted paper to her.

"You know, ever since I came in, I've been trying to place you."

Elizabeth looked up. His eyes were penetrating now, as if he'd shed the clothes of the awkward husband and donned the uniform of an officer of the law. He glanced at the card again.

"You're Claire Gregory's sister, aren't you?"

She completed the order form and tore it from the pad. "Yes," she said, handing it to him. "I'm surprised you remember me. You saw me only once." Elizabeth knew her comment told him she recognized him, too. The near lifting, almost a twitch, of one eyebrow signaled she was right.

"I'm good with faces." He took the paper.

Elizabeth heard the pride in his voice.

"Even if I wasn't, I'd remember Claire Gregory."

Elizabeth's chin started to lift. She forced it to stay level. "Why is that, Officer?"

"If that little scheme of hers had worked, I know one prominent stockbroker who'd be doing time."

Elizabeth gripped the counter as all the breath in her body threatened to leave it. "What scheme? You have it wrong. Claire's the one who'd be in jail."

"Not the way I see it, ma'am." He twirled the black cap in his hands. "I'm sorry." He turned to leave. At the door, he turned back. "Any chance I can pick those up tomorrow? I know it's a rush."

"They'll be ready after twelve," she said absently.

What did he mean, James would be in jail? What scheme was he talking about? James had been the one. He was accused by Claire of using insider information. James had been called before the SEC to defend himself against the charges. Then he and Claire had been involved in the accident and the case against James had fallen apart.

Was he guilty? She was so sure when she first heard it, it couldn't be true. She trusted James. He would never do anything dishonest. Why would he need to? He was a partner, the youngest man to ever join the elite firm. James was intelligent and good at what he did. His clients had no cause for complaint over his handling of their accounts. How did he handle them? she wondered. Did he use information he had, insider information, illegal information, as Claire had accused? When she thought about it James had risen unusually fast. His partnership and his bank account moved with meteoric speed. Then the accident had killed Claire, while James hadn't even been admitted to the hospital. He was treated in Emergency and released. She'd been so angry. She'd flung vile words at him. She'd called him a thief and a murderer. Later on, she'd been sorry. She hadn't meant most of what she said. He hadn't confirmed or denied anything. Why? What did that officer mean?

She had to know.

The accident had occurred past Embassy Row, in the 4000 block of Massachusetts Avenue. It was four o'clock. Elizabeth's desk clock pinged out the hour. The police station's reporting office, which handled the paperwork, would close before she could get there. She wasn't even sure they would have a copy of a three-year-old accident, but she had to try. Grabbing a directory, she located the number and placed a call. Her suspicions were true; the report had been archived. They could get her a copy in five working days, maybe more, depending on the amount of people taking vacation at this time, and there was a charge for the report. Elizabeth checked the calendar. Today was Thursday. If she counted today, she couldn't get it until after Christmas. She wanted it now. Keeping her annoyance out of her voice, she asked the clerk to please request it.

At 4:45 she finished Officer Robinson's invitations and stacked them in a box fitted for their size. When the five o'clock chime sounded, she locked the office door and got into her car. Claire had left some papers, files Elizabeth had put in storage. She'd noticed them a few days ago, when she'd pulled the Christmas decorations out. There were two boxes simply labeled "Claire's Files." They'd arrived the day she'd buried Claire. Elizabeth hadn't even looked at them. The doorman had informed her of their arrival when she'd returned home after a soul-draining day. She'd asked him to have them put in storage, and that is where they'd sat for three years. She'd never opened them. She'd told herself she'd open them later, but she had never found the time. Tonight she couldn't put it off any longer. Whatever demons were inside the boxes, it was time to face them.

By seven o'clock Elizabeth's living room looked like an explosion in a paper factory. She sat barefoot, still in her business suit, among the manila folders, computer printouts, and stacks of paper. Her mind told her this couldn't be true, but there it was in black and white. The charges against James for using insider information were false. This didn't make her feel any better. His crime was worse.

He had embezzled $650,000 and tried to frame Claire.

* * *

Where was she? James wondered. She should have arrived an hour ago. He lifted his beer from the bar and checked his watch. Something had happened. His heartbeat accelerated. Nothing happened, he contradicted himself. She's fine. Using a cellular phone, he dialed the number for Invitation to Love. On the second ring the recording clicked in. He hung up. He'd already left two messages there. He dialed her apartment. Again a machine answered. Draining the glass, he paid the bill and left. Something was definitely wrong.

His foot went almost to the floor as the powerful car shot up Connecticut Avenue. He had swung by the shop. Everything was locked and secure, and her car was missing from its standard parking place. Where could she be? What could have delayed her, and why the hell hadn't she called? Was she sick? Had she been in an accident? His imagination listed excuse after excuse for her standing him up. All the while he fought the thought that something could have happened to her. Not now, he told himself. They were getting close. He knew she was physically attracted to him. Lately, he was sure she was beginning to fall in love with him. Nothing could happen to her now.

James cursed when he found no parking places near her building. Impatient to find her, he pulled in front of the apartment building and threw the car into park.

"Is she in?" he asked the doorman, when he jumped out of the car. His voice held all the force of a drill sergeant's.

"Miss Gregory came in about five-thirty."

James's knees nearly gave out with relief. "Did she leave again?" His tone was softer. He felt bad about barking at the man.

"No, sir."

James didn't wait for anything more. He pulled the glass door toward him and rushed inside.

"Mr. Hill, your car," the doorman called.

James flipped his keys over his shoulder. The man rushed sideways as he went for the outside pass. James continued into the waiting elevator. At Elizabeth's door he knocked loudly and called her name. Anger was getting the better of him. She'd stood him up, not answered her phone, and caused him undue stress. His heart felt tight in his chest and he was wet with perspiration from the adrenaline high she'd put him through.

She didn't reply.

"I know you're in there." He banged again. "Open this door."

The banging startled her. Elizabeth sat up, drawing her legs to her chest and wrapping her arms around them. She lowered her head to her knees and rocked. How could it be true? She'd denied it for three years, told herself the SEC was wrong, that James was the most honest man she'd ever met. He wouldn't embezzle money. Yet he'd done it. She looked at the damning paper as if it were a snake. It lay at her feet, poised, ready to strike. It was all there. Claire had kept the entire file of his transactions. Then Claire had died and James had somehow fudged the records. He'd walked away, his skin intact, absolved of all responsibility, while $650,000 and a woman's life had been lost.

"Elizabeth, please open this door." She heard him. His voice was lower, muffled through the thickness of the barrier between them. It no longer sounded angry. "I just want to make sure you're all right."

All right? she thought. That was a laugh. She didn't think she'd ever be all right again. To think she'd almost fallen in love with him again, after years of trying to forget what he looked like, how his arms felt around her, how good he smelled and tasted. In a week he'd erased all the ground she'd gained and placed her back in that vulnerable position she'd stood in three years ago. She wouldn't open the door. She didn't care what the neighbors thought of him banging on the steel door as if it were a barn.

She rocked back and forth. Tears rolled silently down her face. After twenty minutes he stopped. Then the phone began to ring. She knew it was him, knew he had a phone in his car. She refused to answer. She sat rocking, staring into space. Around her the floor was cluttered with papers, weapons that had stabbed at her sense of euphoria and ripped it to shreds.

Three years ago he'd sworn it wasn't true; that what she'd heard, what Claire had said, wasn't the whole truth. Reaching over, she picked up a paper. Here was the truth: a listing of funds transfers, dollar amounts, dates, times, and James's transaction identification code, as unique as a fingerprint, next to each one. The code was an anagram of their names with their wedding date embedded in it. It could only be James's. Claire had used the word "Majestic" as her identification. It was the name of the apartment building where she lived. She said it was easy to remember and no one would guess what it was.

Elizabeth let the paper go. It floated on the warm air, cutting half moons as it settled at her feet. She stared at it until it blurred before her eyes. Her head pounded with the beginning of a headache. She didn't care. Nothing mattered anymore.

After a while she told herself to think straight. She needed to make decisions, decide what would happen now. She was going to have to break any ties with James. He was a liar, a thief, and maybe a killer. She rejected the latter. Claire's accident had been just that, but the papers before her were another matter. In truth, she should send the files to the SEC. He deserved to go to jail for what he'd done. A fresh batch of tears rushed into her eyes. Elizabeth bowed her head and sobbed. Water ran down her face. She held her head, trying to contain the pounding as more tears came.

She couldn't send him to jail; she realized it now. No matter what, she'd fallen hopelessly in love with him.

Eight

James hadn't slept all night. He paced the bedroom, replaying yesterday's events in his mind, trying to find the one thing he'd done or said to make Elizabeth react as she had. They'd spoken on the phone. She'd told him the day was going slowly. She couldn't wait to leave, and she would meet him for dinner at the Key Bridge Marriott right after she closed. She had sounded glad to hear him. She'd been smiling. He could hear it through the clear wonders of fiber optic phone lines.

He'd sat in the bar waiting. The tiny white lights that twinkled in the ceiling year round gave the place the look of Christmas. He'd imagined Elizabeth there among the star-spangled night. What could have happened to make her refuse to talk to him, or even acknowledge his presence at her door? If it hadn't been for her neighbors checking to see what the noise was about, he'd still be there. Someone had to have come into the shop and upset her, but who? Theresa?

He'd talked to Theresa two days ago. She wouldn't have done it. She was the only person, other than him, who knew the whole story about Claire and she would never hurt Elizabeth by telling her. Grabbing the phone, James dialed Theresa's number.

"Did you talk to Elizabeth yesterday?" he asked, when a sleepy voice answered.

"James, is that you? Do you know what time it is?"

He took a deep, calming breath and checked the digital clock on the bedside table. It read five A.M. Elizabeth was driving him out of his mind. "I'm sorry, Theresa."

"You've been up all night," she stated. "What's happened?"

"Have you spoken to Elizabeth?"

"No, why?"

"Something happened yesterday. I don't know what, but I can't get her on the phone, and she refused to open the door for me at her apartment."

"Are you sure she was home?"

"Her car was parked in the garage and the doorman said she'd come in and not gone out again."

"Do you want me to—"

"No, don't do anything," he interrupted. "I'll find her, and I'll find out what's wrong."

He could hear Theresa's hesitation through the silence of the phone line. "Call me when you find her," she commanded.

"I will." He felt deflated as he replaced the instrument in its cradle.

Morning dawned with a light snow. The weathermen had predicted a white Christmas. At 8:30, James dialed Elizabeth's phone number again. He'd been calling her since seven. He was greeted by two rings and the incessant voice on the answering machine saying she was unable to come to the phone at this time. "Unable or unwilling," he muttered, slamming down the receiver.

Unconsciously he paced the room. Nothing made sense. He needed to talk to her. There was no way he could solve this. Checking his watch, he saw it was nearly time for her to open Invitation to Love. Taking the time to shower and dress, he retraced his route from the night before. She'd already left her apartment when he got there. The shop showed no activity. He sat next to the empty space where Elizabeth usually parked. Where would she go? When he was tense, he usually went to the gym. When Elizabeth needed to be alone, where—? He stopped, his heart thudding against his chest. White flakes collected on the hood and in the angle created by the windshield wipers. When Elizabeth was upset there was only one place she'd go—home.

James backed out of the space and pointed the car toward Wisconsin Avenue. Snow in D.C. impeded traffic as it did nowhere else on earth. The cobblestone street was backed up with bumper-to-bumper cars. He crawled at the pace of a turtle until he passed the library at R Street. Then the road widened and he raced along at fifteen miles an hour behind a line of cars whose drivers appeared to have all the time in world.

A drive that usually took ten minutes took over an hour. Finally he turned onto Cathedral Avenue and raced toward his parents' house. The garage doors were closed and the driveway empty except for the snow. The faint shadow of two sets of tires told him his parents had left long before. Hopefully they had arrived at work before the crowds on Wisconsin Avenue had brought traffic to a near standstill. He parked and got out. Scanning the neighborhood, he searched for any sign of Elizabeth. Then he saw her car. Snow covered it. She'd been here a long time.

Rejecting the entrance door to his parents' house, James jogged around to the back. Across the yard sat a red-brick three-story colonial which Elizabeth and her family had lived in until she was thirteen. The house was empty now. The last family had moved out a month ago. They had added a large pool. It was straight along one side and staggered along the other. A green cover closed it for the winter. The white snow nearly obliterated the green. Behind the pool bushes flanked the back wall. In front of them sat a white-painted garden swing. In this light the swing nearly blended into the white surroundings created by the falling snow. Elizabeth's dark fur coat contrasted with it as she swung back and forth. Her eyes were fixed in front of her. James stopped when he saw her. He wondered how long she'd been there. Her face looked frozen. Her hands were inside her pockets, and snow covered her boots to her ankles.

Quietly he approached. She didn't move. Even if she saw him in her peripheral vision, she gave no acknowledgment.

"Elizabeth," he called softly.

She didn't move. He wasn't sure she knew he was there.

"Elizabeth, we need to talk."

The swing squeaked as it moved, the only sound in the still morning. James stepped inside the swing and sat next to her. Her eyes were fixed, like those of a person lost in an inner world.

"You can't stay here. It's too cold." He was afraid to reach for her. She looked as if she'd shatter if he touched her. "Come on. We'll talk inside."

Elizabeth's head slowly turned to face him. Her eyes were as cold as the howling wind that gusted up and stirred the snow. She gave him a stare that would wither a man. He withstood it, not knowing why it was directed at him.

"Did you do it?" Venom dripped from her lips.

"Do what?"

"Did you steal $650,000?"

James's shoulders dropped. "Yes," he said.

Elizabeth had known if she stayed at the old house long enough, James would remember. He'd remembered the ice cream from moving-in day. They'd grown up together, been engaged. He knew what she did when she was happy and that she always found her way to this house when she was sad. He'd found her here countless times after her parents had died. Although it had been years since she'd needed the anchor of the red brick building, she had no place else to go. She couldn't stay in her apartment with Claire's files staring at her. Here seemed the only place she could retreat to, where memories made her smile and lightened her heart.

She'd seen James the moment he'd come around the patio, but she hadn't moved. The wind didn't bother her; she was numb already and the cold hadn't penetrated to her core until James had spoken.

All night she'd told herself there had to be another explanation. No way was he capable of stealing that much money and blaming someone else for it. Yet each time she convinced herself of his honesty, the hateful piece of paper proved her wrong.

Elizabeth stood up and stepped out of the swing. "Can you explain?" she asked.

He stared directly at her. His eyes were steady and without a hint of guilt. He shook his head.

"What did you do with the money?"

"I can't tell you."

"Three years ago you swore to me you'd done nothing wrong. Now you admit you're a thief." A chill caught her and she shivered.

"Elizabeth, I never lied to you."

"They can't both be true, James. Either you took the money or you didn't."

He stared at her but offered no explanation. Elizabeth felt frustrated. She wanted him to tell her something—anything that would explain the transfer of funds to a personal account and then a sudden transfer out. She couldn't trace where it had gone: to a numbered account in Switzerland, to the private banks of the Cayman Islands—she didn't know.

"Say something!" she ordered, her body reeling in the wind.

"It's not possible for me to explain it, Elizabeth."

"Then you admit it. Everything Claire told me about you was true. You embezzled money and tried to blame her. She'd have gone to jail if she hadn't died."

"I wish I could explain . . ."

Elizabeth waited for him to continue. The wind died down, and momentarily there was stillness. Between them accusation crackled like dry leaves, but neither offered reasonable cause to doubt the facts at hand. James said nothing, but maintained a steady gaze, as if the airwaves between them would tell Elizabeth what she wanted to know. Frustrated, she turned and walked away. Her booted heels clicked when she reached the pavement. James didn't follow or try to stop her. At the gate to the street, she looked over her shoulder. He'd turned his back. His shoulders had dropped, and for the first time, she actually thought he looked defeated.

She wanted to hate him, feel that he was getting everything

he deserved. Yet the only feeling that surfaced was love, disappointment that this man, who'd been given all the advantages of life, had succumbed to stealing.

Pulling the car door open, she slipped inside and started the engine. The windshield wipers spun across the collected snow, affording her enough visible space to see the road. She drove away, a fresh supply of tears washing down her face.

When she pulled into her parking space at Invitation to Love, she saw Joanne's car. Thank goodness, she prayed. She could get the girl started and tell her about Officer Robinson's order, then go out. Joanne was very astute and observant, yet this morning she didn't mention that Elizabeth looked as if she'd been up all night, which was the truth. She took her instructions and cheerily made coffee while Elizabeth slipped back through the door and into her car.

She knew it was a long shot. She expected the police department to tell her the same story they had on the phone the previous day, but she went there anyway. It was the Christmas season, and maybe even a civil servant would take pity on someone who needed to see that accident report as badly as she did.

It wasn't the case. The bored-looking overweight clerk was thirty-something, complaining of her feet and the cost of Christmas gifts when Elizabeth arrived. The woman poured her frustration onto Elizabeth, standing between her and what she wanted like a tank guarding the entrance to Fort Knox. Elizabeth controlled her temper and her need to scream at this woman. She spoke calmly, focusing on the report and not being drawn into the discussion of any other subject. Getting nowhere, she finally thanked the woman and turned to leave.

Upset at losing, she wasn't paying attention as she left the office. Outside the opaque glass door she walked into someone. Looking up, she saw Officer Robinson.

"Ms. Gregory, what are you doing here?"

What did telling him the truth matter? she thought. "I needed a report, but I didn't get it."

"Maybe I can help. Come into my office."

Elizabeth had been right: he was a detective now. She seated herself in front of the desk in a steel chair with a faded gray cushion. Stacks of files covered most of the desk's surface. On the floor were others. An empty coffee cup acted as a paperweight on top of one stack. On the wall were several plaques for meritorious service and a photograph of Robinson shaking hands with Washington's mayor. Elizabeth's assessment of Det. Robinson softened a bit.

"Would you like something to drink?" he asked, taking the coffee cup. "Coffee or tea is about all we have."

"Thank you, no," she said.

"All right, now what report did you want to see?"

"The one from the night my sister died. You were the officer who took the report."

"I was." His statement held no emotion, just a simple statement of fact.

"I never read the report. You told me what happened, but now I want to see it. The clerk in the records office said it usually takes a week, but with the holidays, it would take more time."

Det. Robinson stood up. He went to a gray regulation file cabinet, unlocked it with a key from a large ring, and opened the second drawer. Halfway to the back, he extracted a rather thin file and handed it to her.

"Take your time," he said. "I'll get us some coffee." He took the cup from the desk and left her alone.

Elizabeth held her surprise inside. Why would he still have this? she wondered. Was there something unusual about her sister's death? Were they still investigating it? Did they know about James?

Elizabeth read. Inside the covers of the manila colored folder were just the facts of the accident. There was nothing here to lead anyone to believe it belonged in a locked cabinet. The cars had been driving fast, above 80 mph, according the force of the impact. The ground had been dry, but patches of ice had been present. The conclusion was that Claire's car, car number 1, the report called it, had hit a patch of ice and the driver had lost control. The car had spun around and car number 2, James's, had struck it. The skidmarks on the roadway showed car number 2 had tried to avoid the collision, but the speed at which the drivers had been going had left too little stopping distance before impact. Blood-alcohol levels indicated the surviving driver had been sober. Autopsy reports showed Claire's levels at .03. Two more times Elizabeth read the report. Then Officer Robinson had added a comment that the two cars were either racing or chasing each other, but in his opinion it was an accident and not a deliberate pursuit.

Sitting back, Elizabeth let the report fall onto her lap. She exhaled on a long sigh. At least James was not guilty of causing Claire's death, but she had no clear picture of where they had been going and why they were traveling at such high speeds inside the city.

Det. Robinson came back. He held his ceramic cup with the shield of the DC Police Department etched in silver on the side in one hand and a tan paper cup in the other. He handed her the paper cup.

"You look like the cream-only type."

Elizabeth accepted the cup with a nod. He was right. The coffee was fresh, with just the amount of cream she liked. "Thank you," she offered.

"Find anything interesting?"

She shook her head. "I didn't really expect to," she told him, holding back the information that she didn't really want to find anything damning about James, just something to tell her why he would resort to embezzlement. Why she thought it was related to the accident she didn't know. "I do have some questions."

"Shoot," he said, with a nonchalant shrug. He slid into the worn leather chair behind the cluttered desk.

"There's nothing in this file to warrant it being in a locked cabinet. Why hasn't it been archived with the rest of the records? Or is this case still open?"

Det. Robinson sipped the hot liquid before answering. Elizabeth thought it was a technique he'd mastered to slow down the pace or buy himself time when he was deciding how best to proceed.

"No case is ever closed if new evidence comes to light," he said. "The files in that cabinet," he pointed to it, "are my personal files. Every cop has them. They're the kind of files that report the facts, but down deep inside, sometimes an officer knows there's something that's not finished. It's like getting up from a chess game just before you put the other fellow's queen in check."

"You think there's more to the accident than what's written here?"

"Not the accident."

"Then what?"

Det. Robinson came forward in his chair. He gave her a penetrating stare. Elizabeth withstood it, realizing he was again using a practiced technique.

"Are you sure you want to hear this? Most people who say they want to know everything have no idea what they're asking."

Elizabeth thought about that. Her pulse increased. She felt the pounding begin in her head and knew another headache was imminent. She'd loved Claire and James more than anyone else on earth. The detective might know things Elizabeth would rather not hear, but in the last three years, she'd speculated and wondered. She'd refused to open Claire's files, living in the dark and refusing to see the truth. She wasn't doing that any longer. Weighing the difference between knowing and not knowing, she thought it was better to know, good or bad.

"I want to know," she told him.

He paused again, all the while staring straight at her. Elizabeth held it. He got up then and went to the cabinet. This time the folder he handed her was thick. Papers stuck out of the sides in a haphazard array. Elizabeth wedged the coffee cup onto the edge of the desk and accepted the file.

She read in silence. It was all here. The files in her apartment, copies of them, were in this folder—and more. James's bank account records were here. Transfers between accounts showed deposits and withdrawals within days of each other. Large amounts had been moved. Elizabeth calculated the amounts in her head. Every time she did, the number $650,000 popped up. Finally, she uncovered mortgage loan papers. Again, $650,000. James had mortgaged his house. Why would he do that? Then she found the repayment of the business accounts, on Christmas Eve three years ago, the day after Claire's funeral.

"I don't understand," Elizabeth said aloud. She was talking to herself, but Det. Robinson didn't know that and answered.

"Neither do I," he said. "Why would a man take his own money, transfer it to his business in a group of small business accounts, and within a three-month period, mortgage his house? Why would we find an account in Barbados with his name on it, an account with several deposits adding up to $650,000 that was opened and closed in the same three-month period?"

Something about the tone of his voice told Elizabeth he didn't believe the facts of the folder.

"You think this is a frame?"

"As perfect as if he'd sat and had the artist paint it."

Elizabeth hated to ask, but she'd resolved that she had to know the truth. The detective had alluded to it yesterday in her shop. "Who do you think the artist was?"

She was subjected to the long stare again. Just as Elizabeth was about to scream at him the man answered her question. "Claire Gregory."

Elizabeth thought she'd prepared herself for the answer, but hearing Claire's name made her head reel.

"Claire was my sister. I knew her better than anybody. She wouldn't do this."

The detective sipped his coffee. Elizabeth looked at her cup. The powdered cream thickened on the top of the coffee, leaving a circular pattern that fascinated her. She wanted to concentrate on the rings, but the detective broke into her thoughts.

"I can't prove any of this, but what I think happened is that your sister got into your fiancé's account and started transferring small accounts. She only used accounts that had had no activity for over a year. No one would notice the amounts or the accounts for a while. By the time they did she'd be clean. All roads, or should I say files, would lead to James Hill. She covered herself, by setting up an account with his name on it. If anyone found out, he'd be in the hot seat and she'd be uninvolved. The transfers took place during the early hours of the morning."

Elizabeth remembered the dates and times. "It's not unusual for stockbrokers to work at odd hours. Like the British Empire, the sun doesn't set on world markets. They're open twenty-four hours a day." She attempted a lightness she didn't feel.

"I thought of that, but Barbados is in the same time zone as we are. There would be no need to transfer funds at three o'clock in the morning."

"He could have been also transferring funds from Japanese investments and the Japanese stock exchange would be open and operating at that hour."

Before Elizabeth finished her explanation, the detective was already shaking his head.

"We checked all transfers at that hour. Nothing else happened except the ones to the bank on Barbados."

"It didn't have to be Claire. There are other brokers with access to the office and computer code keys."

"That's where my story falls short. I can't link Claire Gregory with any of the transactions." He paused. "I checked everyone in that firm. They come up squeaky clean. James Hill is to be congratulated on his ability to amass so many honest people in one place."

"But . . ." she prompted.

"Your sister," he said matter-of-factly. "Claire Gregory has no record, no arrest, no convictions, but word on the street paints a blacker picture. She was a petty con artist. After her death we sealed her apartment."

"I remember." It was several days before Elizabeth was allowed inside.

"While we checked into her background we found a diary."

"What diary? I was never informed of a diary."

"It was more like an appointment book. Ms. Gregory had made notations in the margins. The notations led us to the real Claire Gregory."

Elizabeth didn't like the way he said that, but she held her tongue.

"For years she'd . . . appropriated funds from one mark or another." Elizabeth noticed the hesitation. "I have a list of businessmen, some more prominent than others. None of them would go on record. They wanted the entire mess swept under the rug."

"I don't believe you."

"That's your right, Ms. Gregory." He didn't react to her outrage.

"Where is this diary?"

He got up and for a third time went to the file cabinet. Opening the drawer, he extracted a book and a single envelope. He handed it to her. "The amounts of money were small to the marks," he continued, as if he'd just remembered his train of thought. "The embarrassment to their good names would be more detrimental than allowing her to get away with it. So they did."

Elizabeth accepted the book and envelope. Staring at the unaddressed envelope she turned it over in her hand and looked up at the man in front of her.

"Is there anything else you're going to pull out of that cabinet?" Her voice held annoyance, but she didn't care. She was annoyed. Annoyed at Claire and all the damage she'd done. Even if what the detective said wasn't the complete picture of her sister, there was enough evidence there to create doubt in anyone's mind.

Elizabeth opened the envelope. All doubt disappeared. He'd held the trump card until last. Inside were two unused airline tickets: one to Barbados, and another from Barbados to Grand Cayman Island. Claire's name was on both tickets.

"We didn't live well growing up." Elizabeth floundered, thrown by the tickets she held in her hand. "We rarely had enough money to pay the bills."

"But somehow it was always there; the tuition payments, money to send you on the trip abroad your junior year, a designer dress for homecoming parties—"

"Claire got that dress because the woman she was working for didn't want it. She told me." Elizabeth's voice rose.

"I'm sure she did. It was her settlement."

"You're lying."

"I told you, most people don't want to hear the truth."

Elizabeth hung her head. He had to be wrong. "Claire wouldn't have done any of those things. Why would she want to frame James? He'd given her the job, let her have responsibility she deserved. James told me Claire had a real flare for picking the right stocks."

"Your fiancé just became another mark to her, but with him, the money was big time. The carrot was too big to ignore. He covered up for her, just as all the others had done. I imagine his relationship with you had something to do with that."

Elizabeth dropped the tickets inside the folder and closed it. It lay heavy on her lap. The detective's last words made several pieces of the mystery she'd found in the files fall into place.

"He mortgaged his house to replace the money she'd averted. How he convinced the SEC he had nothing to do with insider trading and misuse of corporate funds is beyond me. But he did it." Elizabeth heard the unspoken respect in Det. Robinson's voice.

"You'd have stopped it, wouldn't you?" Elizabeth said, more a statement than a question. "If the SEC had turned James over to the police, you'd have used this file." Elizabeth tapped the heavy package lying on her legs.

He nodded. "Despite the way law enforcement is viewed by the general public, Ms. Gregory, we want justice done. In my opinion, James Hill is a respectable businessman with his clients' interests at heart. Prosecuting him for a crime he didn't commit would be abuse to the system I've vowed to protect and serve."

"So why do you still hold on to this file?"

"In my business, I've seen serpents rear their heads long after everyone thought them dead and buried. There's no statute of limitations on fraud. I keep it as a safeguard."

To the principles in which he believed, Elizabeth realized. She stood up. "Thank you, Detective." One last time she looked at the file, then handed it to him. "Thanks for all your help."

She left the office. The detective looked after her. Elizabeth didn't turn back, didn't see him resume his seat and write "closed" on the outside of the manila folder. She didn't know he walked to the gray cabinet and placed the file in the bottom drawer, where only seven other files resided, all with the word "closed" written on them in the detective's distinctive scrawl.

Her life had changed irrevocably in the last half hour. James hadn't done anything wrong. Why had he let her believe he had? Why hadn't he explained that he'd never stolen $650,000; that he'd been replacing money that Claire had—

Elizabeth choked on the word.

Nine

"You just stood there, not saying a word, and let her accuse you of a crime you didn't commit?"

James sat slumped in his chair, listening to Theresa accuse him of being a fool. He *was* a fool. He wanted to tell Elizabeth the whole truth, but he couldn't. Mark had told him how sad she was, how Christmas upset her every year. When he'd seen her, he'd only wanted her to be happy. His proposition for her to change her holidays from bad memories to good ones had been offered in earnest, yet he'd been the reason she would now forever view this time of year in the worst light. He felt helpless. What could he do?

He lifted a paper on his desk and stared at it but saw none of the writing on it. He dropped it.

"What was I going to say?" he asked, more to himself than to Theresa.

"You could have told her the truth. Elizabeth is a big girl. She can take it."

Theresa's eyes were enormously expressive. Her words made his actions seem inadequate. James shrugged. "It was never my intention to prove my innocence or guilt to Elizabeth."

"Why not? You're in love with her, aren't you?" Theresa stood up and came around the desk. "Don't you know she can never fully trust you unless she knows the truth about you and Claire?"

"Yes," he said, answering both questions.

"Then why didn't you let her know about the money?"

"I suppose I'd have told her last night if she'd opened the

door, but this morning as she sat in that swing, I knew I couldn't tell her the truth. She was in no mood to accept it."

"James."

Theresa's voice was more compassionate than he'd ever heard it sound before. He looked up at her.

"It's time. Both of you have put your lives on hold for three years, all because of Claire's lies. It can't go on. Elizabeth has to be told."

He knew it was the truth. For three years he'd been miserable. The last seven days had been like heaven; then finally, on the eighth day, everything had fallen apart. He couldn't go on like this and he couldn't let this relationship end the way it had three years ago. This time he didn't have the SEC and the police waiting in the wings, looking at everything he'd done since he'd joined this firm. He didn't have his partners wondering about the truth of the accusations. This time more was at stake than going to jail. He'd gambled on giving the SEC only enough information to clear himself, keeping Claire's name out of it, and with Theresa's help they'd played a hand that had won.

His life with Elizabeth was a much more important ante.

Elizabeth drove around in a daze. She needed time to think, put things in order, make some kind of sense out of the information she'd just read and heard. The crawl of the traffic didn't bother her; she had no particular destination in mind so going slowly wasn't a problem. She did call Joanne to say she'd be late, but her intention was to skip most of the day. Other than Det. Robinson picking up his invitations, there was nothing the young girl couldn't handle. Joanne told her she'd had two calls: one from James Hill, and the other from Theresa Simmons. Elizabeth promised to return the calls and rang off. Not yet, she thought. She wasn't ready to speak to James, but that time would come. She had to . . . to what? she asked herself. She'd accused him of being a thief, and he hadn't denied it. Why? Yet she knew better now.

Why would he remain quiet and let the SEC rake him over the coals, look into every aspect of his company, without a defense? It didn't make sense. Claire was the thief. She coughed at having to admit it. Deep down she'd always known, but time after time she'd told herself Claire was working hard to provide for them; the money she got whenever something important came up was legitimate income. Today, any blinders she'd had on had been ripped away by Det. Robinson and his "always open" file. Claire had used James's identification code. She'd transferred funds to the Barbados bank, and James had found out. Why had he let Claire get away with it? Why hadn't he told her? Elizabeth knew why: she was the reason. James hadn't been protecting only his reputation, but hers as well. Any mention of Claire's involvement would have destroyed Invitation to Love. In a government town, the hint of scandal was enough to ruin a business. To have her name linked to the commission of a crime would kill her credibility.

Two hours later, Elizabeth found herself in the parking garage under James's office. His car sat next to an elevator on the third sublevel. Parking in the first space she found, she got out. Her knees cracked, protesting the amount of time she'd remained in one position. Stretching, she closed the door and headed for the elevator. A huge green arrow ran around the wall, ending at the double doors. A laughing crowd exited the small room when the doors opened. Elizabeth heard the last man sing a line from "Jingle Bells." It was nearly noon; most people would be leaving for lunch soon. The office would be empty. She acknowledged the small amount of luck.

James's secretary's desk was vacant when Elizabeth reached it. Strangely enough, no one had stopped her. A few people gave her a curious glance, but she appeared to know where she was going. At his door she raised her hand to knock, but the sound of Theresa's voice stopped her.

She needed to speak to James alone. He'd protected her from the truth about her sister for three years. She wasn't sure what she'd say to him, but she needed to say it when they were alone.

Using stationery on the desk, she wrote a quick note, found a "Confidential" envelope, and stuffed the note inside. On the front she scrawled his name, and as unobtrusively as she'd arrived, she left.

When James knocked on her door later that night, she was as nervous as a teenager awaiting the arrival of her first date. She'd busied herself since arriving home straightening the apartment and practicing what she'd say. She'd lit the gas fireplace, plugged in the tree, made herself coffee, and changed clothes three times. She'd finally decided on a circle skirt of charcoal gray and a red sweater with a large collar. She hung earrings James had often admired in her ears. On her feet she wore her best high heels. At least his size wouldn't make her feel meek. Apologizing would be difficult enough.

She swallowed hard when she saw him. She took his overcoat and hung it in the hall closet. He wore a navy blue business suit, although his tie was gone and his shirt collar was open.

Elizabeth hadn't given him any idea why she'd wanted to see him, but he'd come anyway. She smiled tentatively, glad last night hadn't made him too angry to return. The papers which had littered the floor twenty-four hours ago had been gathered and stacked into a neat pile.

"Can I get you something to drink?"

"Do I smell coffee?"

Elizabeth nodded. "It's hazelnut," she said, as she went to the kitchen.

She returned minutes later with a tray. Silently she poured and passed him a cup. They sat facing each other.

"You must think my behavior a bit strange," she started. "I'd like to apologize."

"Elizabeth, what happened?" James leaned forward.

Elizabeth stared at the pile of documents on the table next to her chair. She lifted the stack of papers and set it on the coffee table between them.

"What is this?"

"It's evidence that proves you diverted $650,000 from your company's inactive accounts to a bank in Barbados."

Shock registered in his eyes. "Elizabeth, I can explain this—"

"I went to the police station today," she interrupted.

James sipped his coffee. Elizabeth remembered Det. Robinson and his technique of buying himself time. James's jaw set and the ruthless face stared at her.

"I wanted to review the accident report of the night Claire died."

James stiffened. His gazed bounced back and forth between the papers and her. "What did you find?"

"I ran into the officer who took the report. He's a detective now."

"You gave him these files?"

Elizabeth sipped her coffee. "No, I didn't."

The breath he let out was audible. She related the detective's story, leaving nothing out. James listened without interruption. When she finished, she stood up and joined him on the opposite end of the sofa.

"Why didn't you tell me it was Claire? You let me believe you'd stolen money and tried to blame Claire for it, when all the time Claire was doing the stealing, framing you, and you were covering for her."

"I wasn't covering for her, Elizabeth," he said. "I was covering for *you.* Theresa berated me for not letting you know the whole truth." He paused. "I knew how you felt about Claire. You thought she'd sacrificed everything for you when all the while she was doing everything in the world to hurt you."

"I don't understand."

James slid closer to her. "The night of the accident, she came to the office. We'd had the annual Christmas party. Everyone had gone, and I was about to leave when she showed up. She threatened to go to the police with lies—tell them that I had embezzled money, sent it to a bank outside the United States. She had everything. It was all there in computer files, my identification code next to everything. On paper, I was a thief."

Elizabeth listened without emotion.

"She'd taken $650,000 before I found out. That wasn't enough money for her. She wanted more. If I didn't give her another $500,000, she was going to tell you and the SEC all about the set-up. I refused to be blackmailed. I knew if I paid her, she'd have an ax to hold over me for the rest of my life. Claire was angry. She swore she'd go to the police and ruin me; no investor in his right mind would ever use my firm after she finished with me."

Elizabeth's breath caught. Claire was her sister, yet the woman he described was foreign to her.

"She wouldn't tell me where the files were hidden," he went on. "I wasn't even sure they really existed. She told so many lies, covering one set with another." James paused. "She said if anything happened to her, the files would be delivered to the police. I was chasing her, hoping to stop her from getting to you, when she hit the patch of ice and spun out of control. After that I waited, knowing every day the police would come and arrest me. With Theresa's help, we managed to cover up the evidence Claire had falsified. Luckily, the SEC believed us when we went before them, and no one lost any money."

"But you did lose some clients."

"They've since returned with even greater investments."

"I'm sorry, James." Elizabeth dropped her head. James moved close enough to slip his arm around her shoulders.

"Don't be. You did nothing to be sorry about."

"I accused you of killing Claire, of—" He put his finger against her lips.

"Claire was an extremely bright woman. Like Theresa, she had an uncanny feel for the market. If she'd only held in the urge to get quick money, I have no doubt she'd be a rich woman today."

Elizabeth let her head fall onto his shoulder. She knew he was right. Claire had so much going for her if she'd only channeled her energies in the right direction, but she was always for the here and now, living from day to day, never thinking of the future or who she might hurt. Elizabeth could only say she'd protected her like a mother. She had given her a huge chunk of her life after their parents had died. She supposed the need to use opportunity when it presented itself was Claire's method of survival. When it was no longer necessary, Claire couldn't stop.

"James?"

He drew her closer and wrapped his arm around her waist.

"Didn't you think I could have understood this three years ago? Is that why you protected me?"

"You didn't mention the files. The police never came with them. I thought Claire had lied about them, too. She'd showed me a copy of the computer transfers, but if I had to, I could have explained them. If she didn't really have any records, everything would be fine for me, but you."

"Why me?"

"You were finally getting somewhere with Invitation to Love. The FBI or the Secret Service would certainly investigate you, Claire, and me. If they found anything illegal, there was no way you'd get the contracts you've secured."

"Detective Robinson had quite a lengthy file on Claire. I'm sure the FBI must have uncovered the same information."

"Probably, but Claire had never been arrested or convicted of anything. She'd had a string of affairs, but that's no crime. Once the SEC said I had done nothing wrong, you were in the clear."

Elizabeth lifted her head and leaned back to look at him. "I'm sorry, James. I'm sorry Claire put you through this."

"It's over now," he said. "She took your love of Christmas away, and because of her it's been restored. Am I right?"

Elizabeth stared at the tree they'd decorated. She thought about the black Santa she'd bought in Georgetown. A wide smile split her face. "I think so."

With one finger James pulled her head back so she looked at him. His mouth touched hers and fire raged through her.

"There's one more thing," Elizabeth said, before she lost all coherence.

"What's that?" James voice was hoarse.

Elizabeth moved out of his arms. She went to the papers and reached for the envelope on top of the pile. She handed it to him.

James opened it and drew out the single piece of paper. "A check?"

Elizabeth stood before the fireplace. The heat behind her warmed her back. "Claire stole your money, you mortgaged your house to repay it."

"Elizabeth," he chuckled. "You're as honest as Claire was dishonest." Going to her, he gathered her close and kissed her quickly. Then he stepped back and tore the check in half, dropping the pieces on the low table behind him.

"Why did you do that?"

"The money has already been repaid, Elizabeth. Theresa found the account and had it closed. The money was sent to a bank in the Cayman Islands, just as Claire had intended it, but to a different account. Two years ago, when there was no threat, the account was closed and the mortgage repaid." He took a step toward her. Elizabeth saw the passion in his eyes. "Thank you for . . . everything."

He bent toward her, but Elizabeth moved. "James." She fidgeted with her hands. "I wouldn't blame you if you walked out the door and never came back."

He didn't say anything. Elizabeth fidgeted more. Her nerves stretched.

"We haven't been very kind to you, Claire and I."

"Elizabeth," James smiled at her. "I left you once. For three miserable years I regretted it. Nothing, not even Claire, will drive me away again."

He stared at her for a moment. Elizabeth had never been more in love with anyone than she was at this moment. His hands slipped around her waist and pulled her toward him. The contact of body to body was electrifying. Her soft breasts flattened against his chest as his mouth dropped to her ear. Shimmers ran through her. Then his lips found hers. Elizabeth went easily into his arms. As James imprisoned her against him, she'd never felt more free. Suddenly there was no ghost between them, no cloud shadowing their love.

Elizabeth's mouth opened at his insistence. His tongue swept inside. Sensation made her weak as it spiraled through her. She arched toward him, clinging as the passion between them became tangible, fierce. James's hands roamed down her back, over her buttocks, and up again. The warmth of the fire behind her added to the fuel his hands made. Her stomach tightened as a gnawing hunger seized her.

"James," she moaned against his mouth.

"I know," he whispered. He turned her toward the bedroom.

"Here," Elizabeth said. "Before the fire."

With his arm around her waist, he pulled her against him. James stood next to her. The glow from the fire highlighted her hair. He lifted the hem of the angora sweater she wore. Quickly he pulled it over her head. Grabbing her hands, he ran his fingers up her arms. She shuddered under his touch. The sweater dropped to the floor. Her dark bronze skin sent a thrill through him. He kissed her shoulders, listening to the soft gasps that came from her throat.

He unhooked her bra and the heaviness of her breasts spilled into his hands. Heat pooled in his groin and he felt himself grow hard against his pants. His hands caressed her. Breath caught in her throat. Rubbing his thumbs across berry-colored peaks, he felt them pebble against his fingertips.

Elizabeth pushed the coat from his shoulders and undid the buttons on his shirt. She pressed her face against his skin. Heat shot through him as her hands spread over his chest and around his torso. He pushed her head back and kissed her. The kiss was long, slow, and as hot as a summer in Washington, when candlewax could melt on the sidewalk. He was dissolving into her, losing the point where one body ended and another began.

They finished undressing as slowly as they could manage, which was with the speed of a quick-draw western hero bringing down his prey. James settled her to the floor and joined her there. He gathered her close to him, his hands stroking her back. Her lips brushed his chest, her tongue tasting, lathing his nipples, sending rapturous sensations through him. She arched toward him, her slender legs tangling with his. His skin was on fire and the tightening coil in his belly was about to reach its breaking point. Rolling Elizabeth onto her back, he lifted himself over her and sought the center of her core. The primal dance between them was wild, uncontrollable, a joining so singularly distinctive, no other couple in history could have ever experienced it in quite the same way. Then a soul-shattering climax took them over the edge and they collapsed against each other in unbridled release.

Elizabeth stirred as James lifted her. Her body was cold since he'd moved from her. She curled her arms around his neck and pressed her cheek to his. As he placed her on the bed, she heard the clock in the foyer. It counted the hour. It was past midnight.

"It's Christmas Eve," she said. "Promise me something?"

He looked at her. In the half light of morning she couldn't see his eyes. "Anything." A smile was in his voice.

"Can we do this every Christmas Eve?"

"I can only promise the next sixty or seventy Christmases. After that, you're on your own."

Elizabeth ran her hand up his arm. His skin glowed in the light coming from the living room. He was rock solid, dark as brandy, and smooth as warm silk. "I love you, James Hill. I've been in love with you since we shared that first bowl of ice cream."

She sat up, hugging him to her, loving the feel of his skin.

"I love you, too, Elizabeth; since the fifth grade, when you had thick braids." His hand brushed through her hair.

"Even through all the mess Claire created, I knew somehow we'd live our lives together."

"That sounds an awful lot like a proposal, Elizabeth." James pressed his mouth against hers. "Are you asking me to marry you?" Each word was uttered between kisses.

"You asked me the last time," she said, when his mouth lifted a moment. "I thought it was my turn."

She gasped as James's hands came around her. His thumbs drew circles along the sides of her breasts. Her blood boiled. Her head fell back, and she thrust her breasts into his chest. God, she felt good. He made her feel like this.

"Are you going to answer my question?" She could hardly speak for the sensations that rioted through her. His hands were heating her—overheating her. In a moment she was going to dissolve.

"Yes, I'll marry you." James's mouth covered hers.

He pushed her back onto the bed and stretched his length over her. Then he began a long, slow mapping of her body. Elizabeth reached meltdown as James joined his body to hers. The invasion was wanted, needed. She didn't think she could survive without it. She closed around him, drawing him into her. The rhythmic love-dance began. Movement as old as time seized her. Together they waltzed, tangoed, jitterbugged, and broke into a slow cha-cha. Elizabeth screamed at the pleasure that filled her, the kind of pleasure she only experienced with James. Her breath came hard, her heart hammered in her ears. James kissed her eyes and cheeks, rolling on his side and taking her with him, keeping them joined.

Elizabeth's legs straddled him. Her insides were so full she thought she'd explode in the aftermath of their lovemaking. God, she felt lucky. She'd been given a precious second chance with the man she loved. She'd never know what forces had made her pull out James's address by mistake eleven days ago, but she'd given her thanks that she'd done it and it had led her here, wrapped in his arms, happier than she'd ever been.

For three years he'd filled her dreams. Even her subconscious knew she wanted only him. Now he was real. Her imagination didn't have to conjure him. He was here and they'd be together from now on.

"I love you, James," she told him.

"Shh," he whispered. "I thought I could wait until tomorrow, but it's already tomorrow."

He slipped off the bed.

"Where are you going?" Elizabeth sat up, grabbing his hand.

"I'll be right back." He kissed the back of her hand and dropped it.

Elizabeth pulled the sheet over her. The morning sun had begun to rise behind the Capitol. She stared at the cracked gold horizon. James came back. She watched his sure gait as he walked naked across the room. He had a great body and no need to feel self-conscious about it. He sat on the bed and switched on the lamp. Elizabeth blinked at the sudden brightness.

"Merry Christmas," he said, offering her a small, square box wrapped in colored paper and completely covered by red ribbon.

The urge to rip the paper away and discover the contents was overwhelming, but she held it back. "Shouldn't we wait until Christmas?"

"I never could wait," he said. "It's why I don't shop until the end of the season." He paused, pushing the box closer to her. "Go on, open it."

Elizabeth sat up in bed, trying to keep the sheet above her breasts. She pulled the ribbon free and used her fingernail to slit the paper. The box had come from the jewelry store where they'd bought his mother's statue. Slowly Elizabeth opened the box. Inside was a small velvet ring box. She pulled it out as if it held the rarest jewel on earth. Lifting the top, she gasped. It was a ring. The stepping stones to the altar.

"How?" Her voice was a hoarse whisper. "When?"

James took the box and pulled the ring out. "I went back the next morning and bought it." He lifted her hand and slipped the ring over the knuckle of her third finger, left hand. The steps moved. They skittered around in a full arc, then back again, like the swinging of a pendulum. Each layer rotated separately, giving the effect of constant and never-ending movement.

"James, it's beautiful." The sheet slipped as she hugged him.

She extended her hand over his shoulder, admiring the ring and the show it presented.

"There's a story behind it," he said.

Elizabeth pushed him back. Her eyebrows rose. "Another Christmas story?"

"This one is a marriage story." He climbed into bed next to her and pulled the sheet over them both. Holding her hand, he began, "The bottom two circles represent man and woman."

"Which one is man and which one is woman?" She looked at her finger, trying hard not to break into laughter.

James grinned and ignored her. "They actually represent man's or woman's search for their ideal mate. Each stone indicates the many seeds and many shores that life touches in its search. They glitter, sometimes blinding the owner."

"To the right man," she offered.

"Or the right woman." He tapped the top circle. "This step is the promise. The commitment that each makes to the other. These stones are angled upward. Light reflects off them, creating a circle that encompasses the top stone, which is the joining of the two lives forever, unending."

Tears misted in Elizabeth's eyes when he finished speaking. All joking and playfulness left her as he spoke. It was the most beautiful story she'd ever heard, and one she'd vow to keep.

"James." Emotion filled her heart and her voice. "I promise to stand within the never-ending light, to join with you forever, to pledge my unending love as long as night blends into day and day blends into night."

Ten

Elizabeth positively glowed. She hadn't been this happy in years. She looked at the glittering ring on her hand. She remembered her pledge to James and his to her. The diamond was only a symbol, but it was enduring, as enduring as their love. The geometric circles twisted back and forth with each movement of her hand. She knew she'd never look at it without thinking of the story James had told her.

Finally the weight she'd carried so long regarding Claire and James was gone. He stood next to her, his arm around her waist, as he greeted his guests. He introduced everyone to her as if she held a place of honor.

Crowds formed in every room. Music played through the sound system. In the great-room couples danced on the temporary dance floor. Bursts of laughter came from the living room as someone said something funny. She could hear the faint sound of a Christmas carol from the direction of the music room. A couple sat on the fifth step of the stairs leading up to the bedrooms, engrossed only in each other.

Elizabeth knew how they felt. It was how she felt about James. Two days ago, on the anniversary of the accident, they had resolved their differences and James had made love to her through the night. Her stomach contracted and sensation pooled in her body at the memory. She smiled up at him and he kissed her on the cheek. Elizabeth directed her thoughts away from last night.

"Why don't we throw all these people out and spend the night alone?" he whispered in her ear.

"I'll take the living room, you do the great-room and the library," she agreed.

Together they laughed and joined the singing crowd in the music room. Mark was seated at the piano, playing as he led the crowd in singing "It's Beginning to Look a Lot Like Christmas." They joined in, playing the perfect host and hostess for a few minutes, before making sure everything was all right in the other rooms.

As Elizabeth passed the foyer on her way to the kitchen, the front door was opened again.

"Merry Christmas, Lizzie."

"Theresa!" Elizabeth rushed across the room to hug her friend. "I'm so glad to see you." Theresa gave her coat to the maid and hugged Elizabeth again. Her dress was Christmas red, with a brilliant white sash around her thin waist. Long earrings danced from her earlobes to her shoulders. She'd swept her hair all to one side and anchored it with a glittering comb.

"I hear you and James finally patched things up."

Elizabeth smiled. "I hear we have you to thank for part of it." Elizabeth raised her hand, displaying the shining jewel James had placed there just hours ago.

Theresa whistled. "James really wants people to know you're his. How many is that? Six-seven-eight?"

"Seven," Elizabeth said, giving her the number of carats in the crowning stone.

"It's beautiful, Lizzie. Congratulations." Elizabeth hugged her again.

"Thank you, too, Theresa. James told me what you did to help him clear himself and keep Claire's name out of the mess she created. I owe you a lot."

"Cut it out," Theresa stopped her. "I did nothing you wouldn't have done. Now, where's the bridegroom?"

James came through from the kitchen as if on cue. "Theresa," he called. "Did Elizabeth tell you our good news?"

"She didn't have to. The reflection off that stone," she pointed to Elizabeth's hand. "was bright enough to lead me here. Now I know how the wisemen found the baby Jesus."

James laughed and took both women by the arm. "Now that everyone is here, let's go make the announcement."

James gathered everyone in the great-room. Before the huge Christmas tree he and Elizabeth took up positions like Christmas ornaments. The lights twinkled behind them; their friends stood in front. Mark and James's parents stood to their right. The smile on Elizabeth's face was wide and happy. She couldn't ask for anything more to make her Christmas perfect. Then James gave it to her.

"My friends," he held a fluted champagne glass in his left hand. The noise in the room reduced to a low murmur. "My friends, I'd like you all to know." The room was absolutely quiet now. "As most of you know, Elizabeth and I have been engaged before."

Elizabeth smiled and the room laughed.

"However," he continued. "We both know a good thing when we find it. Yesterday we decided to . . ." He paused. "To try it again."

From the side of the room Mark yelled "Yeah!" and the room broke into applause. People rushed them, offering congratulations, asking if they'd set a date, kissing her and pumping James's hand.

The tempo of the party increased after James's announcement. Merrymaking went on well into the early morning.

Finally, they said goodnight to the last guest and collapsed on the sofa in the living room. Elizabeth slipped out of her shoes and curled her feet under her. Party debris surrounded them on all sides, yet Elizabeth didn't notice it. She took James's arm and snuggled up to him, her head on his shoulder.

Suddenly the doorbell rang.

"Now, who could that be?" James wondered.

"Probably somebody who forgot something," Elizabeth offered.

He bent toward her and dropped a kiss on her mouth before standing up. "I'll see who it is."

James grinned at the door. It was a delivery man. The envelope he passed him had the familiar Invitation to Love logo on it. He didn't have to ask Elizabeth how she'd gotten a man to come out this late on Christmas Eve—correction, it was now Christmas Day. He tipped him handsomely and closed the door. Tearing open the letter, he found a buff-colored card inside. The message "Marry the woman at the door" was printed in Elizabeth's precise handwriting. He smiled, turned, and opened the door. There she stood.

"This time there is no address mixup," she said. "I'm the woman at the door."

James grabbed her around the waist and pulled her into his arms. The door shut behind them.

"Merry Christmas, Elizabeth."

"Merry Christmas, James."

He kissed her and Elizabeth knew that from this Christmas to her last, as long as she shared them with James, her memories would always be happy.

Dear Reader,

Christmas is such a special time of year. I look forward to it and the warm memories that return as I travel home to see family and friends. Writing *Invitation to Love* enabled me to relive the traditions and the memories and revisit my childhood when the struggle of going to bed that night before Santa was due was suspended for one day. Waking early and rushing to the twinkling tree to find my gifts among the elaborate array of toys and clothes, cooking festive meals, and reading *A Christmas Carol* or *'Twas the Night Before Christmas,* singing carols, and decorating the tree can still bring a smile to my face, even in the heat of summer.

I hope you enjoyed James and Elizabeth's story and that this Christmas and all your Christmases will be filled with good thoughts and good memories.

If you'd like to know more about *Invitation to Love* or other books, please send a business-sized, stamped, self-addressed envelope to the following address:

P. O. Box 513
Plainsboro, NJ 08536

Sincerely yours,

Shirley Hailstock

First Fruits

by

Rochelle Alers

Shelby Carter walked briskly along the snow-covered Manhattan sidewalk toward an Upper East Side luxury high-rise apartment building, trying to escape the gusting, frigid wind sweeping off the East River. She made her way into the vestibule, returning the smile of the young, dark-eyed uniformed doorman.

"Good evening, Miss Carter," he greeted her, touching the shiny brim of his maroon cap.

"Good evening, Henri," she returned.

"Mrs. Morrow is expecting you," he informed her, still flashing his best toothpaste-ad smile.

"Thank you."

She crossed the opulently decorated carpeted lobby to the elevators. Henri's admiring gaze followed her progress. Her short, naturally curly hair was concealed under a bottle-green wool cloche which matched a sweeping double-breasted greatcoat with black frogs. A pair of highly polished black riding boots and a shoulder bag completed her winter ensemble.

Gleaming brass doors opened silently and Shelby stepped into the elevator, pressing the button for the sixteenth floor. The car rose swiftly and quietly, stopping at her floor, and again the doors opened silently. She made her way down a spacious hallway to Naomi Morrow's apartment.

She had accepted Mrs. Morrow's invitation to dinner to discuss what the older woman hinted was a "special project," something art-related.

Two years ago, Naomi Morrow had attended an art exhibit featuring a dozen sculptured pieces of an up-and-coming artist whose work was reminiscent of primitive tribal masks and statues. Mrs. Morrow had purchased the entire collection and a bond between Shelby and the retired school administrator was formed.

Shelby had garnered her share of praise that evening as the purchasing agent for the gallery that had set up the showing. Now, at thirty-four, and fortified with an undergraduate degree in ethnoanthropology, a master's in African studies, and a second master's in art education, she had earned the respect of her contemporaries in the New York City art world.

She rang the bell while admiring the large, fragrant evergreen wreath with miniature red glazed ceramic apples, pinecones, and a red velvet bow hanging outside the door to apartment 16K. It opened and Shelby found herself face-to-face with Naomi Morrow.

She smiled at the petite woman with a smooth honey-beige complexion which complemented her expertly coiffed silver hair. An unlined face and a slim figure belied Naomi Morrow's sixty-nine years.

Extending both hands, Naomi grasped Shelby's shoulders and pressed her lips to her cheek. "How lovely you look. I'm so glad you could make it. Please come in."

She stepped into the foyer, handing her host a decorative shopping bag.

"What's this?" Naomi questioned, peering into a large green bag overflowing with red and black tissue paper.

"An early Kwanzaa gift," Shelby replied. Kwanzaa was still another three weeks away. She pulled off the cloche and slipped out of her coat, hanging them in the closet in the foyer. Tilting her head, she sniffed delicately. "Is that roast turkey I smell?"

"I remembered it's your favorite."

Naomi led the way down three carpeted stairs and into a sunken living room filled with golden light, a blazing fire in a fireplace, curio cabinets crowded with priceless art pieces, and a glossy parquet floor covered with an Oriental rug.

Running a hand through her hair, Shelby picked out the soft curls clinging to her scalp. "You didn't have to bother."

Naomi waved a delicate hand. "Cooking for you is not what

I would call a bother. Why don't you freshen up while I get us something to drink?"

Shelby made her way to one of the two bathrooms in the beautifully decorated two-bedroom apartment. The apartment in the pre-World War II building was designed with towering ceilings, a fireplace, wood floors, and tall windows offering magnificent views of Manhattan's skyline and the bridges spanning the East River.

She compared this view with the one from her apartment on Manhattan's Upper West Side, preferring the panoramic scene of the Hudson River and the New Jersey Palisades from her own living and bedroom windows.

Staring at her reflection in a mirror over a sink in a bathroom decorated in black and gleaming silver, Shelby ran a tube of cherry-red lipstick over her full lips and used a small rounded brush to lift the shiny black curls at the crown of her head. Wetting the brush, she smoothed down the wisps of curls on the nape of her neck and over her ears.

Studying her face, she silently thanked her mother for her flawless dark brown skin and perfect teeth. Her large, vibrant dark eyes, naturally arching eyebrows, hair, nose, and mouth were her father's. Stanton Carter's good looks had always turned heads, and the similar reaction was repeated with his daughter. Shelby Carter had matured into a beautiful woman whose dramatic face and slender body were certain to turn heads whenever she entered a room.

She adjusted a necklace of large black lacquered beads over a long-sleeved white knit dress which lay with perfection over her firm breasts, narrow waist, and rounded hips. Designing the dress had been a challenge for Shelby because of the slightly flaring bias-cut skirt.

She enjoyed sewing almost as much as she appreciated art. There was a time when she couldn't decide whether she wanted to become a fashion designer or a museum curator; however, after careful consideration, she realized she could study art and design clothes; but the clothes she'd design would be for her own personal use.

Shelby returned to the living room, smiling as Naomi set down two porcelain cups on a coffee table. The aroma of orange and cinnamon tea mingled with the sweet smell of burning wood.

"Everything looks and smells wonderful," Shelby remarked, her dark gaze sweeping the living room. Towering potted ficus trees rose up toward the twelve-foot ceiling. Sparkling pinpoints of light from towering skyscrapers, expansion bridges, and stars in a clear winter nighttime sky provided a glittering background through the floor-to-ceiling windows.

Naomi sat on a white loveseat beside Shelby, smoothing down her slim navy blue wool gabardine skirt. Picking up her cup and saucer, she took a sip, nodding her approval. "I think I finally made it right," she said.

Shelby took a sip of her own orange-flavored cinnamon tea. Glancing over the rim, she returned the nod. "Perfect." There was just a hint of orange liqueur in the fragrant liquid.

The two women sipped their tea in silence, both watching the flickering flames in the fireplace behind a decorative screen.

Naomi turned and directed her attention to Shelby. She wasn't certain whether the young woman would accept her offer, but if she did, she knew it would change Shelby Carter's life forever.

"I've given your name to the search committee for the Studio Museum in Harlem for assistant curator."

Shelby went rigid, her hand with the fragile teacup poised in midair. Her head turned slowly as she stared at Naomi. Naomi Morrow was offering what she had dreamt of all of her life.

"I . . . I had no idea you took what I'd said about becoming a curator seriously," she said hesitantly, trying to compose herself. As a part-time lecturer for the Metropolitan Museum of Art, Shelby had often dreamed of becoming a curator for one of the museum's galleries.

Naomi blushed, her bright eyes crinkling with a smile. "I take everything you say seriously, my dear. Besides, with your brains and training, you should've been the assistant curator of the Met's Egyptian galleries a long time ago. But of course, I know everything is political, and I've decided to use my clout just this one time to help you realize your dream."

Naomi Morrow was a trustee with several museums, including the popular Studio Museum in Harlem and the prestigious Metropolitan Museum of Art.

"I don't know what to say," Shelby stated modestly.

"Just 'thank you' will be enough when you're hired."

What Naomi didn't tell Shelby was that her name was the only one the board had selected for the final round of consideration. Shelby Carter's extensive background in African studies, with a focus on African antiquities and her art education in tribal art, prompted the Harlem museum trustees to label the young woman as an "expert" in her field.

Naomi fingered the single strand of pearls resting on her silk blouse. The magnificent necklace had been in her family for four generations, and she had gained possession of the famous Graham pearls on her wedding day. At twenty-one, she'd married Charles Morrow and shared the next thirty years with him until his sudden death from a massive stroke eighteen years ago. Widowed and childless, Naomi had suddenly thrown all her time and energy into her "causes." Her professional career had spanned schoolteacher, principal, superintendent, and art patron, and retiring at sixty after more than thirty-five years as an educator, she set out to make her dreams a reality.

Shelby took a sip of her fragrant tea, smiling over the rim of the cup. The glint in Naomi Morrow's dark eyes said there were more surprises.

"Something tells me that submitting my name for assistant curator at the museum doesn't have anything to do with the 'special project' you hinted at," she said perceptively.

"You're so bright," Naomi exclaimed with a wide smile, "and you're right. It doesn't. But I'll let my nephew tell you about it when he gets here."

Shelby's smile faded. "Your nephew?"

"Yes. Marshall Graham. He's . . ." The doorbell rang, preempting whatever she was going to say. Naomi placed her cup on the coffee table and rose to her feet. "That must be Marshall He's always on time."

Less than a minute later, Shelby caught a glimpse of a tall figure with a pair of broad shoulders filling out the soft wool fabric of a camel's hair overcoat.

Marshall Graham leaned down to kiss his aunt's cheek, but his gaze was directed over her shoulder at the slender young woman sitting on the white loveseat in the living room, the light from an overhead lamp ringing her dark head in gold. Even from the distance he noted her beauty immediately.

He removed his coat and hung it in the closet. The fragrance of an unfamiliar feminine perfume clung to the green coat beside his own coat.

Marshall shifted an eyebrow as he caught his aunt's knowing smile. Leaning down, he said softly, "She's beautiful, Naomi."

Naomi winked at him. "I told you she was lovely," she whispered, leading Marshall into the living room.

"Shelby, I'd like for you to meet my nephew, Marshall Graham. Marshall, Shelby Carter. She's the young woman I've been bragging about."

Shelby stood up, extending her hand and tilting her chin to get a better look at the imposing figure above her. "Hello, Marshall."

Marshall grasped her hand in a firm handshake, his large, dark eyes moving leisurely over her face. "*My* pleasure, Shelby."

Shelby felt a tingling sensation race up her arm as a wave of heat suffused her face. Marshall Graham claimed the exquisite good looks of James Van der Zee's photographic subjects from the Harlem Renaissance.

Marshall's ocher-tinged brown skin was smooth and clear, so velvety smooth it appeared nearly poreless. His black hair was cut close to his scalp, and glints of light picked up the shine of gray along his temples.

He smiled, and his teeth shone white against the brush of a

neatly barbered moustache. But what transfixed Shelby most was his eyes: they literally sparkled. Laughing eyes framed by thick, lush lashes.

"May I have my hand back, please?" she teased lightly.

Naomi laughed aloud as she stared at the startled expression on her nephew's face when he realized he still held Shelby's hand.

"Of course," he replied, appearing somewhat flustered by the woman Naomi Morrow mentioned every time he called or visited.

"Would you like a cup of tea, Marshall?" Naomi asked, breaking the spell between the couple.

"Yes, please, Naomi."

Naomi retreated to the kitchen, leaving Shelby and Marshall alone together.

Shelby took her seat again while Marshall sat down opposite her on the matching white sofa. Crossing one leg gracefully over the other and picking up her cup of tea, she surreptitiously examined Marshall Graham.

A navy blue suit with a double-breasted jacket, collarless white silk shirt, and black low-heeled boots draped his tall slim physique like a lingering caress. The result was tasteful and totally masculine.

Marshall successfully concealed a smile as he watched Shelby watching him over the rim of her cup. He examined her ringless fingers. They were long, tapered, and professionally manicured. If he had known Shelby Carter was so attractive he would have been more receptive to his aunt's insistence that he meet her. It was only when he and Naomi discussed the need to expand the curriculum to include a cultural arts program at the school where he was headmaster that he'd consented to an introduction.

Naomi returned, carrying a tray with a hand-painted porcelain teapot and matching cup and saucer. Marshall rose quickly, taking the tray from her and setting it down on the coffee table.

Picking up the teapot, he stared at Shelby. "Would you like a refill?" Nodding, she extended cup and saucer, and his free hand held her wrist, steadying her hand as he poured the fragrant tea into her cup.

Shelby's gaze met his and her eyes widened in realization. Marshall Graham had the same effect on her as her ex-husband had had. There was an instant attraction the moment she saw Earl Russell; and that attraction had resulted in her marrying Earl when they both were twenty-two. The attraction and the marriage had lasted six years, and now, six years later, she felt the stirrings of desire for the first time in a very long while.

She was uncomfortable with Marshall Graham—a stranger, a man, she didn't know had the power to make her feel something she had forgotten. She had dated over the years since her divorce, but no man—not a one—had elicited anything but a sisterly hug or a chaste kiss.

Marshall released her wrist, refilling his aunt's cup before filling his own. He took his seat and sipped his tea, eyebrows lifting slightly.

"Excellent tea," he remarked, smiling at his aunt.

Naomi stared at Shelby. "It's Shelby's recipe."

His gaze shifted to Shelby. "My compliments, Shelby."

She nodded. It was only when Marshall said her name that she recognized his Southern drawl. "Virginia?"

"I beg your pardon?"

She smiled. The four words rolled fluidly from his tongue like watered silk. "Are you from Virginia?"

Marshall returned her smile. "D.C.," he confirmed. "You have a very good ear for speech patterns."

"I've done a lot of traveling and I've learned to listen to the way people speak to see if I can identify where they're from," Shelby explained.

A buzzer sounded from the kitchen. Naomi put down her tea and rose to her feet. "You two talk while I put the finishing touches on dinner."

"Do you need any help?" Shelby questioned.

"No, I don't. And you, Marshall, please stay and explain *your* project to Shelby."

Marshall waited until his aunt walked out of the room before sitting down again. He stared at Shelby, seemingly deep in thought.

"Your project," she began, breaking the silence.

"My project," he replied, absentmindedly.

What Marshall Graham wanted to discuss was Shelby Carter. He wanted to know everything there was to know about her. His father's sister had only hinted that Shelby was "quite lovely" and "very bright," and that she would be the perfect resource person for his latest school project. And after going over her curriculum vitae, which Naomi had forwarded to him, he was certain Shelby would be able to write the curriculum for Nia Academy's cultural arts program.

"Are you familiar with the Swahili word *nia?*"

"Yes, I am," Shelby replied. "It's the fifth of the seven principles of Kwanzaa. It means 'purpose.' "

"For the past four years I've directed all of my energies toward a single purpose, and that is to give young men of color a quality education coupled with social skills that will help them to succeed when they become adults.

"Nia Academy is a preparatory school for grades one through eight with a very strict dress code. All the young men wear uniforms: navy blue blazer, white or light blue shirts, gray slacks, black shoes, and navy blue ties. And what makes Nia Academy so unique is that it's in Harlem."

"Why Harlem?" Shelby asked, wondering why she hadn't heard of the prep school's existence before tonight.

"Why *not* Harlem?" Marshall gave her a knowing smile. "Would you prefer it be in a Massachusetts, Connecticut, or Rhode Island suburb?"

She shook her head. "Not for people of color."

"Exactly, Shelby. Too many of our young people have gone to these prestigious prep schools and into a world that is so foreign to them that when they return to their own neighborhoods they're not able to fit in. They feel as if they're straddling two worlds. There's the one world, where the students are so privileged that their only concern is where they should spend their summer vacation. Should they go back to Switzerland or the Greek Isles?

"Then we have our children who return to their own communities, where they suffer the ridicule of their peers because they talk differently and perhaps act a little differently than they did before they went away. The pressure is always on for them to prove that they're still a homey and can hang."

Shelby was intrigued with the idea of a prep school in a predominantly African-American community. "Why would a prep school in Harlem be any different from a school like Choate or Chapin, except for location?"

"The curriculum may be similar, but the difference is Nia's emphasis on their heritage. My students all know that Columbus sailed to the Western Hemisphere in 1492, but none of them knew that the navigator of the *Santa María,* Pedro Alonzo Niño, was of African descent. Or that when Vasco Nuñez de Balboa discovered the Pacific Ocean in 1513, thirty Africans were with him, and that these Africans helped Balboa build the first ship to be constructed in the Western Hemisphere."

Shelby's eyes glittered with excitement as she leaned forward. "Aside from the academics, what else are they offered?"

"Dance skills. Not the hip-hop and street dancing they can pick up on their own, but ballroom techniques. They never know when it will come in handy," he added, seeing Shelby smile. "I must not forget the very important sex education courses for the upperclassmen, and last but not least, the course on table etiquette—which fork or spoon to use when dining. They've all become familiar with the differences between a water goblet, a fluted glass for champagne, and one for cordials. I don't ever want them to be confused when they sit down to a formal dinner. The social skills training helps to build esteem and confidence."

"Are they receptive to the social skills courses?" Shelby questioned, totally caught up in the activities of the school.

"In the beginning we were met with a lot of resistance, but each year it gets easier and easier," Marshall admitted honestly.

He smiled, the expression so sensual that Shelby stared at him in a stunned silence. "They don't mind the ballroom dancing because it's always held after class and they get to invite their sisters, cousins, or girlfriends to practice with them. The upperclassmen have become positive role models for the younger students. And what most of them like is not having the pressure of deciding what to wear each day. The latest style of dress becomes irrelevant between the hours of nine and three."

"I'm certain their parents like the dress code," Shelby remarked.

"Aside from the academics, it's what they like best."

"What else do you plan to offer the young men at Nia Academy?"

Marshall gave her a look that set her pulses racing, and she felt herself caught up in the man and the moment. For a brief instant she had caught a glimpse of his vision for Nia Academy.

Leaning forward and bracing both elbows on his knees, he threaded his fingers together and studied the design of the Oriental rug.

"I want a cultural arts curriculum. A curriculum that will include art, music, literature, folklore, and religion." His head came up slowly and the dark, laughing eyes were serious. "My students know what they are, but they don't know who they are, Shelby. I want them to know that they're descendants of a race of brilliant, creative, and honorable people who built advanced ancient civilizations dating from 4500 B.C. and that their accomplishments have continued throughout the ages up to and including 2000 A.D.. And they will know this only if they study their past—every phase of it."

Shelby nodded slowly. "What you want is the main focus of the history of Arabs and Europeans in Africa to be shifted to the Africans themselves. In other words, a history of the blacks *that is a history of blacks.* And the same in the Americas."

"Yes." There was an almost imperceptible note of pleading in the single word.

Shelby had known what he'd wanted the moment he'd outlined

the school's purpose, and she was certain she could write the curriculum Marshall wanted. But she had never made it a practice to accept a project without doing her own research.

"Can you write it?" Marshall asked.

"It's not *can* I write it, Mr. Graham," she replied with a slight tilting of her chin, "but *will* I write it."

His eyes narrowed and he sat up, his back becoming ramrod straight. "You'll be paid well for the project, Ms. Carter."

Shelby compressed her lips tightly, biting back a sharp retort. Marshall thought she was balking because of money. "When do you intend to incorporate the cultural arts courses into your curriculum?"

"Next fall. It's going to take at least three to six months to hire the qualified instructors before everything is put into place. And that includes setting up specialized classrooms for permanent exhibits."

Marshall knew he had done a lot of talking about Nia Academy and he couldn't help himself whenever someone appeared genuinely interested in what had become a priority in his life. He had left a coveted position at Howard University as an associate professor in their history department and had sacrificed his marriage to pursue his dream to establish a prep school for young men of color within their own neighborhood.

Shelby fought her own war of emotions. She wanted to develop the curriculum; she knew the school needed the curriculum; but she also knew that if she undertook the project, it meant interacting with Marshall. His presence reminded her of what she had been denying for so many years.

The stirrings of desire brought back a yearning for an intimacy she had missed for more than six years.

"We'll exchange phone numbers and I'll let you know whether I'll do it," she said, not committing herself.

"When?"

"Soon."

"How soon?" Marshall shot back.

A tense silence enveloped the room, broken only by the sound of crackling, burning wood, followed by a shower of brilliant falling embers. Both of them turned and stared at the fireplace.

Shelby breathed in shallow, quick gasps, trying to ease her tension. Her chest felt as if it would burst. Why was she, she berated herself, getting so worked up over a man whose manner reminded her of her ex-husband's?

Earl Russell had been smooth and confident beyond his years. His friends had referred to him as "slick," yet she saw him as mature; mature and slick enough to get her to marry him within weeks of their graduation.

Act in haste, repent in leisure. Shelby's mother's words came back to haunt her once Earl had revealed his true selfish nature. *And I'm still repenting,* Shelby mused.

The tension was gone from her face when she turned to face Marshall. "I'd like to see your school first. Then I'll give you my answer."

"I can give you a tour tomorrow," he said quickly.

"Tomorrow's Sunday, and I've already made plans for the day. Monday would be a better day."

"But classes are in session during the week," Marshall argued.

"I prefer to observe your school in operation. Besides," she added with a bright smile, "I don't lecture on Mondays."

Marshall let out an audible sigh he was certain Shelby heard. He inclined his head slightly. "Then I'll arrange my schedule to accommodate you on Monday."

Shelby smiled at him. "Very good."

Marshall studied her intently before he returned her smile, a gleam of interest in his gaze betraying his polite expression. Only Naomi registered his look as she walked into the living room.

She studied the two people sitting only a few feet from each other and successfully concealed a secret smile. "Dinner is ready," she said softly, turning and walking back to the dining room.

* * *

Shelby found herself charmed and thoroughly entertained throughout dinner. Naomi and Marshall kept her laughing with stories about the students they had taught.

"It's unfortunate, Marshall, that when you finally get to work with a younger student population it's not in a teaching capacity. I'm certain you would've enjoyed hearing the 'not having the homework' excuses," Naomi said to her nephew with a warm smile.

"College students aren't exempt from coming up with their share of excuses," he reminded her. "And because they're older the excuses go a bit beyond 'the dog ate my assignment' or 'my mother lined the bird cage with my research paper.' "

"What's the most original one you've heard?" Shelby asked Marshall.

He lowered his fork of candied sweet potatoes and smiled at her. He was delighted to see amusement flickering in her large dark eyes. The expression softened her mouth and crinkled her eyes slightly.

His mouth ruffled with a smile, then his lips parted with a wide grin as he recalled some of the more ingenious stories he had heard during his tenure at Howard University.

"I think the most original one I heard was when a student claimed his mother used his research notes to drain the fried chicken for Sunday dinner."

Shelby bit back laughter. "If she didn't have any paper towels why didn't she use a brown paper bag?"

"That's . . . that's because the notes were written down on brown paper," Marshall replied, laughter rumbling deep down in his chest.

"But why would the poor child write his notes on a paper bag?" Naomi questioned, a look of distress marring her smooth forehead. "Couldn't he afford a notebook?"

Marshall stopped chuckling long enough to say, "Because he didn't want to waste writing or typing paper. He said he was an environmentalist and his intent was to save the trees."

"But Marshall, darling, didn't the poor child know that brown paper is also made from trees?" Naomi asked.

Marshall nodded vigorously, holding his chest as tears of laughter filled his eyes. "He had only decided to become an environmentalist that morning."

"How convenient for him," Shelby said, shaking her head and wondering how students, even the ones she'd attended high school and college with, managed to come up with their creatively concocted excuses for not meeting assignments.

"Not convenient enough," Marshall stated, having recovered from his laughing fit. "I took off a full letter grade from his paper when he finally handed it in two weeks late."

"Only a full letter grade?" Naomi asked skeptically. "The rumor around Howard was that Dr. Graham gave out more zeroes than any other professor in college history."

Marshall shrugged his broad shoulders under his jacket. "He caught me at a weak moment." He winked at Shelby.

She gave him a full-mouthed smile. Something told her that the man didn't have too many weak moments. His smile faded slowly as he stared across the table at her. An odd but primitive warning swept through her. There was no mistaking Marshall's curiosity. Her curiosity was also aroused, but she knew the mutual attraction would be perilous—perilous only to her.

The heat that rose from her chest swept up her throat and to her face under the heat of his gaze. Her wildly beating heart was the only audible sound in the room as everything around her faded into a pinpoint of light.

He's nothing like Earl, she thought. Nothing except for an intangible sexual magnetism that made Marshall Graham so much like the man she had fallen in love with on sight and married after a three-month whirlwind romance. At twenty-two, she was going to become a modern-day Margaret Mead. She wanted to be the anthropologist for the twenty-first century, studying tribal people from the continent of Africa.

She had earned her degree in ethnoanthropology and had planned for graduate work in the same field, but Earl had complained that her fieldwork would keep them apart for long periods of time; and not willing to risk her new marriage, she'd conceded, deciding instead to pursue a degree in African studies.

Shelby didn't realize until after Earl had entered medical school that she should have continued her original plan to become an anthropologist because she and Earl had never found time for each other because he seemed to study around the clock; and when he wasn't studying, he was trying to catch up on lost sleep.

It wasn't until Earl had come to her seeking a divorce that she'd realized how much she had sacrificed. She and Earl had decided to wait until they were thirty before starting a family; they were careful, and she was very careful not to conceive; however, once Earl disclosed that a colleague he had been sleeping with since they'd entered medical school together was pregnant with his child, Shelby felt doubly cheated. He had given another woman the child they'd planned to have, and she'd given up her career as an anthropologist.

Shelby Carter had learned a valuable lesson: seek out your own happiness before you try to make someone else happy.

"Is something wrong, Shelby?"

She stared blankly at Naomi, unaware that she had asked her a question.

"I'm sorry," she apologized, her cheeks hot with embarrassment.

"I asked if you're ready for dessert."

Giving Naomi a warm smile, Shelby said, "I don't think I can eat another morsel." She had eaten turkey with giblet stuffing and gravy, a piece of cakelike cornbread, candied sweet potatoes, and a portion of steamed mustard and turnip greens.

"Don't tell me you're going to pass on my deep-dish apple pie?"

Shelby hesitated. Naomi Morrow made the best apple pie. "If you don't mind, I'll take a slice home with me. I'll have it for a midnight snack."

Naomi's smile widened. "Marshall?"

"Like Shelby, I'll also take my portion home with me."

Naomi placed her damask napkin down beside her plate and rose to her feet. Marshall also stood as she began stacking silver onto an empty plate. "Marshall, you and Shelby relax in the living room while I take care of this."

Shelby pushed back her chair, rising to her feet. "No, please. Let me help you."

"Nonsense," Naomi protested. "You're my guest."

Shelby picked up her own silverware, then reached over and removed Marshall's place setting. "I've eaten here so many times that I don't think of myself as a guest."

Naomi's hands stilled. "There's an unwritten rule with the Grahams that says if you don't want to be treated like a guest, then you'll be treated like family."

Shelby gave the older woman, whom she thought of as her mentor, a warm smile. "I'd be honored if you'd consider me family."

"And what would you like to be?" Marshall questioned. "A granddaughter?"

Shelby arched her eyebrows at him. "Your aunt isn't old enough to be my grandmother."

"But I'm old enough to be your aunt. How fitting," Naomi continued, pleased with herself. "Even though I've always doted on Marshall, I've always wanted a niece."

"*Aunt* Naomi, you may think of Shelby as a niece," Marshall said quietly, "but I find it very difficult at thirty-nine to think of another woman as my sister."

Naomi was slightly taken aback by her nephew's reference to their kinship. It was only on rare occasions that he referred to her as "Aunt Naomi."

"Does it bother you, dear nephew, that I'd like to think of Shelby as a niece?"

Marshall stared at Shelby, and the double meaning of his gaze was obvious even before he spoke. "Not in the least. However . . ." He paused, a teasing smile tilting the corners of his mouth upward under his neatly barbered moustache. "As an only child, I never had the experience of dealing with a younger sister. I hope you'll bear with me, Shelby, until I get it down pat."

"Well, since I do have a brother," Shelby countered, "I'll be certain to let you know when you don't get the older brother-younger sister scenario just right."

Marshall leaned forward. "Is your brother younger or older than you?"

"Four years younger."

"Quite different from having an older brother."

Shelby winced. She remembered her friends when growing up who always lamented about their older brothers being too protective. "Are you certain you want to assume this role?"

Marshall's sensual smile was slow in coming, and there was no mistaking his acquiescence. "This is an offer I can't refuse."

"I remember you saying that once before and it changed your life forever," Naomi reminded Marshall.

His aunt was right. He had accepted her offer to leave Howard to take the position as headmaster for Nia Academy, and the decision had cost him his marriage.

"It's a lot different this time," he said. Different because something told him Shelby Carter was different—very, very different from Cassandra.

"Come, big brother," Shelby teased. "You and I are on kitchen duty tonight while *Aunt* Naomi relaxes."

It took some urging, but Naomi finally retreated to the living room while Shelby and Marshall cleared the dining room table.

"I'll rinse the dishes and you can stack them in the dishwasher," Marshall ordered, removing his jacket and hanging it on a colorful hook along the kitchen wall.

Shelby gave him a saucy smile. "Are you certain you're not an older brother? You sure know how to give orders." Her gaze swept over his broad shoulders under the collarless silk shirt. She stared at his face rather than begin a leisurely visual perusal of Marshall Graham's slim, hard athletic frame.

Suddenly his face went grim. "My mother lost a child the year I turned seven. It was a baby boy—a stillbirth. She never recovered from the loss. After she came home from the hospital I don't ever remember hearing her laugh the way she used to. She'd smile, but it was always a sad smile. In my own way I tried to make her forget the loss. And I did everything I could to make her happy. I earned high grades, helped her around the house, and during the tax season when Dad worked late, used to read the stories of Charles Chestnutt to her."

There was a faraway look in Marshall's eyes as he focused on a spot just above Shelby's head. "The loss was hard on my father, too, because he'd lost not only his second child, but also a small piece of his wife. And although I never heard them talk about it, somehow I knew the intimacy in their marriage had died when they'd buried my infant brother."

Shelby hadn't realized she was holding in her breath until her chest felt as if it would explode. "I'm sorry, Marshall. I'm truly sorry for you, your mother, and your father."

His gaze met hers and he smiled. "Sometimes it takes a little longer than we want it to take, but everyone heals. Last year, for my parents' fortieth wedding anniversary, I gave them a gift of a month-long cruise on the *QE II*." His smile widened. "My father confessed the time they spent together was better than their honeymoon."

"You're a wonderful son, Marshall," Shelby said without guile or sarcasm.

"I love my parents very much. All I want is to see them happy."

The conversation ended when Marshall rolled back the cuffs of his shirt and rinsed dishes and silverware before he handed them to Shelby to stack in the dishwasher.

Sharing in the cleaning of the kitchen with Shelby reminded him that his ex-wife never set foot in the kitchen in their Washington, D.C., home. Every social event they'd hosted was a catered affair. Cassandra abhorred housework, yet she hadn't been willing to leave the colonial home to relocate with him to New York.

Marshall left Washington, D.C., giving Cassandra the divorce she sought and leaving her the house she used solely as a showplace for entertaining.

He glanced down at Shelby as she filled the dishwasher cups with liquid, closed the door, and pushed several buttons to begin the wash cycle. There was no doubt that the slender well-dressed woman whose head came just to his nose was more than familiar with the inside of a kitchen.

There was a quiet intimacy of working side by side on a task even as mundane as cleaning up a kitchen. Working together they finished quickly, and smiling at each other, Shelby and Marshall left the kitchen to return to the living room.

"Don't tell me you're leaving so early," Naomi lamented as Shelby glanced down at her watch.

Shelby knew Naomi didn't want them to leave. Whenever she went to the older woman's apartment, they usually spent hours talking about everything from art to the world's political situations.

"It's after eleven, and I have an appointment to meet someone tomorrow morning," she explained.

Marshall stood up, walked over to his aunt, and leaned down to kiss her cheek. "It *is* getting late, and you need your sleep."

Naomi folded her hands on her hips. "Are you trying to say something, Marshall Oliver Graham?"

He smiled down at her, extending his hand and pulling her gently to her feet. "No, ma'am."

Naomi hugged him, her cheek resting on his solid broad chest. "I thought not." She released him, smiling and watching as he retrieved his coat and Shelby's from the foyer.

Minutes later she stood at the door, kissing both of them on the cheek. "Please, Marshall, make certain Shelby gets home safely. And I don't have to tell you to see her to her door," she whispered in a quiet tone.

"I'll take good care of her," he confirmed just as quietly.

Naomi closed the door, smiling and humming "Matchmaker"

from *Fiddler on the Roof.* It had taken her more than a year to bring her nephew and Shelby together; and what she had suspected would happen did happen. It was more than obvious that Marshall was intrigued by Shelby; however, it was up to him to realize that he wasn't destined to spend the rest of his life alone.

Shelby pressed her back against the supple leather seat in the vintage Mercedes-Benz sedan while Marshall expertly maneuvered his car through the nighttime traffic. He waited for a traffic light to change and she felt him studying her profile.

"Do like living here in the city?" he asked, accelerating smoothly after the driver of the car behind him tapped lightly on his horn.

"Very much," she replied. "Everything is right here at your fingertips: restaurants, movie theaters, museums, and art galleries." It was now her turn to stare at his strong profile. "You don't like the city?"

Marshall signaled, then turned off the avenue to the lane leading crosstown through Central Park. "I love it."

"Where do you live?"

"White Plains."

"That's not the city," Shelby countered.

"It's a suburban city."

"It's not New York City, Marshall."

He gave her a quick glance. "Only the five boroughs can be New York City, Shelby."

"You're right about that." Shrugging, she turned to stare out through the window at the passing landscape. A full yellow moon cast an eerie glow on leafless branches reaching skyward like grotesquely shaped skeletal fingers. Gnarled tree trunks took shapes of hulking black bears and crouching felines, and boulders the shape of grazing buffaloes.

"Central Park at night becomes a magical fairyland," she said quietly.

Marshall slowed, permitting her to savor the scenery. "Only if you're not on foot."

She smiled.

"Have you ever taken a hansom ride through the park?"

Turning her head slowly, Shelby looked at Marshall. "No. I've lived here for sixteen years and I've never done it."

He smiled, flashing white teeth. "Don't tell me you're not a native New Yorker."

"I'm a native Californian. My parents and my brother and his family live in the Bay Area, but I have relatives all over the state."

There was a moment of comfortable silence before Shelby spoke again. "Do you miss D.C.?"

"Yes and no," he replied, his tone filled with a strained emotion he couldn't disguise. "I sometimes miss the milder weather and the small-town flavor of a cosmopolitan city. But what I miss most of all is . . ."

"What, Marshall?" Shelby prompted, when he did not finish his statement.

"The food and the jazz clubs," he replied in a half-lie. There was no way he'd admit openly to Shelby that what he felt was loneliness and estrangement. He was more lonely than he was willing to admit—even to himself.

Marshall didn't equate loneliness with celibacy because he hadn't been celibate since his divorce. He'd gone out with women, but he found that they bored him. However, his sense of estrangement had begun when he'd uprooted himself from his hometown, left a position he'd wanted ever since he'd entered Howard University as a freshman, then sacrificed his marriage because he wanted to pursue the second phase of his lifelong dream to head or teach in a specialized school for young men of color. It was only since he'd spent the past four hours in Shelby's presence that his feeling of loneliness had intensified tenfold. He had become so involved with Nia Academy that he hadn't thought of his own personal needs.

"I don't know how many restaurants there are in White Plains that serve Southern cuisine or clubs that offer jazz," Shelby replied, "but I know quite a few of them here in the city. If you want a listing, I'd be more than willing to put one together for you."

"I'd like that very much." What he didn't say was that he'd prefer that she accompany him.

He exited the park, continuing westward until he turned north onto Riverside Drive. "Which apartment building is yours?" he asked, once he neared 112th Street.

"The first one." There were two apartment buildings on the street, both with canopies shading the entrances.

"I may have to circle the block before I find a parking space."

Shelby placed a hand on his arm. "Don't bother to park. Please let me out in front of the building."

He continued past her building and pulled into a space at the corner. "I'll see you to your door."

Shelby opened her mouth to protest, but closed it quickly once she registered the frown set into his features.

By the time she had gathered her handbag and the small shopping bag with a plastic container filled with apple pie, Marshall had opened the passenger door.

She placed her gloved hand in his, permitting him to pull her to her feet. He didn't release her hand as he walked with her to the entrance of her apartment building. Handing him her keys, she waited until he unlocked the door leading to the lobby.

Shelby pushed the elevator button and the door opened. Marshall glanced in, then stepped aside to let her enter before he did. She pressed the button for her floor and both of them stood side by side as the car carried them quickly to the twelfth floor.

"The building has nice art-deco furnishings," he remarked as they left the elevator and walked to her apartment.

Shelby smiled at him. "The buildings on this street are cooperatives and are beautifully maintained. Many of the tenants have lived here for more than thirty years, so when the opportunity came to buy, they snapped up the offer."

She unlocked the two locks and pushed open the door. Heat

and the soft glow of pink light lit up the entry. Turning slightly, she glanced up at Marshall. "Thank you for seeing me home."

Inclining his head slightly, he let his large dark eyes examine her face. "I'll call you tomorrow evening to set up a time for your tour of the school."

Something intense flared through Shelby with his lazy appraisal of her features. A warning flag in her brain snapped up with the word printed in bold red letters—*don't!*

Don't see him again! Don't accept his offer to write the cultural arts curriculum for Nia Academy!

He took her silence as acquiescence, saying, "Goodnight, Shelby."

"Goodnight," she mumbled to his broad-shouldered back as he turned and made his way to the elevator. She watched until he disappeared into the elevator, then closed and locked her door.

Letting out her breath slowly, she pulled off her hat, slipped out of her coat, and hung it in a small closet near the front door. Walking through the living room, she placed the small shopping bag on a table in the dining area. She stood at the window spanning the living room and dining area, staring out at the black surface of the Hudson River and the tiny lights winking back at her from New Jersey.

Marshall Graham had walked into Naomi Morrow's apartment at exactly seven-thirty and he had walked away from hers at eleven-thirty. Four hours. It had taken only four hours to remind her that the memory of distrust and infidelity hadn't vanished completely.

Pulling back her shoulders, she smiled. She would write Marshall's cultural arts curriculum, then she'd move on to the next stage of her life. And hopefully that would be as assistant curator for the popular Studio Museum in Harlem.

Shelby sat on a tall stool examining several small pieces of sculptured jewelry. Her eyes narrowed as she picked up a pendant and turned it over on her palm.

"Gold?" she questioned without looking up.

"Gold leaf over bronze."

This time she did glance up. Her smile matched that of the tall, thin artist who had secured a profusion of curling dreadlocks with a leather thong at the nape of his neck.

"Do you recognize it?" Shumba Naaman asked.

"It's Aztec." Shelby held it closer. "This guy looks like Mictlantecuchtli, Lord of the Dead. And if he is, I would place this little beauty somewhere in Oaxaca around the fifteenth century."

"Right on all accounts, Shelby Carter."

She weighed the pendant, which nearly spanned the length of her hand. "It's an exquisite replica."

"Do you think you can sell it for me?"

She picked up another pendant in the form of a monster with a human head, the body of a snake, and a tail shaped like a bird's beak. The pendant was about six centimeters in height and had been crafted with such precision and skill that only an expert would be able to tell it was a replica.

She examined a golden bell in the form of a monkey. This piece was copied from a sixteenth-century original crafted by the Mixtec. The Mixtec had been the most talented craftsmen in ancient Mexico. They'd lived around the valley of Oaxaca, southeast of the lake. They had carved jade, made exquisite painted pottery, and worked gold with a skill that was unexcelled in the whole of pre-conquest America.

Shumba leaned closer to Shelby, inhaling the sensual fragrance of her perfume. "What do you think of this one?" He held up a pendant in the form of a skull with movable jaws hung with bells.

She took the skull from his long, skillful fingers. Holding up the pendant, she shook it gently. The bells tingled musically. "He's cute, but the movable jaws don't excite me too much." She handed it back to Shumba. "Are all of these cast in bronze?"

"Mr. Jaws is cast in copper. I tried using the same method of casting as the Mixtec. I mixed the copper with an alloy the Spaniards call *tumbaga*. It turned from dull red to yellow after I melted it, then I rubbed it until the copper dissolved from the surface, leaving a spongy film of pure gold which was consolidated by burnishing. It's an expensive method because the *tumbaga* must contain at least ninety percent copper to glisten to a convincing yellow."

"Starving artists don't make pieces in gold, Shumba," she teased.

"I only look as if I'm starving."

Shumba was right. At six-foot-three, he weighed 170. There was a time when he'd weighed in at 210, but after he'd changed his name from Francis Humphries to Shumba Naaman and let his hair grow into dreadlocks, he had become a vegetarian. He'd left his very lucrative position as a stockbroker for one of the top Wall Street firms to be an artist. And as a starving artist he worked out of the spacious SoHo loft which he'd paid for in full from the bonuses he'd earned during the ten years he had "gambled" with the investments of his clients.

Daylight streamed through the windows, highlighting the gold undertones in Shumba's skin and the reddish strands in his sandy-brown hair. His gold-brown eyes were humorous and tender.

There had been a time when Shumba had confessed that he was in love with Shelby. She'd laughed, saying she didn't want to spoil their friendship by becoming involved with him. He had only shrugged, saying she was probably right. Afterward, they'd promised to see each other every other month over Sunday brunch.

"I can sell every piece and you know it," she said, examining a golden replica of a sixteenth-century Inca woman. Putting it aside, she picked up the matching one of a man.

"Those two are solid gold. The little guy is yours."

"No, Shumba."

He took the tiny figure from her fingers, wrapping it in a soft cloth. "I made it for you, Shelby. It's my Kwanzaa gift to you." He grasped her hand and placed the cloth-covered sculpture in it. "Take it. Now the only other thing you have to do is represent me again at my next showing."

Her eyes glistened with excitement. "When do you want to show these pieces?"

"As soon as possible. I'd like to sell everything before I go to Benin."

"If I can get the gallery to set up the showing within two weeks, will that be soon enough?"

"Perfect. I'm scheduled to leave the second week in January."

Shelby spent the entire Sunday afternoon cataloging Shumba's pieces, while he prepared a sumptuous meal of steamed vegetables with homemade sourdough bread and a crisp salad. They toasted each other with several glasses of an excellent dry white wine before Shelby gathered her coat to leave.

Shumba escorted her down to the street, hailed a taxi, paid the driver, then kissed her mouth lightly before he waved her off.

Shelby's thoughts were filled with planning the exhibit for Shumba, and she wondered how many pieces Naomi would buy from this showing.

Pulling out her appointment diary, she scribbled notes on a pad of blank pages at the back of the small spiral book. Using the waning daylight, she jotted down days and dates. She lectured Tuesday, Wednesday, and Thursday at the Met, and usually worked at the gallery on Monday and Friday afternoons.

Flipping open to Monday, she winced. She was scheduled to go to Nia Academy. She hadn't planned to spend the entire schoolday at Nia, which meant she could make it to the gallery before it closed. She wanted to set up the showing as soon as possible.

Closing the diary, she mentally outlined what she had to do before the end of the year. She had done all of her holiday shopping early, mailing off gifts to her parents, her brother, her sister-in-law, and her nieces and nephew. She returned to California for the holidays every even-numbered year. This year, an odd-numbered one, would find her spending the season in New York.

* * *

Shelby unlocked the door to her apartment, registering the soft chiming of the telephone. She rushed into the living room and picked up the receiver. "Hello?"

"Did I catch you at a bad time?"

"No, Marshall," she answered quickly, her pulse starting up an erratic rhythm at the sound of his softly drawling voice.

"I'm available to meet with you at any time you wish tomorrow."

She wanted to cover as many of the school's activities as she could in one day, and she had to get to the midtown gallery by three.

"I'll be there at nine and stay until two."

"I can provide transportation for you," Marshall offered.

Shelby laughed. "That's all right. I have the address and I believe I can find my way to the school without getting lost." Nia Academy was less than a mile from where she lived.

"If that's the case, then I'll expect you tomorrow morning at nine."

"Goodnight, Marshall."

"Goodnight. And, Shelby . . ."

"Yes, Marshall?"

"Thank you."

"You're welcome." She hung up, sinking down into the sofa. She had committed herself.

As she stared across the room decorated in black, off-white, and tan, something clinked in her mind.

She knew nothing about Marshall Graham other than that he was the headmaster of a preparatory school and the nephew of an acquaintance. She didn't know whether he was married or single, and if he was single, whether he was involved with a woman.

Their conversation over last night's dinner had covered topics of a general nature. They'd discussed sports, the results of recent elections, and the evolution of popular music.

And now, only after she'd spoken to him over the telephone, did she know what had had her off balance with Marshall. There was something about him that reminded her that she *was* a normal woman with normal desires.

Without him knowing it, Marshall had become her conscience, reminding her that although her life had undergone an evolution, emotionally, she hadn't.

It was she who should have done the thanking.

Rising to her feet, she took off her coat and laid it over the arm of the sofa. She examined the furnishings in the apartment she'd occupied for the past five years. It was as if she were seeing everything for the first time: the comfortable sofa covered in off-white cotton, a throw rug covering the wood floor in a mud cloth pattern, and matching throw pillows she had bought during a trip to Mali, and the many pieces of sculpted primitive art she had purchased were nestled on off-white glass-topped rattan tables. Lush, live green plants and cacti added a splash of color to the living room, dining area, and bathroom.

She was alive—truly alive. She wanted to be loved, and she wanted to be *in* love; and more than anything, she wanted to share the special intimacy she hadn't had for more than six years.

"Thank you, Marshall Graham," she whispered to the full moon shining in a clear, star-littered winter nighttime sky.

Shelby stood outside the three-story townhouse. A large plaque in gold letters on a black background identified it as Nia Academy. The school was on a quiet residential West Harlem street lined with trees, townhouses, and brownstones. It was an ideal location for a private school.

She noticed one side of the street was restricted to school personnel parking only, and she was able to appreciate the full beauty of Marshall's stately dark-gray vintage 1975 Mercedes for the first time in the bright daylight.

It was ten minutes to nine when she made her way into Nia

Academy and to a front office where two women sat close together, talking quietly over mugs of coffee.

One glanced up and smiled. "Good morning. May I help you?"

"I'm Shelby Carter. I have an appointment with Dr. Graham for nine."

The woman's smile faded slowly as she glanced at a telephone console on the table in front of her. "Dr. Graham's line is busy. As soon as it's free, I'll let him know you're here. Please have a seat, Miss Carter." Her voice was pleasant, her manner professional.

Shelby nodded. She removed her gloves, pushed them into the pockets of her coat, and sat down on a tufted chair in a blue and gold kente-patterned design.

The reception area was spacious, the pale walls covered with the framed prints of Romare Bearden, Jacob Lawrence, and Faith Ringold, and Henry Tanner's "The Banjo Lesson."

Shelby examined the Tanner print, remembering the Met had recently offered an exhibit of Henry Ossawa Tanner's work. The response to his best-known paintings, "The Banjo Lesson," "Daniel in the Lion's Den," and "The Resurrection of Lazarus," had been one of the highlights of the museum's year.

"Miss Carter, Dr. Graham will be with you momentarily."

She turned and smiled at the receptionist. "Thank you." The words were barely out of her mouth when Marshall walked into the reception area, smiling.

"Good morning, Shelby."

The smooth, resonant voice brought a smile to her face and she rose to her feet. Seeing him again was like a punch to the solar plexus. This was the real Marshall Graham—in his universe.

He was dressed in what he'd described as the school's uniform: a navy blue double-breasted blazer with a patch on the pocket in the same navy and gold kente pattern as the one covering the chairs in the reception area, gray slacks, white button-down shirt, and navy tie. His footwear was a pair of black loafers.

He looked every inch the preppie. Her sculpted eyebrows arched; her gaze fixed on the pin on his blazer lapel.

"Good morning," she replied, her smile mirroring confidence and pleasure at seeing him again.

His right hand cupped her elbow. "Please, come into my office and I'll let you know what I've planned for us."

Marshall led her into a large, sun-filled room, his hands going to her shoulders. "I'll take your coat." Lowering his head, his warm, clean breath swept over the back of her neck, eliciting a slight shudder, then a smile from Shelby as his hands caressed her shoulders before he eased the black wool garment from her body and hung it on a brass coat tree in the corner near the door.

Turning around to face her, it was Marshall's turn to gape at the pin on over Shelby's left breast. A slow, sensual smile parted his lips before they inched up, displaying his beautiful white teeth.

"Where did you get yours?" he questioned.

"At the Black Expo last year."

"That's quite a coincidence, because that's where I bought mine." Moving closer, his gaze was fixed on what had been labeled the Middle Passage Holocaust Pin. He and Shelby had each elected to purchase one in pewter.

Most people who saw the pin for the first time were transfixed with the piece of jewelry designed in the shape of the hull of a slave cargo ship. Closer examination showed the outline of human bodies, lying in spoonlike fashion, head-to-toe, commemorating the importation of Africans through the Middle Passage.

"I see you elected to buy the one with the cowrie shells," Marshall said, staring at Shelby's pin.

She nodded. "And you went for the tiny heads." The five tiny heads, each face different, were suspended from nooses. The five tiny cowrie shells shook delicately when her fingers caressed her pin. The pin's designer had selected the number five because it represented "justice" in African forklore.

"Dr. Graham, I have a call from Ms. Pierce." The receptionist's voice came through the intercom on his desk.

Marshall moved over to the desk and pushed a button on the telephone. "Please take a message, Angela."

"I told her I'd take a message, but she insisted that I put her through. She said it had something to do with a date for the fundraising dinner dance."

Marshall hesitated, not wanting to, but knowing he had to take the call. His gaze was fixed on Shelby's face. Motioning, he held up one finger. She nodded and he picked up the receiver.

"Good morning, Nadine." He only half-listened to what Nadine Pierce said as he watched Shelby study the framed diplomas, awards, and certificates on a wall, and several photographs on a credenza facing the desk. "Yes, Nadine, I'm listening," he drawled. His gaze was fixed on Shelby's shapely legs, outlined in a pair of black opaque stockings and mid-high suede pumps.

He found the slim wool black skirt she had paired with a matching long-sleeved tunic flattering to her slender feminine figure. The severe color was offset by a challis scarf in a brilliant orange-and-black paisley. Her neatly coiffed hair was brushed off her forehead and over her ears, and his gaze drank in the delicate symmetry of her features. Tastefully exquisite. The two words summed up everything he had observed in Shelby Carter.

Shelby leaned closer, studying the photographs of a very young Marshall with Naomi Morrow. There was also a photograph of him with people she thought were his parents, on the day he'd graduated from college. There were no photographs of children or of a young woman, and she assumed that he had elected to keep that part of his personal life private.

Marshall ended the call, jotting down a date on the appointment book on his desk. Nadine could have given the information to the receptionist. He punched the button on the intercom. "Angela, please take messages. I'm going to be out of my office for most of the day. So if there's an emergency, page me."

"Okay, Dr. Graham."

He crossed the room, and as he neared Shelby, she turned and smiled up at him. "Where do we begin, Dr. Graham?"

He arched an eyebrow. "There's no need for us to be so for-
ıal, Shelby. The faculty and staff maintain a level of formality
r the students because many of them lack discipline when they
rst arrive at Nia. It'll usually take a couple of months before
ıey conform, and when they do, they're exemplary."

Taking her elbow, he guided her out of his office and down
navy blue carpeted corridor away from the front office. "All
f the offices are on the main floor," he explained. He pointed
ut the offices of the school's psychologist, nurse, and guidance
ounselor. A modern theater, designed with a center stage and
eating in the round and doubling as the auditorium, was also
n the main floor.

Shelby followed Marshall up a flight of carpeted stairs to the
econd level. "Grades one through four are on this floor," he
xplained, walking slowly and stopping to peer through the glass
n the doors of several classrooms.

Shelby stared at a class of eight second-graders who were
stening intently to their teacher as he pointed out countries on
wall map.

A tender look softened her gaze. The young boys were so
mall, yet appeared mature beyond their years. "Do you employ
nly male instructors?" she asked quietly, still staring through
ıe glass.

"No," Marshall replied close to her ear. "We have a few fe-
ıale instructors."

"Do you ever intend to admit female students?"

"Hopefully, one day."

Shifting slightly, Shelby glanced up. "Won't that change your
aison d'être?"

"No. By that time there won't be a need for specialized or
lternate schools for young men of color."

Shelby lost track of time when she sat in on a fourth-grade
cience class that was conducting an experiment on dissection.
he class of twelve young men were divided in teams of two as
hey dissected frogs. Most of them barely noticed her, while
cknowledging Marshall with smiles and nods.

Marshall had to urge her to leave as they made their way to the third floor and the upperclasssmen. The floor was quiet and the halls empty except for a tiny figure huddled near a classroom door. Dark, round eyes in a chubby face grew larger and rounder when the boy spied Marshall.

"What are you doing up here, Malik?"

"I . . . I wanted . . ." His little chin wobbled.

Marshall hunkered down to the child's level. "You wanted what?"

Malik pulled a strip of navy from his blazer pocket. "I wanted to see LaVarr. I . . . I couldn't tie my tie."

Marshall took the tie from the boy. "Does your teacher know you're up here?"

Malik shook his head. "I told him I wanted to go to the bathroom."

"You're not to lie to your teacher, Malik," Marshall scolded softly. He pulled up Malik's collar and slipped the tie under it. "If you wanted your brother to help you with your tie, you should've told your teacher that." Quickly and deftly he tied the tie, adjusting its length. "I'll get your brother to take you back to your classroom."

Malik nodded vigorously while staring up at Shelby. She smiled at him and he lowered his gaze. She waited with Malik until Marshall returned with a boy of about thirteen, an older version of his little brother.

"Good morning, ma'am," he said, nodding at Shelby. His dark, intelligent eyes shifted to Marshall. "Will Malik get in trouble, Dr. G?"

Marshall managed a slight smile. "Not this time, LaVarr. But I want you to practice with him until he's able to tie his own tie. We can't have him buying clip-on ties when he's twenty-five years old and vice-president of a family-owned company, can we?"

LaVarr's smile was one of relief. "No way. Thanks, Dr. G." He gave Marshall a high-five before he led Malik back to his classroom.

"Dr. G," Malik called out. He rushed back to Marshall, also giving him a high-five. "Thanks for tying my tie."

Marshall struggled not to smile. "You're welcome, Malik."

"He's truly adorable," Shelby remarked, staring at the two boys as they made their way down the hall to the staircase.

"Malik's a charmer, Shelby. He manages to wrap all of us around his little finger." Although he'd spoken about Malik, Marshall's gaze was fixed on Shelby's animated features. "Do you have any children?"

"Why, no," she answered quickly. She hadn't expected him to ask about her. However, she had to admit she was more than curious about the private Marshall Graham. "How about yourself?"

His mouth tightened noticeably under his moustache. "I don't have any, either." He studied her thoughtfully for a moment. "Just in case you're wondering, I wanted children, but my ex-wife didn't." He watched her lush lips part slightly with a soft intake of breath. Unknowingly, he had read her mind. "I've been divorced for five years."

Shelby couldn't ignore the build-up of heat in her face. Her thickly lashed eyes were fixed on his Windsor-knotted tie.

"I've got you beat by a year. It's been six years for me," she admitted.

Marshall seemed to move closer while not taking a step. "How long were you married?"

"Six years." She smiled up at him. "And in case you're wondering, we planned on having children, but decided to wait until we were thirty before trying. Then my ex-husband decided he didn't want to wait and . . ." Her expression hardened as her voice trailed off.

This time Marshall did move closer to her, his chest nearly touching her shoulder. Shelby wanted him to take her in his arms and hold her until she healed completely; until she could learn to trust again.

"And what, Shelby?" His voice was low, coaxing.

Her eyelids fluttered slightly, then she tilted her chin and gave him a direct look. "He couldn't wait for me. He'd been sleeping with another woman and she got pregnant." She noted his black eyebrows slant in a frown and she forced a weak smile. "How did we get on the topic of failed marriages?" she asked, glancing down at her watch. It was nearly noon.

Marshall looked at his own watch. "We'll break for lunch before I show you the rest of the school."

He led the way to an elevator at the far end of the hall and a minute later they stepped out to the building's lower level.

The remainder of the afternoon sped by quickly. After sharing a lunch of grilled chicken and a Caesar salad in the lower-level cafeteria, Marshall showed Shelby a modern gymnasium with the latest exercise equipment, an Olympic-sized swimming pool, and a library with an extensive collection of books, ranging from contemporary popular literature and fiction to rare and out-of-print editions donated from private collections.

"Nia has only been as successful in its curriculum and philosophy because of donations," Marshall continued. His right hand cupped her left elbow as he guided her back to his office. "We do a big fundraiser once a year in the spring, and with wonderful results. We have several very generous donors and one benefactor who prefers to remain anonymous. His donation underwrites the administrative overhead expense line in our annual budget."

"Do you offer scholarships?" Shelby asked, sitting down on a loveseat covered in what she had now come to recognize as Nia's navy-and-gold kente-cloth pattern.

Marshall removed his blazer and hung it on the coat tree. Shelby's mouth went a little dry as she stared at the outline of his shoulders against the fabric of his shirt. The tailored gray slacks fit his waist, hips, and long legs with proportioned precision, and his powerful, athletic body moved with an easy grace that made him look as if he floated through a distance of space.

She wondered about the woman who had let this brilliant, handsome, well-groomed man slip through her fingers.

"Most of our upperclassmen are offered scholarships because their parents need to save the money for college." Marshall sat down behind his desk, ignoring the stack of telephone messages he would return later that day. "Our children come from professional, working-class, and poor families. There is a very stringent admissions policy, so we don't and can't take every young man who applies. But if a child is accepted, the fact that his family can't make tuition is never a factor. If we have to underwrite the entire cost of his tuition, then we do it."

Shelby crossed one leg over the other and chewed her lower lip. The ideas were tumbling over themselves in her head. "How involved are your parents with their children?"

"Not as much as I'd like. They come to the traditional open school nights to talk to the teachers about their sons' progress."

She stared directly at Marshall and was successful when she didn't succumb to the intensity of his gaze. It was as if his dark eyes had caught fire and singed her. "How would you like to begin your cultural arts curriculum a little early?"

He rose to his feet, eyes glittering. "You'll do it!" His voice was barely a whisper.

Shelby's smile was dazzling. Marshall reminded her of a little boy opening gifts on his birthday. But she had to remind herself that the tall man was anything but a little boy. "Answer my question, Marshall."

"Hell, yes. I mean, yes," he said, correcting himself.

She rose to her feet and walked over to him. "What do you think of the students at Nia hosting a 'Kwanzaa Expo' for their families and the neighborhood?"

Marshall stared at Shelby, a look of complete surprise on his face. What had been so obvious, too obvious, had never entered his head.

Shelby noted his indecision, wondering if he was opposed to her suggestion, if it had been too preposterous for him to consider.

"Marshall?"

He blinked, then smiled his sensual smile. "That's a wonderful idea."

Her expression matched his. "I take that to mean . . ."

"I mean yes," he cut in. He slipped his hands into the pockets of his slacks to keep from reaching out and clasping her tightly to his body. He found Shelby composed and controlled, yet there was something about her that elicited spurts of passion from him . . . not the physical, sexual passion, but one that made his emotions whirl and tilt until he lost his grip on his rigid self-control.

Shelby crossed her arms under her breasts. "You're not going to have much time to pull it off. I take it the school closes for a holiday recess?" He nodded. "I suggest that you hold it a week before the recess. That way, the students are familiar with all that will go into a Kwanzaa celebration before the holiday arrives. Then they'll be able to duplicate it at home with other friends and relatives."

"That's just what Nia needs to affect a holiday mood after a week of final exams."

"Then the timing is perfect. I have a lot of books and the props you'll need to help you celebrate Kwanzaa."

"When can we get together?"

"Tomorrow," Shelby replied, knowing Marshall would not have a lot of time to organize everything he'd need to host a schoolwide exhibition. "You can pick everything up from my apartment."

His gaze dropped from her face to her breasts, then back to her face. "What time do you leave the museum?"

"Five."

"Then I'll pick you up at the Fifth Avenue entrance."

Shelby noted the clock on his desk. It was nearly two o'clock. "Thanks for the tour. I'm more than impressed with Nia." Turning, she walked to the coat tree.

Marshall was only two steps behind her and reached to retrieve her coat. He held it out while she slipped her arms into it and secured the swingy wrap with a wide matching belt.

"Does this mean you're going to write the curriculum?" he asked, his breath sweeping over her neck.

Shelby looked up at him over her shoulder, unaware of the tempting picture she presented as Marshall lowered his head until his mouth was only inches from hers.

"Yes."

His smile was dazzling while his eyes glittered with excitement. "Thank you." The two words spoke volumes.

Shelby rode the downtown bus, thinking about Nia Academy's commitment to academic excellence, social development, parent involvement, and student goals for continuous self-renewal. Focusing on the school's philosophy temporarily suppressed the awakening realization that she was more than attracted to Marshall Graham.

It hadn't been just his intelligence and overall good looks, but it was the man as a *male;* and seeing him again evoked feelings she recognized as a very strong passion within herself.

How had she, she thought, been able to repress passions which at one time had been as volatile and sometimes unquenchable as an oil field fire, a passion so encompassing that she was stunned when Earl left her marriage bed for another woman's? It was then that Shelby had doubted her role as a wife, and wondered if she had been indeed woman enough to hold on to her man.

The doubts and questions had attacked her relentlessly for a year, and she second-guessed her role as a wife and lover whenever she asked herself if she had demanded too much. Had she not given enough in return? Had she been too conservative in her lovemaking? What was it Earl had wanted that she hadn't been able to give him and he'd found with another woman?

The questions and the self-doubt led to withdrawal. She dropped out and hid herself away from the social circle she had spent years cultivating and became very selective whenever she accepted a date.

The healing process was slow, but she healed; and with the healing came a realization that she had been woman enough; that she had given Earl all he'd needed from a wife and lover; and most important, the fact that she had been concealing a great deal of anger and resentment that she had accommodated Earl when she'd given up her goal to become an anthropologist.

Once and only once had she permitted a man to make her decisions for her, and with disastrous results. Her delicate jaw hardened. It would never happen again.

The tightness in her face eased as she stared out the bus window, noting how easy it was for her to identify different neighborhoods without reading street signs by the types of shops open for business along the avenues. Manhattan was truly the ethnic mecca of the world.

Shelby walked through the door of the trendy East Side gallery and was the recipient of a dazzling smile from a tall, strikingly handsome man with a natural ash-blond ponytail sweeping down his back to his waist.

Hans Gustave's smoky gray eyes swept over her like a quick flash of lightning. "I know that look," he said confidently. "You have something for me."

Shelby made her way through the spacious Madison Avenue art gallery to a back room. She hung up her coat, then withdrew the stack of five-by-eight cards from her leather portfolio.

"What I have is eighteen pieces of exquisite sculpted pieces from Shumba Naaman."

Biting down on his lower lip, Hans pressed his palms together. "Tell me what you've got."

Shelby handed him the cards with detailed descriptions of each piece of sculpture. "They are incredible replicas of Aztec, Mixtec, and Inca amulets and totems."

Sitting down behind a priceless Louis XVI desk, she watched Hans read each card in quick precision. His grin grew wider as he read and shuffled each one. After the sixth one he glanced up. "I want every piece."

"But you haven't gone through all of them."

"I've seen enough. When can I show these?"

"Shumba wants a showing ASAP."

Hans took a matching chair, tapping the cards against the open palm of his left hand. "I can get invitations printed and in the mail by tomorrow, which means if I set it up for a week from this Friday, that'll give everyone on our mailing list a week and a half to clear their calendar and get their checkbooks in order. How does that sound to you?"

"It's a go, Hans."

Shelby spent the next three hours going over the large index cards, editing descriptions for a printed brochure before she and Hans agreed on the list price for each piece.

It was after seven o'clock when she walked into her apartment and flipped on a news cable channel on the television in an alcove of the bedroom. She undressed slowly, trying to digest the events of the world as her brain had shifted into overdrive when she thought of the three projects which would take up all her spare time over the next three weeks.

She had a lot on her plate: assisting the planning and coordination of the Kwanzaa Expo for Nia Academy, setting up the showing for Shumba, *and* writing the cultural arts curriculum for Marshall.

She was going to be very busy; too busy to think about Marshall and how she felt whenever she was in his presence.

Marshall. The thought of his name brought a smile to her lips. *Mr. Perfect.*

So perfect, she mused, that his wife had left him. Or had he said he'd left her?

It didn't matter, she thought, shrugging a bare shoulder. Her association with Marshall was strictly business, and *only* business.

* * *

At five-fifteen Shelby walked out of the Met and glanced down from the top of the stone steps, looking for Marshall. Vehicular traffic along Fifth Avenue had slowed to a crawl as buses, taxis, and cars inched along. Christmas and Chanukah lights glowed from many windows in the apartments of the buildings facing Central Park.

She had taken only a step when a figure moved behind her from the shadows. "Marshall." His name had escaped her lips in a whispered wonderment before she turned around.

"Do you have eyes in the back of your head?" Marshall asked near her ear.

Shelby shivered slightly, turning and staring up at him. "No. I recognized your cologne," she confessed, her gaze racing quickly over his face. Her breath caught quickly in her lungs. Despite the darkness of the hour and the diffuse glow coming from streetlights, she still was able to register a flicker of interest in Marshall's intense eyes.

He was casually dressed in a pair of dark slacks, a charcoal gray and white patterned pullover sweater, and a short gray wool jacket.

"Is that how you identify *men*—by their cologne?" His fingers curved around her upper arm, leading her down the steps.

"Not *all* men," she teased.

Lowering his head, Marshall let his mouth touch her ear. "That's encouraging to know."

"Why?"

"Because . . ." He grasped her hand, guiding her to the street and between lanes of stalled traffic. "Because," he repeated, once they crossed the street, "I don't want to be lumped into the category of the *insignificant* ones."

"What makes you so certain you're not one of, as you say, the insignificant ones?"

Marshall squeezed her gloved fingers slightly. "I say that because I think you like me as much as I like you."

Shelby stopped short, and Marshall nearly lost his balance. "Hold on there, mister. Who are you kidding?"

Tightening his grip on her hand, Marshall pulled her to him until her torso was pressed against his sweatered chest.

"Do you want me to show you how much you like me, Shelby?"

"No!" she gasped, glancing around her and hoping that the passing couples hadn't overheard him.

His hands went to her shoulders and he cradled her to his body. "I thought not, Shelby."

"Marshall." Her voice was small and muffled in his sweater. They were standing on 82nd Street, embracing like so many other lovers on New York City streets did every day.

"Loosen up, Shelby. I was only teasing you. Isn't a *big brother* entitled to tease his sister?"

Pulling back, she stared up at his smiling face. "Of course you are."

Marshall's arms fell away from her body and his smile faded, and even though he had released Shelby, she hadn't moved. They stood, inches apart, their warm breaths mingling in the crisp night air. Seconds stretched into a minute before he spoke again.

"Shelby."

The quiet sound of her name coming from his lips left her tingling. The tingling increased until it was a surging wanting. Her heart pounded in her ears, and amazingly, she felt Marshall's, too. Her gloved right hand went to the middle of his chest at the same time Marshall folded her gently against the solid hardness of his body.

"It's not going to work, Shelby. As much as I try, I can't treat you like a sister or think of you as one."

The spell was broken. The warm wanting was replaced by an icy chill, a chill that began around her heart and spread outward, touching every nerve and fiber of her being.

Had Marshall recognized her attraction to him and decided to establish the rules for their working relationship?

Why hadn't she noted his unyielding self-control before? She was aware of the strict rules and regulations he had set down for Nia, and there was probably no doubt his private life was also maintained by the same strict codes.

Extracting herself, Shelby forced a smile. "That's quite all right. Having one brother is enough for me," she replied, her voice filled with indifference.

Marshall's brow furrowed. "I promised my aunt I would take care of you, and I will."

"There's no need for you to take care of me," Shelby retorted. "At thirty-four I'm quite able to look after myself."

"That's not what I mean," he countered. "I . . ."

"There's no need to explain," she interrupted.

"But Shelby . . ."

"Marshall. I've been on my feet all day, and you and I have a lot to cover tonight. Let's not waste time talking about who you're responsible for."

This time when Marshall's hand went to her arm, his grip was firm, but not friendly. "I thought we could talk over dinner. I wanted to take you to a favorite restaurant of mine."

Shelby had to quicken her step to keep up with Marshall's longer legs. "Perhaps some other time. We can either order in, or pick up something on the way."

Marshall clenched his teeth. Shelby wasn't making it easy for him. He wanted to go over all he needed to celebrate Kwanzaa with the students and their families, but he also wanted to know all there was to know about Shelby Carter.

He knew the professional Shelby from the information he had gleaned from her curriculum vitae; but his aunt had refused to elaborate about Shelby Carter the woman, other than that she was single.

He could still hear Naomi's voice: *"You've spent so much time at Nia that you've lost all the famous Graham male charm, dear nephew. I introduced you to Shelby. Now you're on your own. If you want the woman, go after her!"*

And he *did* want Shelby. He wanted to see her, to talk to her . . . and he wanted to kiss her.

He wanted to taste the moist lushness of her mouth and discover if the flesh covering all of her was as soft and smooth as the skin on her beautiful face.

He wanted Shelby Carter with the same intensity he had once wanted to become a Howard University professor and either a teacher or the headmaster of an all-boys school for young men of color.

"What would you like to eat?" Shelby questioned, breaking into his thoughts as they stopped next to his car.

"It can be your call tonight."

"There's a wonderful Chinese takeout on Broadway, several blocks from my place."

"Chinese it is." Marshall opened the passenger door and waited until she was seated. After he'd settled himself behind the wheel, he stared at her profile. Slowly and seductively, his gaze traveled a downward path, mirroring approval. Beautiful, intelligent, feminine, and sexy. Those were only the first of many other adjectives he had attributed to Shelby Carter as he started up the car and pulled away from the curb and into traffic.

Shelby unlocked the door to her apartment and pushed it open with her shoulder, balancing her shoulder purse and a large bouquet of snow-white lilies. "I can't believe you ordered practically everything on the menu."

"I couldn't decide what I wanted to eat," Marshall replied, following her into the foyer carrying two large bags filled with containers of Chinese food and a third bag with a bottle of wine.

He took several steps into the living room and stopped, feeling as if he'd stepped into a lush, verdant rain forest. All of the white, tan, and black furnishings were set against a backdrop of lush green plants.

Shelby, placing the calla lilies on the dining table, glanced back over her shoulder at Marshall. "Is something wrong?"

He smiled, shaking his head as he made his way to the dining area and placed his packages on the table. "I'm just a little taken aback by your place. It's so beautiful."

Soft pink light from the foyer and from several lamps on the tables in the living room bathed the apartment in a cool, rosy glow. Floor-to-ceiling lace panels in eggshell permitted a view of the Hudson and the New Jersey coastline from the picture window that spanned an entire wall.

The gleaming parquet floor was covered with several area rugs in what he recognized as a mud cloth print. Natural woods and cotton fabrics covered tables, sofas, and chairs, and straw and terra cotta planters held massive banana, colorful coleus, gloxinia, cyclamen, and towering flowering cactus plants.

Shelby shrugged out of her coat. "It's home and it's comfortable."

Marshall agreed with her. Her apartment *was* a home. It was warm and filled with an aura of life. It was tastefully furnished with a combination of the old and the new. The furnishings were contemporary, while the pieces of sculpted art were reminiscent of a time long gone and of people who also were long gone, except for some of the lingering customs, which would remain alive as long as the griots passed along the oral histories.

Her place was so unlike the house where he lived. The house he had had professionally decorated with every convenience possible was large, cold, and empty, now that he was aware of what had been missing. His home was missing the love of a man and a woman—a family.

How, he thought, he had seen to the needs of so many others without seeing to his own? What did he have to prove, playing the selfless martyr?

Shelby watched Marshall as he slowly surveyed her apartment. His reaction was similar to most who were impressed with her collection of primitive artifacts.

"Marshall," she called softly. "Take off your jacket and stay awhile. Make yourself at home." He spun around to face her, his eyes crinkling in amusement.

"You may come to regret that invitation," he said, removing his waist-length gray wool jacket. He turned back to the window. "This is truly a room with a view."

Shelby took his jacket from him and scooped up her coat from the back of the dining chair, heading for the closet in the foyer. "I'll invite you back again when there's a prediction of snow," she said glibly. "I sit on the floor, with all the lights off, and watch it fall for hours," she explained. "It's a natural stress reliever."

She returned to the dining area, watching Marshall as he slipped his hands into the pockets of his slacks. His gaze was fixed on the window.

"Is that an open invitation, Shelby?"

The quiet timbre of his voice served as a warning to remind her of what she'd just offered.

"I . . ."

"Is it?" he repeated, stopping whatever she was going to say. He was frozen in place, only the rising and falling of his chest indicating he was still alive.

"Yes. Of course," she replied, as glibly as she had offered the invitation. "Please give me a few minutes to change my clothes, then we'll eat and go over what you'll need for your Kwanzaa Expo."

Walking past Marshall, Shelby didn't let out her breath until she made it to her bedroom and closed the door behind her.

Fool, she chided herself. What was she doing? How could she invite the man back to her place when all she wanted to do was complete her projects for him and move on? Move on to another man she found less disturbing . . . a man who didn't remind her of Earl . . .

She exchanged her skirt and sweater for a pair of black silk lounging pajamas with an abstract print of gold. She had fashioned the outfit of a long shirt with extended cuffs and side slits and loose-fitting pull-on pants with an elastic waist and drawstring tie. She quickly cleansed her face of all makeup, smoothed on a moisturizer, then brushed her curling hair off her forehead and over her ears. Slipping her bare feet into a pair of black leather ballet slippers, she returned to the living room.

Shelby walked into the darkened living and dining area, only the flicker of candles placed strategically on side tables illuminating the space. The sound of Jean-Pierre Rampal playing Vivaldi's *The Four Seasons* filtered through the apartment. The coffee table was set with a vase of lilies, two crystal wineglasses, several plates, the bottle of wine, and the containers of Chinese food.

Marshall stood with his back to the window, waiting for her. He saw her gaze sweep around the room in the flickering candlelight. The haunting sensual fragrance of vanilla lingered in the space. The fat candles were scented with a similar ingredient in Shelby's perfume.

"You said to make myself at home, and I did."

She bit back laughter. "So you did. Everything looks beautiful."

Floating across the room with his fluid stride, Marshall met her, extending his hand. "Dinner is served." She permitted him to seat her on the floor in front of the coffee table. Marshall also knelt, sitting down with his sock-covered feet tucked under him. He waited until she picked up a pair of chopsticks before he filled her wineglass with a chilled white Zinfandel.

"What would you like to begin with?" he asked.

Shelby's large eyes glittered with anticipation. She had thought of Marshall Graham as conservative and stodgy. How wrong she was, because he'd shown her he was anything but stodgy when electing to sit on the floor to eat. The candles, wine, flowers, and classical music revealed a lot about the man: he was a romantic.

She tried to remember all that he'd ordered. "I'll start with a steamed vegetable dumpling."

Each of them ate a dumpling before sampling a medley of stir-fried seafood and vegetables, chunks of lightly fried chicken with a hot spicy sauce, and sliced boneless duck bedded in snow peas, broccoli, red bell peppers, and water chestnuts. Her gaze met his over the rim of her wineglass as he balanced a portion of white rice on his chopsticks.

"Your students should be made aware that Kwanzaa lasts for

seven days—December twenty-sixth to January first. They also should learn about twenty words and phrases in Swahili if they're to make the celebration an authentic one," she said, before taking a sip of the delicious chilled wine.

"Class projects can include making or buying the seven symbols of Kwanzaa. They can make a *mkeka,* or placemat, by hand from strips of cloth or paper," Shelby continued. Marshall had lowered his chopsticks and stared intently at her.

"Nia should purchase a big cup or goblet. The Swahili word for the cup of togetherness is *kikombe cha umoja.* Everyone who takes part in the celebration sips juice or wine from the *kikombe."*

"What else do we need for the celebration?" Marshall questioned, taking a sip of his own wine.

"Mazao, or fruits and vegetables. *Mazao* represent the harvest for all work. When these are placed on the *mkeka,* African Americans honor themselves and the work that they do.

"The *muhindi,* or corn, represents our children. A family places one ear of corn on the *mkeka* for each one of their children."

"What about us, Shelby? We don't have any children."

"We would still put corn on our *mkeka."*

Marshall couldn't pull his gaze from Shelby's face. The golden light from the candles flattered the delicate bones of her jawline, illuminated the brightness of her eyes, and made her appear ethereal, almost unreal.

"What else?" he asked softly.

Shelby felt her heart racing. It was as if she were poised on the top of a mountain, waiting to plummet back to earth.

"The *kinara,* or candle holder, is the center of any Kwanzaa celebration," she replied breathlessly. "The *kinara* represents our ancestors, who lived many years ago in Africa. The *kinara'*s seven candles are called *mishumaa saba.* The candles are a beacon because they light the way. A black candle is at the center, with three red candles on the left and three green on the right."

"Shouldn't they know what the colors stand for?"

"I saw a *bendera* in one of the history classes. I'm willing to bet every student at Nia knows that black stands for black people staying together, red for their struggle for freedom, and green for their future."

"Only some of them may remember."

"If that's the case, then I'll be certain to include it when I write up the lecture."

"What's the seventh symbol?"

"The *zawadi,* or gifts. The *zawadi* are usually for the children."

"Can the *zawadi* be for adults?"

Shelby nodded. "Children, parents, siblings, or loved ones. On the first day of Kwanzaa, a child lights the black candle in the center of the *kinara.* One more candle is lit each day, beginning with the red candle, then the green candle, closest to the center. When the day's candle is lit, the child talks about one of the reasons for Kwanzaa.

"These reasons are called the *nguzo saba*—the seven principles. The principles are goals for African Americans to strive for. Posters defining the *nguzo saba* should be put up around the school during the week-long celebration."

A clock on a table chimed the hour and both Shelby and Marshall turned to stare at it. It was eight o'clock, and she marveled at how quickly the time had passed.

Marshall turned back to look at her, his mind filled with an eager excitement that he would see her again. He'd formulated a plan, but what he had to be careful of was that she not suspect his intentions.

"It's getting late, Shelby, and tomorrow is a workday—at least, it is for me."

"It is for me, too," she confirmed.

"Then, if you don't mind, we can go over the seven principles tomorrow. At what time are you scheduled to leave the museum?"

"Wednesday is my late night. I don't leave until six-thirty. What I can do is write up a draft of everything we've covered tonight. I'll also include the seven principles, their translations, and what each represents."

"You don't have to do that."

"I think it would be best," she insisted.

Marshall showed no sign of relenting, saying, "I have to see you anyway."

"Why?" Marshall didn't answer her, and she felt increasingly uneasy beneath his scrutiny. The look he gave her was familiar and disturbing. It was as if he could look inside her and see the real Shelby Carter.

He could see a woman who had hidden her emotions behind a facade of indifference to men; a woman who successfully hid her passions and emotions from every man who'd shown an interest in her; a woman whose body screamed silently for a release of the leashed sexuality she had repressed for years.

"I need you to sign the contract for the project. The contract's language reads that you'll be paid one-third on signing, a second third when you submit a draft of the proposed curriculum, and a final third on the approval of the curriculum committee."

Shelby knew she had to complete the cultural arts curriculum for Nia Academy quickly. She couldn't afford to spend many more "dinner meetings" with Marshall and not succumb to his charm and blatant masculinity.

"Okay, Marshall," she said quietly. "I'll meet you at six-thirty."

He stood up, coming around the table and helping her to her feet. "I'll help you clean up."

"No!" she nearly shouted. "It's all right. You have a long ride ahead of you. I'll clean up. Thank you for dinner." *Go home, Marshall Graham,* she said to herself.

Marshall slipped his feet into his loafers. "I should be the one thanking you." He moved closer until he left her no room at all to escape. The backs of her legs were pressed against the coffee table.

Lowering his head, he held her shoulders in a firm grip and brushed a gentle kiss across her ear. "Goodnight, Shelby."

Her fingertips grazed her ear after he'd released her and walked to the closet to retrieve his jacket. The thick brush of his moustache was intoxicating, and at that moment she wished her ear had been her mouth.

"Goodnight, Marshall." He glanced at her over his shoulder, smiled, and then opened and closed the door.

Shelby stood staring at the closed door for a full minute before she locked it. The warning voice in her head taunted her again. *Don't see him again. He's dangerous. He's trouble.*

But how could she not see him if she had committed herself to writing a curriculum proposal for him? She had given her word, and to her, her word was as binding as a contract.

Contract! The word slapped at her. Marshall wanted her to sign a contract and they'd never discussed or negotiated a fee.

She shook her head. She was slipping. In the past, she'd never committed herself to a project unless she had negotiated a fee that she felt was comparable to her experience and training.

"Get it together, Shelby," she whispered, making her way back to the living room to clear away the remains of dinner.

Everything she'd shared with Marshall was put away, except for the vase of lilies. After Marshall had paid for the food, she'd waited at the restaurant for it to be prepared while he'd left to pick up what he'd referred to as a "few things." The few things turned out to be a bottle of chilled wine and a bouquet of flowers.

A wry smiled twisted her mouth. If she had been looking for the "perfect" man, she probably wouldn't have been able to find one. On the other hand, Marshall Graham came close to what she defined as "perfect," and she was afraid. Not afraid of Marshall, but of herself and what she felt whenever they were together.

Had she really matured emotionally in six years? Was she really ready to become involved with a man again?

Sitting in bed with a pad and pencil and outlining the Kwanzaa celebration for Nia, she pushed the questions to the recesses of her mind, but they attacked her relentlessly as she slept.

Her dreams were filled with visions of Marshall—his smooth ocher-tinged brown skin, his close-cut graying black hair, the brilliance of his large, laughing dark eyes, his cologne, and the silkiness of the thick black moustache that concealed most of what appeared to be a sensual male mouth.

She woke up two hours before her alarm went off, exhausted and disoriented. She stayed in bed, staring up at the ceiling until sleep claimed her again . . . this time without the disturbing dreams.

Shelby sat across the table from Marshall in his favorite restaurant. The Garden was an atrium-designed restaurant with an abundance of live plants and flowers that reminded her of an oasis. The fragrance of pale orchids hung from planters filled the air.

Marshall watched Shelby's expression as she glanced around the private alcove. The space contained only four tables, with seating for two at each.

Her gaze met his. "I can see why this is your favorite restaurant. It's beautiful."

He nodded. "A beautiful setting for a beautiful woman." His penetrating gaze and compliment were as soft as a caress, and what Marshall was unaware of was that he'd stoked a gently growing fire in Shelby.

Her lashes shadowed her eyes for a quick second, the gesture demure and provocative. "Thank you." Her voice was a breathless whisper.

Marshall smiled, his arching eyebrows inching up. It never occurred to him that there was an innocence in Shelby that wasn't apparent when he was first introduced to her. There was no doubt she could hold her own professionally, but it was the woman that entranced him.

He stared at the commemorative pin she wore on the orange wool dress over her left breast before bringing his gaze back to her face. Reaching into the breast pocket of his jacket, he withdrew an envelope and handed it to her.

"There're two copies of the contract. I need you to sign both and give them back to me. You'll receive one copy and a check for your first installment after the school board meets Monday night."

Shelby noted the dark blue and gold embossed logo of Nia Academy on the thick sealed envelope. "Is it all right if I bring this back to you on Monday?"

"Perhaps you can get it to me over the weekend."

Her brow furrowed. "What's this weekend?"

"My aunt's birthday is Saturday, and I've planned something very special for her big 7-0. I know she's quite fond of you, and I'd like for you to help me host a party in her honor."

"Where?" She was too startled by his suggestion to flatly reject his offer.

"At my house. I've sent out invitations to all her friends and former colleagues and hired a caterer and a small combo for the musical program."

Shelby's eyes sparkled. "Is this a surprise?"

"Yes. I told her I was taking her out for her birthday, so she believes it's going to be only the two of us."

"How are you going to get her there if you have to be home to greet the guests?"

"I've arranged for a car service to pick her up. I told her I was taking her to a place where black tie is the norm for dinner and dining. She's prepared to stay overnight."

"It sounds like a wonderful surprise."

"I'm hoping it will be. Well, Shelby?"

"Well, what?"

"Will you be my hostess?"

All her uneasiness regarding Marshall Graham slipped back to grip her. What she wanted to do was throw the envelope back at Marshall and walk out of the restaurant. She wanted to forget he'd ever existed. But she couldn't. An invisible thread bound her to him through Naomi Morrow, the kind elderly woman who had become her mentor, friend, and surrogate aunt.

"Yes."

Her reply was wrested from a place where logic and reason

ceased to exist, and she murmured a silent plea, praying fervently she would not make the same mistake twice.

Reaching over the table, Marshall held her hands possessively between his large, well-groomed fingers. Shelby stared at his hands covering hers, and if she had glanced up she'd have recognized his caressing gaze making passionate love to her face. However, neither of them noticed the woman approaching their table.

"My, my, my. Isn't this a touching scene?"

Shelby's head came up quickly. She stared up at a woman whose attractive face was marred by a sneer pulling down the corners of her lush mouth.

Leaning over, the woman placed her gloved hand on Marshall's while kissing him flush on the mouth. "Hello, sugar."

Marshall released Shelby's hands, rising to his feet. A muscle ticked in his lean jaw, and there was no mistaking his annoyance. He glared at the woman with straightened hair pulled tightly off her toffee-hued face. "Nadine."

Nadine arched an eyebrow. "Oh, so you *do* remember my name. You said you would call me, but it looks as if you've been occupied with other *things*."

Shelby's back stiffened. She'd never been referred to as a *thing*. Her gaze met Nadine's dining partner, and he offered an apologetic smile.

Nadine slipped her arm through her date's, pulling him to her side. "Cameron, this is Marshall Graham. He's the headmaster for Nia Academy. Marshall, Cameron Porter."

The two men shook hands, murmuring the appropriate polite responses. Marshall turned and stared down at Shelby.

"Shelby, this is Nadine Pierce. Ms. Pierce is chairperson for our fundraising committee. Nadine, Shelby Carter."

Shelby nodded. "Nadine." She extended her hand to Cameron. He grasped it firmly and held her fingers a moment too long for propriety. "Cameron."

Cameron Porter placed a hand in the center of Nadine's silk-covered back and steered to her toward a table in the alcove. "Let's not tarry, Nadine. You know I'm starved."

Nadine gave him a dazzling smile, then glanced back at Shelby. "That's a darling little dress you have on. I'd love to carry something like that in my boutique. Would you be so kind as to tell me where I can pick up a few like it?"

"I'm so sorry," she replied facetiously. "It's a one-of-a-kind original." There was no way she was going to tell her that she had designed the dress.

"Such a pity," Nadine crooned.

Shelby's smile was wide and false. "Isn't it.?'

Marshall took his seat, letting out his breath as Cameron steered Nadine to their table. "I'm sorry about that," he apologized softly.

Shelby fingered the large gold hoop in her left ear, remembering he had taken a call from Nadine Pierce on Monday. There was no mistaking the woman's venomous hostility and jealousy.

"Are you in some way involved with Ms. Pierce?"

Marshall's eyes flashed anger, and for a long time he stared at her. "My involvement with Nadine is strictly business."

"Does she make it a practice to insult every woman she sees you with?"

"Well . . . no."

Shelby raised her eyebrows. "I see."

"Do you really?" Marshall shot back.

"I'd have felt better if she'd referred to me as *Miss Thing.*"

"I've never known Nadine to be overtly rude to anyone." He waved away the waiter who'd approached the table to take their order. "Nadine's involvement with Nia serves as a vital link between the school and the business community. Her methods may be unorthodox at times, but her efforts have generated more than a half million dollars in contributions from business organizations. If you want, I'll talk to her about her being rude to you . . ."

"Don't bother, Marshall," Shelby interrupted. "I can defend myself."

"I bet you can, Shelby Carter."

She registered a smile crinkling his eyes. "You've offered to protect and defend me. What else is left for you to do for me?"

Make love to you, he mused. Thinking of making love to her elicited an instant response in his groin. "I don't think you'd want to know at this juncture, Miss Carter." His smile had turned into a lecherous grin.

Explosive currents raced through her body, heating and melting away her resolve, and leaving in its wake a slow, drugging wanting.

From the moment she was first introduced to Marshall there had been a strange waiting: waiting to discover whether he was married or single, and waiting to find out whether he was involved with another woman; it was more than apparent he wasn't, if he asked her to be his hostess for his aunt's seventieth birthday celebration.

"I don't think so," she replied, reading his mind. "I'm not interested."

His grin vanished, replaced by an expression of innocence. "Now, what did you think I meant?"

Rather than reply, Shelby picked up the menu, studying the selections. "How's the lamb, Marshall?"

"The lamb's great. But you didn't answer my question. What did you think I meant?" He enunciated each word.

She prayed she was right, saying, "You want . . ."

He leaned closer. "I want what?"

Her lashes shadowed her eyes, sweeping down and brushing her high cheekbones. The light from the small table lamp was flattering to her features. It glimmered on her flawless sable-brown skin and soft, moist mouth.

"You want me," she said in a small voice.

Marshall nodded. "To do what with?"

Her head came up, and there was fire in her challenging gaze. "What every man wants to do to a woman."

"I'm not every man, Shelby," he stated, so quietly that she

had to strain to hear what he'd said. "But you're right. I *do* want you, but only on your terms. The choice has to be *yours.*"

"Aren't you gallant? Why make me responsible for everything, Marshall?"

"Then it'll be my way."

"No way, Marshall Graham."

He eyed her critically. "What's it going to be? Take your pick . . . my way? Or yours?"

Shelby realized Marshall was offering her the chance of becoming whole again. He wanted her to trust not only him, but men in general.

"My way," she said, after a long silence.

Marshall picked up his glass of water and touched it to hers. "I'll drink to that." He drank half the glass of water, then reached for his own menu. "The grilled lamb with mint jelly looks good." Glancing up, he winked at her and she smiled back at him.

He gave their orders to the waiter, Shelby ordering club soda with a twist of lime, while Marshall opted for mineral water.

Over dinner she outlined the *nguzo saba* for each day of the celebration, translating the Swahili and describing the seven principles in detail.

"The fifth day should be of great significance to the students because their school is named for the principle Nia," Marshall said solemnly. "And that's what Nia has tried to do. It's purpose being to make our young men as great as they can be."

"You seem to be doing a wonderful job with them."

He bit down on his lower lip, seemingly deep in thought. "It hasn't been easy. Everyone connected with Nia have made a lot of sacrifices to make it a success. I think of myself as twice blessed to have a selfless and dedicated faculty and staff."

The evening sped by quickly and Shelby felt completely at ease with Marshall for the first time. It would be up to her to determine where their relationship, if there was to be one, would go.

He drove her home and saw her to her door. Shelby smiled at him. "Thank you for a wonderful evening."

"My thanks to you, too. I'll pick you up Saturday afternoon at one. Be prepared to spend the night." Leaning over, he kissed her ear, then spun around on his heel and retraced his steps to the elevator.

"What are you talking about? Marshall!"

"Goodnight, darling," he answered, without turning around, and disappeared into the elevator.

Damn, she swore to herself. He'd tricked her. He'd gotten over on her without her being aware of it. Next time, Marshall. Oh yes, there would be a next time.

Shelby spent three hours in the area adjoining her bedroom, completing the proposal for the Kwanzaa Exposition. When she'd taken possession of the apartment five years ago she'd hired a carpenter to remove the folding doors to a walk-in closet, creating a spacious alcove where she'd set up a table for her sewing machine, television, and computer workstation.

Pushing a button, she printed out what she had saved on a disk. Duplicate copies of the contract Marshall had given her earlier that evening lay on the bedside table.

She had to read the fee Nia offered her to complete the cultural arts curriculum twice before she realized the amount was more than half of what she earned annually at the museum. She remembered Marshall saying, *"You will be paid well for the project."* He had not lied to her.

She was expected to submit a preliminary draft within sixty days of signing, and a final copy by April first. Shelby smiled. She could make both deadlines easily. She always took a leave from the museum and the gallery the last week of the year. Yes, she thought, she had plenty of time to complete the project.

* * *

Shelby ticked off the listing of things to do on a page in her appointment diary. She'd made arrangements for a pick-up from Shumba and delivery to Hans of the sculpture with a bonded messenger service that specialized in transporting precious gems and priceless art. The completed Kwanzaa packet and signed contracts were in an oversized envelope, along with a book of recipes for an African American celebration of culture and cooking and a large *mkeka* in a kente-cloth pattern she'd made as a donation to Nia for Kwanzaa.

She had also chosen a dress to wear for Naomi's party and packed a bag containing clothes she'd need to spend the night at Marshall's house.

The clock in the living room chimed one at the exact moment her intercom buzzed loudly. Marshall was always prompt. She buzzed him into the building.

It was a very different Marshall who walked into her apartment. He was dressed in a pair of worn jeans, a black wool turtleneck sweater, and jogging shoes. She stared openly at the dark stubble on his unshaven cheeks, finding him even more stunningly virile than before.

Marshall was equally entranced as his gaze swept over Shelby. It was the first time he had seen her not wearing a dress. She had paired black tailored wide-wale cords with a bulky white ski sweater and black leather hiking shoes. He smiled at the neat feminine figure she presented.

"I'm ready," she announced, walking back to the living room. She picked up a ski jacket and slipped her arms into it. She hadn't missed Marshall's obvious examination and approval.

Marshall picked up her overnight bag by the door. "Did I tell you to pack a swimsuit?"

Shelby spun around and stared at him, her expression mirroring surprise and shock. "I thought I was going to White Plains, not White Sands."

"You *are* going to White Plains," he confirmed.

"But why would I need a swimsuit, Marshall? It's all of twenty-eight degrees, with a prediction of sleet later tonight. Sorry to disappoint you, but I happen not to be a member of the Polar Bear Club."

Marshall set down her bag and walked over to her. Reaching out, he cradled her face between his hands, giving her no choice but to stare up at him. All that she didn't know she felt for him swept over her at that moment.

There was no way she could resist the man cradling her so gently. She had known him exactly one week, and in that week he had unwittingly forced her to examine herself.

She couldn't continue to live in the past. Earl was Earl and Marshall was Marshall. How could she ever have thought that they were anything alike?

Earl had done nothing to her that she hadn't permitted him to do. He hadn't forced her to give up her study of anthropology—she'd done it willingly to please him; and she didn't have to agree to wait until she was thirty before becoming a mother—she'd also agreed to that willingly.

Marshall had permitted her a choice: her way or his way, and she had opted for her way. It was up to her to see him; it was up to her to permit him to kiss her; it was up to her to share her body with him. And most important, she would have the freedom, without doubt or guilt, to offer Marshall her love.

"Do you own a swimsuit, Shelby?" His voice was soft and seductive. She nodded numbly. "Then, please go and get it." His hands moved to the back of her head, his fingers threading through the short curls. He lowered his head slowly and deliberately, then did what he'd wanted to do ever since he'd first seen Shelby Carter. His mouth moved over hers, exploring and tasting her lush, moist lips. He felt her hands curl into fists against his ribs, slacken, and finally open to close again, grasping the back of his sweater as she parted her lips to his searching, demanding tongue.

Shelby inhaled the familiar cologne on his clothes and body, felt the heat searing her body through his clothes, and marveled in the feel of the thick, silky hair on his upper lip. She was soaring, floating, and drowning all at the same time. Her tongue met the velvet warmth of his.

Marshall's hands swept down her back and his fingers curved under her hips, pulling her closer. He felt her trembling and his passion grew stronger.

Blood pounded in his brain and the heat and fire seared his loins. He wanted Shelby Carter with a longing that was totally foreign to him. He wanted her not for a cause or reason or because of a lifelong dream. He wanted her for himself. She was the first woman he wanted because she was wholly woman. All of the other women he'd known were his sexual counterpart—female.

Shelby pulled back to catch her breath, and in that moment, sanity returned. She pushed against Marshall's thick shoulders, breathing heavily. "Stop! Please."

He raised his head, but he didn't release her. He folded her gently against his chest, permitting her to break the hold if she chose to. The sound of their heavy breathing echoed in the stillness of the apartment. Marshall closed his eyes, sighing in relief as she pressed her cheek against his shoulder.

Shelby smiled as one of Marshall's hands came up and cupped the back of her head in a comforting gesture. His heartbeat throbbed wildly against her ear before slowing to a steady, measured rhythm.

A deep feeling of peace entered her, and she wondered if she should feel some guilt. Marshall was the first man she had kissed who was able to summon the passion she had hidden away for six long years.

Pulling out of his loose embrace, she smiled up at him. "I think I'd better get that swimsuit now."

Marshall watched her walk toward her bedroom, hoping the swimsuit was not a bikini.

"The house is at the top of the hill," Marshall informed Shelby, as he downshifted the four-wheel-drive vehicle up a steep, winding road.

Shelby was unprepared for the panorama unfolding before her eyes. She turned in her seat and stared out the back window at the Hudson River and a magnificent view of the Tappan Zee Bridge, but it was the sight of the house on the hill that stunned her.

Marshall's house was a series of connecting modern pale-gray structures with what appeared to be two floors of glass and skylights. The house reminded Shelby of the nooks, crannies, twists, turns, turrets, and charm of a nineteenth-century Connecticut farmhouse-turned-bed-and-breakfast she had once stayed in.

Puffs of smoke drifted from several chimneys, disappearing in the raw late-fall air. Towering pine and blue spruce trees provided the only color on a hilly landscape dotted with starkly bare maple, oak, and white birch trees. Patches of snow still remained after the first snowfall of the season ten days before, although all traces of it had already disappeared in Manhattan.

Marshall opened the passenger door, curved an arm around Shelby's waist, and swung her effortlessly to the ground. A smile crinkled his eyes as he registered her staring up at him. His smile faded slowly, replaced by a slight frown.

"Do you realize that this is the first time I've ever looked at you in daylight, Shelby? It seems as if we can only get together at night."

Her smile was mysterious. "Maybe we're vampires and we're not aware of it," she teased.

His gaze shifted from her eyes to her mouth. "I think not. I'd prefer to think of you as a witch . . . a beautiful witch who's cast a spell over me where I'm unable to resist your charms."

"What charm, Marshall?" she asked, tilting her chin.

"You haunt my dreams, Shelby," he replied, his words echoing her dreams. "Since I met you, I've undergone the worst case of insomnia I've ever experienced," he admitted. And he was also experiencing another condition he hadn't had since he was a teenage boy.

Marshall's expression was so serious that she wanted to laugh; but she didn't. She placed a delicate hand on the sleeve of his sweater. "You should see a doctor about your insomnia. Perhaps he could prescribe a sleeping aid."

What about my other condition? he asked himself silently.

She stared at him, drowning in the black pools of shimmering velvet staring back at her. "You're going to need more than a prescription for a sleeping aid if you continue to stand out here without a coat," she said quietly.

"If I get sick, will you take care of me?"

"No."

Dropping an arm over her shoulder, Marshall led her toward the house. "You're a hard woman, Shelby Carter."

"And you're not a hard man?"

"Not with someone I care very deeply about."

She was unable to reply to his retort. She cared for Marshall, more deeply than she was willing to admit; however, she couldn't care more for him than she could for herself. She could not give again; she could not give more than she hoped to receive. But on the other hand, if Marshall was willing to offer her what she was willing to offer—trust and fidelity—then she'd consider becoming involved with him.

"I believe in giving sixty-five percent in a relationship, Shelby."

"That would only leave you with thirty-five percent. You'd wind up on the losing end," she protested, wondering if he'd done all the giving in his marriage the way she'd done and wound up the loser—the willing victim.

"Not if you give me sixty-five percent. That way both of us would be winners. We'd both have a hundred percent."

She stared at his sweater-clad back as he unlocked the front door, replaying his equation in her mind. He was willing to give her more than half of himself because he believed if she became involved with him she would give him more than half of herself.

"Did you get sixty-five percent from your ex-wife?"

The broad shoulders under the black wool sweater stiffened, then relaxed. "Yes, Shelby," Marshall replied, not turning around. "She gave me sixty-five percent, but I asked her for something else she refused to give up. And it wasn't until the divorce that I realized she *couldn't* give it up."

He pushed opened the door and pulled her gently into the spacious warmth of his house. "I made a very serious mistake once, Shelby. I *will not* make it again."

She wondered what mistake had been tragic enough to end a marriage. Had he insisted she become pregnant? Had he been unfaithful to her?

The questions regarding Marshall and his ex-wife vanished quickly as Shelby stared up at the cathedral ceiling and a second-story level with roof windows and skylights. Polished natural wood floors, covered with colorful dhurrie rugs, a wood-burning stove off the entrance, and recessed lights provided a warm glow. He had elected to decorate his home in black and pale gray with splashes of peach and coral, and the resulting effect was masculine and visually pleasing.

Marshall placed a large warm hand on her shoulder. "Make yourself at home while I bring in your bags."

She walked into the living room, drawn to a wall of windows rising to the second story, smiling. She remembered she had said the same thing to him the night they'd dined amid soft music and candlelight.

She had thought the scene from her apartment windows magnificent, but now she quickly changed her mind. The vistas from Marshall's house were spectacular and breathtaking. She was barely able to discern the movement of vehicular traffic crossing the Tappan Zee Bridge to upstate New York. The landscape across the Hudson River revealed roofs and chimneys of houses nestled in verdant evergreen-covered hills.

Marshall returned with her overnight bag and a garment bag containing her dress for the evening's dinner party. "Come with me. I'll show you to your room."

She followed him up a curving wood staircase while trying to take in everything around her. Her professional gaze took in the blending of the mix of styles. Marshall had decorated using Queen Anne-style chairs with glass-topped, very classic modern tables and antique quilts as wall hangings, and everywhere she looked there was a sense of spaciousness and light.

"This will be your bedroom." He stepped aside. She walked into a large, octagonal-shaped room with Palladian windows. A king-sized wrought-iron bed dominated the space. The bedroom was filled with warmth—from the white-and-coral-print bed dressing to the vase of fresh pale pink roses, a rack filled with magazines, a wicker basket overflowing with packets of herbal teas, and another basket filled with rose-scented potpourri.

Shelby glanced up at Marshall over her shoulder. "It's charming."

His gaze widened as he stared down at her profile. Again he was stunned by her natural beauty. Her clean-scrubbed face was exquisite. Aside from the passion he had sampled earlier that morning, Marshall wondered what would make a man unfaithful to a woman who appeared to have it all.

Shelby Carter was not only beautiful, but she was brilliant, totally feminine, interesting, and sensual. She claimed the most sensual eyes and mouth of any woman he had ever seen. She stirred passions he wasn't aware he possessed.

And those passions weren't just physical. She made him feel alive, much more alive than he'd felt in years. He wanted to travel with Shelby, visiting museums while she taught him all she knew about art. He wanted them to concoct exotic dishes, then eat whatever they'd cooked over candlelight and with quiet music. But most of all, he needed her to fill the void in his life, because now he knew he did not want to spend the rest of his life alone.

He wanted to remarry. He wanted to have children.

"Do you want lunch?" he asked quietly.

She shook her head. "No, thank you. I'll wait for dinner."

"I'll let you settle in, then I'll give you a tour of the house."

Shelby was awed by the tour. Built to Marshall's specifications, the connecting buildings contained an exercise and weight room, an indoor pool, and a library housing thousands of books. Some were priceless rare out-of-print volumes on European history. He saved the best building for last—a large modern greenhouse.

"Nighttime temperatures are set for a tropical seventy degrees," he explained, watching Shelby as she inhaled a cluster of *lemona ponderosa.*

She moved on to an area where he had planted fruit trees. The ripe, lush fruits hung heavily from cherry, apple, plum, and pear trees.

Walking slowly along a broad path, she noted a Japanese garden and a twelve-foot topiary of acacia, then stopped and stared at the dark green leaves of several vegetables, recognizing collards, the curling ends of kale, and the large, firm heads of cabbage.

"You're a regular greengrocer, Marshall," she teased. The fruits and vegetables fascinated her, but it was the flowering plants that held her enthralled. The greenhouse held a profusion of fuschia, orchids, hanging geraniums, roses, camellias, and a beautifully delicate yellow flower Marshall had identified as an *allamanda cathartica.*

He grasped her hand firmly as she reached out to touch it. "It's extremely poisonous," he warned. "In all of its parts."

She pointed to a brilliant red flower. "How about this one?"

Marshall tucked her right hand into the bend of his elbow, holding it possessively. "No. That's a begonia. The 'firebrand' is one of the most brilliantly colored of all begonia cultivars. I grow it for the color."

Shelby stared up at him, seeing his gaze sweep lovingly over his plants and flowers. "Who in your family is the horticulturist?"

"No one. My mother's a librarian and my father's an accountant. Some people like photography and others *art.*" He shifted an eyebrow when she smiled. "The architect who designed the house is a friend. And when I told him that I wanted a place with an indoor pool and gym, he also suggested the greenhouse.

He explained that the heating and cooling system for each building could be regulated independently, but I could save on heating the pool with a special system using solar panels. He decided to experiment using the same procedure with the greenhouse. It works because the nighttime temperature for the greenhouse and the building with the pool are always the same.

"I sort of fell into growing plants," he admitted. "I started with a single rose bush, then tomatoes, and now, three years later, it's a jungle."

"All that's missing are tropical birds."

"They would eat my fruits and vegetables," he replied solemnly. "And I shudder to think of the mess they'd make in here."

Shelby's gaze swept up the wide spotless paths. "What do you do with all your fruits and vegetables?"

"I give them away to an organization that prepares meals for the elderly and homeless."

"That's wonderful." Shelby kept pace with Marshall as he led her back through the greenhouse and the building containing the shimmering blue tiles lining the pool.

Her body under her corduroy pants and ski sweater was coated with a layer of moisture from the warm, humid air enveloping the two buildings. "At what time do you expect the caterers?" she asked Marshall.

"They're coming at four, the invited guests between five and six, the band at six, and my aunt at seven. Why do you ask?"

"I just want to know how much time I need to get ready."

"It's only two-thirty. You'll have plenty of time. What would you like to do?"

"Swim a couple of laps."

Marshall released her hand and cradled her face between his palms. "Only a couple?" he teased quietly.

Shelby tilted her chin, her gaze caressing his lean, handsome face. "I'll be lucky if I swim a lap. I'm out of practice."

"I'll give you a head start."

"Are we racing, Mr. Graham?"

"Why? Do you want to?"

She took a step closer until her breasts were only inches from his sweatered chest. "Do I look that naive to you? You probably swim *at least* two laps every day."

Marshall didn't tell her that he'd swum a half-dozen leisurely laps every morning since the pool was installed.

"I do all right," he admitted.

Shelby's eyes narrowed. "I bet you do."

"Put your suit on and show me what you've got."

She stared unblinkingly and moved away from him and out of his loose grasp, wondering if he was aware of the double entendre.

"You're on."

Marshall registered her challenge and led her back to the main house. A quarter of an hour later, they stood at the edge of the pool. "You count," he offered, unable to take his gaze off her skimpily clad body in an Olympic-style black tank suit.

The body-hugging Spandex garment was more revealing and provocative than a bikini. It was not the first time he'd been awed by her femininity, but it was the first time it had been displayed so wantonly.

Her body was slender, yet there were no straight lines. Her legs were long and slender, her waist narrow, her hips full and rounded, and her breasts ripe and lush, pushing sensually against the fabric of her suit.

Shelby stared at the opposite end of the pool rather than look at Marshall. She felt the heat of his gaze on her, and even though she didn't return his stare, she could still see his nearly nude body in her mind.

Marshall Graham claimed the body of a swimmer: broad shoulders; long, ropy arms; flat midsection; slim, firm hips; and long, muscled legs. She wondered whether she should've challenged him.

"Ready whenever you are," she said, taking in a deep breath. She moved closer to the edge, her toes gripping the Persian-blue tiles. Marshall also moved into position.

"Now!" she shouted.

His body cleaved the water quickly, but if he had glanced over at Shelby, he'd have noticed the curving arc of her body and the near splashless entry as she dived into the warm pool water.

It had been nearly sixteen years since Shelby had swum competitively, and the rush of adrenaline spurted through her body, giving her what she needed to overcome Marshall's obvious superior strength. She had barely touched the opposite end of the pool before she pushed off to retrace her smooth-measured strokes.

Marshall began his second lap before the realization set in: Shelby was more than a casual swimmer. He increased his pace but knew instinctively he was no match for her. He swam for exercise and relaxation; she swam to compete.

He was nearly twenty seconds behind her by the time he'd finished. She had hoisted herself out of the water and now sat waiting for him—breathing heavily.

He pulled himself up and sat beside her, shaking his head. "Where did you learn to swim like that?" he asked, his chest rising and falling from the exertion. Reaching over, he pulled her to his side.

Shelby rested her head against his hard shoulder. "I was captain of my high school swim team. It's been sixteen years since I last competed."

His free hand curved her chin, tilting her face to his. Water dotted his moustache and spiked his lashes. The soft, warm light from wall lamps and the gray of the sky through roof windows shadowed his features as he slowly lowered his head.

"You're good, Shelby Carter. Very, very good."

Her own lashes, spiked with moisture, lowered. "You don't mind that I beat you?"

He shook his head. "I only mind that you didn't tell me you were a pro."

"Even if I had," she said, staring at his mouth, "I still would've beat you."

"Only this time," he whispered. "We're going to have to do

this again some other time. Meanwhile, I'm going to practice until I *do* beat you."

Shelby had to smile. She had bruised his male ego. "I don't give repeat performances."

"But I do." Marshall didn't give her a chance to ask what he meant when he eased her down gently to the tiled floor and brushed his lips across her ear, registering her sharp intake of breath.

His lips feathered over her jaw and down further to her throat. His body covered hers when her arms moved up and circled his neck.

Shelby lay between Marshall's legs, feeling his heat and the hardness between his thighs. Closing her eyes, she gave in to the rising desire scorching her everywhere he touched, moaning once before his mouth claimed hers in a strong, hungry possession that sucked the breath from her lungs.

His tongue pushed incessantly against her mouth until her lips parted. His mouth was as busy as his fingers, slipping the straps of her swimsuit off her shoulders and down her arms.

The passion she had successfully banked for so many years surfaced, short-circuiting her nervous system where every nerve ending screamed for release.

Marshall's mouth was everywhere. He kissed her throat, her shoulders, and her breasts. Her nipples swelled and ached as his teeth teased them into turgid nodules of dark-brown flesh.

Her own hands swept up his muscled back and over his smooth chest. She didn't trust herself to venture lower than his waist, where his aroused sex strained against the scant covering of Spandex.

Marshall's respiration increased, his breathing heavy and labored, as he moved his hips against Shelby's in a slow, deliberate rotating motion. He wanted her; he wanted her so much that he feared he was going to explode.

"Shelby," he gasped, from between clenched teeth. Raising his head, he stared down at her, waiting for a signal. He needed something—a word, any gesture that would indicate she'd permit him to come to her as her lover.

Shelby struggled to bring her turbulent emotions under control as a shudder shook her body. Opening her eyes slowly, she stared up at the face only inches from her own. How could she have thought that Marshall Graham was anything like Earl? Not only did they not look alike, but their approach to lovemaking was completely different, because somehow she'd sensed Marshall was waiting; waiting for her to give approval for him to continue. Earl would never have waited.

"No." She shook her head for emphasis. "It's too soon, Marshall," she explained, her voice a husky whisper.

Sitting up, he gathered her close and she lay across his lap, her head resting on his shoulder. "I'll wait until you're ready," he replied quietly. Marshall smiled and pressed a kiss to her temple. She had not rejected him.

Shelby extracted herself from Marshall's loose embrace and stood up. He also rose in one fluid motion, staring at her with an expectant expression on his face. If she allowed herself to become involved with Marshall, she knew there was a chance for her to grow whole again, to learn how to trust a man again.

She had only known Marshall a week and she had no intention of making the same mistake twice. Her mother's warning came rushing back—*"Act in haste, repent in leisure."* Six years was a long time to do penance, and she knew the time for being repentant was behind her.

She gave him a warm smile. "I have to get dressed."

Marshall opened his mouth to respond, then closed it quickly as he glanced up. The sound of sleet tapped rhythmically against the roof windows. He moved over to the expansive windows surrounding the poolhouse. Sleet was falling, and a driving wind swirled it in a forty-five-degree slant.

Shelby joined him at the window, watching as the frozen precipitation quickly blanketed the winter grass with a sheet of white.

"It wasn't supposed to snow until late tonight," she said, unable to believe how much wet snow and ice had already accumulated.

Marshall dropped an arm around her shoulders and his fingers grazed the length of her neck in a soothing motion. "If it changes over to all snow, it won't be so bad. But if it's sleet or ice, then that's going to be a problem. The roads up here are treacherous whenever there's sleet."

Shelby noted his frowning expression. "What are you going to do if it doesn't change over to snow?"

His fingers tightened. "I don't know."

Her gaze shifted back to the window. Trees and the open meadow beyond the rear of the house were shrouded in an eerie gunmetal gray, making visibility nearly impossible.

"The caterers are due here at four," Marshall said, breaking the silence. "If the weather doesn't break, then I'll have to make a decision whether to try to go ahead with the dinner party or cancel it."

It was the catering company who made the decision for Marshall. They regretfully informed him that they were closing early because all the roads were covered with ice, which made it virtually impossible to drive without sliding into other vehicles.

Shelby, who had showered, shampooed, and changed into a pair of jeans with a sweatshirt and running shoes, sat on a tall stool in Marshall's kitchen, watching the weather channel on a small television on a countertop as he telephoned the guests to tell them the evening's festivities were canceled. Most had expressed relief that they wouldn't be obligated to try to navigate the ice-covered roads to help Naomi Morrow celebrate her seventieth birthday. After he'd called the limousine company to inform them not to pick up Naomi in Manhattan, he called his aunt.

He spoke briefly with Naomi and ended the call wishing her a happy birthday. The last call was to the small band he'd contracted for the night's musical program. Replacing the receiver in its cradle, Marshall turned to Shelby.

"I promised you a party, and we'll have a party." He flashed a bright smile. "That leaves me to put together something for dinner. I'm far from a gourmet chef, but I can assure you that you won't come down with ptomaine."

Shelby hopped off the stool, smiling. "I'll help you."

Marshall defrosted and marinated two shell steaks. Then, at Shelby's suggestion, he picked enough kale from the greenhouse garden for them. She steamed the kale with olive oil and garlic and roasted small cubes of red potatoes with dried thyme, dehydrated onions, and parsley until they were done to a crisp golden brown.

Standing behind Shelby and looking over her shoulder, Marshall curved his arms around her waist. "It looks delicious."

She speared a small cube of potato and held it out to him. "Try it."

He ate the potato, chewing slowly and nodding. "It's fabulous." He swallowed, never taking his gaze from Shelby's face. Her naturally curling hair had dried, feathering over her forehead and ears. She usually brushed her hair off her face and the style made her appear older and more sophisticated. With her fresh-scrubbed face, curling hair, and casual dress, he found it difficult to believe she was thirty-four years old.

Sharing the cooking duties with her reminded him of what he'd never had with Cassandra. He hadn't thought of himself as a demanding husband. In fact, he had given in to Cassandra even when he hadn't wanted to. He'd never asked anything from her except that she relocate.

He had told her of his dream before they'd married, and she had agreed to go with him whenever the opportunity presented itself. But in the end, he'd realized she'd deceived him. He'd also deceived and deluded himself, because he had married Cassandra knowing she would never follow him. The lure of D.C.'s social life was too strong for his ex-wife to give up. The influential D.C. Grahams helped the ex-Mrs. Marshall Graham improve her social standing in Washington immeasurably.

"I think the steaks should be ready now," Marshall stated, trying not to think of how he was going to spend the night with Shelby Carter sleeping under his roof only several feet away from his own bedroom.

Shelby turned back to the stove and spooned the potatoes and kale into serving bowls, placing them on the dining room table.

Marshall had already set the table with china, silver, and stemware. He popped the cork on a bottle of deep purple Cabernet Sauvignon and filled two wineglasses.

A hanging light fixture with an authentic Tiffany shade spilled golden light onto the table, while the familiar haunting voice of Sade filled the downstairs space with music. However, the sound wasn't enough to eradicate the sound of the howling wind and the occasional snapping of ice-covered branches as they cracked and crashed to the frozen earth.

Marshall and Shelby sat at opposite ends of the modern glass-topped table, eating and drinking silently.

Shelby felt the heat from Marshall's gaze on her face each time she glanced up. The flattering light from the fixture highlighted the rich gold in his smooth brown skin and the sprinkling of gray throughout his close-cut, neatly barbered hair. Her gaze lingered on his moustache and mouth, remembering the feel of the thick, silky hair on his upper lip and the mastery of his mouth when he claimed hers.

Marshall's kiss hadn't been just a touching of the lips or a joining of their tongues. It was as if he had known instinctively how much pressure to exert, just where he would kiss her, and when to deepen the kiss or pull back.

Marshall Graham wore his sensuality like a badge of honor, displaying it for every woman who'd have to be blind not to recognize it.

Everything about him was subtle. His self-confidence, exquisite manners, quiet virility, and arresting good looks were impossible to ignore.

Shelby sipped her wine slowly, staring down the table at him. *He could be so easy to love,* she thought. *If only I could trus him,* she mused silently.

She opened her mouth to ask him whether he'd been unfaithfu to his ex-wife, but decided against it at the last moment. It wa too personal a question to ask. And she hadn't known him lon enough to feel comfortable asking.

She was fully and totally relaxed. The two glasses of dry re wine, the succulent grilled steaks, and the steamed tender kal and crispy potatoes left no room for dessert.

"I went over the Kwanzaa proposal. It looks easy enough t implement without a lot of planning," Marshall said, breakin the silence.

"I tried to keep it simple. The students won't have to make *mkeka* because the placemat will be my donation to Nia for th celebration. You can either buy several *benderas* or have th students make the red, black, and green flags in their art classes

"I included the listing of stores where you can buy Africa artifacts only as a suggestion. All of these stores usually hav the *kinara* candles and the *kikombe cha umoja* as a part of thei regular stock," Shelby continued.

"Nia's *kikombe cha umoja* will be filled with grape juice in stead of wine," Marshall said, smiling. "City regulations won' permit us to have alcoholic beverages on the premises."

"Have you decided to celebrate Kwanzaa the entire week be fore the school closes for the holidays?"

"We're only going to hold classes for three days that week so I've decided that we'll celebrate the first principle Monda night and invite the parents, family members, and friends of th students, and anyone else who wants to attend. We'll start i around seven and serve dinner after the opening ceremonies."

"Very appropriate." The first principle was *umoja,* and th aim of *umoja* was to strive for and maintain unity in the famil community, nation, and race.

"Will you be able to make it to our first-night celebration?" Marshall asked.

"I wouldn't miss it," she confirmed.

"Are you doing anything for Kwanzaa?" she asked Marshall.

"I haven't made any plans. Why do you ask?"

"This year I'm staying in New York for the holidays, and when I do, I usually get together with several friends and we always have a big celebration for the first night. I'd like to invite you to come along, if you don't have anything planned for December twenty-sixth."

"What do you do for the next six days?"

Shelby went on to tell him that she and her family always observed the seven days, but in New York, most of her friends were usually too busy to observe more than a day or two.

"I wouldn't mind celebrating all seven days with you," Marshall volunteered.

"Are you certain you want to do that?" she questioned.

"I'm more than certain. I haven't celebrated Kwanzaa since I left Howard."

Shelby offered him a quick smile. "Okay, it's settled. You'll come with me to my friend's place for the first night, then we'll decide about the next six nights."

"Do you and your family usually exchange gifts all seven nights?"

"Only the children get gifts all seven nights. They're normally small, inexpensive items, but the kids are thrilled with the notion of getting something new each night."

Marshall propped his elbow on the table, resting his chin on a fist. "I wouldn't mind getting a gift every night for seven nights."

"My, my, my," Shelby teased. "Aren't we subtle?"

He shifted an eyebrow. "You would also get a gift for each of the seven nights."

"We don't have to exchange gifts," she protested. "Besides, gift-giving is for the children."

"Didn't you say that even if someone doesn't have a child they can still place *muhindi* on their *mkeka?* One ear of corn for each child." She nodded slowly. "If I can put an ear of corn on my *mkeka,* then I can buy a gift for someone I think of as very special for each of the seven days of Kwanzaa."

Shelby stared at him as a new and unexpected warmth swept over her. She knew Marshall liked her and that the liking went beyond their professional working relationship. He had hinted that he cared deeply for her, and now he had admitted that she was special.

Could she really take the chance to lower her defenses, the barriers, she had set up to keep all men at a distance? Could she risk opening up her heart and offering Marshall the love she was certain was there?

It had taken only a week, but Shelby was more than certain that her feelings for Marshall were a combination of attraction, anticipation, and desire.

There was no doubt that she was attracted to him and that she desired him. And if her self-control hadn't been so staunchly in place, she was certain she would've succumbed to his lovemaking beside the pool.

She glanced away, her lashes shadowing the passion in her eyes. "I guess that settles it. You can expect a gift for each of the seven nights."

Marshall pushed back his chair, rising to his feet. He took less than a half-dozen determined steps that brought him to her side. He eased back her chair and helped her rise.

Shelby was in his arms, her face pressed to the clean laundered smell of a shirt covering his solid shoulder. "You've given me all the gifts I'll ever need," he whispered against her ear. "Having you for seven nights is enough."

It was only when Marshall openly verbalized his feelings about wanting to spend a week with her that Shelby admitted to herself that she *was* falling in love with him.

What was there for her not to love? He was attractive, intelligent, and dedicated to his career, and he treated her like an equal. He was secure enough to respect her profession, and he had not asked more from her than she was willing to give.

She, too, had all the gifts she needed for her own first fruits: Marshall Graham.

Her arms tightened around his waist as she pressed closer to his length. She inhaled the familiar scent of his aftershave. She remembered admitting that she could identify him by his cologne.

Pulling back she smiled up at him, admiring the velvet softness of his clean-shaven cheek. Her gaze visually traced the line of his jaw, then moved with agonizing slowness down to his mouth and chin.

"Have you decided to reschedule your aunt's dinner party?"

A sensual smile showed his beautiful teeth. "No, I haven't. But I've decided it won't be a surprise, and hopefully by that time she'll have more than a birthday to celebrate."

His head came down slowly as he claimed her mouth in a slow, burning passion that robbed her of her breath. Shelby clung to him, her body vibrating with liquid fire. It took only seconds before her flame was passed to Marshall, and both of them were awed and trembling when she pulled back. She clung weakly to his stronger body.

She was too caught up in her awakening passion for Marshall to register his statement—"Hopefully by that time she'll have more than a birthday to celebrate,"—not knowing the words would come back to haunt her.

Shelby spent the night at Marshall's house, sleeping soundly while he tossed restlessly on his bed in a bedroom across the hall.

She awoke to a scene from a Currier and Ives Christmas card. The storm had left the landscape a winter wonderland with icicles coating trees, shrubs, and power lines.

Turning away from the window and pressing her face into her pillow, she hoped for another hour of sleep, but sat up quickly when she heard a steady tapping on the closed door.

"Shelby, are you awake?"

Pulling a down-filled comforter up to her throat, she called out, "Yes."

"Meet me at the pool in five minutes," Marshall announced, issuing a challenge through the door.

She laughed. "Don't you ever give up?"

"Five minutes, Shelby Carter, or I'm coming in."

She jumped out of bed and raced to the adjoining bath. Five minutes later she slipped on her swimsuit after washing her face and brushing her teeth. She hadn't bothered to brush her hair. She simply ran her fingers through the curling strands, then went down the stairs toward the pool.

The house was warm and comfortable, the heat generated from several wood-burning stoves defying the cold wind and ice claiming the countryside.

Shelby beat Marshall again, this time by a greater margin. She kissed his grim, tight mouth, patted his broad chest, then turned on her heel and made her way back to the main house, leaving him sitting on the edge of the pool and staring at her trim body.

Marshall sat at the oval conference-room table, writing aimlessly on a pad. One of Nia's board members read from a typed report outlining the proposed school budget for the upcoming school year.

The woman's voice droned on as Marshall listed several items under a column labeled "Shelby." He had accounted for only three of the seven gifts he planned to purchase for her. He didn't know her dress size, so that meant he could not purchase an article of clothing.

He drew another column and listed several department stores: Barney's, Bergdorf Goodman, and Bloomingdale's. A second column listed specialty shops: Chanel, Tiffany, and Polo/Ralph Lauren. He thought about several mail-order houses with the added feature of ordering and having his purchase shipped overnight. His brow furrowed. He had a little more than a week to complete his list and shop.

He wrote down another three items, then turned the pad over. Six down and one to go. He considered a gift basket of lotions and oils or a gift certificate for a complete beauty makeover at Georgette Klinger, but didn't write it down. The name F.A.O. Schwarz popped into his head and popped out just as quickly. F.A.O. Schwarz would have to wait for another time.

The week passed quickly for Shelby. She shopped for her Kwanzaa gifts for Marshall, began writing Nia's cultural curriculum, and called Hans Gustave every day for an update for Shumba's Friday evening showing.

Marshall had called her late Monday night to let her know that the first installment on her proposal was approved and a check would be mailed to her the following day.

He asked to see her again, but she declined, saying her calendar was booked solid for the week and that she wouldn't see him until the evening of Nia's Kwanzaa celebration. There was complete silence. After he rang off, she could tell by the coldness in his voice that he was not pleased.

She'd hung up, thinking, my way or no way, Marshall.

It wasn't that she hadn't wanted to see him, but she was forced to change her schedule after she'd received a letter from the Studio Museum requesting she be available for interviews the first week of the new year.

Things were happening too quickly, and there was no way she wanted to repeat the mistake she'd made with Earl with Marshall. She had to make certain all the pieces fit.

The elegant Madison Avenue art gallery was ablaze with lights, the murmur of voices, and the crush of art critics, collectors, and the curious; and even though it was the most decorative of holiday seasons, most of the attendees were dressed in black.

Shelby Carter was no exception. She wore a black chiffon dress that flowed fluidly around her ankles. The matching silk slip, jewel neckline, and long sleeves were simple, yet proclaimed an understated elegance. Her jewelry was a pair of large pearl earrings. Sheer black stockings and a pair of black suede pumps with matching satin bows completed her tasteful ensemble.

Marshall spied her before she could turn to stare at him. She held a flute of champagne in one hand while the other was lost in the grip of a tall man who held it possessively.

A swift shadow of anger gripped Marshall's features before he schooled his expression not to reveal what he felt at that moment. In one brief instant he felt a foreign emotion he could identify only as jealousy. The man holding Shelby to his side had the woman he wanted.

He wanted her—not just her body, but *all* of her; and in that moment Marshall Graham knew it was for always.

"There's Shelby," Naomi Morrow whispered quietly. Her fingers tightened on her nephew's arm. "And that's Shumba Naaman, the sculptor." She pulled Marshall toward Shelby and the artist whose entire collection she had purchased at his last showing.

Shelby recognized Naomi and smiled as she walked toward her. The smile faltered slightly when she saw the tall man dressed in black escorting Naomi through the large crowd, but it was back in place by the time he stood over her, scowling slightly.

Extracting her hand from Shumba's loose grip, she curved a free arm around Naomi's shoulder and kissed her cheek. "I'm so glad you could make it."

Naomi returned the kiss. "You know I wouldn't miss this little soirée. You look beautiful," she added, close to her ear.

She released Naomi and extended her hand to Marshall, her gaze taking in everything about him in one glance. He was breathtaking in a black silk shirt with a band collar, a black wool unconstructed jacket, matching loose-fitting slacks, and Italian loafers. She focused on the commemorative pin on his lapel rather than on his face. His large, dark eyes burned with a strange fire she had never seen before.

"Hello, Marshall." She was surprised her voice was soft and evenly modulated while her insides quivered. She hadn't seen him in nearly a week, and the absence made him more startlingly attractive than she remembered.

Marshall took the proffered hand and brought it to his lips. His gaze locked with hers as he took in everything that was Shelby Carter: her artfully made up face; her curling dark hair swept up and calling attention to her high cheekbones; and the exquisite shape of her delicate jaw. He inhaled the familiar fragrance of her perfume on her wrist, smiling for the first time. It had taken him more than an hour of smelling every fragrance at Bloomingdale's before he'd found it.

"Shelby." His voice was low and seductive. He released her hand, but not before he'd turned it over and pressed his mouth to her inner wrist.

Shelby felt the heat from his mouth and her eyes widened as pinpoints of desire fired her body. She saw Marshall's gaze shift from her face to her breasts. She felt them grow heavy, felt the nipples swell against the silk of her slip.

Damn you, she raged silently. How could he make love to her in a room filled with people?

Shelby recovered quickly, not seeing the questioning glances Shumba and Naomi exchanged. She managed to introduce Shumba to Marshall without further incident, and she only let out her breath when the two men had greeted each other politely.

Naomi took over as she wound an arm through Shumba's and led him away, saying, "I'm not going to buy everything this time. I've heard that someone called me a 'selfish old woman.' I don't mind being called old, but I do resent the selfish part."

Shumba laughed and patted her hand affectionately. Leaning down from his impressive height, he whispered in her ear that he had put aside something he thought she would truly love.

Marshall stared at his aunt's departing back, then turned to Shelby. He watched as Shelby took a sip of champagne, then he extracted the glass from her fingers. Slowly and deliberately, he turned the glass and drank from the spot where her lipstick had left a faint smudge of color, his gaze fixed on her mouth. He drained the glass and put it down on a freestanding column that doubled as a table.

Moving behind Shelby, he pressed his chest to her back. "Is he your boyfriend?" he questioned quietly.

Shelby's breath caught in her throat. She felt Marshall's heat, the solidness of his chest and thighs against her. The clean, sensual scent of his cologne enveloped her until she had trouble drawing a normal breath.

"He's a friend."

"How good a friend?" The fingers of his right hand closed on her waist, then inched up slowly until they rested under her breast, grazing and caressing chiffon and silk. Marshall's body responded quickly, hardening when he realized Shelby was not wearing a bra under the thin layers of black.

"A very *good* friend," she whispered. She curbed the urge to lean back against his body, but it didn't stop Marshall as his arm slipped under her breasts and eased her back until she lay against him—her back to his chest, her buttocks to his groin.

"I see." The two words revealed nothing yet said everything.

"Let me go, Marshall."

"Why?" His breath was warm near her ear.

"Because my boss is staring at me."

Marshall raised his head and met the dark gray eyes of a tall man with a blond ponytail. He smiled and waved to Hans. Hans returned the gesture, smiling.

"See, Shelby? No harm done. He approves." He dropped his arm and smiled down at Shelby, noting her frown. "Don't frown, darling. It causes wrinkles," he teased.

"I'm not worried about wrinkles, Marshall Graham. Did you come here tonight to harass me or to embarrass me?"

Marshall sobered quickly. "I came here because my aunt invited me. She told me you were putting on an exhibition she thought would interest me. What she didn't tell me was that the artist would be hanging on to you as though you were a priceless piece of sculpture he couldn't let out of his sight."

Mixed feelings surged through her, and she knew she couldn't vent those emotions . . . not in a room filled with people.

Her gaze narrowed. "Jealous, Marshall?"

Marshall leaned over, his strong fingers gripping Shelby's shoulders. "Hell, yeah!" he whispered savagely, before releasing her and stalking away.

Shelby made it through the evening in a daze, smiling and chatting like a programmed robot. She and Marshall did not exchange another word, even though she found him staring at her each time she turned in his direction. A maddening smile played at the corners of his sensual mouth.

He had admitted he was jealous and the thought thrilled her. He had to feel something for her to be jealous of Shumba. She hadn't slept with either man, and that meant Marshall's feelings went beyond lust or sex.

The showing ended at ten with all of the success Hans, Shumba, and Shelby had wanted and expected. The three sat talking quietly amid tables covered with the remains of fresh melon slices, large, succulent strawberries, varied cheeses, smoked whitefish, salmon, lox, and several varieties of imported crackers and breads. Empty bottles of champagne, red and white wine, and soft drinks were packed in cartons stacked along a wall in the back of the gallery.

"It was a sellout again, Shumba," Hans reported.

Shumba, his long legs propped up on a chair, pointed at Shelby. "Thanks to Ms. Carter."

Hans raised a half-filled glass of champagne. "A toast to Ms. Carter."

Shumba raised his glass of seltzer. "Ms. Carter."

Shelby nodded to both men. "Thank you, gentlemen, but this Ms. Carter is going home. I'm exhausted. Hans, please get me a cab."

Hans called a car service while Shumba gathered Shelby's coat and purse. She took the envelope that contained the commission Hans gave her and pushed it into the purse.

She said her goodnights and slumped onto the back seat of the car as Shumba and Hans stood out in the winter cold, watching her until the driver pulled away from the curb.

She didn't realize she had closed her eyes until the driver pulled up in front of her apartment building.

"Happy holidays," she replied, as she exited the car.

Walking quickly to her building entrance, she stopped short, nearly tripping when she recognized the tall man waiting for her.

"I thought perhaps you had gone home with your *very good friend,*" Marshall drawled.

Her heart pounded in her chest. "What are you doing here?"

He shrugged his broad shoulders beneath his overcoat. "Waiting for you."

"Go home, Marshall," she drawled behind a yawn. "I'm exhausted."

He grasped her arm, taking the keys from her gloved fingers and opening the front door. "I'll put you to bed."

They made their way into the lobby. "I don't need you to put me to bed. I'm quite capable of finding my way, thank you."

"I'm a very good tucker-inner."

She followed him into the elevator, smiling a tired smile. "I bet you are."

Marshall lowered his chin and flashed her a sensual grin. The grin faded when he realized Shelby was telling the truth. She looked exhausted. Her face appeared thinner, drawn. His plan to seduce her where she would permit him to make love to her vanished quickly.

All he wanted to do was to take care of her.

Shelby walked into her apartment, hung up her coat, and walked to her bedroom. She forgot about Marshall standing at the living room window, staring out at the shadowy outline of New Jersey, as she showered and prepared for bed.

She heard the haunting sounds of music coming from her living room before she burrowed under the quilt and drifted off to sleep. It would be the first time in days that she'd be guaranteed more than four hours of sleep.

Marshall sat on the sofa in the dark, knowing he should leave, but he couldn't. Seeing Shelby earlier, watching her graceful and elegant motions, had made him aware of what he had been fighting. He was in love with the woman!

He had fallen in love with a woman who'd deliberately spurned his every advance until he'd thought he was going to lose every shred of his iron-willed control.

He had admitted he was jealous while he couldn't admit that he loved her—at least, not to her face.

Running a hand over his face, Marshall wondered why he found it so difficult to tell Shelby that he loved her. He never had that problem with Cassandra. But then, Cassandra wasn't Shelby. Cassandra could never hurt him the way Shelby could. He only realized that when he thought about how easy it had been to give in to Cassandra and walk away from her.

But could he walk away from Shelby? Could he give her up, now that he'd found her?

"No," he whispered into the darkness.

He didn't know how long he sat, but the three CDs he'd put on the player were finished. Rising to his feet, he removed his jacket, laid it across a chair, then moved back to the sofa and folded his long length on it, shifting until he found a comfortable position and drifted off to sleep.

He had barely closed his eyes when he found himself awake with Shelby standing over him. Her warm, familiar feminine fragrance wafted to his nostrils.

Her fingertips grazed his jaw. "If you spend the night on that sofa, you'll need a chiropractor in the morning. Come to bed," she said softly.

Swinging his legs over the sofa, he sat up. "What time is it?"

"Don't worry about the time, Marshall. If you need a toothbrush, there's a supply in the wall cabinet in the bathroom."

Marshall stared at her figure, retreating in a silky-looking nightgown trimmed with lace. He couldn't make out the color but knew it was a dark shade because it blended in with her skin coloring.

He undressed in the living room, laying out his clothes on the sofa. He made his way to the bathroom, brushed his teeth, and showered. By the time he walked into Shelby's bedroom, he was wide awake.

He made out the shape of her body under the quilt as he slipped into bed next to her. She moaned softly and moved into his embrace.

Marshall held her, holding his breath while he dared not move. She had trustingly come to him and he didn't want to do anything to destroy that trust.

She shifted and snuggled for a more comfortable position, her face pressed to his chest. He felt her press against his naked body and he let out his breath slowly.

It was a time for comforting and protecting, and he knew if Shelby had invited him to her bed, she would also invite him to share her body. This was not the time to share their bodies. Closing his eyes, he drifted off to sleep again.

Shelby reveled in the hard male body imprinted on hers. It had been too long since she'd lain in the strong, comforting embrace of a man. There were times when she treasured being held as much as she enjoyed the physical fulfillment she sought from sex.

She tried to explain to Earl that sex wasn't lovemaking, but his carnal appetites were too skewed to differentiate between the two.

She smiled in the darkness, listening to Marshall's even breathing. Marshall had surprised her with his open display of possessiveness at the gallery. She had thought of him as stoic, conservative, and quite in control of his emotions and actions.

Nia's headmaster had nearly lost it!

* * *

Bright sunlight inched up the bed, spilling over the two people sleeping in spoonlike fashion. Shelby awoke first, registering the body pressed to her back and the warm breath on her neck. She knew Marshall was also awake because the rhythm of his breathing changed.

"I was wondering what color it was," said the soft male voice near her ear.

"What was?"

"Your nightgown." It was a rich mahogany brown with an ecru lace trim.

She smiled. "I don't have to guess about the color of your pajamas, do I?"

"They are always the same color. Bare-butt dark milk chocolate," he teased.

Shelby's smile widened. "I wouldn't know about that. I've never seen it."

Marshall released her and swept back the quilt and sheet. He rose to his knees, permitting her a side view of his naked body.

She swallowed painfully as she saw what his swim trunks had concealed. She had registered his magnificent erection. He turned and presented her with his back. She pinched his firm hip seconds before he flipped her over and fastened his teeth to her buttocks.

"Stop, Marshall. That hurts," she mumbled.

Marshall's fingers grazed her thighs and eased the silky garment up to her waist. His hands spanned her waist as he turned her over effortlessly until she faced him. Concern filled his dark eyes. "Did I really hurt you?"

Shelby reached up and smoothed away the frown furrowing his forehead. "No. I don't think you'd ever hurt me."

"You're right about that, darling. I would never hurt you." He lowered his body, supporting his greater weight on his elbows. "I would never deliberately hurt you, Shelby, emotionally or physically."

Shelby placed her fingers over his mouth. "Don't talk, Marshall."

He stared down into her large eyes, searching in her gaze for what he knew she could see in his—love. "What do you want me to do?" he asked against her fingers.

"Don't make me beg, Marshall," she whispered.

He needed no further prompting. Covering her body, Marshall cradled her face and kissed her. The pressure of his mouth on hers was gentle as he coaxed her lips apart.

He took his time tasting her mouth and throat while moving down to her breasts as he gathered the silk gown around her waist and pulled it over her head. He felt Shelby tremble and heard the rush of breath from her open mouth when he fastened his mouth to the ripeness of one firm brown breast, sucking until she felt her womb contract.

His fingers inched up her inner thigh and Shelby panted, then turned her face into the softness of the pillow to muffle her moans when his finger entered her celibate flesh.

Marshall was experienced enough to know that he had to prepare her small, tight body before he took her. He wanted to bring her pleasure, not pain.

She closed her thighs tightly against his invading hand. "Easy, darling. I won't hurt you," he crooned quietly. She opened her eyes and stared up at him. "I'll try to make it good, Shelby. For both of us."

Marshall's hands and mouth charted a course over the dips and curves of Shelby's body, lingering at the moist area between her thighs until she was nearly mindless with the passion he had aroused in her. And she did beg him; beg him to take her before she dissolved in a trembling mass of hysteria with the searing need that had been building ever since she'd met him.

Marshall waited until he had aroused Shelby where she was unable to disguise her body's reaction that she had nearly reached the point of fulfillment.

He entered her wet, pulsating flesh, moaning loudly when he felt her claim his own turgid sex throbbing for release.

Their joined bodies set a rhythm that was heard only by the two of them, and in unison they climbed the heights of ecstasy that shattered into brilliant fragments of fulfillment.

Shelby clung to Marshall, languishing in the flooding of uncontrollable joy and wonderment. Her lips quivered against his as she failed to verbalize that she loved him.

Marshall held onto Shelby, carefully reversing their positions. His heated blood cooled, the lingering throbbing subsided, and he closed his eyes, unable to believe the passion she'd aroused in him. It was as if she had reached deep inside of Marshall Graham to capture what no other woman had ever claimed.

Shelby Carter had wordlessly exacted the awesome, uncontrollable passion he'd erected as a shield against the pain of rejection. He had given her more than sixty-five percent of himself; she had claimed the total one hundred percent.

He held her close to his heart until they both succumbed to the sated sleep of lovers.

Shelby walked into Nia Academy and was greeted warmly by one of the secretaries in the front office. They smiled, handing her a visitor's pass. Then an upperclassman escorted her to the auditorium. The school was decorated with their blue and gold kente print, helium-filled balloons in the same blue and gold, and *benderas*—the red, black, and green flag created by Marcus Garvey for African Americans.

She sat in the amphitheater-styled auditorium with guests, students, parents, faculty, and staff, listening to Marshall as he welcomed everyone to Nia's first Kwanzaa celebration. The overhead spotlight flattered his gray-flecked close-cut hair and his smooth skin.

Shelby smiled, remembering how they had lingered in bed two days before, leaving only to eat and bathe. They had talked, watched a movie, and made love another two times before she'd suggested he leave so she could complete her weekend chores. He'd kissed her passionately at the door, driven back home, and telephoned her as soon as he'd walked through the front door of his house. He thanked her for the two gifts she had given him: herself and her passion.

She was pulled back to the present when eight students, representing each grade level, advanced to the stage and explained the principles of Kwanzaa.

Shelby felt her heart swell with pride as she observed the composed young men, dressed in their school uniforms, articulately deliver their prepared speeches to their peers, parents, and neighborhood community of what Kwanzaa meant to them.

Tears were visible in the eyes of many of the parents, and pride shone from the expressive faces of the instructors who labored unceasingly to help make the young men at Nia the best they could be.

The fruits and vegetables were placed on the *mkeka,* the candles were lit, the students sipped juice from the *kikombe cha umoja* amid the fruits and vegetables on the placemat. Each boy presented another with a *zawadi,* or gift, and this gesture concluded the Kwanzaa ceremony.

The assembled crowd rose, applauding enthusiastically, then filed out of the auditorium. Students who were assigned to the reception committee escorted everyone to the gymnasium for the remainder of the celebration, which was rumored to be the "real fun part of Kwanzaa."

Long tables set up around the perimeter of the gymnasium sent tantalizing smells wafting into the air. Shelby noted the serving dishes contained hot and cold dishes, all labeled with their countries of origin.

She noted a dish labeled *yassa*—spicy marinated chicken in an onion sauce from Senegal, yogurt-sauced chicken curry from Morocco, *tapo*—a Honduran fish stew with plantains and yucca, and familiar favorites from the United States: Southern fried chicken, Texas-style chili, cracklin' bread, Tuskegee Institute sweet potato bread with raisins and walnuts, duck and smoked sausage gumbo, macaroni and potato salads, cornbread, biscuits, shrimp creole, and steamed collard, mustard, and turnip greens.

Amid the surging crowd of celebrants, Shelby caught a brief glimpse of Marshall as he stopped to greet and talk to parents, students, and staff. She stood patiently in line, waiting to fill her plate with the food being served by the white-clad caterers, who patiently explained the ingredients in some of the less-than-familiar dishes.

Twenty minutes later, Shelby sat on the bleachers, her plate balanced on her knees. She swallowed a portion of Hoppin' John, concluding it was the best black-eyed peas and rice she had ever eaten. The dish had been prepared with spicy pork sausage, shrimp, onion, and red pepper.

She chatted amicably with the father of a student on her right, listening to him extol the excellence of Nia's philosophy of education and socialization. He proudly recanted how his nine-year-old son had begun to cut classes at his former public school because he thought he was "wasting his time listening to a boring old teacher." The father said he'd promptly enrolled his son at Nia. The boy managed to drag himself out of bed to attend classes even when he was sick.

Shelby saw Nadine Pierce walk into the gymnasium with a flair of brilliant red and black sweeping behind her. The stylishly dressed Nadine wore a cape-coat that had been fashioned with exquisite detailed piping and epaulets. Nadine spied Shelby and flashed a wide grin before she slipped an arm around Marshall's waist inside his blue blazer.

She turned away, jealousy racing through her chest, rather than look at the man she had fallen in love with cradling another woman to his body. It was she he had cradled to his body, offering her a second chance for love; she hadn't known when it had happened, but she *had* fallen in love with Marshall. And this love was different from the one she felt for Earl. It contained none of the frantic passion or the smothering possessiveness.

What she'd experienced with Marshall was a strong, secure, and comforting passion that she would never tire of. Marshall Graham was a man she would never tire of and who would never bore her.

Heads bobbed and toes tapped in rhythm to the taped music playing updated versions of classic holiday songs. The sound escalated as several parents raised their voices, singing along with the Temptations singing "White Christmas." The mood became even more festive when everyone joined in to what had become a Motown sing-along.

Shelby looked around for Marshall but did not see him in the crowd. She glanced at her watch. She wanted to congratulate him on a successful Kwanzaa celebration before she left.

Gathering her coat and purse, she smiled and excused herself as she wound her way through the crowd. Students and young people gathered in the halls, talking quietly to one another. She walked into the front office and found it empty. She heard Marshall's voice coming from the direction of his private office—his voice and that of another.

"I can't believe this, Marshall," said a woman in a soft, drawling Southern cadence. "We were married for years, and even though I never wanted a baby, there were times when we got careless. But I never got caught. Now, I'm thirty-eight years old, unmarried, and pregnant. Why, Marshall? Why now, and not five or six years ago? A baby probably would've saved our marriage."

"Cassandra," Marshall replied, his voice soft and comforting. "You know we ended our marriage for different reasons. And being pregnant is not the end of the world. I don't know why you think that having a child is a death sentence. You know how I felt and still feel about fathering a child. I've never changed my mind about having children."

Shelby was stunned, not only from what she'd heard, but because she found herself eavesdropping on what was a private and intimate conversation between a man and his ex-wife. A man she had fallen in love with.

Spinning around quickly, she retreated from the office, biting down hard on her lower lip. She tasted blood by the time she found herself on the sidewalk outside the building.

It had happened again. The man she was in love with had gotten another woman pregnant!

Instead of taking a taxi back to her apartment, she walked. The cold wind chilled her face, but she didn't feel it. She was too numb to do anything except replay what she'd overheard in her head.

Shelby didn't cry because she couldn't. There had been a time when she had shed so many tears that she knew she could never cry or grieve for a lost love again.

Why couldn't she have waited, she chided herself once she found herself in bed. She should've waited to sleep with him. But Shelby knew it still would not have changed anything. Unknowingly, she had fallen in love with Marshall before she'd ever offered him her body.

The telephone on the bedside table rang, startling her. Her heart pounding in her chest, she counted off the rings before the answering machine switched on.

"Shelby, this is Marshall. I'm sorry I missed you before you left. Please call me when you get in. Love you."

The two words shattered her resolve and the dam broke. She cried, the sobs deep and wrenching. Marshall Graham loved her even though he had gotten his ex-wife pregnant.

How could she have made the same mistake twice?

Marshall felt as if someone had kicked him in the head. Pain and tension had stretched his nerves until he was mindless with the fear that something had happened to Shelby.

He pushed the food around on his plate, seeing and not seeing. She hadn't returned his calls; he was told that she wouldn't return to the museum until after the new year, and he had waited in front of her building for hours, praying she would appear.

"Either eat it or throw it out, Marshall."

His head came up and he stared at his frowning aunt. "I'm sorry, Naomi. I'm not too hungry." He kneaded his temples.

"You're not hungry, you have a headache, and you're too stubborn to tell me what's going on," Naomi shot back.

He pushed back his chair, rising to his feet. "Nothing's going on," he mumbled.

"Sit down, Marshall. Now!"

He obeyed her, glaring across her dining room table at her. His hand was shaking when he reached for his glass of wine. The liquid soothed his dry throat, but only temporarily.

Naomi's dark eyes examined her brother's only child. She saw what she should've recognized three weeks ago: Marshall had changed. There was intensity and restlessness that he hadn't shown in years. The last time she saw it was when he had made his decision to end his marriage and relocate to New York.

"It's Shelby, isn't it?" she questioned perceptively. She hadn't missed the interaction between her nephew and Shelby at Shumba Naaman's showing. There was no doubt that something was going on between her protégée and her nephew.

Slumping back in his chair, Marshall nodded slowly. He couldn't lie—at least, not to his aunt. "Yes."

Naomi shifted an eyebrow. "You really like her, don't you?"

Marshall shook his head slowly. "No. I love her."

"Does she know this?"

"I don't think so."

"You don't think so, Dr. Marshall Oliver Graham. For someone who's earned a Ph.D., you're not too bright. And why haven't you told the lady that you love her?"

He closed his eyes. "She won't let me."

"Why not?"

Marshall's temper exploded. "What is this? An inquisition?"

"Don't sass me, Marshall. Just answer my question."

The set of his jaw indicated his stubbornness. He felt like getting up and walking out of his aunt's apartment, but didn't. They were family. Naomi Morrow was the only family he had in New York. And because she was alone, he had elected not to return to Washington, D.C., and spend Christmas with his parents and cousins.

"Because she won't return my calls," he admitted reluctantly. He went on to tell his aunt all that had happened since the night he was introduced to Shelby Carter. He did not disclose that he had slept with Shelby, but he suspected Naomi was more than aware of it.

"I don't believe she went to California to visit her family," Naomi said, after Marshall explained his dilemma. "But I do know that she always takes off the last ten days of the year."

Naomi stood up, and Marshall rose with her. "Let *me* call her to wish her a merry Christmas. That should confirm whether she's still in New York."

He paced the length of the dining room while Naomi retreated to the kitchen. What he felt for Shelby was akin to an itch that only she could scratch.

How, he asked himself, had she gotten to him without his knowledge? Why Shelby and not some other woman? What was it about her?

Because Shelby Carter is a challenge, a voice taunted him. He found her beautiful and feminine. She was versatile and intelligent. She was fiercely independent, as well as passionate.

He managed a smile. And most of all, she was uncompromising. She never pretended even to let him win during their swimming competitions.

"Marshall." He stopped pacing and turned to stare at Naomi. "She's at home."

"She's been home all this time?" His voice, though quiet, had an ominous quality.

"Don't lose it, Marshall," Naomi warned. "Shelby said she's been working around the clock to complete your curriculum before the end of the year."

"Today is December twenty-fifth. She doesn't have much more time before the year's over."

"And after that, Marshall?"

The forefinger of his left hand stroked the side of his nose, then something Naomi said registered. "Yes!"

Naomi stared at Marshall as if he'd taken leave of his senses. "What are you talking about?"

His smile was dazzling. "Tomorrow is the twenty-sixth, and the first day of Kwanzaa. We're supposed to spend Kwanzaa together."

"Tomorrow?"

"No. The entire holiday—all seven days." His eyes were glittering with excitement as he threw back his head and let out a burst of laughter.

Marshall reminded Naomi of the serious child he had always been who would on occasion exhibit an effusiveness which never failed to shock his family.

"Do you think seven days is enough time for you to win the young lady over?" Naomi teased, feeling some of his enthusiasm.

Marshall picked her up, swung her around, and kissed her cheek before he lowered her to the carpeted floor. "More than enough." There was confidence in his words.

"If that's the case, then I think I should give you something. Come with me," Naomi ordered, taking Marshall's hand and leading him to her bedroom.

He recognized the dark blue velvet pouch when she extended her hand. "Thank you, Aunt Naomi. It helps to know you have that much faith in me."

Naomi cocked her head at an angle, smiling. "Why not? You've inherited the famous Graham male charm. What else would you need?"

"A Mrs. Marshall Graham." Marshall smiled back, and surprisingly, his headache had vanished.

The ringing of the telephone pulled Shelby from her sleep, and before she could react, she picked up the receiver. "Hello."

"Happy Kwanzaa, Shelby!"

Her somnolence vanished. "Marshall?"

"How many Marshalls do you know?"

She groaned silently. "Only one. Happy Kwanzaa, Marshall."

It wasn't fair. He'd caught her when she wasn't fully awake. The glowing red dials on the bedside clock read six-ten. The sun hadn't even come up.

"What time should I pick you up for the get-together with your friends?"

Shelby stared at the faint outline of the gaily wrapped gifts lining the work table in the alcove. There were seven—one for each day of Kwanzaa.

"Six." Her voice was low and flat.

"Is the dress casual?"

"Yes."

"Then I'll see you at six."

Marshall hung up, his call lasting no more than sixty seconds. Shelby replaced her receiver and lay in bed, staring up at the darkened ceiling. It was about to begin, and in seven days, it would be over. She had committed herself to sharing the seven days of Kwanzaa with him, and once the first day of the new year came and went, so would her time with Marshall Graham.

Shelby opened the door for Marshall, stepping aside as he walked into her apartment. He was casually dressed in a pair of charcoal-gray slacks, a slate-blue V-neck sweater, and a dark-gray suede jacket. At first glance the jacket appeared more velvet than suede.

He handed her a flat box wrapped in gold foil. *"Umoja,* and Happy Kwanzaa."

"Umoja." She repeated the Swahili word for "unity" or "staying together." Closing the door, she followed him into the living room and handed him the gaily wrapped box on the coffee table. "Happy Kwanzaa, Marshall." The shape of his gift box was similar to the one he had given her.

Shelby felt a little uneasy. Marshall's midnight gaze lingered on her face before moving leisurely over her blouse and slacks. The last time he was in her apartment they had spent most of their time in bed.

She held up her gift. "Should I open it now?" Marshall nodded and she moved over to the sofa and sat down. She felt, rather than saw, him watching her as she carefully peeled off the decorative bow and gold paper. Her heart started up a double-time rhythm when she saw the silk Hermès scarf nestled in tissue paper. The fabric was exquisite, the print vibrant.

Her head came up slowly. "I don't know what to say," she said breathlessly.

Marshall sat down beside her. His gaze caressed the delicate bones in her face. " 'Thank you' will be enough."

A tremulous smile touched her lips. "Thank you, Marshall."

Leaning over, he pressed a kiss to her temple. "You're quite welcome." He unwrapped his gift, his smile mirroring his approval. He held up a length of fabric for a bow tie and a cummerbund in the same print as the Nia Academy logo.

"Where did you find this?"

Shelby placed her gift on the table and clasped her hands together on her lap. "I made it. I hope the cummerbund fits."

Marshall stood up, removed his jacket, and fastened the cummerbund around his waist. It was a perfect fit. He raised an eyebrow. "You have a good eye—and good taste."

What Marshall didn't know was that it had taken her nearly six hours of browsing through every fabric store she knew that sold kente-cloth patterns to match the one on Nia's letterhead.

"I'm glad you like it, Marshall."

He took off the cummerbund and replaced it in the box with the bow tie. "Where are we going and what time do we have to be there?"

Shelby stood up. "We're going to SoHo. We should be there before seven." What she didn't tell Marshall was that Shumba Naaman was hosting the first-night celebration.

Marshall sighed in relief after spending more than two hours at the sculptor's loft apartment. He and Shelby had attended as a couple while not appearing to be a couple. She was polite *and* estranged.

He had spent hours observing her as she'd talked quietly with Shumba and the other invited guests. She had once referred to the talented artist as a very good friend of hers and Marshall believed that was what they were.

"What do you have planned for tomorrow?" he questioned during the drive uptown.

Shelby turned to stare at his profile. "Nothing."

He bit back a smile. "Would you like to spend days two and three at my place?"

"I can't. I'm trying to complete your curriculum."

"Why the rush?"

"I have other things to do. I can't afford to spend two days away from the project."

"When do you expect to complete it?"

"Hopefully, before the first." What she didn't say was that she was pushing herself to complete his project by January first because then she would be able to walk away from him and erase all memories of the man who'd brought back the pain she had forgotten.

"Would you mind if I make the plans for the next two days of Kwanzaa?"

Closing her eyes, she pressed her back against the leather seat of his vintage Mercedes. "No. I don't mind."

"Dress formally." Those were the last words he said until he left her at her door, bidding her goodnight. There was no goodnight kiss or embrace.

Shelby spent the night tossing and turning restlessly, her dreams filled with images of Marshall—his caresses, his kisses, and his slow, methodical, and purposeful lovemaking.

She'd missed his dry wit and his occasional jealousy. She wanted to hate him for his infidelity, but she couldn't.

"Why didn't he tell me?" she asked aloud in the darkened

bedroom. Why couldn't he have told her that he was still seeing his ex-wife? That he was sleeping with her?

Sighing heavily, Shelby managed a small smile. One down and six to go. She prayed she could make it.

Marshall stared at Shelby, his mouth gaping slightly. He inhaled and let out his breath slowly. "Wow!"

Shelby gave him a sensuous smile. "Should I say thank you?"

He moved closer, grinning. "I'm the one who should say thank you." Shelby was stunning in a gold crêpe de chine dress that clung to every line of her body until it flowed around the toes of her black satin pumps. The garment claimed long sleeves and a high neckline, and when she shifted, it revealed an expanse of bared back to her waist.

Marshall handed her a decorative package with a large black velvet bow. "For you."

The burgundy color on her lips shimmered. "Thank you." She gestured to Marshall. "Please come in."

He walked past her and spied his gaily wrapped gift on the coffee table. Picking it up, he shook it gently. "Do you want to give me a hint?"

Shelby shook her head, visually admiring him in formal dress. His black wool tuxedo fit his broad shoulders with tailored precision and the stark white band-collar shirt with onyx studs eliminated the need for a bow tie, even though he had opted for a black cummerbund.

He noted her stare. "I do own a shirt with a wing collar," he admitted sheepishly.

"Open your gift, Marshall." Her command was quiet and filled with laughter.

They sat side-by-side on the sofa, opening their gifts. Shelby laughed. Marshall had given her a large box of assorted Godiva truffles.

"I'll have to swim a dozen laps to work off these calories," she said, staring up at him through her lashes.

Marshall noted the subtle bronze and moss green shadows on her lids and the plum blush accentuating her high cheekbones. His obsidian gaze lingered on her hair, swept off her ears and forehead. A styling mousse had taken most of her curl out of her hair, creating a style that would have been much too severe on a woman with features less delicate than Shelby's.

Picking up a truffle, she held it to his mouth. "What flavor is this one?"

He held her wrist as she fed him the truffle, drawing her forefinger into his mouth and sucking gently. Marshall watched her eyes widen as his tongue moved sensuously up and down the length of her finger.

Everything that was Shelby Carter—the haunting fragrance clinging to her flesh, the shimmering gleam of her flawless face, the soft curves of her body in the silky dress, and the essence of her femininity that lingered with him even when they were apart—swept over him, buffeting him like a tidal wave sweeping up everything in its wake.

"Marshall!"

The sound of her hoarse whisper broke the spell. He released her finger and Shelby sprang from the sofa. He moved quickly, capturing her arm and spinning her around.

"Don't touch me, Marshall!"

He stared down at Shelby, baffled by her vehement outburst and the look of revulsion on her face. "I don't understand what the hell is going on. Perhaps I'm missing something, but I seem to remember that ten days ago you invited me to your bed. And in that particular bed you and I shared something that was very personal, special, and quite intimate. I don't recall, but correct me if I'm wrong, us having an argument or a misunderstanding.

"Fast forward to the present. I'm afraid to touch you, much less kiss you. And I dare not even *think* of making love to you." His fingers tightened around her upper arm. "Talk to me, Miss Carter. What did I do wrong?" He enunciated each word.

Shelby stared back at him, her temper rising in response to

his angry statement. "I don't ask for much in a relationship, Marshall . . ."

"What relationship, Shelby?" he countered, interrupting her. "You haven't given us an opportunity to *have* a *relationship.*"

"And don't interrupt me," she shot back. He nodded and she continued, "I repeat, I don't ask for much in a relationship. But I demand respect and fidelity."

Marshall released her arm, frowning. "What are you talking about? I haven't slept with, kissed, or even *looked* at another woman since my aunt introduced us."

"What about before that time?"

His gaze widened and he managed to look sheepish. "I'm not a monk, Shelby. I've slept with a few women since my divorce."

"Do those *few* include your ex-wife?"

"Cassandra?"

"Is that her name?"

"Yes. Why?"

"Have you slept with her since your divorce?"

"Of course not." His eyes narrowed and he stared back at her in silence. "What does Cassandra have to do with us?"

At that moment Shelby wanted the floor to open up and swallow her whole. How could she tell Marshall that she had eavesdropped on his conversation with his ex-wife? That she suspected the baby in Cassandra's womb was Marshall's?

"Shelby?"

She jumped slightly at the drawling sound of her name. Turning her back, she wound her arms around her waist in a gesture of protectiveness. There was complete silence except for the soft, even sound of breathing. There came another foreign sound and she spun around.

Her mouth gaped, then snapped closed. Marshall had kicked off his shoes and slipped his arms from his tuxedo jacket.

"What are you doing?"

"What does it look like?" He answered her question with one of his own, removing his cummerbund.

"Put your clothes back on."

"Why, Shelby? I'm not going anywhere until I get some answers. It sounds as if you've tried and found me guilty without a fair trial. And the sentence appears to be exile. You've deprived me of my right to be made aware of the charges leveled against me *and* the right to defend myself. Governments have been toppled from their very foundations because of similar practices, Shelby Carter."

He removed the studs from his shirt, dropping them on the coffee table before he shrugged out of his shirt. His hands went to the waistband on his dress trousers and Shelby panicked.

"No."

Marshall stalked her, unzipping the trousers. "Talk fast, Shelby, or I'm going to *live with you* until you do."

She did, leaving nothing out. She told Marshall what she had overheard when she'd gone to his office, while he stared at her in stunned relief. The heat in her face swept lower and her entire body burned in embarrassment.

Whatever anger or annoyance Marshall had experienced vanished quickly with Shelby's confession. The laughter started in his chest and bubbled up until he nearly collapsed with relief. The more he laughed, the more her humiliation increased.

"It serves you right," he stuttered. "Being nosy is not an admirable trait."

"I wasn't being nosy, Marshall Graham. I just happened to overhear a private conversation."

He sobered quickly. "But if you'd stayed long enough to hear the rest of the conversation, you'd have heard me tell Cassandra to marry her child's father because they did love each other."

Reaching out, he pulled Shelby to his bare chest. "Cassandra and I have remained friends. She came to me because she needed another opinion from a friend. I don't love her anymore, but I don't hate her, either. Both of us finally realized we married for all the wrong reasons. I knew she never wanted children, even though I did, and she knew what my professional aspirations were. She told me flat out that she would never leave D.C. Most of us delude ourselves, believing we can change the other person."

"Are you hoping that perhaps I might change my mind and let you win whenever we swim?" she teased. Shelby was certain he could feel the runaway beating of her heart through the fabric of her dress.

He pressed his mouth to her ear, inhaling deeply. "Of course. Have you no pity for my bruised male ego?"

"No," she whispered, smiling.

"Was there even the slightest chance that you might have been a little jealous of Cassandra?" he crooned.

Shelby smiled, planting light kisses on his broad chest. "Hell, yeah," she replied, repeating the very words he'd uttered at the art gallery.

He pulled back, examining the sensual smile on her lips. "You care?"

She nodded. "I care a lot."

"How much?"

"This much." She wound her arms around his strong neck, pulling his head down. Her lips parted as she kissed him with all the love she could summon for Marshall Graham.

He moved his mouth over hers, devouring its moist softness, drinking deeply to replenish the love he felt for her.

The kiss ended, both of them breathing heavily. Marshall's dark eyes crinkled. "That's a whole lot of caring." One hand came up and covered her breast. "What are we going to do tonight? Dine in or out?"

Shelby was unable to hide the love she felt for him. She was certain it showed in her eyes. "Dine out. Days four and five are mine, and I've planned two very special nights of dining in."

Marshall released her, successfully concealing his disappointment. "May I open my gift first?" She nodded.

The box contained a Vermont teddy bear wearing a blue blazer, gray slacks, a white button-down shirt and navy blue tie. Marshall's unrestrained laughter filled the apartment for the second time that evening.

"It's perfect, Shelby."

"So is its owner."

Marshall nodded modestly. "Thank you, darling. For the bear and the compliment."

The next four nights became a blur with the exchange of gifts and the evening celebrations. Shelby gave Marshall a bottle of his favorite cologne, Eternity for Men, a leatherbound appointment book for the next year, engraved with his monogram, a supply of scented beeswax candles for their candlelight dinners, and a subscription to a magazine for horticulturists, along with an exquisite bonsai plant.

Marshall's exceptional taste was reflected in his gifts to Shelby: a bottle of Shalimar perfume, an illustrated anthology of art and poems of love from the Metropolitan Museum of Art gift shop, a double strand of delicate gold links dotted with tiny diamonds, and the tiny gold sculptured woman he had purchased at Shumba's exhibition. He admitted to Shelby that Shumba had told him that she had the matching male counterpart.

The seventh and final night was celebrated at Marshall's house, the living room ablaze with the scented candles.

Shelby lay on the rug in front of the fireplace, staring up at the shadowed face of the man she loved.

"I didn't think I would finish the curriculum in time, but I wanted it out of the way so that there wouldn't be anything between us if we couldn't work out our differences."

Marshall ran his forefinger down the length of her nose. "What differences, darling? The only problem was that you overheard something you didn't understand. And it's taken me nearly two weeks of penance to pay for that!"

"I had to make certain what I feel for you is real, Marshall. I couldn't sleep with you again until I worked out my problem of learning to trust a man again."

"I would never be unfaithful to you." He punctuated each

word with a light kiss on her mouth. "You're everything I'd ever want or need in a woman."

"Imani," she whispered. "Faith, Marshall. The faith to believe in ourselves, our people, and those we love."

"Imani," he repeated.

Shelby reached into the pocket of her dress, handing Marshall a tiny box. "Happy Kwanzaa." He opened the box and removed the sculpted gold Inca man and woman. "She missed you," she said quietly. "But it was her decision to come back with her husband."

Marshall closed his hand around the sculpted pieces, smiling. "Thank you. I think she'll be very content with her husband."

He handed Shelby the velvet pouch by his feet. "Happy Kwanzaa, darling. I love you."

She opened the pouch and removed the strand of magnificent pearls she had seen many times around Naomi Morrow's neck. Her gaze mirrored confusion. "Why?"

"The Graham pearls have been worn around the neck of a beautiful Graham woman for more than a hundred fifty years."

Shelby's lower lip trembled. "But I'm not a Graham woman."

Lowering his head, Marshall gave her a hopeful smile. "You could be, if only you'd marry me."

Her eyes filled with tears of joy. "Are you proposing to me?"

"It sounds like a proposal to me," he replied in a smug tone. "I want to be able to celebrate the next fifty first fruits of the harvest with you, if you'd have me."

Her smile was dazzling. "I love you, Marshall."

"I think you're supposed to say yes, Shelby."

She threw her arms around his neck, whispering, "Yes, yes, yes!"

Friend and Lover

by
Angela Benson

One

"Just a minute," Paige Taylor yelled to whoever was ringing her apartment doorbell at nine A.M. the day after Christmas. She'd just gotten in herself, having taken the six A.M. flight from Boston to Atlanta. She'd planned on spending the day being upset with Dexter Fine, her fiancé, for canceling their plans to spend the holidays together. As usual, he'd used work as an excuse. This time, he'd had to visit a client in Los Angeles.

Of course, her father had taken Dexter's side and chastised her for not being supportive of her hard-working fiancé. She was getting angry again just thinking about it. She closed her suitcase and shoved it in her already crowded bedroom closet and ran to open the door.

"Just a minute," she said again, in an annoyed tone that she hoped the intruder recognized. She jerked the door open and saw an elderly woman standing in her doorway. The chastisement on her lips fell away. The woman had to be eighty, if she was a day. She couldn't have been more than five-four, a hundred pounds. She looked rather feeble standing there with her gray hair pulled back in a bun, wire-rimmed glasses, support hose, and orthopedic shoes. The woman was so much the stereotypical senior citizen that Paige was immediately sorry and embarrassed for her rudeness. "I'm sorry, ma'am," she said. "May I help you?"

The older woman opened her mouth to speak, but she was interrupted by a booming male voice coming from down the hallway. "Big Momma, I thought I told you to wait for me at the elevator." Before Paige saw him, she knew it was her friend Reed. She'd recognize his deep, rich, Barry White-like voice anywhere. When she saw him, she wondered why he was carrying three suitcases, one under his arm, and one in each hand. The one under his arm had caused his black bomber jacket and sweater to rise, giving a glimpse of his flat, brown stomach.

"Reed, what are you doing—?"

Reed quickly dropped the suitcases by her door and pulled her into his arms. "Go along with me until I can explain," he whispered in her ear. "I missed you, sweetheart," he said, loudly enough for the woman Paige now guessed was his grandmother to hear. "I hope your father and mother were well."

He pulled back from her and she saw the plea in his eyes. What was going on? she wondered.

He looked at his grandmother. "Didn't I tell you she was something, Big Momma?"

His grandmother slapped him on the arm. "You have no manners, sonny. You didn't even introduce me. The girl looks like she's scared to death."

Reed grinned at his grandmother and Paige knew then that they shared a special relationship. "Big Momma, this is Paige Taylor. Paige, my grandmother, Willie Pearl Lewis. You can call her Big Momma, or you can call her Grandma Lewis."

Paige extended her hand. "It's nice to meet you, Grandma Lewis." "Big Momma" was a bit much, in her opinion.

Grandma Lewis looked at Paige's outstretched hand and shook her head. "You young folks! I'm not shaking my granddaughter-in-law-to-be's hand. I want a hug, and a better one than you gave your fiancé," she said with a huff, and pushed her patent leather handbag further up her arm to embrace Paige.

It wasn't a strong hug, because it seemed Grandma Lewis didn't have a lot of strength, but it was a loving hug. Paige felt the love all the way to her bones.

When Grandma Lewis pulled away, Paige felt that she'd lost something vital. As if she knew Paige's thoughts, Grandma Lewis winked at her. "You're a special girl, Paige. My grandson finally did something right."

Reed put his hand to his heart. "I'm hurt, Big Momma. All this time I thought I could do no wrong."

Grandma Lewis looked at him and smiled. "Now, greet your fiancée like you love her. If your grandfather, rest his soul, had come to visit me after being separated for Christmas Day, I'd want more than that poor excuse for a hug you gave Paige."

Reed reached in his pocket and pulled out a dried sprig of mistletoe.

"Reed—" Paige lifted her hand to stop him, but before she could finish the sentence, he had pulled her into his arms.

He hugged her and whispered, "Do it for my grandmother. Please. I'll explain later."

"You owe me, big time, Reed Lewis," she whispered back.

Paige thought she'd done what he'd wanted when he pulled back from the hug, so the kiss surprised her. It was the first time she'd kissed a guy with a mustache. There was something very sensual about the contrast of the feel of his lips against hers and the lingering caress of his mustache against her skin.

She heard herself moan, and felt Reed deepen the kiss. Her arms automatically encircled his back.

"That's enough, children," Grandma Lewis said. "I don't think my heart can take any more of your welcoming."

When Reed pulled away and smiled down at her, Paige felt as though she was looking at him for the first time. His deep-set light-brown eyes were hooded by thick black eyebrows and long eyelashes that probably made some women jealous. That didn't mean there was anything feminine about his face, though. To the contrary, his face was all male, from the wide forehead to the strong cheekbones and the square chin. When he smiled, his features turned soft and inviting. And his ears—she wanted to use them as handles to pull his face back to hers.

Hold up, Paige, she said to herself. This is Reed, your old friend Reed, you're talking about. What's happening here?

Reed mouthed the words "Thank you," then gave her a quick

hug before picking up the suitcases in the hallway. "My apart ment's flooded and we have no place to stay. Can we bunk wit you for a few days?"

Paige was still thinking about that kiss and wondering wher Reed had learned to kiss like that.

"Doesn't look like she's going to let us in, Reed," Grandm Lewis said.

"Oh." Paige stammered and stepped back so they could ente her apartment. "Come on in." She smiled at Grandma Lewis "Make yourself at home."

As Reed passed her, Paige whispered, "You've got a lot o explaining to do, and you'd better do it fast."

Reed pressed his ear against Paige's bedroom door in an at tempt to hear what she and his grandmother were talking about but he could hear only bits and pieces of sentences.

He listened for a few more seconds before giving up an moving back to his seat on the sofa.

He propped his feet up on Paige's glass-topped cocktail table smiling as he thought about the grief she'd give him when sh saw his feet there.

His smile eased into a frown as thoughts of the last time he' been in her apartment filled his mind. It had been three month ago, after they'd attended the Hawks's season opener.

"Take your feet off my table," she'd said, pushing his jeans clad legs to the floor. "You act like you have no home training and I know your mother taught you better than that."

He'd grinned at her, liking the way her big, brown eye sparked when she pretended to be upset. "Hey, my mother wa more concerned with making sure her men were comfortabl than she was about some old furniture." His use of the word "old" was a jibe, since all the furniture in her apartment had been replaced in the last year. She'd called it remodeling. He'd called it a waste of money. Too much white and too much fluf for his taste.

His remark had only gotten a smirk from her before she'd one off for a quick shower. Then the phone had rung. He knew e shouldn't have answered it, but he had. It had been Dexter. Ir. Fine.

"Lewis, what are you doing in my fiancée's apartment this ite at night?"

Because you're not here, where you ought to be were the ords that came to Reed's mind, but he didn't speak them. Not ut of any respect for Fine, but out of respect for his friendship ith Paige. "We went to a Hawks game, Fine. Nothing for you worry about."

"I'm not worried about you, Lewis," Fine said in a smug oice. "Put Paige on the phone."

Reed punched his hand into the back of the upholstered white ofa, wishing the sofa were Fine's face. God, how he hated the uy. In his opinion, Fine was in no way good enough for Paige. he guy didn't have a heart. "She's in the shower. Do you want e to go get her?"

Reed took satisfaction in the silence that his question caused. Tell Paige I'll call back later."

Tell Paige I'll call back later, Reed repeated in his mind. The uy was too arrogant for words. "Right," Reed said, and hung p the phone.

"Who was it?"

Reed looked up to see Paige standing in her bathroom door, er calf-length green terrycloth robe wrapped around her, her till-wet thick black hair plastered to her neck. He felt a tightness n his groin and thought for the thousandth time in their four-year elationship that Paige didn't have a clue about the effect she ad on him.

"So, who was it?" she asked again.

He cleared his throat. "Mr. Fine," he spit out, and immediately egretted it.

She pursed her lips and he knew she was holding back her nger. "Why didn't you call out to me, Reed? You know I would ave spoken to him."

Reed flopped back down on the sofa, angry that Fine ha ruined his evening with Paige. "He said he'd call back. There no need to get bent out of shape."

She walked over and sat next to him on the sofa. "I'm n getting bent out of shape. What did you say to him?"

Reed looked away. "I told him you were in the shower."

She stood up then. "Why do you do this, Reed? Dexter is th man I'm going to marry. You have to accept that."

"Never," Reed whispered under his breath.

"I heard that, Reed," Paige said, walking toward the door. " think you'd better go now."

He stood up and opened his arms to her in supplication. "I' sorry, Paige. I didn't mean anything by it. It's just that the gu rubs me the wrong way."

Paige dropped her hand from the doorknob. "Don't you se what your attitude is doing to me, Reed? I want our friendshi but Dexter is going to be my husband."

Reed knew what was coming and he dreaded the words, bu he couldn't stop what he had set in motion. He and Paige ha been coming to this point ever since he'd first expressed hi reservations about Mr. Dexter Fine. "So, what are you sayin Paige?"

She maintained the eye contact. "Don't make me choose be tween you, Reed."

Reed felt as if she'd slugged him in the gut. He had no dou who she'd choose.

As he thought back on that evening, he wondered again ho Paige could be so blind that she couldn't see through the guy.

Now, three months later, Fine was up to his old tricks agai It was the holidays, and the guy was nowhere to be found. Ree knew where'd he'd be if he had a fiancée like Paige: he'd b right by her side. Better yet, he'd be in her bed. With her.

Reed stopped the direction of his thoughts. It'd taken him while to recover from that kiss he'd shared with Paige. H couldn't handle thoughts of being in bed with her without deal ing with the physical reaction it caused in him.

He wanted Paige. As a friend. As a lover. As a wife. But she wanted him only as a friend.

Well, Reed told himself, he had one week to change her mind.

Paige closed her bedroom door quietly and walked back into the great room. Reed had made himself at home. He sat on the sofa with his legs propped up on her table, reading one of the magazines from the white wicker basket next to the sofa. His bomber jacket was thrown over the back of the sofa. "Take your feet off the table and start talking," she said, as soon as she sat down.

Reed flashed a hundred-watt smile, and Paige felt her insides quicken. What was wrong with her? If she'd seen Reed smile once, she'd seen him smile a thousand times. Why was he having this effect on her now? "What are you grinning at?" she asked, to mask her roller-coaster emotions.

He moved his feet off the table and nodded toward her closed bedroom door. "Big Momma."

Paige returned his smile. "She's really something."

"That she is." Reed sobered. "Thanks for letting us stay here, Paige. I know it's an imposition."

Paige nodded, thinking again that she needed a bigger place. Her family and friends agreed, and they told her so frequently. "This is a one-bedroom apartment, Reed. How are three people going to live here?"

Reed inclined his head in the direction of the bedroom door. "Well, it seems Grandma has staked out her place. I'll flip you for the sofa."

Paige laughed. "I don't think so. This is my apartment. You get the floor."

Reed dropped the magazine on the table and looked up at her. "Now, what would Big Momma say about that? We're supposed to be engaged."

A warm feeling curled in Paige's stomach. She ignored it.

"How can I forget? Whatever made you tell your grandmother we were engaged in the first place?"

Reed shrugged his shoulders before standing and turning his back to her. "It just happened."

"Come on, you can do better than that." She noticed the way his jeans curved across his buns and thought for the first time that he had a very nice butt. Very nice.

He turned around to face her. "She hadn't been feeling well and she kept talking about the great-grandchildren she'd love to see before she left. I felt like I had to give her some hope." He sat down on the sofa next to her. "Your name just came up. I never thought she'd come to meet you."

Paige nodded. "She seems feeble, but she doesn't look like she's that sick."

Reed brightened. "It's amazing. It's almost like the news of our engagement gave her a second wind. That's why this week is so important. She needs something to hold on to, Paige."

"But why me, Reed? What about some of those, ah, women that you've been dating?"

"Not quite grandmother material. You've said as much yourself."

Paige couldn't argue with him there. She'd often spoken to him about the quality of the women he dated. "You think I'm grandmother material?"

His gaze caught hers and held it. "Definitely."

The potency in his words made her want to turn her gaze away, but she couldn't. It was as if she were trapped by his eyes. "Oh . . ."

Reed brushed his hands down his jeans-covered thighs, stood, and shoved his hands in his pockets, breaking the spell. "So are you going to go along with the ruse?"

Paige was grateful for the change in topic. "Why are you asking me to do this, Reed?"

"Because you're my friend."

She heard his unspoken, *And friends help friends out. "Are* we still friends?"

He jerked his head in her direction. "Why do you ask something like that?"

"I think you know."

"You're talking about Mr. Fine?"

She heard the distaste in his voice, but choosing to ignore it, she merely nodded. It was about time she started thinking of her fiancé.

"But he's so—"

She lifted a hand. "Stop right there, Reed. If you want me to do this for you, you have to do something for me."

"So, we've moved from friendship to blackmail? Is that what we're doing, Paige?"

She wasn't going to let him shame her into doing what he wanted. "Let's call it two friends entering into a pact to help each other."

He sighed in defeat. "Okay. What do you want?"

"I'll play the ruse for your grandmother, if you'll agree to spend New Year's Eve with me and Dexter."

Reed laughed a dry laugh. "That doesn't sound like fun to me, Paige. Three's a crowd, or haven't you heard?"

She rolled her eyes, wondering why Reed was being so obtuse. "You get to bring a date. That's the whole point. It'll be a double date. Me and Dexter, and you and one of your women."

"Talk about double standard."

"What do you mean?"

He pointed a finger at her. "You. I'm a bad guy for my opinions about Mr. Fine, yet you make snide remarks about *my* dates all the time."

"But you aren't serious about them, Reed. I talk about them the way you do. Now, is it a deal or not?"

"I don't believe you'd tell my grandmother the truth. You aren't that heartless."

"You're right," she said. "But I'm appealing to you as a friend. Will you do it for me? I'm not asking for much—just a beginning. New Year's Eve, a double date. What do you say?"

Two

Reed stared at her, taking in the determined set of her beautiful face. Her thin brows were arched, her nostrils slightly flared, her lips set in a straight line. He didn't have a chance. Though it pained him to do it, Reed knew he had to agree to her plan. She wanted a double date on New Year's Eve. Well, he'd give her a double date.

"You've got a deal." He stood up again. "Now, what do you want for dinner? I figure I could pick up some take-out."

Paige wondered at Reed's quick acquiescence, but she decided to take his words at face value. "We can't give your grandmother take-out." She got up and walked into the kitchen and opened the refrigerator. She didn't know what she was looking for, but she felt she needed to do something while her emotions settled down. "I'll prepare us a nice dinner. It shouldn't take long."

Reed followed her. "You don't have to cook for us. Big Momma likes Chinese and Mexican."

Paige pulled a head of cabbage from the vegetable tray and closed the refrigerator door. "I prefer to cook. Besides, I want Grandma Lewis to think I can take care of her grandson, and I know, in her mind, that includes cooking."

Reed leaned back against the counter. The idea of Paige taking care of him brought back his smile. Of course, he could think of other ways she could take care of him. "So, you're going to play the domestic for Grandma."

Paige put the cabbage on the cutting board, got a knife from a cabinet drawer, and began to chop the cabbage into four sections. "Maybe I like being domestic."

"Maybe Mr. Fine likes your being domestic," Reed said before he thought, and regretted the words as soon as they'd left his mouth.

She didn't bother turning to look at him. She filled a boiler with water and placed in on the stove top. "Yes, Dexter likes my cooking." She turned to look at him. "And I like cooking for him."

A sarcastic *Right* was on the tip of his tongue, but he didn't say it. "And when did you get this desire for cooking? I thought you were the eat-out, take-out queen."

Paige smiled. Reed was right. She remembered all the nights the two of them had gone out for a late meal after a twelve- or fourteen-hour day at the office. And her weekends were no better. She and Reed had tried every restaurant in Atlanta. She had a cabinet drawer full of take-out menus and squirt packages of every condiment imaginable. "Things change, Reed."

"So I see."

She turned around. "What do you mean by that?"

Reed shrugged as if the answer didn't really matter to him. "You've changed, that's all." His unspoken *Since you've met Mr. Fine* hung in the air between them.

"Everybody changes . . . even you."

He walked up behind her. She was right about that. He'd changed in ways that she had no clue about. "How have I changed, Paige?" he asked.

She felt his breath on the back of her neck and all of a sudden the kitchen was too small for the both of them. She wanted to leave the room, but that required turning around. And she knew if she turned around, she'd be face-to-chest, literally, with him. And that, for some reason, scared her.

"Paige," he asked again, "aren't you going to tell me how I've changed?"

She shrugged her shoulders, wishing he'd move back to the counter. He was too close. "When you first came to Atlanta, your goal was to be the best trial lawyer in Atlanta. And the highest-paid."

He grunted and moved away from her.

She breathed a relieved sigh and turned to face him before adding, "Now you're working in the public defender's office. I call that a drastic change."

"And you never approved, did you, Paige? You thought it was the wrong decision."

Paige returned her attention to the cabbage. The water was boiling now. She diced the cabbage sections and put them in the boiler, thankful for the time the act gave her to think. It wasn't that she thought he was wrong. She just hadn't understood his decision. She hadn't judged him, although she'd known it wasn't a decision she could make.

He tapped the toe of his loafers against the floor. "Are you having hearing problems today, or what? Say something, Paige."

She put the last of the cabbage in the boiler and covered it with a lid before turning to answer him. "No, that's not what I thought."

"Sure," he said. His tone made it obvious that he didn't believe her. "Isn't that one of the things you find attractive about Mr. Fine—that he's a hotshot lawyer who can impress the hell out of your daddy?"

Anger flashed in her pretty brown eyes, but she didn't say anything.

"That's another way you've changed. You don't have as much spirit as you used to." He laughed. "I remember the arguments we used to have. You used to argue about everything. Did Mr. Fine change that, too? Does he want a docile little woman? Is that what you're trying to be?"

"Why do you always bring the conversation back to Dexter? We were talking about you. Are you jealous of him, Reed?"

Indignation rose up in Reed like a tide. He was jealous of Dexter, all right, but not for the reason that Paige thought. "Why would I be jealous of Mr. Fine?"

Paige shrugged. "Maybe because he's so successful . . ."

"And I'm not?" he finished for her.

"I didn't say that. Dexter's success just has a lot of perks associated with it."

"And mine doesn't?"

She shrugged again. "I think it gives you personal satisfaction."

"You're right. It does. I was trying to run away from my past when I was at McCurdy and McCurdy."

"And working in the PD's office is not running?"

"What do you mean by that?"

"You could have accomplished just as much with M & M as you have in the PD's office. Maybe even more, with the prestige of the partnership behind you."

The censure in her voice made him angry again. "You think I was wrong, don't you?"

She didn't answer.

"Paige, you're a snob."

"I am *not* a snob. I just don't think one has to be poor to make a difference in life."

"So now you think I'm poor." Man, this was worse than he'd thought.

"That's not what I'm saying. It's just that there's more than one way to make a difference."

Reed shook his head. "Not for me. The kids I see every day, well, I was one of them. If no one had helped me, God knows where I'd be. They need me, Paige, and I need them. I thought you knew me well enough to know that."

Paige was ashamed, but she really didn't understand Reed and his reasons for doing what he did. She understood men like her father and Dexter. They measured a man's worth by the size of his wallet and the number of people he controlled. She didn't necessarily buy into their philosophy, but it was all she knew, all that she'd ever known.

Paige wished again for a larger apartment. When she'd moved into this building, she'd told herself it was only temporary. The

Buckhead location was close to her office at Lenox, and that was all she'd been concerned with. Now, four years later, she was still here. She had to get a bigger place. Soon.

As she sat on the toilet in her bathroom, thankful for the privacy, she realized she'd been a fool to tell Reed he and his grandmother could stay here. She'd been a fool to trust Reed. He didn't approve of Dexter, and he never would. She remained convinced that if he was really her friend, he'd find some way to accept Dexter.

Besides, Dexter wasn't a bad guy; he was a good man. A bit inflexible, but a good man. So what if he expected her to support him in his career and was sometimes insensitive to the support she needed from him? So what if he occasionally put work before his personal obligation to her? As he always said, he was doing it for them. A successful career for him meant a more stable home life for them and the children they would have. That made sense, didn't it?

Well, she admitted to herself, sometimes she *did* resent Dexter's thoughtlessness. She did think he could be a bit more in touch with her needs. But what man was in tune with a woman's needs? Her father surely wasn't. He'd never been.

In fact, Dexter was a lot like her father. She assumed that was why they got along so well. Her father thought Dexter was the best thing to happen to her.

"You're not getting any younger," he'd said on more than one occasion. "You may never get a chance with a man of Dexter's caliber again. Don't mess it up."

His words had hurt at first, and she'd been tempted to "mess it up" just to spite him. But she couldn't. She couldn't "mess it up" and let her father down. Not again. It seemed he always found fault with what she did. Nothing was ever good enough. *Summa cum laude,* Law Review, McCurdy and McCurdy—none of it had made him take notice. But Dexter Fine had gotten her father's attention. She'd finally done something right. She'd been careful not to screw it up. She had learned to manage Dexter, just as she'd learned to manage her father.

She did care for Dexter. He had his good points. He didn't run around with other women. He was financially and emotionally stable. And he loved her. In his own way, he loved her. She was sure of it.

And she loved him. So what if it wasn't the love that romance novels said made your toes curl and made fire burn in your belly? Dexter remembered her birthday and the anniversaries of their first date and their first kiss, and he always gave her a gift to celebrate those occasions. So what if sometimes business kept them from celebrating on the actual dates? She knew he loved her. She didn't need those trappings to prove it.

She stood and looked at herself in the bathroom mirror. Why had she allowed Reed and his questions to get to her tonight? He didn't understand her or her relationship with Dexter. Reed had his own opinions on the matter, and as far as he was concerned, his answer was always the right one.

There had been a time when she'd loved that about him. She had loved the arguments his pigheadedness had led to. In fact, she'd thrived on them. Reed had been a great friend. Her mouth turned down in a frown. "Had been" was the right set of words. She didn't know what they had now. If only he wasn't so critical of Dexter . . .

She shook her head and ran a hand through her hair. What was Reed's problem? Why was it a crime for a woman to marry a man her father actually liked?

Reed stared at the bathroom door. She'd been in there a good twenty minutes and he was tired of waiting for her to come out and finish their conversation. He knocked on the door. "Paige, you haven't flushed yourself in there, have you?" he asked.

He heard the faucet come on. Then he heard it go off. The door opened and she walked out.

"You're going to have to learn bathroom etiquette if the three of us are going to live in this small apartment. How long do you think that'll be, by the way?"

"I'm not sure," he said, shrugging his shoulders. He didn't want to get too specific. "No longer than a few days. Big Momma goes back home on New Year's Eve."

"That's five nights, Reed."

"I know how many nights it is. Don't worry, we'll all be fine here."

She poked a finger at his chest. "Well, the next time you have the urge and I'm in the bathroom, take a quick trip down to the gas station."

He grabbed her finger and stopped her poking motion. "The nearest gas station has to be more than a mile away."

"I hope you're in good shape." She pulled her finger away and brushed past him.

Willie Pearl slipped out of bed and padded to the door of Paige's bedroom, grateful her granddaughter-in-law-to-be had finally left her alone. She'd thought the child would never leave. She put her ear to the door, trying to determine what was happening on the other side. She heard the voices of Paige and Reed. Though she couldn't make out the words, she was pretty sure they were arguing. She lifted her ear from the door and slowly moved back to the bed.

She eased herself back down on the side of the bed and shook her head. Something was wrong. Paige had looked more than surprised to see her; the child had been positively shocked. And Willie Pearl hadn't missed the widening of Paige's eyes when Reed had kissed her in greeting. If she hadn't known better, she'd have bet the farm that it was the first time Reed had kissed Paige. Fortunately, she would also have bet the farm that they'd both enjoyed the kiss. She smiled at the thought.

Her smiled drooped when she finally put her finger on what was bothering her. Paige wasn't wearing the Lewis engagement ring. *What is going on here?* she wondered. She knew she was no longer a member of the now generation, but surely things hadn't changed that much. Surely young people still respected and valued a family heirloom for an engagement ring.

What was wrong with Reed? Why hadn't he given Paige the Lewis engagement ring?

Before she could muster up much anger toward Reed, another question popped into her mind. What if it was Paige's fault? Maybe Paige was more interested in expensive baubles than the love and commitment signified by the family ring.

Willie Pearl quickly dismissed the thought. Paige hadn't seemed the type. She'd only just met the girl, but Willie Pearl sized people up pretty well and fairly quickly. No, Paige was an old-fashioned girl. Just the girl for her grandson. She'd known it as soon as she'd met her. Paige and Reed were meant to be together. She was sure of it. But she was also sure something was wrong.

She sighed and leaned back in the bed. God help her, she was going to have to teach these young people about love. She smiled before picking up the phone to call her best friend, Ida Mae Thompson. Between the two of them, they'd teach these pups more than they'd ever thought they'd need to know.

Three

"More cornbread, Grandma Lewis?" Paige asked, offering her the platter.

Grandma Lewis shook her head. "No more for me, child. I'm full." She picked up her napkin and wiped her mouth. "You're a good cook. I didn't know young people today took much stock in cooking. Especially down-home food like cabbage and cornbread. I'm impressed."

Paige couldn't help but smile. Her culinary skills had been acquired from her late maternal grandmother. Though the memories were vague, in her mind's eye Paige could see herself standing on a chair in her grandmother's country kitchen, helping her prepare supper for the family. Those had been good times. "Thanks so much, Grandma Lewis. It's nice to know that someone appreciates my cooking skills," she said with a meaningful glance at Reed.

Grandma Lewis looked at Reed who was seated across from her. "You don't appreciate Paige's cooking?"

Reed placed his napkin on the table. "I appreciate everything about Paige, Big Momma." He turned his gaze to Paige. *"Everything."*

Paige looked down at her plate. The sincerity in that single spoken word went directly to her heart. If she hadn't known better, she'd have believed that Reed meant what he said. But he didn't. This was all a show for his grandmother.

Grandma Lewis cleared her throat and Paige turned her head in her direction, glad not to have to look at Reed.

"Then why isn't the woman you're engaged to wearing the Lewis engagement ring?" the small woman demanded of Reed.

Paige looked at the dazzling three-carat diamond on her left hand, the engagement ring Dexter had given her. She'd told him it was too much, but he'd ignored her words and said nothing was too much for her. Her father had agreed. The bigger, the better. "Look for a man's money and you'll find his heart," her father had said.

Paige looked from the ring to Reed, surprised when he turned and flashed her his most charming smile. She felt an immediate pang in her belly. What was wrong with her? she wondered.

She also wondered, as the silence between them lengthened, how Reed was going to answer Grandma Lewis's question.

Looking flustered, Reed passed the buck. "Maybe you should ask her?" he said, pointing to Paige. "I did what I was supposed to do."

Paige kicked him under the table. It took all her strength to keep from screaming at him. How dare he throw the question back in her lap? This was the first she'd heard about a Lewis engagement ring. This was Reed's problem. She was doing him a favor. She was tempted to tell Grandma Lewis the truth, but the look on the older woman's face stopped her. She didn't want to hurt Grandma Lewis, she wanted to hurt Reed. So she kicked him again.

He winced, and Grandma Lewis saw it. "So, what is it, Reed? Is it so painful that you can't talk about it?"

Reed nodded in the direction of Paige's hand. "It had to be resized. It kept falling off her hand. The jeweler gave us that one as a loaner."

Paige shook her head, glad Grandma Lewis's attention and question were again directed at Reed. No way was the older woman going to fall for that. She frowned at Reed. That was a dumb thing to say, she mouthed silently.

Grandma Lewis's eyes widened. "A loaner ring? I've never heard of such. Besides, it's so *big*."

Paige knew exactly what Grandma Lewis meant. The ring was big. So big it was almost gaudy.

Reed laughed. "It's costume jewelry, Big Momma. The jeweler's a friend of mine. He made it up for Paige. She didn't want to wear it, but I told her it was a test of her love. As you can see, she's willing to make any sacrifice to show her love. Even to the point of wearing that godawful ring." He grinned confidently.

Paige threw him a withering glance that said, "Don't go too far, buddy." She knew Reed was taking potshots at her ring. It wasn't the first time, either. But since Grandma Lewis seemed to accept his answer, Paige had to respect Reed's quick thinking. But she didn't have to like it.

"So, when are you getting her real ring back?" Grandma Lewis asked.

Paige shot a quick glance at Grandma Lewis. She was a sharp cookie. She looked again at Reed, wondering how he was going to answer that question.

"I'm glad you asked." Reed scooted back in his chair, got up, and went for his jacket, on the back on the great room sofa. When he returned to the kitchen, he had a box in his hand. A ring box.

Paige looked up at him. What was he doing now? she wondered. But she knew. In that box was the Lewis engagement ring.

Reed's gaze met hers as he walked to her. Paige's eyes followed his every movement as if she was entranced.

When he reached her seat, she'd turned around so that she faced him.

He dropped to his knees in front of her. Paige wasn't surprised. It was as if they had done this before. In some other life, maybe. She shook her head to clear her thoughts. What was she thinking about?

Reed opened the box, pulled the ring out, and placed the box on the table. He held the ring out to her, and she was immediately taken with its simplicity. It was a small diamond, no more than a quarter-carat, and the band was worn from years of wear. It was the most beautiful ring she'd ever seen.

"This ring has been in my family for more than four generations. It's passed down to the eldest son in each generation." He paused and looked over at Grandma Lewis. "Big Daddy gave it to Big Momma." He turned warm eyes back to Paige. "My father gave it to my mother, and I give it to you. It is a token of the love I feel for you, a love that will last generations. As long as there is breath in my body, I will love you. And when my body no longer breathes, I will still love you. And with each generation of Lewis men that gives this ring as a token of their love, it will be a symbol of the love that I still feel for you."

Paige couldn't speak and she couldn't take her eyes from Reed. His words had taken hold of her heart and squeezed. She knew if she opened her mouth, she'd begin to weep. She didn't know why. She just knew that those words were words she'd been waiting a lifetime to hear. But this wasn't real, was it? She and Reed were just playing a game for his grandmother.

Reed didn't wait for her to say anything. He picked up her hand resting on her knee and slipped the engagement ring Dexter had given her from her finger. Somewhere in the back of her mind, Paige knew she should stop him, but she didn't. She couldn't. She had to think about Grandma Lewis.

Reed caressed her fingers, then lifted them to his mouth and kissed each one, never taking his eyes from hers. She began to get warm all over. What was Reed doing to her?

After he kissed the last finger, he slipped his ring, the Lewis engagement ring, on her ring finger. He kissed the palm of her hand and placed it back on her knee. She knew from the expression in his eyes that he wanted her to say something, but she couldn't form the words. She had an overwhelming desire, no, an overwhelming need, to pull Reed into her arms and hold on forever.

As if he'd read her thoughts, Reed leaned toward her and wrapped her in his arms. Until he had touched her, she thought that was what she wanted. Now, she knew she wanted more.

Reed pulled back from the embrace and she felt bereft. Thankfully, the feeling didn't last long. The slight nod of her head answered the question she saw in his eyes. He leaned in again and this time, he captured her lips in a kiss.

And then Paige knew this was what she really wanted.

She leaned her body into his, seeking to lose herself in him. It felt so right. It *was* so right. And then it was over. Reed was pulling away from her. Why? She wasn't ready for it to be over. She wanted more.

Grandma Lewis's voice brought her back to reality. "If you two keep this up, it's going to be a long few days and I'm going to feel like I'm in the way."

Paige tore her eyes from Reed and looked back at Grandma Lewis. The tears in the older woman's eyes pushed her over the edge.

She quickly stood. "I have to go to the bathroom," she said and fled the room. She felt Reed's eyes on her with each step she took.

Rooted in his kneeling position, Reed stared after Paige long after she'd closed the bathroom door. He'd done it. He'd told her how he felt, and a part of him believed she knew he wasn't acting, that he was speaking of his love for her. And, God help him, he thought she had feelings for him, too. He'd guessed that she did, he'd hoped it, but he'd never been sure. Now, he was. He just wondered what she was going to do with those feelings.

"Do you want me to go to the grocery store?" Big Momma asked.

Her words pulled Reed's thoughts from Paige back to her. The tears in her eyes conflicted with the smile on her face. "Why do you need to go to the grocery store?"

Big Momma wiped at her tears with her dinner napkin and inclined her head toward the bathroom door. "I don't need anything. Maybe you and Paige need some time alone."

Reed shook his head. That was what he and Paige *didn't*

need . . . at least, not now. He got up from his knees and went and placed a kiss on his grandmother's cheek. "No, ma'am. Stay right here." He smiled. "I love you, Big Momma."

She patted his head as she had done so many times when he was a child. "And I love you, too, Reed. I'm so happy for you and Paige."

Reed sat down in the chair next to his grandmother. "You're happy for us, huh?"

Big Momma practically beamed at him. "All I've ever wanted for you, Reed, is for you to be happy. You worried me for a while there, but now it seems like you're on the right road, and I believe Paige is a big part of that."

How Reed wished that were true. He now believed that he'd only be happy with Paige in his life. As his friend. As his lover. As his wife. "Well, I'm glad you're not worrying about me anymore. I'm a big boy; I can take care of myself."

"That's what had me worried," Big Momma said.

Reed knew what his grandmother referred to. "I wasn't that bad, was I?"

Big Momma nodded. "You were worse than that."

"But I've got it together now," Reed defended. "I know what I want."

Big Momma stood up, pushed her chair to the table, and stood behind it, placing her hand on its back. "You've always known what you wanted, Reed, but it's only been the last few years that you've decided to live the life you wanted instead of the life that was expected of you. Now that you're living the life you want, I don't have to worry about you."

Reed smiled. His grandmother knew him very well. Too well, sometimes. She was as right this time as she usually was. She'd been the first one in his family to understand his reasons for leaving McCurdy and McCurdy for a job as a lowly public defender. Everybody else, family and friends, had thought it was the craziest move he'd ever made. They'd only thought of the money and the prestige that Reed was giving up, instead of what he'd be getting. Only Big Momma had seen that. And she'd been the one to give him the encouragement he needed to make the decision of his heart.

He hadn't regretted it for a moment. Leaving McCurdy and McCurdy had been the start of a new life for him. The work he did every day now meant something more to him than the payment on a luxury car or the mortgage on a house that would never be filled with the laughter of his happy children. No, his paycheck now was a bonus for doing the work he loved, work that made a difference in people's lives. Some people wondered if they made a difference. Reed *knew* he did. He knew it when some kid, using a tough-guy persona to hide his fears, was able to admit, after a close game of one-on-one, that he wanted more out of life than a prison sentence and children from one coast to the other. He knew it from the tears of joy in a mother's eyes when she saw the son she'd almost given up hope on get his GED.

Even with all that, Reed had felt something was still missing from his life. And it hadn't taken him long to figure out what that something was. Paige. At first, he'd thought he was only missing his best buddy. But slowly, he'd begun to realize that Paige was so much more than his buddy. She was the best friend he'd ever had. It wasn't until her relationship with Fine had moved to an engagement that he'd realized he wanted more than friendship with her.

He hadn't known how to handle this discovery at first, but seeing the careless way Fine treated her affections made him realize he had to let her know of his feelings. He wanted to be open with Paige and just tell her how he felt, but he knew that wasn't enough. He knew that Paige's relationship with Fine had more to do with her love for her father than her love for Fine. Because of that, he knew any decision to end the relationship would be doubly hard for her.

Reed thought about Paige's father. He knew Mr. Taylor didn't like him. Oh, he'd tolerated him well enough until he'd quit the M & M job. But as soon as he'd made the move to the PD's office, Taylor had given up all pretense of civility. Paige never said anything directly, but he knew Taylor didn't think he had "success" in him, at least, not success as Taylor defined it.

It had been around that time that Paige's relationship with Fine had intensified. Taylor liked Fine. Oh, yes, indeed. Fine had even done some work for him. And Taylor had decided that Fine was the right son-in-law for his only daughter. And Paige had fallen into the trap her father had laid for her. She had become engaged to a man she didn't love, just to please her father.

Paige was an intelligent woman, but she was being naive about this. Sometimes Reed wanted to yell at her to "wake up and smell the coffee," but he didn't because he knew the struggle that she waged internally. He'd waged it himself. Paige needed to decide to live her own life, not the life her father wanted for her. He'd done it, and he knew she could, too. Eventually. Unfortunately, he couldn't wait that long. He *wouldn't* wait that long

"I think I'm going to get ready to turn in, Reed. I want to take a bath. Do you think Paige will be much longer in the bathroom?"

Reed didn't know how long Paige would be. "I'll go check on her," he replied. He looked toward the bathroom door, in no rush to get there. He was unsure of Paige's response to the scene they'd played for his grandmother. He knew she was running from her feelings. How long would she run?

When he reached the bathroom door, Reed raised his hand to knock, but before he could, the door opened and he came face-to-face with Paige.

"Excuse me," he said hesitantly, dropping his hand to his side. Her face was freshly washed and he had the feeling she'd been crying. His heart nearly stopped. He hadn't meant to make her cry.

She brushed a strand of hair back from her face. "Don't you remember what I told you about that gas station?" she asked.

Reed stared at her for a quick two seconds before silently acknowledging that he understood what she was doing. She was going to pretend that it hadn't happened. "It's not me. Big

Momma wants to take a bath. Actually, I think she was worried about you."

Paige focused her eyes on Reed's brow, and though he willed her to look him in the eye, she didn't do it. "Well, as you can see, I'm fine. Why don't we get back to the kitchen so Grandma Lewis can see that for herself?"

When she moved to brush past him, Reed caught her arm. "Thanks," he said simply.

She snatched her arm away as if he'd burned her. Her eyelids fluttered closed, then quickly opened. She looked straight into his eyes and said, "Anything for Grandma Lewis."

Four

Paige moved on rubbery legs down the hallway to the kitchen. *What is wrong with me?* she continued to ask herself. Why was Reed affecting her the way he was? She was an engaged woman, for God's sake, and Reed was just a friend.

Just a friend. Somehow, even as she spoke the words in her mind, she knew they weren't true. Reed had never been "just a friend." Their relationship had always carried an undertone of sexual attraction and tension, but neither of them had pursued it, though they'd been mature enough to acknowledge it, mature enough to say they could handle it.

Why was Reed trying to change things now? Why couldn't he leave well enough alone? Her life was finally going right. Her family was happy with her. She was engaged to a man any woman would want. Why was Reed bothering her now?

Bothering her . . . that was an understatement. Reed was pulling out all the stops. She wasn't fool enough to think that he'd just happened to have the family engagement ring handy. And that speech! That speech had her worried. Had Reed been playing a role for his grandmother, or had he been telling her his true feelings? For a moment or two, while he'd knelt there in front of her, she could have sworn he was being sincere.

"Grandma Lewis," Paige said, as she entered the kitchen, "the bathroom is free now. You can take your bath."

Grandma Lewis got up from the table and kissed Paige on the cheek. "Thank you, sweetheart. Reed really found himself a charm when he found you. Welcome to the family." She pulled

Paige into her arms for another loving embrace. Paige closed her eyes and savored the warmth of the older woman's hug. When she opened her eyes, she looked beyond Grandma Lewis's shoulder directly into Reed's eyes. She wanted to look away from him, to tell him to leave her alone, but she couldn't break eye contact.

Grandma Lewis eased away from her and Reed came forward. "How are the two loves of my life?" he asked, drawing Grandma Lewis into his arms. "Why is everybody getting hugged except me?"

Paige watched Grandma Lewis envelope her six-foot, 180-pound grandson in her frail arms. Reed had to bend over to lean his head on his grandmother's.

When Grandma Lewis pulled away, she looked at Paige. "It's your turn now," she said.

Paige quickly darted her eyes to Reed. *No,* she shouted silently. *I can't do this now.*

But you will. Reed didn't open his mouth, yet she heard him as if he had spoken with a microphone. As he advanced toward her, her heartbeat hammered and her pulse raced. It was too much. She wasn't going to be able to do it.

Reed was within a foot of Paige when Grandma Lewis stretched out her hand and stopped him. "On second thought, I think you two have done enough of that. You'd better wait until I go to bed. I wouldn't want you to start something you can't finish." She gave Paige a broad wink.

Paige's mouth dropped open and Reed grinned.

Primly straightening her dress, Grandma Lewis continued, "Don't look so shocked, Paige. I was young and in love once." She turned and headed for the bathroom. When she reached the bathroom door, she turned back to add, "Oh, I forgot to tell you. I don't sleep with my hearing aid, and I can't hear a thing without it." With that, she closed the bathroom door and was gone from sight.

The sound of male laughter caused Paige to turn to Reed.

"What's so funny?" she asked, not allowing herself to dwell on Grandma Lewis's suggestion.

Still chuckling, Reed began clearing the table. "Big Momma. She just gave us permission to get busy tonight."

"Get busy?"

Reed shot her an unbelieving glance. "Get busy—you know, make love."

Paige propped her hands on her hips, determined to play ignorant. "Now you've gone too far, Reed. You know that's not what your grandmother meant. She was just telling us so we'd know why she wasn't answering if we called out to her."

Reed scraped the plates clean and placed them in the dishwasher. "Tell yourself what you want, but I know what she meant. She's *my* grandmother, after all."

"She's a sweet little woman who'd probably have a heart attack if she even thought we were sleeping together," Paige said.

Reed laughed. "You never can tell about Big Momma. As soon as you think you've got her figured out, she shows you something new."

"Well, I don't think she'd go that far. She reminds me of my mother's mother. She died a few years ago, and I still miss her."

Reed leaned back against the sink and relaxed his arms across his chest. "I know you must. I don't even like to think about the day Big Momma won't be around."

Paige could still see her grandmother's face. How she wished she were still around.

"You can share Big Momma with me, Paige," Reed said in a soft tone. "She already loves you."

Though Paige had known Big Momma for less than a day, she knew Reed's words were true. The older woman *did* love her. "She thinks I'm going to be her granddaughter-in-law. Would she love me if she knew the truth?"

Reed dropped his hands to his side and turned back to the dishes. "What do you think?"

At that moment, Grandma Lewis came out of the bathroom, waved to the two of them, and padded into the bedroom.

"So?" Reed asked.

"Okay, I think she'd love me if she knew the truth."

Reed turned back and grinned at her. "Good answer," he said. "Now we're getting somewhere."

"What do you mean, I have to sleep on the floor?" Reed demanded. Paige was relieved he wore pajamas, though she admitted he did look attractive in the green-and-blue plaid flannel wear. "*Why* do I have to sleep on the floor?"

"Because you're not sleeping with me, Reed," she said, dropping down onto the sofa that she had unfolded to make a bed. "And I'm taking the sofabed. You can take any other place you like."

Reed sat down on the bed next to her. "Why don't you sleep on the floor? I don't mind sleeping with you. *You* have a problem sleeping with *me*."

Paige punched her pillow, wishing it was Reed's face. "Earth to Reed: this is my apartment, remember? I make the rules here." She threw a pillow and a couple of blankets on the floor. "You've made your bed, now lie in it."

"Ha, ha, ha," Reed said. "Very funny." He got up from the bed and began to put a makeshift pallet in place. "I can't believe you're doing this to me. What will Big Momma think if she comes out and finds us like this?"

Paige turned off the lamp on the end table. "Don't even try it, Reed. Your grandmother will probably think I'm a nice, sweet girl, saving myself for the marriage bed."

"Ouch," Reed said. "Why'd you turn the light off? You knew I was making my bed. Now I've bumped my damn toe."

Paige grinned, glad Reed couldn't see her in the dark. "What are you whining about? I had no idea you were such a baby. Go to sleep."

Reed mumbled a few unintelligible words.

"What did you say?" Paige asked.

"I said I wish you'd turn on the damn light. I think I broke my foot."

"Yeah, right."

"I'm serious, Paige."

"All right," Paige said, reaching for the light. "I'll turn on the light."

Paige had to grin at the sight she saw. Reed sat on the floor, rubbing his hand across his right foot. God, did he look like the lost little boy. "What is it, Reed?"

"I told you. I think I broke my foot."

She rolled her eyes at him. "You did not break your foot."

"How can you tell from way over there on your comfortable bed?" he challenged.

"I don't believe you. You're acting like a big baby. Do you want me to go get your grandmother for you?"

Reed gave a low moan. "You're a real comedian tonight, aren't you, Paige? I thought you were my friend."

Paige threw her arms into the air. "I give up," she said, getting out of bed and walking over to him. "Let me see your foot."

She dropped down on the floor next to him and reached for his foot, placing it across her lap.

He moaned again. "Go easy. I told you, I think it's broken."

She examined his foot. His big toe was bruised, but that was about it. "Believe me, Reed, if your foot were broken, you'd be making a lot more noise than you're making now." She pushed his foot off her lap. "You've just bruised your toe."

"Are you sure?" he asked, rubbing his toe some more.

Paige stood. "I'm positive. Now, may I turn out the light and go back to bed?"

"I still don't understand why I can't sleep in bed with you. After all, we're only friends. It's not like we're attracted to each other."

Paige walked over, turned off the light, and climbed into her bed. "Goodnight, Reed."

"I didn't know you were so cold-hearted, Paige."

"I'm going to sleep now, Reed."

Reed mumbled again, but Paige refused to ask him to repeat what he'd said. She hoped he'd go to sleep if she ignored him.

"Paige," he called out a full two minutes later.

"Reed, I'm trying to get some sleep," she said in a voice full of impatience.

"I'm not sleepy," he said. "Talk to me."

"Count sheep. I guarantee you'll be asleep within fifteen minutes."

"Do you remember the day we first met?" he asked, in the dark.

"Reed . . ." Paige threatened.

"I remember it just like it was yesterday," he said, with no concern for her threat. "You paraded into the office in your brand-new thousand-dollar suit and everyone knew Miss Ivy-League Lawyer had arrived." Reed laughed. "You were so full of yourself."

Paige couldn't stop her laughter. His description of her was right on target. "I was young then. Besides, you weren't exactly Mr. Modesty yourself. You and your Armani suits and your Morehouse attitude."

"Hey, I'm just a confident kind of guy."

"More like a know-it-all," Paige said under her breath.

"Hey, I heard that. Can I help it if I have a wealth of knowledge on a variety of subjects?"

"Go to sleep, Reed."

Reed tugged at the covers on her bed. Even though she couldn't see him in the dark, she knew he was sitting up. "You can't just insult a man and then go to sleep."

Paige smiled. "Watch me." She felt more than heard Reed lie back down.

"Just like a woman," he mumbled.

"I forgot. You're sexist, too."

"Now, I resent that. You know I have only respect for women."

"Yeah, I can tell that by the women you date." She regretted the words as soon as they'd passed her lips.

"I don't think you really want to discuss our tastes in the opposite sex, do you?"

She turned over on her side, facing him, and propped herself up on her elbow, but of course, she couldn't see him in the dark. "Why do you hate Dexter? Has he ever done a thing to you?"

"It's not that I hate him. It's just that I care so much about you. Tell me, do you really love Mr. Fine?"

She ran her fingers through her hair in exasperation. "Of course, I love him."

Reed sat up again. She felt it. "Then why haven't you set a wedding date?"

"You're sounding like my father, Reed. It doesn't suit you."

"I just bet Mr. Taylor is wondering when the wedding of the century will take place."

He was right about that, but she wasn't going to tell him so. Her father was relentless about this wedding. He'd even gone so far as suggesting a date. Fortunately, Dexter had told him that the wedding was their business, not his. "Well, Daddy is not getting married—*I* am."

"I'm glad you realize that."

Paige straightened her back. "And what's that supposed to mean?"

"Nothing, Paige," Reed said. "I'll let you go to sleep now."

"You can't just say something like that and go to sleep."

"It's past our bedtime. We're starting to exchange lines."

"Chicken," she challenged.

"You don't want to hear this, Paige," he warned.

"You're just too scared to say it," she taunted.

"Paige . . ."

"Out with it, Reed."

"Okay, you asked for it. I think your father is more in love with Mr. Fine than you are."

"What kind of sick comment is that?"

"You know what I'm talking about."

She took a deep breath. "So you think I'm marrying Dexter out of some sick need for my father's approval?"

Reed clapped his hands and gave a hollow laugh. "Give that woman a banana."

"You think I'm that immature? How can you stand to be around me, then?"

"I don't think you're immature," he explained. "Confused, maybe."

"Thanks for your confidence in me."

Reed tugged on the covers again. "It's not that. I understand exactly where you are. It's the same place I was, until I left McCurdy and McCurdy. I was always trying to do the right thing. But then I decided I'd rather be happy. I think you're still trying to do the right thing. And I want you to be happy."

"You don't think Dexter will make me happy?"

Reed snorted. "Not in this lifetime."

"Well, I disagree. Dexter and I will have a great life."

"What you'll have is the longest engagement in history, and then marriage to a guy who'll have you bored out of your mind in less than a week."

Five

Reed rolled onto his stomach in an attempt to get away from the annoying tug at his arm. He just wanted to sleep. God knew it had taken him long enough to fall asleep on the hard floor of Paige's apartment.

"Get up, Reed," the annoying voice said again. Reed wanted nothing more than to clasp his fingers around those lips the way he'd clasp a bug.

"Go away," Reed said. "I'm trying to sleep."

Now she was tugging on his arm. "Get up. I told Grandma Lewis that we were going for a morning run."

Figuring she wasn't going to give up, Reed turned over onto his back.

Paige's smiling face was the first thing he saw. She was so beautiful, her face freshly scrubbed and her hair pulled back in a ponytail. His complaints almost fell away. Almost. "You know I go to the gym at the end of the day, not at the beginning. I'm not going running."

Paige tweaked his nose like he was some naughty nine-year-old. "Yes, you are. Now, hurry and get dressed. I like to get in at least five miles before breakfast."

Five miles! Reed wasn't into running. He much preferred lifting weights at the gym. Besides, he ran around all day. His body didn't seem to need more. "Well, you go ahead and do your miles. I'll stay here with Big Momma."

In her squatting position, Paige rocked back and forth on her heels. Reed wanted to reach out and rub his hand down one of her taut brown thighs. Those calves were appealing, too. "You probably couldn't keep up with me, anyway," she challenged.

Reed responded to the twinkle in her eyes. Was his old Paige resurfacing? "With one leg, Paige. I could outrun you if I had only one leg."

"Big talk." She grinned at him, her large eyes filled with teasing challenge.

Reed knew he was doing what she wanted him to do, but he didn't care. Now, he wanted to do it, too. "Give me ten minutes." He threw back the covers, jumped up from his pallet and made his way to the bathroom.

He was back facing Paige in a few minutes. Not missing her quick appraisal of his form, he caught her eye. "See something you like?"

She smiled. "Yes."

Hot damn! he thought. Maybe he was getting somewhere.

"Where'd you get those running shoes?" she asked. "I thought you weren't a runner."

Well, hell, he thought again. Maybe he wasn't getting anywhere. He lifted three fingers to his forehead. "I was a Boy Scout, and I'm always prepared."

She sauntered toward the door, giving him time to view her perfectly rounded bottom perched atop her long, lean legs. "Let's go, boy scout. It's time you earned a merit badge or two."

Reed followed after her. They warmed up on the stairs of her building before starting a leisurely jog down the sidewalk. When it seemed to him they had been running for hours, he asked, "How much farther?"

"We're almost at the halfway mark. How are you holding up?"

He needed oxygen and a minute or two to catch his breath, but he wasn't going to let Paige know that. "Okay." He could only muster one word. He had to conserve his energy. The feeling in his legs gave new meaning to the word "watery."

"Good," was her only reply, but it seemed that she'd picked up her pace. He had to go deep to find the reserve to keep up with her. There was no way he'd be able to keep up this pace until they made it back home.

"Ouch," he said, moving off the sidewalk and plopping down on the grass.

A good ten feet ahead of him, Paige turned, continuing to run in place. "What's wrong?" she asked, running back to him.

Reed unlaced his sneakers and pulled off his socks. "I think it's my toe. I must have put too much weight on it too soon."

Paige didn't stop running in place. "Why didn't you just say you were tired? You didn't have to come up with a lame story about your toe."

Reed wasn't going to admit to anything. "Believe what you want, Paige. I know what I feel. You can keep running. I'll meet you back at the apartment later." He looked around with what he hoped was a pain-filled expression. "I hope I don't have to take a cab."

Paige dropped down on the grass next to him and gave a burst of laughter. The sound made the morning seem brighter to Reed.

"You're not in as good a shape as you thought, are you?"

Reed continued to rub his foot. "I haven't gotten any complaints on my physical condition."

Paige pulled her knees up to her chest and clasped her arms around them. "Hey, your body looks pretty good now, but I don't want to think about you five, ten years from now."

Reed pulled up his T-shirt and patted his hand across his washboard-flat stomach. "I don't think you should worry. I'm good for ten years, at least."

Paige got up and began to run in place. "Don't get too cocky, Reed. You know what they say, washboard today, beer belly tomorrow." She turned and resumed her jog.

No, suggesting the jog had not been a good idea, Paige thought, slowing her pace. She knew that now. She'd questioned the wisdom of asking him as soon as he'd turned over and looked up at her. She'd been convinced of it when he'd lifted his T-shirt.

He was one fine brother. That was one of the first things she'd thought when she'd met him. She'd often wondered what would have happened if they hadn't worked together.

Paige picked up her pace and tried to clear her mind of such thoughts. She was engaged to Dexter. She was going to be Mrs. Fine. Reed was her friend, and she wanted to keep his friendship, so that's what she should concentrate on.

When she reached the steps of her apartment building, she did her cool-down and dropped down onto the steps to wait for Reed. He hadn't been fooling her with that "hurt toe" excuse.

She smiled. The brother just couldn't keep up with her.

Willie Pearl was sitting on the side of the bed, putting on her shoes, when she heard the phone. She let it ring a couple of times, hoping Paige or Reed had gotten back from their morning jog and one of them would answer it.

She knew they weren't back yet when the answering machine picked up.

"Paige, it's your father. I thought you'd be back from your run . . ."

Willie Pearl picked up the phone. "Hello," she said, then she realized she didn't know his name.

"Who's this?" Paige's father asked.

"Willie Pearl Lewis, Reed's grandmother. It's so good to talk to you, ah, Mr. Taylor. It's a shame our families haven't met."

"Reed Lewis's grandmother?" Mr. Taylor asked.

"Of course," she replied. "Who else would I be?" Willie Pearl didn't know what to make of Mr. Taylor's response. She was beginning to think he was not a nice man. He hadn't even told her his first name. "Paige is a lovely girl. I know she'll make my grandson a happy man."

"A happy man?" Mr. Taylor practically yelled the question. "Where's Paige? Put her on the phone now."

Now Willie Pearl *knew* he wasn't a nice man. Mr. Taylor was pushing her a bit too far. She began to feel a little sorry for Paige, if the child had grown up with such an ornery father. "Paige and Reed went running this morning. They're not back yet."

"Paige and Reed?" Mr. Lewis yelled again. "Where's Dexter?"

"There's no need for you to yell, Mr. Taylor," Willie Pearl said. "I can hear. Who's Dexter, anyway?"

"Who's Dexter?" Mr. Taylor repeated.

Willie Pearl was about to repeat her question when she heard the door open, followed by the voices of Reed and Paige. "Hold on a minute, Mr. Taylor. Paige and Reed just got back. I'll get her for you."

Willie Pearl placed the receiver on the nightstand and walked out to meet Reed and Paige.

"Good morning, Grandma Lewis," Paige said.

Reed greeted her with a kiss. "Good morning, Big Momma."

"Good morning." She looked at Paige. "Your father is on the phone and he's upset about something. You'd better talk to him. He seemed to get angry, then he asked about someone named Dexter."

Paige shot a quick glance at Reed before rushing into her bedroom. She heard Grandma Lewis ask Reed, "Who is Dexter?" before she closed the door and walked to the bed.

Taking a seat, Paige lifted the receiver, held it to her heart while she took a deep breath, and then, once she was calm, she spoke. "Good morning, Daddy," she said, glad that the words came out smoothly.

"What the hell is going on there, Paige?" her father asked. "What is Reed's grandmother doing in your apartment? And what is she talking about—you'll make *Reed* happy? Why were you out running with Reed? I thought your friendship with Reed was over, anyway. Has Dexter gotten back from L.A. yet?"

Paige rolled her eyes to the ceiling while her father rattled off his questions. It was just like him. He always had to be in control, always had to know everything.

"Are you going to answer me, Paige?"

She released the breath she had been holding. "I'm feeling very well, Daddy. I'm glad you asked. How are you and Mom?"

"Damn it, Paige," her father began. "I'm sorry. I'm fine and your mother's fine. Now, what about my questions?"

"It was good seeing you two over Christmas. I know Dexter enjoyed himself."

Her father laughed. "If you weren't so much like me, Princess," he said, "I don't think we'd get along."

Paige laughed, too. She loved her father and she knew he loved her, but sometimes she had to set boundaries with him. She found that difficult to do at times, since she cherished his approval. Still, she was able to manage it . . . most of the time. "I hope you weren't mean to Grandma Lewis," Paige said.

Her father cleared his throat. "I could have been a bit more cordial," he confessed. "She caught me off-guard with her comment about you making her grandson happy."

Her father didn't say any more, but Paige knew he was dying to repeat his earlier questions. "If you agree to apologize to her, I'll tell you what's going on. But you have to agree."

"I'm an attorney, Paige. No deal until I know the details."

"Fine," Paige said. "No deal."

The older man laughed again. "You win, counselor. I'll apologize."

Paige smiled again. "Reed and his grandmother are staying with me because his apartment is flooded."

He gave a "humph." "I know public defenders don't make much, but Lewis ought to have enough money for a hotel room. Why is he staying at your place?"

Paige explained the ruse she and Reed were playing.

"You're *what?"* her father exclaimed. "I don't believe this. What does Dexter have to say about it?"

What does Dexter have to say about it? Paige repeated in her mind. Why did her father always think about Dexter first? "There's nothing for him *to* say. Reed and his grandmother will be gone before Dexter gets back from L.A. Don't make a big deal out of it. I'm just doing a favor for a friend."

"I don't know, Paige . . ."

"Well, I do," she interrupted. "Now, put Mom on the phone

so I can say hello. And don't run away. You still have to apologize to Grandma Lewis."

"Who's Dexter?" Big Momma asked again.

It took all of Reed's will to pull his gaze from Paige's bedroom door. More than anything he wanted to know what she was telling her father. He shrugged his shoulders. He'd just have to wait until she came out.

"So, who is he?" Big Momma asked for the third time.

"Dexter? Oh, he's a friend of Paige's."

Big Momma's eyes widened in question. "Why would Mr. Taylor ask about him? Why, he seemed more interested in this Dexter than he did in you or me."

Reed smiled like it was nothing. "You have to get to know Mr. Taylor. He's a gruff kind of guy. He thought Dexter was better suited for Paige than me." At least that part was true, Reed thought. "He hasn't given up on the two of them getting together."

"Even though Paige is engaged to you?"

Reed shrugged. Lying to his grandmother made him uncomfortable. "He'll come around. I know he loves Paige. He just has to understand that I love her, too."

Big Momma nodded. "Is that why you haven't had them out to meet the family? That has kind of bothered me, Reed. You're engaged and no one in the family has met your fiancée. The two families need to meet and get to know each other."

And they would have met if he and Paige had really been engaged. He'd love to bring her home with him so she could see where he grew up, so she could better appreciate who he was. He knew his mother and father would love her, just as he'd known Big Momma would love her. And Tom. Tom would flirt outrageously, but then, that's what little brothers did. Soon, he thought. Soon he'd be able to introduce Paige to his family and to the world as his fiancée. He knew it. "We'll get together, Big Momma. I promise. Paige and I will have a lifetime together."

Six

"I told Reed we need to get the families together, " Grandma Lewis was saying.

Standing next to Grandma Lewis, Paige couldn't hear her father's response, but she was confident he was appropriately non-committal. Grandma Lewis's nod confirmed it.

"Excuse me, Matthew," Grandma said, "seems like Paige has another call coming in." Grandma Lewis nodded again. "I understand if you have to go. I can't wait to meet you and your wife." Grandma Lewis smiled, nodded again, then handed the receiver to Paige.

Paige quickly pressed the switchhook. "Hello," she said. She handed the phone to Grandma Lewis. "It's for you."

"For me?" Grandma Lewis asked, reaching for the phone.

Paige nodded. "It's Ida Mae Thompson."

"Hi, Ida Mae," Grandma Lewis said into the phone. "I'm doing fine." She looked up at Paige and smiled. "You just have to meet my new granddaughter."

Paige returned her smile before backing toward the door and leaving the room, closing the door behind her.

"How did Mr. Taylor handle it?" Reed asked, before she had closed the door good.

She saw the concern in his eyes. "Don't worry, Reed. It's okay. I know how to handle my father."

"I guess I'd better get dressed, then," he said. "I want to take Big Momma for a ride to the country. I've got something to show her." He paused. "Do you want to come with us? I think you'd like my treat for Big Momma as much as she will."

"I don't know," Paige said. "Where are you going and what are you showing Grandma Lewis?"

"It's a surprise."

The twinkle in Reed's eyes made Paige smile. Though she wanted to go, she shook her head and turned away. "I don't know—" There was something about the look in his eyes that made her very uncomfortable.

Reed touched her shoulder to turn her around. "Come with us," he pleaded. "You'll love it." When she would have given another objection, he added, "Do it for Big Momma."

Paige didn't hold back the smile that spread across her face. "You don't play fair, Reed Lewis."

He tapped a finger to the tip of her nose. "We public defenders can hold our own with you hotshot private-practice guys, and don't you forget it."

It took all of Reed's legal training and control to keep his secret for the one-hour drive to his surprise. His emotions were mixed. He wanted Paige to love it, and he was pretty confident she would. But what if she didn't? No, he said to himself, he wouldn't think that way. She'd love it.

The smell of her perfume and the sound of her laughter surrounded him. Though Paige had wanted Big Momma to sit up front with him so she could "see the sights better," Big Momma wouldn't hear of it. She'd taken her seat in the back, forcing Paige to sit in the front with Reed.

Paige was turned around in her seat so she could talk with Big Momma. It warmed Reed's heart that the two most important women in his life had fallen in love with each other so quickly. But then, he'd expected that.

"You can't convince him to tell us where we're going?" Big Momma asked Paige.

Paige looked over at him. "Tell us, Reed. We've been driving for a long time. Where are we going?"

Reed kept his eyes on the road. He didn't trust himself to look at her. "I'm not telling."

Paige turned back to Big Momma and shrugged. "No luck. I guess we'll have to wait."

"I don't think you're trying hard enough, Paige. Reed's grandfather could never keep a secret from me. Womanly wiles and all that."

Paige's mouth dropped open and Reed laughed. "Don't give her any ideas, Big Momma. I have to keep my attention on my driving."

Reed took a quick glance at Paige. The shade of red that colored her face made him laugh again. He patted her on her thigh. "That's for going easy on me, sweetheart."

When Paige placed her hand on Reed's to remove it from her thigh, he turned his hand over and clasped hers. He picked up both their hands and rubbed her cheek with the back of his. "I love it when you blush," he said.

For a second, Paige was trapped again in the game she and Reed were playing for Grandma Lewis. God, he did seem sincere.

She wondered if he was as affected by this charade as she was. She certainly hoped so, but the look in his eyes told her he was in complete control. She didn't like that.

She pulled their hands down from her face and turned them over so that his was facing her. She pulled his hand to her lips and kissed each knuckle with the tip of her tongue. His skin was warm to her touch. When she caught the look in his eyes again, it, too, had grown warmer. She smiled, satisfied now that she wasn't the only one uncomfortable. She leaned over and brushed her lips across Reed's. "Where are we going, sweetie?" she asked again.

Reed opened his mouth to tell her, but his grandmother's laughter from the back seat stopped him. "You're good, granddaughter," Big Momma said, still laughing. "And all it took was one kiss." She laughed again. "You're weaker than your grandfather, Reed. It took at least two kisses before *he'd* spill the beans."

Paige shifted back to her side of the car. She was smiling, but there was a question in her eyes. What was it? Reed wanted to ask. But Big Momma's presence stopped him. He could only hope that her kiss had affected her half as much as it had affected him.

A few minutes later, he turned off the main highway onto a tree-lined dirt road. "We're almost there. You two can stop with your plotting."

Reed drove down the road for about a mile before Paige saw the clearing surrounded by the dense pine trees. He heard her "Aghh" and he knew she was going to love it. "Have you two figured it out yet?"

Big Momma piped up from the back seat. "My guess is somebody is getting ready to build a house."

Reed drove the car off the road onto the clearing and parked. "You're right about that, Big Momma. Do you think my lady likes it?"

"I don't know, sonny," Big Momma said, opening the door so she could get out of the car. "You have a fifty-fifty chance. Some women like to be included in picking out the site for their home. I have a feeling you and Paige need a little privacy." With that, Big Momma got out of the car and walked toward the spot Reed had picked for the home he wanted to share with Paige.

He looked over at Paige. Her hands were clasped in her lap and her eyes were focused straight ahead. She hadn't said anything beyond her first moan. "So, do you like it?"

"Are you going to build a house here?" she asked, still looking straight ahead.

Reed turned sideways in his seat, willing her to do the same. She didn't. "I want to," he said simply.

"When did you buy the property?"

Uneasiness rose up in Reed. "I've had an option on it for a while. There hasn't been much activity in the area until now. I have to make a decision by the first of the year." She was silent. "What do you think?"

She looked at him. Maybe stared at him was a better description. The look on her face was stern. Then, all of a sudden, she smiled. "I love it." She turned, opened the car door, and ran out to Big Momma, whom she pulled into her arms and gave a big hug.

Reed watched the women from his seat in the car. He smiled. Paige had remembered. And she was happy. Things were definitely looking up.

Paige needed the feel of Grandma Lewis's arms right now. Her emotions were definitely on the road to taking over. What was going on here? Why had Reed chosen this site?

Paige almost pulled away when Reed came up behind her and wrapped an arm around her waist. His whispered *"Remember, we're engaged"* stopped her, causing her to smile at him instead.

"This sure is a pretty piece of land, sonny," Grandma Lewis said.

"I knew you'd like it," Reed said, squeezing Paige's waist with his hand. When she looked up at him, he just shrugged his shoulders and mouthed, *We're engaged.*

"How do you like your surprise, Paige? Do you think you'll like living out here, or are you a city girl?"

Paige felt Reed tense up. "I think I've always been a country girl at heart, Grandma Lewis. When I was younger, I spent every summer with my grandmother in Alabama. She lived in a big house in the country." She looked up at Reed and silent words of understanding passed between them. "The spot was something like this."

Grandma Lewis smiled. "I guess that means you're happy with my grandson's surprise."

Paige placed her hand across the one Reed rested on her waist. "Very happy. Reed couldn't have picked a better surprise."

She felt Reed's lips touch the top of her head and the sensation went straight through to the tips of her toes. She had to get out of his grasp. "Are you up for a tour of the property, Grandma Lewis?" Paige asked, reaching for the older woman's hands.

Grandma Lewis shook her head. "I don't think so, dear. I'm content just to sit here." She pointed at a tree stump. "You two walk around. I'll be fine until you get back."

Paige wished she hadn't suggested the tour, but she knew she couldn't get out of it now. She was going to miss Grandma Lewis's presence. Somehow, it helped to keep her emotions in check.

"Let's go," Reed said, urging her forward. "There's a lot to see."

Paige nodded and let Reed lead her on a tour. She saw the sights, but her thoughts were more consumed with Reed. When had he started wearing that cologne? She'd never noticed it before. She wondered what it was. And his clothes. The soft wool covering the hard muscles made her want to burrow herself into his arms.

"So what do you really think?" Reed asked.

They were standing at a lake about 300 feet from the clearing for the house. "I think it's beautiful, but I can't believe you're going to live out here all by yourself."

He dropped his hand from around her waist. "What makes you think I'll be by myself? Maybe I'll be married by the time the house is finished and I'm ready to move in."

Married? She'd never heard Reed talk about marriage before. "So, this," she spread her hands to indicate the area, "isn't just for Grandma Lewis's benefit."

He shook his head. "Like I said, I've had an option on the property for a while. If things go the way I plan, I'll be giving a yes answer on January first."

Paige was afraid to ask about his plans. Instead, she nodded and began walking along the bank of the lake. Reed followed her. "You're making a lot of changes in your life, aren't you?" she asked after a while.

Reed plopped down on the bank, careless of the natural-colored denim slacks he wore. Paige was tempted to sit next to him, but chose instead to stand.

"I'm growing up, Paige," he said simply.

"What do you mean by that?"

He picked up a blade of dried grass. "I know what I want, and now I'm going after it. No more playing the field, trying everything just for kicks."

She nodded. "Going to the PD's office was just your first step, huh?"

He threw the blade of grass toward the water. "Something like that."

She remained silent.

"Do you know what you want, Paige?" he asked.

She didn't answer. "Your grandmother's waiting. We'd better get back." She turned and walked back to the clearing where Grandma Lewis was seated.

Reed watched Paige drink her hot chocolate. He smiled at the whipped cream that settled around her lips. She must have noticed his smile, because her eyes widened and her tongue slipped out of her mouth to lick the cream away.

The sight of her tongue caused Reed's thoughts to go back to the kisses they'd shared. He'd felt that tongue in his mouth and he wanted to feel it again. He wanted to taste her again. He wondered what a kiss would taste like after the hot chocolate. Then he thought about strawberries and champagne. That's what he wanted. He wanted Paige. Naked. In bed with him. And strawberries. He'd dip one in the champagne, put it in his mouth, and share it with her. He'd clean the juice that rolled from the corners of her mouth with his lips. And when she finished the berry, he'd kiss her, savoring her taste and that of the berry. Then . . .

"Reed," Paige was saying. "We're talking to you and you're miles away. What were you thinking about?"

"Just dreaming," Reed said. That was true. "What were you saying?"

"Do you want to play another game?" Grandma Lewis repeated.

"Not me. I'm beat," Reed said, looking at the Afronopoly board in front of him. Paige had suggested the game, the African American version of Monopoly.

Grandma Lewis stood up. "Not me. I want to call Ida Mae before I go to bed. I have to tell her about the house you two are going to build."

Paige closed the Afronopoly board and put it back in the box along with the game pieces. "Tell Mrs. Thompson I said hi," Paige said. "I'd love to meet her. The next time you come to visit, you'll have to bring her with you."

Grandma Lewis practically beamed. "Ida Mae'll love that." She went over and kissed Paige on the cheek. "You are a sweetheart. And the drive today was a lot of fun. Thanks for suggesting that we go downtown and see the Christmas lights at night. It was beautiful." With that, Grandma Lewis turned and went to her bedroom.

"That was nice of you," Reed said. "But it could present a problem."

Paige put the cover on the game box. "How's that?"

He pointed to the Lewis engagement ring on her finger. "She thinks we're engaged, Paige."

"Oh," she said. "I forgot." As soon as she said the words, she realized how silly they sounded. How could she forget the game they were playing?

"I forget sometimes, too," Reed said softly.

Paige looked over at him. He was too attractive for his own good. And too sweet. First, the ring. Now, the house. Reed was doing a number on her. She wondered if he knew it. "We've been friends a long time, Reed."

"Best friends," he clarified.

She heard the "Until Mr. Fine," though the words did not pass his lips. Before she could make a response, the phone rang. She picked it up in time to hear Grandma Lewis say, "Hello, Taylor residence."

"Who's this?" was Dexter's gruff response.

Paige looked quickly at Reed before standing up and turning her back to him. "It's for me, Grandma Lewis," she said, glad Dexter had called before Grandma Lewis got on the phone with Ida Mae. She didn't want to think what conversation would have passed between Dexter and Grandma Lewis if she'd beeped him in at the call-waiting tone.

"Okay, dear," Grandma Lewis said.

Paige waited for the click of Grandma Lewis replacing the receiver before speaking. "How are you, Dexter?"

"Who's Grandma Lewis?"

Paige thought for the hundredth time that Dexter was too much like her father. "I've missed you, too, Dexter," she said. As she spoke the words, she felt Reed's eyes boring into her back. She didn't want to think about Reed now. Her fiancé was on the phone.

Dexter was apologetic, as she expected. But once the pleasantries were over, he was back to his question. "Who's Grandma Lewis?"

Paige considered the question and decided a direct answer was best.

"What? Reed Lewis and his grandmother are staying in your apartment? Where is he sleeping?"

"I resent that question, Dexter. I expect you to trust me," Paige said, her hands fisted.

She could imagine Dexter pinching his nose. "Paige," he said slowly, "sometimes you can be so naive. It's not that I don't trust you. Don't you know that Reed Lewis has the hots for you and always has?"

That statement surprised Paige. "Dexter, Reed and I are friends. We've been friends forever."

"Like I said, you can be naive sometimes. Think about it, Paige."

"You're either going to trust me, Dexter, or you're not. It's up to you."

Dexter sighed. "Okay, Paige, you win. Again."

Seven

Reed got up from the sofa and ambled into the kitchen. He took a glass from the cabinet and opened the refrigerator. So, Fine had finally decided to call. It was about time. And the jerk had the nerve to give Paige grief about him and his grandmother being here. Well, Paige should be giving him grief about deserting her during the holidays. Reed grabbed the orange juice carton from the top shelf, opened it, and filled his glass. He put the carton back in the refrigerator, closed the door, and leaned back against it while he drank the full glass in one gulp.

He could hear Paige on the phone, though he couldn't make out her words, since she spoke in soft, hushed tones. He hated to think of her sharing intimate conversation with Dexter. He was not going back into the great room until she hung up.

As he stood there in the kitchen, he wondered again at his plan. He knew he was having an effect on Paige, but he couldn't measure the extent of the effect. He should have kissed her earlier today. The timing had been perfect, but he hadn't taken advantage of it. Why, he asked himself, hadn't he kissed her?

Though he asked himself the question, he knew the answer. He hadn't kissed her because he wanted her to want him as much as he wanted her. He didn't want something stolen, something she would regret later. If he had kissed her today, it would have been a kiss of acknowledged passion, and he didn't think she was ready for that. But she'd be ready soon; he was sure of it.

"That was Dexter." Paige stood in the entrance to the kitchen, her hands in the pockets of her jeans.

Reed placed his empty glass on the counter next to him. "I know. I gather he's upset."

Paige shrugged, hands still in her pockets. "You know Dexter."

Reed only grunted. "So. When's Mr. Fine coming home?"

"He should be back tomorrow or the day after."

Reed straightened up from his position. "Wonder why he's cutting his business short."

Paige went to the refrigerator, opened it, and pulled out the orange juice carton. Reed got a glass from the cabinet and held it for her. "Was it because *we're* here?"

Paige poured her juice. Should she tell Reed what Dexter had said about him having the "hots" for her? "That's part of it."

She placed the juice carton back in the refrigerator and closed the door. Reed handed her the glass of juice. "And what's the other part?" he asked.

"Dexter thinks you could have, how can I say this, more-than-friendly thoughts toward me." Paige dropped down in one of the kitchen chairs.

Reed took the chair next to her. "And what do you think?"

Paige ran her finger around the top of her juice glass. "We're friends, Reed. That's what I told Dexter."

"Friends." Reed repeated the word as if it were dirty. "And what if I wanted to be more than friends?"

Paige looked at him. "But we decided . . ."

"I know what we decided." Reed jumped up out of his seat. "But that was then and this is now, so answer the question. What if I want to be more than friends?"

Why was he asking her this now? What did he want from her? "I'm engaged, Reed."

"Tell me something I don't know," he said, taking his seat at the table again. "You still didn't answer my question."

Paige could slap herself for not telling Reed straight out that there was no chance for them. She was engaged, for God's sake.

So why hadn't she told him? She knew why. She hadn't told him because she was tempted. Tempted to think about a life with Reed. As a friend. As a lover.

Reed. She shook her head. When she hadn't answered his question, he'd strutted out of the kitchen like she'd just said she was in love with him. God, she'd never be able to keep him in line now. Maybe she didn't want to.

She climbed into the sofabed, having already placed Reed's blankets and pillows on the floor for him. She closed her eyes and prayed he wouldn't want to talk when he finished in the bathroom.

Fifteen minutes later, she heard him enter the room. She held herself very still, hoping he'd think she was asleep. She didn't want to talk tonight. She needed to think, to decide what she wanted to do.

She could feel him looking down at her while she pretended sleep. For a moment, she hoped he would lean over and kiss her goodnight, but he didn't. He clicked off the light and slid into his bed. It was going to be a long night.

Paige woke earlier than usual the next morning. She'd tossed and turned all night. It was a wonder she hadn't kept Reed up right along with her.

She jumped out of bed with forced enthusiasm and dressed for her morning run. She decided not to wake Reed. No, this morning she needed time to herself. Maybe the cool morning air would help clear her head.

When she got back to the apartment an hour later, nothing was clearer, but she did feel refreshed.

"You didn't wait for me this morning," Reed said, as soon as she entered the apartment.

She slipped off her jacket and placed it on the back of the sofa. *I needed some time away from you.* "I didn't want you to risk hurting your foot again."

Reed lifted a brow to indicate his disbelief. "Thanks for the consideration."

She flopped down on the sofa, propped her feet up on the coffee table, and closed her eyes. "Don't mention it."

Reed sat next to her and propped his feet up on the coffee table, too.

She opened one eye. "Take your feet off the table, Reed."

Reed looked at her. "Your feet are up there."

She closed her eye. "You keep forgetting that this is *my* apartment, so take your feet down."

He mumbled something unintelligible and she didn't bother to ask him to repeat it. Then she heard him remove his feet from the table.

"You're going to make a lousy parent," he said clearly.

Again, she opened an eye. "What makes you say that?"

He pointed at her feet propped on the furniture. "Because you have to teach by example. You can't go around telling your kids, 'Do as I say, not as I do.' "

She closed her eyes. "You're right, but there's one thing you've forgotten."

"What?"

"You're not a child, and I'm not your parent."

Reed mumbled again. "Do you want children, Paige?"

She hadn't expected the question. "Sure."

"How many?"

She shrugged her shoulders. "I don't know, three or four sound good."

The picture of a pregnant Paige floated through his mind and caused his groin to tighten. "Three or four. By today's standards, that's quite a few."

"So? I like children and I think I'd be a good parent."

"And you think Mr. Fine will be a good father?"

That question irritated her, because her feelings on the matter were mixed. She knew the kind of father Dexter would be. She was certain he'd be exactly like her father. Exactly. She hadn't quite decided if that was good or bad. Not that her father wasn't a good parent; he was. He was just so demanding, so controlling.

"It's taking you too long to reply. I think I know the answer."

"Then I guess I don't need to reply." Paige kept thinking about Dexter as a parent. The two of them had discussed the role she would play in their children's upbringing, but they hadn't discussed his at any length. She hoped he'd cut back on his work obligations, but deep inside she knew that was a futile wish. Again, Dexter was too much like her father. Work would always come first.

Of course, Dexter would never admit that, and neither would her father. Their answer was, "I'm working *for* my family, so the family comes first, not the work." Paige had heard that logic many times when she was growing up. And though she was certain her father loved her, she wished she'd had more of his time. Then, maybe she wouldn't have had to try so hard to win his attention by doing things to make him proud.

"I want kids, too," Reed said, interrupting her thoughts. "I could deal with five or six, myself."

Paige opened both eyes then. "Good luck finding a woman willing to have that many for you. God, Reed, the woman will have to stay pregnant."

Reed smiled what she could only term a masculine grin. "Hey, in order for her to stay pregnant, she has to keep getting pregnant. I don't have a problem with that. No siree, I don't have a problem with that at all."

Paige sneered. "Just like a man. Sometimes, you can be so crude."

"What are you getting so upset about? It's not like we haven't talked about sex before."

Paige knew that, but right now the idea of Reed making love with some other woman made her angry. She didn't want to picture him in bed with some woman, his strong arms wrapped around her, his mouth covering hers, his body atop hers, his manhood inside her. No, Paige didn't want to think about that.

She knew her emotion was unreasonable, but it was how she felt. "That was then. This is now."

"What's the problem?"

The problem was that when Paige closed her eyes, she didn't see Reed with some other woman, she saw Reed with her, his strong arms wrapped around her, his mouth covering hers, his body atop hers, his manhood inside her. She could even feel . . .

She jumped up from her seat on the sofa, hoping those thoughts would leave her mind. "Look, I'm going to shower and get dressed."

Reed watched Paige pick up her jacket and go into the bedroom, but his thoughts were still on her, pregnant with their child. As soon as the bedroom door closed behind her, he switched to thoughts of getting her pregnant.

God, they'd be good together; he just knew it. When he recalled how heated their arguments used to be, he knew their lovemaking would be even more heated. Yes, Paige would be great in his bed. That hard-soft athletic body of hers would definitely keep him up for the night. And he'd do his best to keep her satisfied. He smiled at the thought.

He could see her face in climax in his mind. It was heady to think she would trust him enough to let go totally. But that was what he wanted. He wanted her under him. He also wanted her to love him and to trust him. He had been around long enough to know that love and trust would take their lovemaking to heights he could only imagine.

As always, when he thought about Paige, his body began to react. He longed for the day when he wouldn't have to "deal with it" or "work it out." No, he wanted his sexual desire for her to be quenched by burying himself inside her. But the time for that had not arrived. Yet.

He grabbed his jacket from the hall closet. He needed a long run this morning.

* * *

"I don't know what happened," Willie Pearl said over the phone to her friend Ida Mae. "Things were great when I went to bed last night, but dinner tonight . . . I don't know."

"Willie Pearl, don't worry too much about them young folks. They'll work it out if they're as much in love as you say they are."

"I don't know." Willie Pearl sighed. "I just wish there was something I could do. They're such a good couple. Reed has needed someone like Paige in his life for a long time. And from the looks of things, Paige has needed him. I don't want them to mess it up. You know how foolish the young can be."

Ida Mae laughed. "We were young once and we didn't turn out too bad."

That was true, Willie Pearl thought. Ida Mae had been married more than fifty years when her man, Harry, had died. And she and Grady had been wed more than sixty years. "I hope these two are as smart as we were."

"They are." Ida Mae cleared her throat.

"What is it, Ida Mae? When you clear your throat, it means you have something else to say. Go ahead, say it."

"You promise you won't get mad at me?" Ida Mae asked in a soft voice.

Willie Pearl sighed. Ida Mae always did this, and it almost drove her batty. "I won't get mad. I promise."

"Well, ah, they could be frustrated."

"I don't see why," Willie Pearl explained. "I told them that I didn't sleep with my hearing aid. They can do all the courting they want to after I go to bed."

Ida Mae cleared her throat again.

"What is it, Ida Mae?"

"Courting means more today than it did when we were young."

"Come on out with it, Ida Mae," Willie Pearl said.

"You know . . . sex."

Willie Pearl was quiet while she considered that statement.

"Well, I see what you mean, Ida Mae. Do you really think that could be the problem?"

"Think about you and Grady when you were courting."

"Grady and I never—you know, before we were married."

"Neither did Harry and I, but times have changed, Willie Pearl, and besides, they *are* engaged."

"I guess you're right, Ida Mae. And that being the case, they're going to have to stay frustrated, because I'm not going anywhere."

Eight

He loomed above her and his gaze met hers. He was asking for permission. Her mouth couldn't form any words, so she reached up and pulled his head down to hers. When his lips met hers, she knew she had made the right decision. This was right. They were right together.

His tongue teasingly coaxed her lips apart and slipped into her mouth. The invasion, if you could call it that, was sweet. Her surrender was total.

While he ravaged her mouth, her hands explored his body. He felt so good, so different from her. Where she was soft, he was hard. Except for his hair. It was soft, babysoft to touch. And that contrast to the feel of his hard body pressed against hers only made her want him closer.

Her hands moved down his back, feeling the flexing of his muscles. It was a heady feeling to know she was the cause of his arousal, to know his desire for her caused him to tremble and shake.

Her hands moved further down to his tight buttocks. She squeezed them as best she could and was rewarded by a low moan from him. She smiled. This was what lovemaking was all about—pleasing each other.

Suddenly, he removed his mouth from hers. She leaned up in bed to follow him. She wasn't ready to let him go yet.

"It's all right," he said softly. "I'm not going anywhere."

He just leaned back into the night and looked at her nakedness. She was surprised that she didn't feel bashful. Quite the contrary: she felt wanton, wanted. The look of pleasure and desire in his eyes made her feel beautiful.

"You're beautiful," he said, as if he'd heard her thoughts. "So beautiful. I've waited so long for you. Too long."

He was beautiful, too, and she wanted to tell him, but she couldn't. She could only stare at him. The soft fur on his chest, the taunting arousal between his legs. This man was hers. And she was not letting him go until they'd shared the ultimate expression of love.

She lifted her arms to him. "Now, Reed," she said, finally able to speak.

Reed? The sound of her own voice woke Paige up. She was dreaming about Reed. *Oh, my God!*

She looked in his direction, but she couldn't see him in the dark. She hoped he was asleep and hadn't heard her call his name. She hoped all she'd said aloud was his name. She'd be mortified if he knew about her dream.

She held herself still for a good five minutes before releasing a sigh. *Thank God, he slept through it,* she said to herself.

She turned on her side but was afraid to close her eyes. She didn't know what picture she would see. Or maybe she knew which one she would see and she wasn't ready to deal with it. She turned onto her back and stared up into the dark.

"It's hard, isn't it?" came Reed's voice in the dark. His words caressed her skin, just as his hands had done in her dream.

"Why aren't you asleep?" she asked.

"I think you know the answer to that, Paige."

Did that mean he'd heard her in her sleep? God, she hoped not. "We did have a long day," she said.

"How long are you going to deny what's happening between us?" he asked. She heard the fabric of his blanket scrape against the carpet as he sat up.

She pulled the covers closer around her, trying in vain to protect herself from the emotions lying very near the surface of her being. "It's the close proximity and the role-playing. Things will get back to normal once your grandmother leaves."

She heard him get up from his pallet. He flicked on the light and sat down on the sofabed next to her. "That may be what it is for you, but it's more than that with me."

She sat up. She felt too vulnerable in her reclining position with him looking down at her. "Reed—"

His mouth against hers stopped her words. She knew she could break the kiss if she wanted to; she knew she should break it; but she couldn't. Maybe if she hadn't had the dream. But not after the dream. She wanted his kiss. And more . . . so much more.

When Reed pulled away from her, her lips trembled. "Was that role-playing?" he asked.

She looked down at her hands. "What are we doing, Reed?"

He put his finger to her chin and lifted her face. "I'm falling in love with you. What are you doing?"

Her heartbeat raced at his words. "We can't."

"Can't we?" He leaned in closer and captured her lips again. This time his hands joined in the action. He caressed her shoulders through the blue polka-dot granny gown she wore. At that moment she wished she'd worn something sexier, something easier to remove from her body.

Reed didn't seem too bothered, though. He caressed the skin around the collar of the gown. When his hand touched the top button, he gently slipped it free. He continued undoing the buttons until her breasts were within reach of his hands.

He broke the kiss, but before she could complain, he dropped his mouth to the tip of her right breast.

"Oh, God, Reed," she said, loving the feel of his lips against her nipples.

He moved from one breast to the other, tending to each as if it were a valued possession. While his lips tended her breasts, his hands slipped the gown from her shoulders and she was exposed to her waist.

When his hand slipped inside the waistband of her panties, she came to her senses. "Reed, we can't," she said, without much conviction. She wanted this as much as he did.

"Why can't we?" he asked, between nips at her breast.

She moaned again. *"Reed . . ."*

His hand slipped farther into her panties. When he touched her wetness, she knew she had to stop this before they went too far. "Grandma Lewis," Paige whispered. "She's in the next room. What if she gets up?"

Paige's words slowly penetrated Reed's mind and when they did, they were like a wet blanket on his desire. His grandmother was in the next room, for God's sake.

Reed pulled his mouth from her exposed breasts and dropped his head to rest against her warm cleavage. She felt so good. And it felt so right to be with her like this. Like he had come home.

The soft touch of her hands against his head, though nice, had to stop. "If you don't stop rubbing my head like that, Big Momma is going to wake up to some wonderful noises."

"Oh," he heard her say, and the rubbing stopped.

He smiled against her breasts, gave each one a final kiss, and lifted his head. For the sake of his sanity, he pulled her gown back up on her shoulders and buttoned it. "You're going to have to wear this gown for me again, after Big Momma leaves. You've definitely come up with a new definition for sexy," he teased, fiddling with the ruffle around her collar.

When she stopped the smile that threatened to spread across her face, every muscle in Reed's body tightened. "What is it, sweetheart?" he said.

"This shouldn't have happened," she said, in a voice so soft he almost didn't hear her.

"Oh, no, you don't," he said, pulling her into his arms again. "I'm not going to let you regret what just happened between us."

"But I'm an engaged woman, Reed."

He caressed her shoulders. "Maybe this means you're engaged to the wrong man."

* * *

Paige didn't want to get up for her run this morning. She wanted to stay in bed, cuddled up against Reed for as long as she could. There was something right about it. Something good.

After their long discussion of their feelings last night, he'd gathered her in his arms and held her. In a way, there was nothing sexual in his holding her, but in another way, it was purely sexual. She shook her head and smiled at herself. Did she have to analyze everything? Maybe Reed was right: she should just listen to her heart and forget the rest.

Yet she couldn't do that. She'd made a commitment to Dexter and she owed him the time it took to decide what she really wanted. And it didn't seem to her that making a quick decision to spend her life with Reed was the right thing to do.

Maybe Reed was right and she was engaged to the wrong man, but she wasn't going to end an engagement with one man and immediately go into an engagement with another one. She couldn't do that. Could she?

Whether she could or not, she wouldn't. She was going to give it time, to see where her feelings for Reed took her.

She snuggled back against him and he responded by tightening his arms around her. She smiled and went back to sleep.

Reed woke up happy, happier than he'd ever been. He had the woman of his dreams in his arms, and he was in her bed. This was the best vacation he'd ever had.

He turned his face into Paige's neck and inhaled her sweet, clean, fresh scent. Now that Paige knew his feelings and shared them, he could wait for the inevitable consummation of those feelings.

He knew Paige was unsure of herself, but that didn't scare him. He'd had months to come to grips with his feelings for her; she'd had less than a week. And she was engaged to another man.

He tightened his arms around her waist. He didn't like thinking about Fine. He couldn't wait for the day when Paige would give that guy his ring back. He smiled. She wasn't wearing Fine's anymore, anyway. She was wearing his ring. She even slept in it. He wondered if she knew she did, or if it was an unconscious move. It didn't matter to him which it was. He just knew it made him happy to see the ring there, to see that she had become attached to it in such a short time.

Reed knew he should get up and crawl back into his pallet, but he didn't want to leave Paige. He wished she would wake up so he could tell her again how much he loved her. "I love you, Paige Taylor," he whispered, needing to say the words even though she couldn't hear them.

The sound of the doorbell made Paige stir and caused Reed to hop out of bed. *Who could be visiting at this hour of the morning?* he wondered.

He grabbed his robe and headed for the door, thinking only to keep the intruder from waking Paige and his grandmother. "Just a minute," he whispered, when the bell rang again. He knew the intruder couldn't hear him, but he said the words anyway.

Reed unlocked the door and pulled it open.

And he came face-to-face with Dexter Fine.

Nine

"What the hell are you doing here?" Fine's loud voice filled the hallway. Reed looked back to make sure Paige was still asleep. She was.

Reed didn't know whether to laugh or slam the door in Fine's face. He chose not to do either. Instead, he chose to smirk. "Keep your voice down, Fine. You know what I'm doing here."

"Later for you, Lewis. Where's Paige?" Fine asked, lifting on his toes to look past Reed's shoulder. At that moment, Reed felt the psychological advantage his height gave him. And the fact that his wide build effectively prevented Fine from barging into the apartment did wonders for his ego.

Reed really didn't like the proprietary air that Fine had where Paige was concerned. Fine didn't own her. Not her body, and definitely not her heart. No, her heart belonged to him—even if she didn't know it yet. "Paige is asleep, Fine. Why don't you come back later? She should be up in about an hour or so."

"Like hell. I've come to see my fiancée, and I *will* see her," Fine challenged.

"Dexter, is that you?" came Paige's sleep-filled voice.

Reed turned around to speak to her and Fine took advantage of that moment to slip past him and into the apartment.

Fine stopped in his tracks when he saw Paige. "Paige?" Fine yelled.

Paige reached for her robe, but it was too late. Fine had already seen the incriminating evidence. Reed didn't know whether to feel sorry or glad that he'd so bungled the buttoning of her gown that she looked like she'd hurriedly tried to cover herself. From the look in Fine's eyes, he had put two and two together and come up with much more than what had happened between them last night.

Unable to think of anything else to do, Reed moved to stand protectively in front of Paige. "Don't yell at her. She's not a child."

Paige pushed him out of the way and glared at him. "And I can speak for myself, Reed." He was glad she had found her robe. He didn't like the idea of Fine looking at her in her gown.

"What's going on here, Paige?" Fine asked. It was obvious to Reed that Fine was doing all he could to keep a rein on his temper.

"Nothing," Paige said, with no conviction. "I already explained that Reed and his grandmother were staying here for a few days."

Fine's eyes moved deliberately from Paige to Reed, then back to Paige. His accusation was loud, though unspoken. "Where's *he* sleeping?"

Reed dropped down on the sofabed and Paige shot daggers at him with her eyes. "I really don't appreciate your attitude, Dexter, and under other circumstances I wouldn't answer that question. But I'll be generous this morning." She pointed to the sofabed. "I sleep here," she said. "And Reed sleeps on the floor over there." She pointed to the pallet with its rumpled covers.

Reed leaned back on the sofabed. He caught Fine's eye. No way was Fine buying Paige's story. Especially not with Reed leaning back on the sofa like he owned it.

"Reed," Paige said, causing him to take his eyes from Fine. "Dexter and I need a few minutes alone."

Reed sat up straight. Was she asking him to leave the room? "You can say whatever you need to say to him in front of me."

Before Paige could respond, Fine started yelling again. "What the hell is that ring on your finger? Where's your engagement ring?"

Reed couldn't help himself: he grinned. "Do you want me to explain that one to him, Paige?"

She frowned at him. "No, I do not," she said, punctuating each word.

Reed thought if she continued to frown at him like that, her facial expression would probably be set that way for life. Fortunately, she still looked adorable. He was smart enough not to tell her, though. *"Ex-cuse me,"* he said, with mock hurt in his voice. He reclined back on the sofabed and crossed his legs.

"You were telling me about the ring, Paige," Fine said, as if he were speaking to some child who couldn't understand complicated thoughts. Reed was amused that Fine had fallen back into a super-calm mode. Personally, he thought the guy needed to show passion. He knew he would if he were in Fine's shoes. Reed was convinced all over again that not only did Fine not deserve Paige, but he wouldn't know what to do with her once she was his.

Paige tightened the belt on her robe and crossed her arms in front of her. "I'm not answering any more questions."

"It's about time you put this guy in his place," Reed said.

She glared again. "I'm disappointed in you, Reed. Why are you trying so hard to make Dexter believe the worst? I thought you were my friend."

Her words hurt. The pain in her voice hurt, too. He was her friend. He loved her. "Paige—"

She lifted her hand. "Don't even try it. You're as selfish as Dexter, as my father. I thought you were different."

He *was* different, he screamed silently. "Paige—"

She cut him off again. "I'm going to get dressed for my morning run. I hope to God that both of you will be gone when I come out of the shower. I know that won't happen, but I want you both out of here when I come back from my run." She turned on her heels and stormed into the bathroom.

Reed looked at Fine. "What the hell are you grinning about?" he asked.

"You can't beat me, Lewis," Fine said, his calm composure still in place. "You're not even in my league."

Reed wanted to hit him, but he decided to play it his way. He could be calm, too. "Whose ring is she wearing?"

Those words were meant to incite, and by the flash of anger that crossed Fine's face, they did just that. Reed didn't bother to hide his satisfaction.

"She's playing a role now, Lewis. But as soon as your grandmother leaves, she'll come back to her senses." Reed didn't like the confidence in those words.

"Maybe she *has* come to her senses. Maybe she was playing the role with *you*."

Fine laughed, and if Reed hadn't been looking at him, he'd have believed something was funny. "You don't really believe that, do you?"

Reed didn't answer. Why should he?

Fine walked to the front door. "Let me give you a tip, Lewis, attorney to attorney. Look at the facts. Paige has known you for four years. Before this week, has she ever shown anything other than a friendly interest in you?"

The answer to that was no, but Reed knew it was a complicated no. He and Paige had always been attracted to each other, but they had decided not to act on it.

"No answer, huh?" Fine went on. "Think about it. And don't think I'm doing this for you. I'm doing it for Paige. She wouldn't want to hurt you."

"Get the hell out of here, Fine," Reed said, tired of the guy's philosophizing.

Fine opened the door. "I'm leaving, but only out of respect for Paige. She asked me to go along with this charade for your grandmother and I'm going to do it, but don't for one minute think I'm going to give Paige up. There's no way she's not going to be my wife."

Paige wondered how she'd ever allowed herself to become engaged to Dexter. It must have been a moment of weakness, because right now, she could slap him. "You're not listening to me, Dexter," she said for the fifth time. She had gone to his condo after freshening up after her run. Now, seated on the plush burgundy leather sofa in his living room with the engagement ring he'd given her on the antique table between them, she saw how different they really were.

"I *am* listening," Dexter said. He paced in front of her, hands in his pockets, as though he were lecturing to her. "You're just not making sense."

"I think I make perfect sense. You just don't want to understand." His pacing was driving her mad. "Sit down, Dexter. Your standing is not having the desired power effect."

Dexter stopped pacing and stared at her as though she had two heads, but he did sit down. Not next to her, but in the chair across from her. That was what Dexter always did. He never needed to be next to her. Physical closeness was not one of his needs. That was just one of the ways he differed from Reed, but now was not the time for thinking about Reed.

"So you want to end our engagement? Does this mean something happened between you and Lewis?"

She shook her head. Dexter seemed more concerned with what had happened between her and Reed than he did about her feelings for him. "Not in the way you mean. I didn't sleep with him, but I wanted to."

"You thought about sleeping with him? That doesn't mean anything. You didn't do it, that's what counts."

How could she and Dexter be so different? she wondered. "It means something to me, Dexter. I can't be engaged to one man and continually have erotic thoughts about another. I can't do it."

"Hell, Paige, everybody has erotic thoughts, fantasies. I'm not threatened by those." Dexter's calm exterior was beginning to crumble.

"But what if it's more? What if what I feel for Reed is more than friendship?"

Dexter stood again and resumed his pacing. "So, you think you're in love with him? Three days and you think you're in love with him? You've known him for four years, and in three days you think you're in love with him. Get real, Paige!"

"Do you love me, Dexter?" she asked.

He stopped pacing and stared at her. "Of course, I love you. I asked you to marry me, didn't I? I gave you an engagement ring big enough to choke a horse, didn't I? Of course, I love you."

Paige remembered Reed's declaration of love. Dexter's didn't exactly measure up. "Why do you love me, Dexter?"

He sat down again. She could tell he was uneasy with her questions. "I love you because I love you. Why are you asking all these questions now? You didn't ask them when you accepted my proposal."

"Maybe I should have," she responded softly.

Reed climbed into the sofabed he'd shared with Paige last night, wishing she was there with him. The knowledge that she wasn't with Dexter was small consolation. He needed her with him.

When she'd called earlier to speak to Big Momma and not to him, he'd been relieved and angry. Why hadn't she wanted to talk to him? It had taken all his acting skills to put up a nonchalant pose for Big Momma.

She'd said she'd gone by her office and gotten caught up in a problem that needed her attention. She'd have to stay there until they worked it out. Reed didn't believe that, and he didn't think Big Momma did, either. What was she doing? he wondered.

He closed his eyes and tried to sleep, but that was impossible. He knew he wouldn't be able to sleep until he talked with her. He had to know how her talk with Dexter had gone. Though he was sure she wasn't with Dexter now, he was sure she had spoken with him earlier. It wouldn't have been her style to handle it any other way.

He heard her key turn in the lock about fifteen minutes later.

The clock said eleven-thirty. He wanted to jump up and meet her at the door, but he allowed himself only to sit up in bed.

"So you finally made it in." The words sounded like an accusation, though that wasn't what he meant by them.

She strode into the room and dropped her bag on the table behind the sofa. "Why is it that no one seems to realize I'm an adult, capable of making my own decisions? I can even tell time."

"Okay," Reed said, climbing out of bed. "I'm sorry, but I was worried. Do you want to tell me what happened with Dexter?"

Her now frequent frown returned and she sat down on the side of the sofabed. "What makes you think I went to see Dexter?"

He sat down next to her and brushed his hand across her hair. "I know you."

She shook her head and his hand fell away. "You *think* you know me."

He didn't like that she pulled away from him, but he wasn't going to pursue it. At least, not now. "Okay, I'm not going to argue with you. But I think you owe me an explanation."

"An explanation," she said, hopping up from the bed. "I owe you an explanation." She pointed her finger at him and spoke in hushed tones. He knew that was so she wouldn't wake Big Momma. "Let me tell you something, Reed Lewis. You behaved like a big jerk earlier today, and I don't owe you *anything. You* owe *me.*" She poked her finger into his chest. "And you owe me *big.* Because of a favor I did you, my engagement is over. Do you hear me? It's over!"

He heard it and he wanted to scream his happiness from the rooftops. She'd ended her engagement to Dexter. "You make it sound like that wasn't what you wanted. It was, wasn't it?"

She propped her hands on her hips. "What I want is for every man on this planet to leave me alone, and that includes *you,* Reed Lewis. I'm going to take my shower now, and when I get back, I want you out of my bed and on the floor, where you belong."

"Paige," Reed protested, "you don't mean that. Your engagement with Dexter is *over.* Don't you see? Now we can be together."

Paige shook her head woefully. "I can't go from one man to another just like that, Reed. Though you didn't think much of my engagement to Dexter, I did. I was going to marry him." She was near tears now. "I was going to spend my life with a man I didn't love. Do you know how shallow that makes me feel? Just leave me alone, will you?" She turned and fled the room.

Ten

Grandma Lewis placed the last of the breakfast dishes in the dishwasher. "Thank you so much, Paige, for allowing Reed and me to stay with you like this. I know you haven't had much privacy since I've been here."

Paige closed the Arts section of the newspaper and placed it on the kitchen table. "I've loved having you here, Grandma Lewis. Don't you know that? I don't want you to think anything different."

Grandma Lewis switched on the dishwasher and turned around to face Paige. "And I've enjoyed being with you and Reed. It's good for the old folks and the young folks to get together."

"You'll have to come back."

Grandma Lewis shook her head of silver curls. "You'll have to come visit me. I know you'll love the farm."

"I know I will, too."

"Oh, my," Grandma Lewis said, placing her hands to her mouth. "I forgot all about my pictures. I brought pictures for you and Reed."

Grandma Lewis headed off for her bedroom and Paige followed her.

"Where did I put them?" Grandma Lewis asked herself, as she rummaged through the tote bag she'd brought. "I can't believe that I've waited until the end of my trip to think about them."

"I'm just glad you remembered them. Try the chest," Paige

suggested, when the older woman had no success with the bag. "Maybe you put them in with your clothes."

Grandma Lewis went and opened first the top drawer, then the second. "That's one thing about getting old. The memory goes." She found her packet in the third drawer. "Here they are." Grandma Lewis practically beamed. She walked over and sat on the foot of the bed, patting the spot next to her for Paige to sit. "I didn't put them in an album because I wanted to leave that for you and Reed."

Paige sat next to her. "You're giving us these pictures?"

Grandma Lewis smiled, wrinkles puddling around her bright eyes. "Why, yes, dear. Actually, I'm giving them to you. It's sort of a pictorial of Reed's life. I thought the photos might help you understand Reed a little better. I know you love him, but understanding comes with time."

Paige hugged Grandma Lewis to her. She was sure Grandma Lewis was right. She loved her father and she definitely didn't understand him. She didn't want to think about loving Reed . . . not yet, anyway. "That was so sweet of you."

"Sweet, nothing, you're going to be a part of this family and there are some things you should know."

Paige felt like a fraud. All Grandma Lewis had done since she'd been here was try to make her feel like a real member of the Lewis family. And how had Paige repaid her kindness? By lying to her, by making her think she was engaged to her grandson. Now, it seemed like a cheap trick.

"Grandma Lewis," Paige began, "there's something I need to tell you."

Grandma Lewis grabbed Paige's hands. "There's nothing you need to tell me, sweetheart. I know you and Reed are having a few problems right now, but I also know that you love each other."

"But—" Paige began.

"But nothing," Grandma Lewis said. "You can't tell me anything that I can't see in my heart. I know as sure as I'm sitting here that you and Reed are going to make it. You two just don't know it yet, but you will. Soon."

There was nothing Paige could say to that. Grandma Lewis had painted a picture of her and Reed that couldn't be changed. "Well, show me the pictures, then."

For the next two hours, Grandma Lewis showed pictures and told stories of Reed's life. When she was done, Paige wanted to know more. She wanted to meet Reed's parents and his brother. She wanted to visit Grandma Lewis's farm. She wanted to see the high school where Reed had been a track star and valedictorian. She wanted to see and experience the world that he'd grown up in.

Grandma Lewis had been right: the pictures had helped her understand Reed. It was now very clear to her why he'd joined the public defender's office. She understood that for Reed it was much more than a job. It was a way of giving back, a way of making a difference. Her respect for him and the courage it had taken to make that decision grew by leaps and bounds. She'd have to tell him so and maybe do some apologizing in the process.

She and Grandma Lewis spent the rest of the day together, just talking and doing girl things. It was wonderful. It reminded Paige of the times she had spent with her own grandmother. Once again, she realized how much she missed her. Not that her mother wasn't there for her, but grandmothers were different. They just loved you and let you be. She missed that. She saw now that her grandmother had provided a much needed balance to her father's overbearing concern.

Though Paige enjoyed her day with Grandma Lewis, she missed Reed. He'd been gone all day. She hadn't asked about him or his whereabouts, and neither had his grandmother. She was surprised when he showed up an hour or so before dinner. Though "Where have you been?" were the words uppermost in her mind, she chose to open with, "Hi, Reed."

He returned her greeting and followed it up with a kiss on the cheek for her and Grandma Lewis. "Did my girls have fun today?" he asked Grandma Lewis.

"Yes, we did. And thank you for giving us some girl time. We needed it."

Reed looked at Paige with questioning eyes. "We had a great time," she said. "And Grandma Lewis gave me a combination Christmas-New Year's Eve-engagement-wedding gift."

"What was it?" Reed asked.

"It's a secret," Paige and Grandma Lewis said at the same time. They'd decided that Paige would buy a photo album and present it and the pictures to Reed on their wedding night. It had been Grandma Lewis's idea, and Paige hadn't had the heart to tell her no.

Reed laughed. "It must be something naughty, if you're both being so secretive. Am I gonna like it, Big Momma?"

"I think you will. You'll have to wait and see."

He looked over at Paige, eyes twinkling. "Maybe I can coax you into spilling the beans."

Paige remembered the coaxing she had done during their drive to the country. She definitely didn't want that right now. "Of course, you could convince me to tell, sweetie, but don't do it. Grandma Lewis and I want this to be a surprise."

He pressed his lips to hers anyway. "That's the price for stopping my coaxing." When he pulled away, he grinned at her like a schoolboy with his first crush. She couldn't stop the smile that spread across her face in return.

"Dinner will be ready soon," Paige said, needing a cover for her emotions. "Grandma Lewis and I worked all day preparing your favorite foods."

Reed smiled at his grandmother. "I bet I can guess whose idea it was."

Grandma Lewis opened the door of the wall oven to check her apple cobbler. "It may have been my idea, but Paige was all for it. You've got a good one in her, Reed." She winked at Paige. "You'd better treat her right."

"You keep telling me how well I've done in finding Paige," Reed said. "Why don't you tell her how well she did in finding me? After all, you're *my* grandmother, not *hers*."

Grandma Lewis tapped Reed on the forearm with her rolling pin. "That's where you're wrong. I'm her grandmother, too, now."

"I've lost my grandmother," Reed lamented. "What else am I gonna lose in this marriage?"

"Aw, hush up, sonny," Grandma Lewis said. "You're talking nonsense."

"Now, I can't even talk." Reed caught Paige's eye. "Boy, I don't know if I'm going to like married life."

"You'll like it," Grandma Lewis said, "especially with a smart, pretty girl like Paige."

Reed got up from the table and headed for the living room. "I can see there's nothing I can say tonight. You've woven a spell around Big Momma, Paige." Paige smiled and opened her mouth to comment, but Reed added, "Just like you've woven one around me."

Paige closed her mouth. The words she had been about to speak were now meaningless. Reed meant what he said. He wasn't joking. She was sure of it.

The sound of the doorbell saved Paige from having to comment on Reed's statement.

"I'll get it," he said.

Paige turned her attention back to Grandma Lewis. "I don't know if I'm going to let Reed have any of this apple cobbler. I may just eat it all myself."

Grandma Lewis pinched Paige's arms. "Go on with you."

"Mr. Taylor," Paige heard Reed's surprised voice. "It's good to see you again, sir."

"It's your father," Grandma Lewis said, taking off her apron and brushing down her dress. "Let's go greet him." She headed off toward the front door.

Paige rushed behind her.

Reed turned around as they approached and Mr. Taylor entered the apartment. "Big Momma, this is Mr. Taylor, Paige's father. Mr. Taylor, this is my grandmother, Willie Pearl Lewis. You can call her Grandma Lewis or Big Momma."

Paige leaned forward and kissed her father's cheek. "Remember your promise," she whispered, then said for all to hear, "This is a pleasant surprise. Come on in so you and Grandma Lewis can get acquainted."

Mr. Taylor handed his overnight bag to Reed and took Grandma Lewis's elbow and led her to the sofa. "It's about time we met, Mrs. Lewis."

" 'Mrs. Lewis' is much too formal. You must call me Big Momma or Grandma Lewis. After all, we're practically family."

Mr. Taylor cleared his throat, then frowned at Reed. At least now Reed knew where Paige had learned the look. "I guess you're right about that, Grandma Lewis."

Grandma Lewis gave her best smile and Paige thought she saw a smile touch the corners of her father's mouth. Maybe Grandma Lewis could win her father over.

Reed excused himself from the room and beckoned Paige to follow him into the bedroom. As soon as the door was closed, he pulled her into his arms and gave her a hungry kiss.

"What are you doing, Reed?" Paige asked, after she caught her breath. She stood with her arms around Reed's waist.

He began a trail of kisses down her jaw. "If you don't know, I'm not going to tell you."

Paige tilted her head to give Reed better access to her neck. "We'd better get back out there."

"Why?" Reed asked. "So your father can stare me down all night?"

Paige pulled back so she could look at Reed. "It wasn't that bad."

Reed pulled her closer and resumed his attack. "I wasn't in there that long. Face it, Paige, your father hates me."

"He doesn't hate you," Paige said, caressing Reed's jawline with her hand. She liked the feel of the stubble on his face.

"You talk too much," Reed said, before taking her lips in his.

Paige decided he was right. There was nothing else for her to do except concentrate on his kiss.

* * *

Reed kept looking at the door. He didn't know if he wanted to get up and leave through it, or throw Mr. Taylor out of it. Right now, the latter was more appealing.

He had studied Taylor covertly all through dinner. He guessed women would find the man attractive. With his graying temples, bright eyes, ready smile, and pearly white teeth, Taylor could have been a poster child for Lawyers-Are-Us. The way Paige and Grandma Lewis hung onto his every word made Reed want to throw up. So the guy was well-read, well-traveled and well-dressed. Reed could accept that. Why couldn't Taylor accept him?

It wasn't that Taylor was being rude. To the contrary, he was treating Reed as though he really liked him. And that rankled. How could a man of Taylor's obvious intelligence think that Fine was a better man, a better catch, for Paige? Reed just didn't understand it.

"I'm so proud of Reed," Big Momma was saying. "Not many young people today would sacrifice money for principle, but my Reed did." The pride in her voice made Reed smile. It was either smile or tear up, and he wasn't about to tear up in front of Taylor.

"You should be proud of him," Taylor said, as though it was expected of him.

"And so should you," Big Momma continued. "He'll make a fine husband to your daughter." She looked over at Reed and smiled. "My grandson knows what's important in life. He'll never neglect Paige or the family they'll have."

Taylor looked over at Reed. "It takes money to support a family," he said.

Now the true Taylor was coming to the surface, Reed thought. Reed sought Paige's eyes, but they were directed on her father. There was a plea in them. She didn't want her father to say something to upset Big Momma.

But Reed wasn't concerned about Big Momma. He knew there was nothing Taylor could say that could shake her confidence in him. No, it wasn't Big Momma he thought Taylor would influence. It was Paige.

That was what that kiss earlier had been about. He didn't want Paige to forget the feelings he aroused in her, the feelings they aroused in each other. His kiss had been more than a sexual act; it had been a statement of his love for her. As she listened with rapt attention to her father, he didn't want her to forget him and the life he wanted for them.

"I'm sure sonny knows that," Big Momma said. "But he also knows that money can't make you happy."

At this moment, Reed was proud of his grandmother.

"But it can help," Taylor added.

Reed thought Taylor was going to say more, but he didn't and neither did Big Momma.

"Dessert?" Paige asked, a little too brightly. Though she held her own with her father, Reed knew it took a lot out of her to do so. He was familiar with trying to stand your ground, while also trying to win and keep the love and respect of someone you loved and respected.

Reed pushed back his chair and placed his napkin on the table. "I'll help you." He followed Paige into the kitchen.

As soon as they were out of view of their elders, he pushed her against the wall and kissed her.

"What was that for?"

He moved away from her. "I don't want you to forget what's important. I love you, Paige. That's what counts."

Eleven

"Why can't he go to a hotel?" Reed asked in a hushed tone.

Paige placed the blankets and pillows in his hand. "That's the same question he asked when I told him you were staying here."

"He's a hotshot attorney; I'm a lowly PD. He can afford a hotel; I can't."

Paige added a couple of sheets to the stack Reed was holding. "Stop whining, Reed. Now, take those things in the great room. You and Daddy will have to flip for the sofa."

"Well, don't be surprised if you wake up in the morning and one of us is no longer here."

Paige laughed. "I hope you two don't kill each other."

Reed grimaced. "You've got that right."

"Oh, Reed," Paige said, punching him playfully on the arm. "It won't be that bad. You two may grow to like each other."

"Well, we're off to a bad start as it is. Because of him, you're sharing the bedroom with Big Momma and I'm still on the floor in the living room."

She kissed him softly on the lips. "Don't complain so."

"Kiss me again and I'll stop," Reed said in a husky voice. He wished his hands were empty so he could wrap them around her.

Paige leaned over the armload of bedclothes he held and planted a kiss firmly on his lips. He dropped the bedclothes on the floor. "To hell with this," he said, pulling her body into his.

Paige responded to his kiss freely, glad she had broken her engagement to Dexter, glad she no longer felt guilty. She still wasn't sure where things were going with Reed, but she wanted to find out.

She pulled away first. "Now, pick up the bedclothes and go talk to my father. Remember, no more complaining."

"I love her," Reed said in the darkness. He had kept his word to Paige and not complained. He'd even tried to be nice to Taylor, but Taylor wasn't having it. Since Big Momma and Paige had gone to bed, the older man hadn't said more than five words to him.

"So does Dexter," Taylor answered.

Reed pushed back his blanket, got up from his pallet, and turned on the light. He pulled a chair up next to the sofabed. "We need to have this out, man to man."

The bright light invading the darkness caused Taylor to squint. He mumbled, then sat up in bed, the covers neatly folded around him. "Okay," he said. "Let's talk man-to-man. What can you offer my daughter, other than dreams?"

"Love, Mr. Taylor," Reed said, extending his arms in supplication. "Faithfulness. Trust. I can make her happy."

Taylor wasn't impressed. "Dexter can offer her that and much more."

Reed leaned back in his chair. "You can't make me believe this is about money. You've never liked me. Even when I was at McCurdy and McCurdy, you didn't like me. What is it about me that threatens you?"

Taylor gave his most arrogant laugh. "You don't threaten me, Lewis."

Reed steepled his hands in front of him. Though he'd never considered it before, he was now convinced that he was a threat to Mr. Taylor. "I'm not trying to take her away from you. I want to be a part of your family, just as Paige will be a part of mine."

Taylor narrowed his eyes. "You'll *never* be a part of my family."

Reed was taken aback by the anger in Taylor's voice. What

had he done to alienate the man? He shook his head. "It's your loss, Mr. Taylor, because I'm not giving up on Paige. I love her, and I believe she loves me."

"Then why is she engaged to Dexter?" Taylor asked.

It was Reed's turn to laugh. "Don't tell me you didn't see the ring. It's not Dexter's ring she's wearing, it's mine."

Taylor was not moved. "Paige is playing a game with you, Lewis. Your grandmother found a warm spot in her heart, and you're playing on it. But mark my word, as soon as your grandmother is gone, Paige will come to her senses."

Taylor's words were the same words that Fine had used, and that caused insecurity to rise up in Reed, but he wasn't going to give Taylor the satisfaction of knowing that. "We'll have to see, won't we?"

Taylor slid back down in the bed. "I guess we will," he said, before turning his back to Reed.

Reed sat in the chair, staring at Taylor's back for a long while. He didn't understand it. What had he done to cause such hostility? He thought and thought and he continued to come back to the same answer: for some reason, Taylor was threatened by him.

For the life of him, Reed couldn't think why.

When Paige got up the next morning and readied herself for her daily run, Reed and her father were both up. Her father was dressed for a run; Reed wasn't. "Did you guys sleep well?" she asked.

"I did," her father said, kissing her on the cheek. He turned back to Reed. "How was your pallet, Lewis?"

Reed walked over and kissed Paige on the lips. "Good morning, sweetheart," he said, as he pulled away.

"Good morning, Reed," Paige said, stirred by the kiss, yet also understanding the reason for it. Something had passed between her father and Reed during the night, and it hadn't been good. She looked from one to the other before deciding not to ask any questions.

"You're not going running with us?" She looked at Reed. The uncertainty in his eyes made her reach out and touch his arm to reassure him.

He smiled as if her touch made a difference and shook his head. "Not this morning. I'm sure your father wants to spend some time alone with you. And I want to be here when Big Momma gets up. You know, she's leaving today."

Paige's smile faltered. "I'm going to miss her. I've really enjoyed having her here."

"I know," Reed answered.

Paige detected a tinge of sadness in his voice. "Is something wrong, Reed?" she asked.

Reed forced a smile. "No, nothing's wrong." He looked at Taylor. "You two'd better get going. We'll be here when you get back."

Her father smiled. "He's right about that, Princess. Let's go."

Paige followed her father out of the apartment, her mind still on Reed. She wished she could have spoken privately with him, but she knew she had to talk with her father first.

They ran in silence for the first mile. Her father was still in good shape so he didn't have a problem keeping up with her. She wasn't surprised when he stopped in front of the Donut Shoppe.

"Let's stop for breakfast," he said. It was a command, not a suggestion.

Paige agreed because it was better they had it out now.

She saw Dexter as soon as they were inside. All she could do was stare at her father. There was no way she'd ever believe this was a coincidence.

"Good morning, Paige," Dexter said, when he reached their side. He extended his hand to her father. "Matthew, it's good to see you. Paige and I had a wonderful time over Christmas. How's Lillie?"

Paige felt her annoyance grow as her father told Dexter about her mother's plans for New Year's. When the waitress asked how many, she was tempted to answer one. "Three, please. No smoking."

They sat in a booth near the front—Dexter and her on one side, her father on the other. Paige focused her attention out of the wall of windows, studying the joggers who passed by. She knew if she looked at her father, she'd scream.

Dexter nudged her arm and handed her the menu. "What do you want, darling?"

Paige took the menu and stared at him. She was tempted to ask him why he was still calling her darling, since their engagement was now off, but good manners made her hold her tongue. "Thanks," she snapped.

As her father and Dexter talked, her thoughts wandered to Reed. She wished she could be home with him, instead of here.

"Paige," her father said, "Dexter is talking to you."

Paige turned. Dexter was talking about the New Year's Eve party they had planned to attend.

"I didn't think we were still going to that, Dexter," she said, in as kind a way as she knew. Surely, he didn't think their plans were still on.

"Why not?" her father asked. "You two talked about this party all during Christmas."

Paige looked at Dexter with pleading eyes, hoping that he'd answer her father so she wouldn't have to. Dexter didn't move. He just smiled at her with an "I got ya" smile that she'd seen him flash before in the courtroom, but directed at a hostile witness, never at her. And that's when it hit her: Dexter didn't think she'd stand up to him with her father present. He'd called her father and brought him here to make her toe the line. She was sure of it.

When she looked at her father, she was hurt to the core to see the satisfaction on his face. He thought he was going to get his way. It didn't matter to him what she wanted. All that mattered was what *he* wanted.

She placed her menu firmly on the table. "Dexter and I aren't going to the New Year's Eve party together because we're no longer engaged."

Her father dropped all pretense of calm. "When are you going to stop this nonsense, Paige?"

"Nonsense?" she repeated. "You call my decisions nonsense? I think you're out of line."

Her father's confident pose slipped a little. "You're the one out of line, young lady. What are you doing breaking your engagement to Dexter because of that Lewis character?"

If Paige had been sitting on the outside of the booth, she would have gotten up and left. But since she couldn't leave, she had to speak her mind. She looked at Dexter. "I'm sorry, but I don't love you, Dexter. I never should have allowed things to go as far as they have."

Dexter reached for her hand. "We don't have to talk about this now, Paige," he said, obviously realizing that he was taking the wrong tack with her. "We don't have to go to the New Year's Eve party. We can discuss this after the new year."

Paige snatched her hand away. "Aren't you listening to me? I said I don't love you. I don't want to be engaged to you, and I *don't* want to spend New Year's Eve with you!"

Dexter got up and slapped his napkin on the table. "If you want Lewis that much, you can have him, but don't come running to me when he can't give you the life you want."

Paige slid out of the booth and stood nose-to-nose with Dexter. "I don't know how I could have ever thought I loved you."

"All right, you two," her father said. "Don't say something you'll regret later."

Paige looked at the man who was her father and wondered how he could sit there and ignore her words, her feelings. "I think we've passed that point, Daddy. You can stay here with Dexter or you can come home with me, but you've got to make a choice."

"She loves you, Reed," Big Momma said. The two of them sat on the sofa in Paige's great room. Paige and her father hadn't come back from their run yet and Reed didn't have to guess what they were doing.

"I hope so," Reed said, letting his facade slip. "There's something I have to tell you, Big Momma."

She placed her care-worn hand over his. "There's nothing you have to tell me. There's something I have to tell you."

"But—"

"No buts," his grandmother interrupted. "I'm not yet blind, Reed. I know things aren't as they should be between you and Paige."

"You're right about that."

"Oh, hush up," she said. "I know something else. That girl loves you and you love her. And she's not going to let her father or that Dexter guy convince her otherwise. You have to have faith in her, Reed. If she's the woman you think she is, she'll make the right decision."

Reed felt hope spring up in his heart. Once again, he thanked God for his grandmother. "How did you get so smart?" he asked.

"I've always been smart," Big Momma replied. "It just took you a while to figure it out."

Reed and Big Momma were laughing when Paige stormed into the room. "What happened?" Reed asked, immediately attuned to her feelings. Her face closed up and he knew she wasn't going to answer.

She put on a fake smile. "Nothing." She walked over and kissed Big Momma. "Good morning," she said, and then she leaned down and gave Big Momma a big hug. The hug lasted so long that Reed knew Paige sought comfort in his grandmother's arms. For the first time since his grandmother had come to visit, Reed wondered if her visit had been a good thing. Had Paige fallen in love with him, or with his grandmother?

Twelve

Paige hadn't spoken to Reed since they'd seen his grandmother off earlier today. He had taken his things with him when he'd left her apartment. She'd hoped he would call, but inside, she'd known he wouldn't. She could still hear Grandma Lewis's words in her ears.

"It's your turn," she'd said, and then she'd rushed to the gate to board the plane.

Paige had wanted to ask her what she'd meant, but she hadn't had time. Reed had escorted her out of the airport and driven her back to her apartment. They hadn't talked much. In fact, he'd said only a few words.

He'd dropped her outside her apartment and driven off, with not so much as an "I'll call you later."

She began to wonder if all the things he'd said had been part of his plan for Grandma Lewis, but she quickly discarded that thought. No, Reed had explicitly said that his feelings for her were real. By God, he'd said that he was in love with her. Was she in love with him?

She heard her father enter the room. He looked suitably contrite about the fiasco with Dexter this morning. He'd tried to make up for it by being especially nice to Grandma Lewis before she'd left. That helped, but it didn't make things right between them.

"Would you like to go out for dinner, Princess?" he asked.

Princess . . . he'd called her that for as long as she could remember. To him, she was still a little girl. "Not tonight, Daddy. You should be getting back for Mom's party."

Her father sat down next to her. "I don't think she wants me there."

Paige was surprised by the moist brightness in her father's eyes. "That's silly. Why would you think something like that?"

Her father dropped his eyes to his hands. "I told her what happened over breakfast this morning. She thinks I was wrong."

This was a first. Her mother always supported her father. That was the one thing she could count on growing up. They'd always presented a united front. She was glad her mother had chosen to break rank this time. "What do you think?"

He looked up at her and the unshed tears in his eyes almost made her forgive him. Almost. She forced herself to wait for his answer.

"I love you, Paige," he began. "I just want you to be happy."

She knew this was hard for him, and it touched her heart that he was making the effort for her. "Reed makes me happy. I love him, Daddy." The words came out unplanned. But they were true. It was what she felt in her heart. She loved Reed.

Her father laughed before wiping the lone tear that fell from his eyes. "I was afraid you'd say that."

She dropped down on her knees in front of him and pulled his hands into hers. "Why do you dislike him so much, Daddy? Reed's a good man. He'll make me happy, and I'll make him happy. Why can't you see that?"

Her father rubbed her hands with his own. "I remember the first time I met him." He chuckled. "I didn't like him then."

"What did he do, Daddy?"

"Princess, it wasn't what he did. It was who he was."

Paige didn't understand. "Who he was?"

Her father dropped her hands and stood. "It's a man thing. I knew from the minute I met him that he played by his own rules, that he wasn't a man to follow the dictates of others. Reed makes his own rules."

Paige's heart beat faster. "But that's a good thing, Daddy. Aren't you like that?"

He laughed a real laugh then. "That was the problem. We were too much alike. With him in your life, you wouldn't need me. I didn't want to lose you."

Paige sat back on her heels. "You won't lose me. You didn't think you were losing me when I was marrying Dexter. Why do you think it with Reed?"

Her father placed his hands in his pockets. "I'm ashamed to admit this, but Dexter's not a very strong man. He'd do what I wanted him to. He'd make you happy, or by God, I'd make him make you happy. Reed is more of an unknown."

Paige smiled, finally believing that this whole mess would have a happy ending. "What you see in Reed is passion, Daddy. Dexter doesn't have that. And I need it."

Her father turned his back to her. "Am I going to lose you, Princess?"

She walked up behind him and rested her head on his back. "You're not going to lose me," she repeated. "I'm not going anywhere. I'm just getting married. At least, I hope I am."

"Oh, he'll marry you, all right. The man won't give up."

Paige hoped that was true, but if it was, why wasn't Reed by her side now?

It was almost midnight. In less than ten minutes the new year would ring in. Everybody was celebrating . . . everybody but him. What was he doing? He was sitting alone in his apartment, wondering if the woman he loved was thinking about him as she rang in the New Year with her ex-fiancé.

He hoped she wasn't with Fine, but where else would she be? He'd thought about getting dressed, getting a date, and showing up at the party just to spite her, but that seemed such a juvenile thing to do. He was beyond that. He wanted a serious relationship with Paige. He'd laid his cards on the table. The next play was hers.

Reed got up and turned on the television. If he wasn't going to be a part of the action, he could at least be a spectator. He flopped down on his well-worn brown plaid sofa and stared at the screen. All he saw was Paige's face.

When the doorbell rang, he debated opening it. Who would be visiting on New Year's Eve? Probably some partygoer looking for an address.

Paige was standing in the doorway when he opened it. She was dressed in her trenchcoat and house shoes. A part of his brain registered the shoes, but that thought was overcome by the fact that she was at his door and not out with Dexter. He just stared at her.

"Aren't you going to invite me in?" she asked. Did he detect uncertainty in her voice?

He stood back and she sauntered into the room, taking a seat on the sofa. "What are you watching?" she asked.

He couldn't remember. All his thoughts were of her and what her presence meant. Did he dare hope it meant what he wanted it to?

When he didn't answer, she looked up at him and he saw the question in her eyes. "Is this a bad time?"

Hell, no, he thought. "No," he said. "What are you doing here, Paige?" He was tired of games. He needed to know how she felt. He needed to know what she wanted from him.

"You promised to spend New Year's Eve with me, remember?"

He remembered. He also remembered that it was supposed to be a double date. "Where's Dexter?"

She fixed her eyes on him. "Dexter's history."

He wanted to pull her into his arms, but he forced himself to wait. "I don't have a date, either. So I guess that means a double date is out, then."

She smiled. "Like you said, three's a crowd. I guess it's just you and me."

Reed pointed to the television screen. "And Times Square."

"They don't count. It's just you and me, Reed. Nobody else counts."

He understood she was telling him that her father was no longer a factor in the equation. "Are you sure?" he asked, fearful to let hope fill his heart, just to let that hope be dashed at some later time.

Paige stood and wrapped her arms around his waist. The bulkiness of her coat was a barrier he wanted removed. "I love you, Reed Lewis," she said into his eyes.

His heart felt as though it would explode. "You do?"

"I do."

Reed pulled at the sash of her coat. "Then why don't you take this coat off so we can ring in the new year the right way?"

Paige grinned at him and he felt all his insecurities fade away. "I'll take it off at midnight," she said.

"I can't wait that long."

She moved a step back from him. "Look at the television, Reed. Ten—nine—eight—"

Reed watched as she undid button after button with her countdown. When she reached one, the coat dropped from her shoulders to the floor.

Hot damn! he thought. She was wearing the granny gown.

About the Author

When Angela Benson sold her first book, *Bands of Gold,* to Pinnacle Books it was a dream come true. Since then, Angela has continued to dream. And she's seeing those dreams come true. Reviewers proclaimed her second novel, *For All Time,* a book "all women should read." Her next book, *Between the Lines,* is slated for release in May 1996.

A graduate of Spelman College and Georgia Tech in Atlanta, Angela is a retired engineer who now writes full-time while she works on her second graduate degree. She uses her professional training and experience to provide realistic characterization and motivation for her strong and independent, yet vulnerable, heroines.

A native of Alabama, Angela currently resides in the Atlanta suburb of Decatur. When she's not weaving her own tales of romance, Angela can be found curled up on her couch reading her favorite romance authors.

Angela loves to hear from readers. Write to her at P.O. Box 360571, Decatur, GA 30036.